A TURKEY AND ONE MORE EASTER EGG

The Paradise Secret

By

Davey J Ashfield

Dedicated to:

Clyde, who kept me alive and sane during the darkness.

And always to Francine,
who was, and is, my light in that darkness.

CONTENTS

ACKNOWLEDGMENTS

To the beautiful people of Asia who made me welcome and kept me smiling, particularly those in Singapore and those in St George's Church who found me in a mess and showed me the light and the way.

Also to the families of those who work away from their loved ones, in often dangerous places, for long and difficult times.

To all who ever helped me at work and to all those we have lost and those who remain great friends. It was a special time in a special place: Gone with the wind.

My candle it burns at both ends
It may not last the night.
But oh my enemies and ah my friends
It gives a wondrous light
- Roald Dahl

One ring to find them all
One ring to bring the all
One ring to rule them
And in The Outback bind them all.

CHAPTER ONE

Houston, Texas, USA

Gator Tom

Some years ago…

"Have you ever killed a man, son?"

Jack looked up from the urinal at the tall, greying, red-haired, elderly man urinating next to him and felt the hairs on his testicles shrink in parallel with those precious organs to which they were attached.

"Not to my knowledge, Red," Jack replied, wishing that he could finish peeing, zip up and quickly get out of the toilet into the safer ground of the office and normal people.

The tall American man stared down at the young consultant through his one fixed and sparkling blue eye. His gaze was like a gimlet and seemed eternal as he continued to stare the shivering man out. Jack was unsure if Red was going to expand on his astonishing unprompted statement or continue with the last conversation about quality management. As Jack had no idea why Red had changed from discussing welding procedures to homicide within a few seconds of starting to pee out the morning's caffeine, he remained silently trying to squeeze his pee out as fast as his prostate would allow him.

Jack felt his gonads shrink a little bit more under the tall man's constant auger-like stare. Red moved his eye down a lot closer to

Jack's face and Jack noticed the shiny black eye patch on the other eye glowed in the fluorescent light of the toilet. The younger man looked down into the urinal and hoped the crazy man would zip up and go but Red put his large grizzled hand on his shoulder prompting him to look up from his shrinking manhood and Red finished what he started.

"I have. I've had men try to kill me and I've killed men. Sure hope I don't have to do that again but maybe one day I'll do the same if those sons of bitches in human resources don't start listening to me."

He zipped up and turned to wash his hands. Jack just stood with his intact privates in his hand wondering what planet he had just landed on. Red opened the toilet door and without any more explanation of his statement or angst about the friends from HR, he turned and said, "Come on, Jack. I'll introduce you to Gator Tom, the Big Man."

Jack zipped, washed and followed him out to the relative safety and sanity of the Houston office 45th floor. As Jack followed him he wondered, what next?

The last hour he had sat listening to Red in his huge office tell him about his undoubted experience of building big construction projects across the ass ends of the world which had been both enlightening and worrying. Enlightening because he had undoubted experience in building massive structures and worrying as this was interspersed with tales of his past involvement in war with foreigners. He could only guess that from the toilet revelation that Red was planning a similar war on the corporate HR department.

As they walked Jack was curious to learn the strange ways of the Americans that he would have to work with and he asked Red why Tom was called Gator Tom.

"Hell man, Tom is one tough cookie, son. He once was trapped whilst fishing in the bayous by a small gator. He slit its throat with his double-edged Gook knife. He skinned it and still wears the boots to this day. Since then he's been Gator to his buddies. You all got gators over in England, son?" Red replied.

Jack confirmed that the only animals that may bite you over in his green and pleasant land were the women. He also confirmed that they didn't have Gooks either, so no need to carry double-edged Gook knives.

Jack had only recently arrived in Houston, having been selected to support one of the largest oil and gas construction projects in the world as a management consultant. His purpose as an independent consultant was to work with all parties to build teamwork and ensure effective communication between the many different contractors and suppliers of all cultures across the globe and ensure war didn't break out with the multinational participants.

He was employed by a Seven Sisters oil company to carry this out across most of Asia Pacific and the head offices in Houston, London, Singapore and Perth. Today was the day he was to meet the corporate project boys from the Company and Main Engineering Contractor in the gleaming ivory towers of Houston. Already, after meeting Red, Global Vice President of Construction, he was beginning to understand the scale of the task ahead.

Red took him to an office which was marginally smaller than his own and overlooked downtown Houston. Red opened the door and a man resembling a Cape buffalo stood up from his desk and blocked out the searing Texan sun that poured through the windows. Jack blinked a couple at times as this huge figure came out from behind his desk and shook hands with Red. The immense man stared at the new comer with a breaking warm smile as he walked towards him. Curiously, before he outstretched his hand of friendship, he grabbed his testicles and adjusted them with his hand, and then with a smile he offered Jack the same hand with a rhetorical greeting.

"Howdy, buddy. I'm Tom. You must be Jack, the limey entertainments officer."

Before Jack could correct him and try to get some form of professional credibility and self-esteem back into the relationship, Red butted in.

"Yup, Tom, this is Jack. Somehow that crazy Kraut project manager and those goddammed HR bullshitters want us to love each other or some other bullshit management speak. We gotta work with him Tom, so let's try and help him get settled in, buddy."

Before Jack could try to gain credibility and possible empathy with these two giants of men, Tom just nodded and put his huge arm around Jack's shoulders and pulled him towards a circular table with six chairs around it. Jack's shoulder joint collapsed under the pressure.

"Hell man, that's no problem Red. I like Limeys, worked with them all over the world. Sure, I'll put him straight Red."

"OK, Tom. Let's take him to lunch, see Spinner later and then we'll hit happy hour in the Holiday Inn for a few beers and shots."

"Sure, Red. Take a seat, Jack. You want coffee?"

Jack answered in the positive for yet more caffeine. He was beginning to realise that in America a large bladder and perfect kidney function were essential. As was a reinforced steel handshake and a pair of shoulders that were able to stand forces of up to 100 newtons.

Red left the office. He was a tall figure with an imposing presence, once with full red flaming hair from which he got his name, but now greying. He had told Jack he'd come from Kentucky and had been with the company over forty years, and his homicidal tendencies and age didn't seem diminish his stature or the welcoming smiles and greetings from the office staff as he passed. Possibly mad as a box of frogs but well-loved was the amazed consultant's initial impression. Jack noted that he must spend more time trying to get Red reconciled to the modern ways of empowerment, cross-cultural communication and integration with their friendly partners; even if it may well be bullshit to most in the industry. He took it as a challenge to his relationship management skills to win this industry giant over. Time would tell if he succeeded.

Tom, however, despite his first greeting, was more flexible and certainly seemed more malleable and friendly once they had passed the usual formalities of greeting. His scrotal scratching ritual had disturbed Jack quite a bit but he was new to this crazy world of the oil industry and contracting, so he was determined to learn and succeed.

Tom was the project construction manager, overseeing all the remote construction managers in the various countries where parts of the main project would be built. These were mainly Indonesia, China, the Philippines, Vietnam, Korea and Thailand with smaller fabrication and main equipment suppliers coming from over twenty other countries, including Japan, France, Russia and the USA. Like Jack, Tom would be based in the main engineering design office in Singapore. The final project would be assembled in Australia and would be a world challenging first in taking gas and oil from floating things offshore and coal gas onshore and turning the gas into liquid. The size, complexity, the huge social and environmental challenges and the multicultural nature didn't seem to concern the Big Man.

"Hell, Jack, I've worked all over the world. Most of the time asshole places. This one is gonna be built in paradise, man. You ever lived in Asia, buddy?"

"Just visited a few years ago, Tom. And I only visited for short periods on business, never lived there. Is it good?"

"Hell, it's heaven, man. I've been married to three of the beauties. Cost me three houses. One I haven't even seen in Thailand. I got kids everywhere. My latest fiancée is Indonesian and waiting for me out there with the new young uns. I can't wait to get mobilised – girls, bars, golf, beer everywhere, buddy. Guess you coming with us to Singapore?"

"Yeah, after a few weeks working with the senior team here, I'm mobilised there too," Jack replied, feeling quite excited by this news.

Gator looked happy but revealed some of his concerns.

"Great, bud. Only problem with Asia is the girls. My latest wife I met in the bars, so I guess she knows me too much and will cut my balls off if I'm caught even talking to them. Last trip to Singapore she stalked me on the Ho Chi Minh trail every night on my way up the trail to our condo after the beers in the Four Floors of Whores. She leapt on me from behind a mango tree after a night out in the Towers. After she'd clawed my right eye out she chased the Filipino maid who was only walking with me to her condo. She threatened to cut my balls off in bed in the night. You got to be careful, buddy. You married?"

Jack replied that indeed he was married with three kids and they were coming out too. However, he was beginning to worry about the Ho Chi Minh trail and his sight and also his testicles again. This was not a great day so far for the gonadal region. Gator Tom continued with his travel agent sell.

"The only thing wrong with Asia, buddy, is the food. The last time I worked in Korea if I hadn't stopped eating that foreign shit I would have had an ass like the beginning of Bonanza."

5

In those few words the culinary culture of the east and its effect on the human digestive tract was explained by the man who was to live solely on an epicurean diet of Tiger beer and the groundnuts which were supplied free by the lovely Philippine bar girls in whose bars he habitually lived.

He was a giant of a man and was soon to prove that a diet solely of Tiger beer and nuts had little effect on size. Jack was soon to be was reminded that the largest animal on the planet lived on plankton and Gator Tom was not far off the size of a small humpback. He was to become an icon of cultural alignment theory during Jack's initiation to the Lion City, Singapore.

The anal reference related to the sixties' American cowboy series where it used to begin with a map of the Ponderosa, the Cartwright family ranch, and a very small flame emerging from the centre of the map which got larger and larger, burning the whole map whilst the music played, "Dum diddle um, diddle um, dump diddle um diddle um…"

The burning reference apparently related to Tom's problem with his anal region after the odd small bit of Asian spice or two. 'Ass like the flag of Japan' is probably more descriptive for the younger generation who did not enjoy the delights of Hoss, Adam and Little Red Cartwright.

He explained more succinctly his aversion to Asian cuisine, particularly Korean food.

"Goddamn, after a few weeks of eating that Bulgogi shit I began to start barking and when I started to lick mah own ass, ah said **** this and went back to vegetables. But hell, not that Kimchi: man that stinks like a frog armpit… but the girls, well now you're talking, boy."

He smiled a beautiful Donny Osmond white smile in a head the size of a bison and calmed down after his epicurean rant.

Tom came from Lafayette, Louisiana. He was indeed a coon ass, a Cajun, as those folks from the swamps and deltas of the Pelican State appeared to be named by the intelligentsia of the 43rd floor. He had studied engineering at Louisiana State University and had played as a line backer for LSU Tigers and also trialled for Houston Oilers. He had been in the US Marine Corps and he was one of the biggest men Jack had ever met at his tender middle age. His head was massive; as an old colleague had once noted of a man with a similar sized figurehead: "Jack, he had a head like a sniper's dream."

Tom also had the strangest trousers the Englishman had seen. His huge abdominal girth, which wasn't fat but just huge, was contained by a six-inch-wide trouser band and he seemed to need no belt. Jack was to notice that whenever he met anyone, he'd lift his balls up from his huge crotch with his shaking hand before offering it in friendship. It was to become a trait that he was determined to try to eliminate through effective counselling and mentoring consultancy. Also as he observed in those first weeks, Tom also tended to stand holding his balls and adjusting his crotch whenever he was presenting to an audience; this behaviour Jack decided may not be seen as culturally correct to his Asian partners and colleagues, male or female, whom he was going to lead to excellence in construction.

On reflection after leaving the office, and in his hotel isolation from this bizarre office, Jack considered that possibly the ritual ball grabbing may show some form of human bonding, or empathy unknown to the current management gurus that he was supposed to represent. But despite his initial worries about Red's homicidal tendencies and Tom's genital comforting, he concluded that he was still learning about this oil business and possibly they were all perfectly normal. A false truth in today's political spin that will be confirmed in this epic story if you keep reading till the end: Jack was soon to find out that very few people in this business and those who supported it were, what the medical books and that endearing crazy person he'd meet later, the Doc, would call, well... normal.

Tom continued with Jack's education, telling him about the various bars, girls, and weird men he'd known across South East Asia whilst reading and shredding papers in his paper shredder. The consultant noticed that this was the only appliance in the big man's office – the shredder and his cell phone. There was no sight of engineering drawings, construction procedures, personal protective equipment or any paperwork, only his shredding material box.

Tom broke off from shredding to sign cheques and put them in his outbox. Jack naively asked him if he was shredding confidential data and paying project expense claims for his staff.

"Hell no, Jack... these are credit card bills from the bars from my last trip to Singapore and child support demands from the other wives. Goddamn, I've got children all over the world, all got to be paid for and if the Ninja ever saw the credit card bills from the Four Floors of Whores or Here and Now she'd have my balls off in a second. You make sure you get a paper shredder, buddy, when you get to Singapore, or buy Incatel-lined Jockies."

Jack made a mental note to do just that.

Tom finally wrote his cheques and shredded his bar bills which he showed copies of to the amazed consultant. Most of them were for many beers and also many, many tequila shots for the host of bar girls that he said surrounded him every night. Jack noted that he must get paid very well as the sums were not small, as like his new friend, they were huge.

Tom finally stood and asked his visitor if he had learnt enough from him about the project. Jack had heard little about the construction execution plan, his construction organisation or indeed anything remotely to do with steel, wires or welding at all, just how wonderful Asia was. But somehow he thought now wasn't the time to challenge this behemoth over his execution plan, let's ease into this role and try to win these megaliths of the industry over first. It was after all, early days, and he was getting paid for listening to pleasant conversation (well, apart from the toilet room interrogation from Red, which continued to worry him.) Tom concluded the interview.

"We're off to see Spinner for lunch with Red now. You'll enjoy chewing the fat with the man. Spinner and Red are legends in the bidness, worked together in offshore West Africa and started the North Sea off for you Brits. Both are nearly eighty, I guess. Goddamn, then I gotta then bring you back to meet Jon, your new boss. We'll go for beer after. You'll need it after meeting that son of bitch, son."

As he finished he laughed loudly, shaking his huge head in some form of comforting or warning gesture.

They did indeed pick up Red and after a short drive they pulled into a large car park under a massive skyscraper and took a lift to the main reception where they were greeted by a lovely attractive lady who gave them security passes and led them into a lift. She had a security pass which allowed her to press a button for a floor that was just marked 'Presidential Suite' and they flew up eighty-five floors to enter a huge reception area.

As they entered Jack asked Gator Tom why Spinner was called Spinner.

"Hell, Jack, the man bet a high roller in Dallas his house and truck for the oilman's drilling rig on the spin of a quarter. That's how he got started in the bidness. Some balls has Spinner."

The floor was just like the arrangement of JR and Bobby Ewing in that great epic TV show, *Dallas*. On one side of the office was one gorgeous blonde-headed secretary with legs up to her coccyx; the other the same. The space in between was about the size of an American football field. The walls were covered with all the animals that the boys from Texas on Batam Island (later in the story) hadn't managed to shoot, as they were now extinct and decorating these walls.

They walked to the right of the office and Red asked the lovely girl if Spinner would see them. She replied that he was in his anteroom and was ready and waiting. She opened the door and they were led into the biggest office Jack had ever seen. They were greeted by a very tall, wiry, older man. His hair was white and his face grizzled. He wore jeans with a huge ornate buckle and a denim shirt and his long leather boots were embroidered snake skin.

Red made the introduction.

"Spinner, this here is Jack. He's come to help us on the project."

Jack shook hands, Spinner's grip belying the fact he was about eighty years old.

Spinner released his vice-like grip and said, "Let's go through to the office and talk some bullshit," and he opened another set of double doors. They walked into the second biggest office Jack had ever seen, with views across the whole of downtown Houston, and they were politely asked to sit down at a table with large armchairs around it in the corner of the office.

Jack looked around and there were yet more stuffed endangered species on each wall and paintings of drilling rigs, obviously his favourites, and a picture above his desk of Spinner and a couple of others in overalls, hard hats and covered in oil and grime, next to a drill platform floor. Jack found out during the initial conversation that the guy next to him was George Bush Senior and they had worked together in early days when Bush had been in the drilling business with him.

They sat down and Spinner spat into a spittoon next to the table. He put his immaculate booted feet onto the table and pressed buttons by the side of his armchair which raised and lowered his feet until he was comfortable. His P.A. had already brought him a thick black coffee, and he took a drink and turned to his American friends.

"Who's this guy, Red?"

"He's one of them management consultants, Spinner. Yet another one who knows nothing of the bidness."

Hum, Jack thought, *thanks Red.*

"Where's he from, Red?"

Spinner didn't address Jack directly but his long-term buddy from '*When the West Was Won*'.

"He's a limey," Red answered, spitting into the spittoon at his side.

"Hell, ah thought so. Goddamn, Red, have you no decent people in your company? All you bring to see me are homo limeys or that crazy kraut. Brits? What they doing in the bidness? I thought we whupped their asses once and for all in eighteen twelve?"

Oh dear, Jack thought yet again. This job was not going to be easy for sure. Gator Tom kindly stuck up for his Limey colleague.

"Ah think this one might be OK, Spinner. He likes a beer and he doesn't talk like he's got ******* marbles in his mouth."

"Well, he'll be the first limey I've known that's any use," Spinner replied and then continued with another groundbreaking statement about the 'bidness'.

"Son, in the oil bidness there is one thing that rookies and limeys need to learn and that's if you can't shit get off the ******** pan. Y'all know that?"

Jack decided to try to get some credibility by explaining to them all that he had ran offshore and onshore contracting businesses, and knew all about drilling contractors.

It seemed to work as the conversation went away from the absolute incompetence and effeminate ways of English people to days gone by when America ruled the world of offshore exploration and drilling and Spinner and Red could hire and fire anyone at the drop of a Colt 45. They chewed the fat about 'Nam' and 'Gooks' and 'Ayrabs' and the smell of napalm, and talked about all things military and violent but never about the project.

It seemed that Spinner had the contract to drill all the wells for the offshore project, so as far as Red and Tom were concerned Spinner delivered what he said he would; therefore there was no need for plans, statistics and reports; this was the oil 'bidness'.

Jack enjoyed the couple of hours spent with Spinner. He even managed to get Spinner to talk directly to him and not through Red, although the conversation, like all the people you'll meet in this story, was bizarre to say the least. He asked him about a certain poor animal's stuffed head which was stuck on his wall that seemed to be looking directly at him.

"What's that animal, Red? It looks a lot like a gazelle or something."

They all looked up at the once beautiful brown and white striped creature's head. Red pointed with his large, grizzled fingers and answered.

"Yeah, it was some sorta antelope, can't remember now. Shot it in Africa in the seventies after 'Nam. I was real lucky to shoot it. I was told it was nearly extinct."

Jack looked at the once magnificent creature and thought maybe he was looking at the last one on our Lord's earth. The eyes in the other heads all seemed to stare at him accusingly, just like Red's one-eyed stare, asking him for some rhyme or reason for the madness of shooting an endangered creature just to ordain an office wall thousands of miles from its native land.

He felt a surge of guilt flow through his limbic system as he ignored the virtual pleading of the stuffed heads and said nothing in response to Spinner's absurd revelation. He felt a bit ashamed of himself that he couldn't challenge the elderly oilman on his right to obliterate a beautiful species of this earth. So he bottled it and muttered another futile question.

"Do you shoot now, Spinner?"

"Hell man, only got time to shoot limeys," he answered with a loud laugh and slapped 'the limey in the room' on the leg with his huge hands to the guffawing of Red and Tom in the background and he continued in his jests.

"Son, down here in Texas it's still legal for a man to take his truck, dawg, house and his firearms and leave his wife nothing: so it's obvious that here it's still legal to have open season on limeys!"

All three of them laughed and slapped each of their thighs. Jack thought they were going to burst into the *'dee Camptown races sing mah song... do dah, do dah'* like in *'Blazing Saddles'*.

"Heh Spinner, show Jack your Alaskan boy's den. You gotta see this Jack, ain't many people got what Spinner got," asked Red, breaking off from his guffaws.

Spinner got up and went to his desk and drew out from one of the drawers a photo album. He strode back, his long lean legs and boots taking a couple of seconds to cross the room despite his ancient age. He opened the book on the table and asked the Englishman to look.

"I live in Alaska a lot of the year now; hunt and fish mainly, kinda given up on the screwing."

He burst into laughter, as did Red and Tom, slapping their thighs again in their merriment. Jack smiled warmly, still looking up at the poor stuffed heads, all of whom seemed to be mocking him. Spinner pointed at a large picture of a room which seemed to be full of every endangered species on the planet. The pictures of his trophy room were like the Smithsonian Museum. However, unlike the Ben Stiller movie, *'Night at the Museum'*, these critters were never coming back to life.

There were grizzly bears, brown bears, crocodiles, lions, tigers, and whales, but also a lot of sheep. It seemed he liked shooting sheep. It was obvious why he lived mainly in Alaska; he had probably shot most of the wildlife in his native Texas.

"Me and the boys just love taking a case or two of Bud and a bottle of Jack and just sitting in here shooting the shit about hunting. Sometimes we try to remember what it was like to talk about screwing."

They all laughed again and Tom said, smiling, "Spinner, tell him about Lars and the hunting."

Spinner put the photo album down and smiled. He spat into his spittoon and began his tales.

"One day a stranger came to the township in Alaska. He asked Bobby, my buddy the barman in the one and only bar, 'What do you folks do around here?' Bobby just carried on drying his beer glasses and didn't look at the guy but he told him the truth and said – 'Hunt and screw.'

"The stranger asked Bobby, 'What do you hunt?'

"Bobby told him straight – 'Something to screw.' He left the town quickly in his truck melting snow as he went."

He laughed and so did Jack, still not sure that this was true but up to now with these three it could well be fact. But Red wasn't finished his stories.

"One of my rig managers, Sam, left us after twenty-five years, sick of the stress, and moved out to the wilds. He saw the postman once a week and got his groceries once a month. He was living in perfect peace and quiet without too much interference from his neighbours. After six months or so of almost total isolation, someone knocks on his door. He opens it and there's a big, bearded man standing there. 'Name's Lars, your neighbour from forty miles away, having a birthday,' this huge man grunted to him.

"He continued, 'Party Friday – thought you might like to come, about five.'

"'Great,' says Sam, 'after six months out here I'm ready to meet some local folks. Thank you.'

"As Lars is leaving, he stops and says, 'Gotta warn you – there's gonna be some drinkin'.'

"'Not a problem – after twenty-five years in business, I can drink with the best of 'em,' says Sam.

"Again, as he starts to leave, Lars stops and says, 'More'n likely gonna be some fightin', too.'

"Sam said, 'Well, I get along with people. I'll be there. Thanks again.'

"Once again Lars turns from the door. 'I've seen some wild sex at these parties, too.'

"'Now that's really not a problem,' says Sam. 'I've been all alone for six months! I'll definitely be there. By the way, what should I bring?'

"Lars stops in the door again and says, 'Whatever you want. There's just going to be the two of us.'

All three oilmen went into apoplexy at this story and Jack laughed in tandem, hoping that this meant he was now in their team and circle of trust. The stuffed heads turned away in disgust and condemnation.

It was like being a fly on the wall of J.D. Rockefeller's office and on the set of Apocalypse Now, interspersed with Ernest Hemmingway's tales of mass extermination of large land and marine animals. Jack thought he was going to enjoy this trip but he decided that maybe he'd give Spinner and Red a miss though, when it came to cultural alignment workshops and supporting the sustainable development programs he had to introduce. God, this was going to be a difficult job.

They went for lunch and ate, as usual in Houston, far too much. They took Jack to a restaurant where you carved your own steak off the joint of a beast the size of one of Red's stuffed grizzly bears. If you ate more than the heaviest yet eaten you got your lunch for free. There was a picture on the wall of the current winner. He was the current line backer for the 'Oilers', Jack was told. He made Tom look small.

Jack asked the carver man if he could try to win as he felt hungry and thought, *Let's show these Yanks how a good British boy eats.* Maybe he could win some credibility back after the assassination of his character and his country in the office. He asked the man to place the knife on the huge joint just a bit further than the steak the line backer had eaten. The carver placed it about a foot along the joint.

"That's about ninety ounces, buddy," and challenged, "do you want it or not!"

Jack looked aghast, ninety ounces was about half a stone of beef. He had not seen a whole family of eight eat that much for Sunday lunch with Yorkshire puddings, nor the lions on David Attenborough's wildlife programs eat as much. Feeling defeated and inadequate yet again, he turned the challenge down and asked for a piece about an inch wide. The carver just looked at Red, who was staring Jack out through his one eye.

"Is he with you, buddy? Get a lot of limeys in here, think they kin eat. Bull…shit! They are just like those Californian tree huggers, most of them."

And turning to Jack: "Whatta you ****** want?"

Jack sat down with his newfound colleagues and tried to enjoy his lunch, his ego dented and wondering how much more he could be humiliated. When he left half of his huge one-inch-wide steak on his plate, along with the football field of salad and potato farm of fries, he realised he had a long way to go.

Finally they said their goodbyes. Again, there had been little talk about drilling or progress reporting. Jack was beginning to believe what Tom had said earlier; maybe he was just there to arrange the entertainment.

Tom turned to him in the car.

"I guess you want to go meet your boss now?"

"Sounds great, Tom, what time and where do we meet?"

"I'll take you now and come and get you soon, Jack. You don't want to spend too much time with that crazy son of bitch. Hell man, he'll have you writing execution plans all ******* afternoon and night. We got to party, boy, it's a man's bidness and people matter, not ******* plans and procedures, that's the way this bidness works. He lives on another planet, Jack."

Tom laughed after revealing his affection for the project manager and continued with a rhetorical question.

"And we gotta work for the son of a bitch. Hah-hah. Which imbecile picked him to lead real men who already know the bidness inside out?"

"I think it was the president of the company, Tom: your ultimate boss," Jack said with a smile and a small hint of sarcasm.

"Goddam lunatics are running the asylum now. Come on, let's go and I'll show you where he's locked up," Tom said, laughing and with that engaging smile which Jack assumed confidently had captured the hearts and minds of many of his colleagues and also, his lovely wives.

They arrived back at head office and walked to the lift up into what was the main project management office. They walked past the project staff sitting at their work stations. Jack was planning to get to know most of these very well over the next five years and didn't realise at the time how their lives and his would entangle in both the pain and pleasure of life overseas and with a leadership and team that were in many ways bizarre, or possibly just insane.

They arrived at a corner office which seemed to have views across the whole of downtown Houston. Tom opened the door and they entered. Sat at his desk was Jack's client and new boss, Jon. He had met him before in London when they had agreed on what was required from him and what his vision was to deliver a world-class project. Jack liked him and certainly respected his keen mind and determination to do the right thing and get everyone aligned to the challenging goals they would set for all participants. Jon offered him a whole new world of management experience and also a life-changing opportunity for his family and him to work and live in Asia.

Jon was dressed in what Jack came to realise was his usual attire of smart pants, long-sleeved white shirt and red tie. A medium-build man with slightly greying hair and wearing black spectacles. He was a German-born engineer who had studied in America and joined the company straight from university but had worked most of his life from London, the Middle East and Asia Pacific. He had a reputation as a very hard and strict task master and was named by those who had benefited from his leadership after Bismarck, The Iron Chancellor. He was well educated and massively experienced with the company.

Unlike Tom's desk, Jon's had rows of files, drawings and paperwork neatly stacked in order either ready to action or ready to be filed or transported. Laptops, printers and no shredders were apparent. There were posters on the walls depicting the design models of the various mini projects that made up the main processing facilities offshore and onshore. Further posters showed the engineering and design progress curves and key performance statistics. Jack made a mental note to ask Tom if he had any of these.

Tom adjusted his crotch and introduced himself to Jon.

"Howdy, Jon; I got Jack with me, thought he could have a word before we take him downtown for a few beers."

"Thank you, Tom. Did you take him through your draft execution plan?"

Jon peered at Tom over his glasses. Jack noticed there was no small talk or social interaction.

Jon picked up his personal organiser that was on his desk and fixed his gaze on Tom, who was looking uncomfortable. He looked up after checking and continued his interrogation of Tom.

"It is due to be completed in the document control review system by Friday for internal review. I'd like Jack to review it with you before then and have some input to your organisation plans. What did you think of it, Jack?"

Oh shit, Jack thought. *This is difficult.* He really didn't want to drop Tom in and lose any hint of trust or friendship on day one in the bloody office. Tom looked at him he thought in a threatening way but to his undying credit Tom showed that he was indeed a real man and told John the truth; well, a sort of truth.

"Goddamn, Jon; ah didn't have the time to go through all that today. I just gave him a brief summary of what we intend to do in each country."

Jon looked at Tom in a doubtful way but his brown eyes seemed to glint over his glasses and a wry smile came over his face. He was obviously getting to know Tom over these past few weeks that he'd been working with him.

"I see. Well, make sure you get your lady to print a copy off so that Jack can read it tonight in his hotel and we'll reconvene tomorrow to go through it."

Yet again, Jack thought, Oh shit. It looked like the beers tonight were off. He was beginning to realise why they called Jon, The Iron Chancellor.

"Hell Jon, I got a meeting with Red and the HR people tomorrow morning to agree the contractor rates and terms. It'll have to be another day."

Tom looked suspiciously like he was telling porkies.

John looked at his laptop and pressed a few buttons. To Tom's everlasting pain, he never expected Jon to look at the Microsoft

Outlook project diary. He looked downfallen.

Jon looked up and stared at Tom.

"I can't see any meeting in the diary, Tom. Are you sure you are not mistaken?"

Tom raised his crotch a little and also his voice a notch.

"Goddamn Jon, Red arranged with HR and it's in my personal diary and probably his. You know Red, he doesn't count any truck with these modern electronic bullshit diaries and things."

Jon looked at Tom with a piercing stare and Jack thought, *For God's sake, Jon, give the lad a break.* He was still learning about his Iron Chancellor and still very naïve, of course. Torture and humiliation were just some of the many management tools for Jon to ensure he got his deliverables, as Jack and many of his laboratory rats were to find out shortly.

"Well, I will have a conversation with Red and I shall enlighten him on project procedure. I will make a note to that effect." Jon noted the fact in his personal planner. "I will also come back to you with a time to review your execution plan with Jack before Friday. Thank you, Tom. I'll ring you when I have finished with Jack."

Tom was summarily dismissed and left, cursing under his breath as he passed by. Jon offered his new victim a seat. Jack started to realise that Jon was not going to be an easy man to work for. Jon sat opposite him around a circular table. He opened his personal planner which he seemed to keep with him at all times and he asked Jack a loaded direct question.

"What do you think of our two American construction leaders?"

Jack wasn't sure what to say as he was still trying to absorb some of behaviours and comments from his new colleagues and certainly didn't want to poison any relationships, so he tried to be diplomatic.

"Found them very polite and helpful, like most Americans I've worked with, Jon. We haven't had too much time to talk about the project yet or their plans."

Jon threw himself into his project management mantra.

"That is obvious to me. You are not here to talk to them but to make sure they do what they are paid to do. On projects we can have no one that needs training, developing, counselling. I expect everyone to do their staff work and deliver their goals and objectives. Anyone who doesn't I will run off."

Jack was confused as he thought part of his job was to support, counsel and train people to improve communication, team spirit and reduce conflict and he told Jon so. He also told him that he thought that he wished him to assist Jon in his own leadership coaching. He was advised of his misunderstandings again.

"No. I need no coaching and you will not waste your time on anyone else. If they don't deliver their staff work then I will run them off. On projects, everyone has to plan their work, record it and deliver it. If they don't they will be on a flight home."

He looked at his consultant with a weak smile again. Jack was wondering if this was a wind up to get him to react, so he kept quiet. He was soon to learn as his time with Jon evolved, sometimes it was best to know when you had lost the intellectual argument. Jon closed his organiser and seemed to relax somewhat after his lecture and he went back to answer his first question himself.

"I think you have been kind about our two colleagues you've met. You must learn to be honest... all Americans are crazy. All construction people in this industry are Neanderthals. We have to educate them, Jack. On this project we need to ensure we get no influence from their corporate bosses here. Once I have them all on my project in Asia, I will run any off who don't deliver. You must try to keep them all aligned and on track to deliver despite most of them being deranged. If you fail... I will run you off."

Jack was really beginning to wonder what on earth he had let himself in for. This didn't seem to be what they had talked about in London, nor in his consultancy contract. But it was early days and he thought, why rock the boat yet? There were years to go, if only he could survive; so he replied tentatively.

"Well, at least we know where we stand, Jon. I will endeavour to meet your goals."

"Yes you will." Jon concluded the lecture.

The phone rang and Jon took the call.

"OK, I will see him now; just tell him to come in."

"I'll head off then, Jon, and let you get on," Jack said and moved to stand up. He was halted by a sharp retort.

"No, sit down. I think you may learn something from this conversation."

He sat down wondering what on earth his leader meant. Into the office walked a young, lean-figured, Hispanic-looking man. He looked nervously around and then at Jon, and sat down. Jack noticed a slight shake in the hand that was clasping a document.

"Come and sit down, Tony. This is Jack, he is going to work with us to help build teams and ensure the foreigners, like you, get along with us."

Jon was in full cross-cultural bonding mode again.

"Hi Tony," Jack said, extending his hand hoping to ease the obvious worry shown in the young man's face and body language.

"Hi Jack, have you just arrived, sir?"

Jack was still getting used to being called 'sir' by Americans. He was always amazed at the manners and humility of Americans who always seemed to respect anyone of older age or authority with the title. The English were beaten with canes and hard objects by their teachers and school principles to make them address their betters as 'sir'. To call anyone 'sir' in his culture was to show that you were subservient and afraid. So they just wouldn't...despite the constant flagellation by teachers. It was indeed a pleasure to have a more sensible reason to call someone 'sir': that was, politeness and respect. Jon, however, had no intention of polite small talk or empathy and he interrupted Jack's answer.

"We have no time to talk about Jack. You must get back to work after this conversation as it is obvious you need to change your behaviour and your work process."

Tony sat down and shuffled the document he'd brought on the table. His head slightly bowed. Jon continued the torture.

"Now then Tony, yesterday I did not have the time to conclude our debate in the Exec Meeting as it was running later than I scheduled. I will fix that next week. I have asked you to come back this morning to explain what your role on this project is. I will not expect in future that you debate with me on the process of document control. I expect you to deliver the plan and process that I have signed off, not argue with me over technical details. Do you understand?"

It seemed that Tony had deemed to question the great man's knowledge of that mind bogglingly boring subject of document control. Jon stared at Tony through his glasses and Tony looked up and tilted his head from side to side in some way of calming his nerves or temper.

"Yes sir, I guess I have to understand."

"Good, that will be the end of it then. Let me explain something to you which you may well find motivating and enlightening about projects."

Jon stood up and opened the door and as he did so he put his arm around Tony and told him project theory lesson number two hundred and twenty-two.

"On projects, we have highly intelligent, highly paid individuals. We call them engineers. We also have less intelligent, less well-paid people. We call them document controllers. You are one of those and you are paid to serve engineers, not the other way around. Do you understand now, Tony?"

"Yes sir. Thank you for helping me," Tony replied and walked out of the office, head a lot lower than when he came in. Jon closed the door and sat down again.

"He seemed to go away well motivated, Jon," Jack said, tongue in cheek, wondering how he'd take the sarcasm. Maybe running him off seemed to be possible.

"I believe he did."

Jon confirmed with a very satisfied grin on his face and he continued, "Come on, I'll take you down to the construction Stone Age as I'm heading for a meeting with Red. I need to confirm if he really did book a meeting with HR."

Dear me, Jack thought, *this man does not give up, he is like a bloody Rottweiler with a human leg bone – poor Tom.*

They left his office and took the lift. In the lift already were two very smart, tall, good-looking, middle-aged, suntanned males.

"Good morning Jon," one of the men greeted them.

"Good morning Randy."

Randy turned to his partner and said, "Bruce, this is Jon, our Scorpio project manager. Bruce is our Corporate Social Responsibility VP. "

"Hi, Jon." Bruce held his hand out and Jon shook his hand, saying, "Good morning Bruce. I am pleased to meet you."

Jon turned to Jack.

"Jack, Randy is the Chief Executive Officer." And turning back to look at Randy he opened his hand and pointed to his new consultant. "This is Jack. He is here to do some of that corporate social responsibility stuff on the project. He may look like a street fighter: but I have hired him as I believe he may have some brains as he has a PhD."

Marvellous, Jack thought. *He meets the CEO and a corporate VP who may well be instrumental in him staying on this project and maybe getting much more future work, and he with a brain the size of a planet, and Jon calls him a street fighter.*

Randy and Bruce both shook hands and as the lift door opened and Jon left. Randy turned slightly and grabbed Jack's arm and whispered into his ear, "Jack, you may need your street fighting a hell of a lot more than you need your PhD to put Jon's team back together – best of luck, son."

As they walked towards Tom's office again Jon took his leave and said he'd arrange the construction execution meeting with Tom. Jack mused that it would probably humiliate and destroy both of them and that Jon certainly didn't forget about anything, for sure. He told Tom the bad news.

"Goddamn son of a bitch, does he not know that Red is a ******** VP of this company and we won't be writing ******** execution plans once we start getting gas ashore? I think he'll be long gone, Jack, run off if he upsets Red. Red goes way up to the top. Anyway, who gives a **** about plans? I've designed 'em , built 'em , commissioned 'em and also ran the mother*******s to bring gas and black gold ashore without a plan! So we gonna build them Red's and my way, bud. Ah hope you can come with us, Jack; I think Red likes you and I think we can be – what you limeys say, erhm – mates?"

Tom said he'd take Jack to his hotel, the Holiday Inn, to freshen up after a long day talking. He said that he and Red would meet him for a drink after work around 6pm. Jack thought, *That's good time to relax, freshen up after the jet lag and a few cold beers*. Thoughts of reading any execution plans for Jon were never spoken about; Tom obviously thought he'd fixed it with his private conversations with Red.

Indeed they had a pleasant evening as 'happy hour' in Houston was a delight for someone like Jack who was used to a few beers in a smoky pub with nothing but hairy assed men talking about football and how shit their wages were. In his world there were no women to be seen in working men's pubs nor was there any food, only crisps and maybe nuts on the bar and then only in posh places. In Aberdeen a study was done of the public bars and hotel bars of the free nuts and snacks on the bar. The nuts were laden with urine and certain infections, it was discovered, as few men washed their hands after going to the toilet and then on returning dipping their fingers back in the nut bowl. Needless to say no sane person ate food in Britain in pubs after work. It was beer and then home if you were married, if not, a trip to the Chinese or Indian take away at closing time to stuff curry and chips down your throat. But here in Houston it was magic.

The hotel bars were full of gorgeous ladies, legs up to their coccyx, blonde or auburn hair down to their navels with amazing figures and dressed to kill. The sad part was that all of them were with elderly Texan men. Rich men too and all looked like JR from Dallas or Spinner. Stetsons, jeans and boots were still de rigour uniform and the girls hung off their arms. Jack was mesmerised by them all.

The bars were full of free food, wonderful Tex Mex food too – nachos, chilli, fajitas etc. – and seafood to die for. Jack decided to actually eat whilst in Houston while drinking and he tucked in before Tom and Red arrived.

Red informed him on arrival that he'd had his 'conversation' with Jon.

"Goddammed man, expects me to change mah plans for a ******* document. Ah told him no way. But Tom and I spoke before and we have now arranged for you to head off with Tom to N'awlins tomorrow to see Danny, the main engineering contractor project manager. He's there to look at a friendly fabricator we all know who may be setting up in Asia to get some of our work. Thought you'd like to meet him sooner and also get the hell away from Jon for a few days."

"Gee Red, that's great news, never been to New Orleans for ten years, should be great," Jack replied, smiling with a warm glow from the several Bud Lights that they had poured down his neck.

"It's a great town, Jack, spent a lot of mah life there. Not as good as the bayous mind and the coon ass boys I grew up with in those swamps, but good town to party."

He swallowed a beer with his huge hand in one swallow.

"Sometimes when I sit here I think how I miss my old home and the boys back in Louisiana. Jack, ah miss ma little old home. Hell, man, give me a butane burner right now and a greased pig's ass and I'd burn the ass hairs right off and screw the thing."

Jack looked at this giant of man, who was surrounding yet another bottle in his massive fist and managed to find out what his attraction to greased pigs was.

It seems the favourite pastime down in the bayous is to smear grease all over a small gruffer and then chase it around the yard until you catch it. It is said to be fun trying in vain to grab a tiny pig with your hands slipping off the greasy lard smeared on it, which probably came from its poor mum when she was roasted for last Sunday's dinner. But Jack feared in Tom's neighbourhood even Burt Reynolds and his *Deliverance* mates would have been worried after hearing the statement about his habit of greased pig chasing 'chez' the big man and the eventual outcome of the chase.

Some weeks later in Singapore he suggested to Jack that he come with him back to Dixie next leave and meet his family sometime in the vacation. As Jack reflected on his statement of greased pig fun he decided to decline and thought it best he take the hell of Bali or Phuket as a holiday, it may well be safer. Especially when Tom said his cousin had a banjo!!

A small squat man wearing the ubiquitous Stetson and gator skin boots came over and began chewing the fat with the two icons of construction. He was finally introduced to Jack by Tom.

"Jack, this here is Jerry. Jerry is big in paint and we'll probably be using his paint on the job. Spinner and him go back a long time. He's got some new shit he'd like us to use on the job."

Jack shook the gentleman's hand and stupidly asked what his 'new shit' was. He was blown back a bit by the heated response.

"Man, in the oil bidness biggest problem these liberal assed days is getting rid of the paint waste. The bidness has changed due to those tree-hugging bastards in California and those ******* Democrats in Washington interfering with us good old boys down here in God's country. We know more about the bidness than those sons of bitches ever will."

Jerry took a swig of his beer and slammed the bar.

"Goddamn, in the old days we just used to throw the tins over the side. Never killed no one and there were more tarpon and dolphins around then than now."

Jack thought, *I guess there would be plenty sea creatures, until the tributyltin, arsenic and cadmium and the other lovely poisons in the paint got them.* Jerry continued his rant and seemed to have developed a solution for the tree-hugging brigades in Washington and California.

"Anyway, I have mah own bidness as well as selling paint. I've invented a product that eats the waste paint. I culture bugs that eat hydrocarbons. So when you paint offshore you place a few pints of mah solution into oil drums full of paint waste. The bugs eat the paint and the bugs piss out solvent that you can reuse. It'll revolution the bidness, buddy, and I'll make millions."

Tom looked at Jack and noticed a glimmer of a laugh on Jack's face and he seemed to read his mind as to what Jack's response was going to be. Tom intervened:

"Well Jerry, it seems we are all going into the 'bug bidness', buddy."

They all raised their beer bottles and toasted Jerry's new microbe venture.

"Jack, would you like to come to my ranch at the weekend for a clam bake and do some shooting?" Jerry asked the amused Brit, very kindly Jack thought.

"I'd love to, Jerry, if I'm still here. What do you shoot there? Rabbits? Pheasants?"

Jerry looked shocked at the thought.

"Hell no, Jack! We shoot zeehbra."

"Surely not real zebra, Jerry. You got some virtual reality software and gear there, mate?" said Jack, astonished, but quickly realising he was in a very strange place with very strange people, and hoping for a sensible explanation to the bizarre statement.

Jerry looked even more shocked.

"What the hell is virtual reality, man? Some form of techno shit from California? Ain't gonna buy into anything from those liberal, commie-loving mothers. Hell, I got real zeehbra – all the way from Africa. I also got some impala and a buffalo."

Jack couldn't really all comprehend this, his mind was now completely numb with the thought of beautiful animals from the Veldt roaming the Texas ranch, only to be shot by Jerry and his crazy buddies. Jerry could see his potential guest was puzzled and thoughtful.

"Guess you Brits dohn't hunt zeehbra on your ranches? Here we all take a few beers down to the hide. Mah ranch hands let the animals loose from their paddocks and march them past the hide. My buddies and me then blast the suckers with whatever firearm we feel like using. Ah got every type you'd want in the hide – rifles, automatic, handguns, hell I even got a handheld FM-92 Stinger if ever I get an elephant shipped over. The hands will skin and butcher them and we can eat them on the barbecue with the clams. Great sport, buddy; you have to try to get there Saturday."

Jack agreed that it may be great sport but he'd have to see if his schedule would allow it, knowing that he really had to get out of this place sooner rather than later. Shooting unarmed zebra gently strolling past a host of drunken rednecks armed with more firepower than a small third world country just didn't seem quite fair to him.

The beer was taking its toll and Jack's guard was dropped somewhat in that he started talking with lady who was standing next to them. She looked amazing, Julia Roberts's type, and she loved talking to an Englishman. Jack realised that American ladies love an English accent. Why? He had no idea because in his experience they were exposed to Englishmen only through movies, and every movie he had ever seen from Hollywood depicted Englishmen as homosexual, perverted, evil wrongdoers. Or they are genocidal maniacs, incompetent military leaders, or cheeky cockney garbage men. Even the Disney movies have every animated bad guy with a posh English accent; you watch them; the tigers, snakes, octopuses, crocodiles, spiders, hunchbacks, sadists, sadistic pirates, evil fairy godmothers, cruel dog breeders, you name it, the English are evil, cowardly and soft.

So why this gorgeous lady wanted him to whisper sweet nothings to her all evening in his non-posh English accent was a mystery to him. After a few more beers, he thought maybe it was his body like a temple and Brad Pitt looks.

He was enjoying the evening and the lady's attention, as you do. She went off to the ladies' room. A guy walked up to him as she left and asked him a worrying question.

"What are you doing with mah girl?"

Jack looked at him and said that he wasn't doing anything but enjoying a chat and anyway he didn't know she was his girl. The Texan just smiled and said that indeed she was; but not to worry and he walked away. Jack thought this was strange behaviour but by now he was realising that there were strange people in this town. The lady came back and he pointed out the man who was standing some way away in the bar and told her what he'd said and asked if he was indeed her boyfriend.

"He's not with me; I've never seen him before," she answered.

Oh, he thought, *weird,* but he carried on chatting with her. Red had left by now and Tom was talking to some guys from a contractor at the other end of the room. After about ten minutes the guy came back and took Jack's arm and repeated his question.

"What are you doing with my girl?"

Jack looked at him and gave him a fixed stare and turned to the girl and asked, "Do you know this guy?"

"I've never seen him before, he's not with me," she replied.

Jack turned to the guy and told him in his best tough British accent to **** off; as you would.

The Texan just smiled and said he was just joking and walked off. *Bizarre,* Jack thought and carried on with what was much more pleasant than talking with grizzled octogenarians about wiping out endangered species or rampant male homosexuality in the backwoods of Alaska or slippery porcine bestiality.

Twenty minutes later, he heard a commotion behind him and turned to see that Tom had lifted the same guy off his feet by his neck. His huge right hand was gripped all round his neck and he had his arm twisted up his back. Tom dragged him by his neck with his arm in a peculiar, almost certainly broken position through the room and out of the main door.

"What the hell was that all about?" Jack asked unbelievingly to the girl.

"Man, I've no idea, honey, but wasn't that the guy you told to **** off?"

"I think so," he replied.

"Forget it, honey, let's have another drink and talk to me in that funny accent again… ah just love hearing you talk."

So he did.

About ten minutes later Tom came back. He stood next to the lady, adjusted his crotch and spoke to her.

"Ah'm mighty sorry, ma'am for that ruckus, but I think it's time Jack and me left this party. We gotta go to N'awlins tomorrow on the early red eye. "Come on Jack, let's hit the sack."

Jack said his reluctant goodbyes and walked through the bar with the big man and asked him what was 'all that ruckus' about.

"Jack, you got to learn here in Texas ain't like England. Don't know who that fella was or why he was after you but the lady tipped me the wink about him earlier that he'd been stalking you so I was watching."

"Tom, I can handle myself. I wasn't scared of him, mate, happy to take him on any day," Jack said forcefully, the booze helping in his macho stance.

"I can see you can look after yourself, buddy, but this guy was walking towards you with loaded thirty-eight! Lucky I was watching him, just got to him in time I guess. I've taken him to security but they've just thrown him out. Here, it's normal for guys to carry handguns, so I think it's best you go to bed, lock your door and don't open for anyone till I pick you in the morning."

"For ****'s sake Tom, what the **** was wrong with him? And the gun, dear God! Bloody hell, man. Heh, thanks buddy, I owe you one."

Jack put his arm around half the giant's chest – he couldn't reach his shoulders and it wouldn't go around anyway. Tom patted him with his huge mitt and grinned.

"OK Jack, see you 5.30 a.m. Ah bet you don't forget your first day in Houston with the good old boys. Sleep well."

He was correct. Jack never forgot that first day and he only slept well once he'd bolted the door and put a chair against it. What tomorrow would bring? God only knew. He was soon to find out…

CHAPTER TWO

New Orleans, Louisiana, USA

Buffalo Alf

One day later...

They took the red eye to New Orleans at the crack of dawn and were greeted on arrival at the Louis Armstrong airport by the engineering contractor's construction USA manager, Jim. He was yet another large man. Jack reflected that he hadn't met any small men here, or indeed any working women, apart from the ones that were beauty queens on the arms of the large men. Jim was also elderly. Again, the consultant reflected that most he'd met in this business were old. There were not a lot of young people.

Jim offered Gator Tom his hand.

"Howdy Gator, sure glad you could make it today."

Tom adjusted his crotch and took Jim's hand in his huge paw.

"Looking forward to getting outta that hell hole of an office, Jim, and do some real work. What you got planned, buddy?"

Jack stood waiting to be introduced, thinking maybe he didn't exist, this had all just been a dream and he was still stuck in the hell of Aberdeen freezing his balls off and being abused by miserable intoxicated Scotsmen on Union Street. Tom seemed to remember that he was actually there and turned around to introduce him to Jim.

'Heh Jim, sorry but this is Jack. He's a limey from London. Come to try to get us to love each other. Hell, man, we all get along in this bidness – these limeys! – always looking to love each other: Sons of bitches must think we are all gay boys out here – the Brits, they invented it, man!"

He slapped the object of his affection on his back, laughing loudly and Jack staggered forward a few feet under the blow. Friendly fire, he thought, and wouldn't fancy an unfriendly slap. Jim laughed and put his hand out.

"Howdy Jack, just breaking your balls, buddy. You'll meet Danny soon. He's a Brit but I sure wouldn't want to screw him; the ugly son of a bitch!"

Jim and Red both howled and Jack took his hand, recovering from the friendly-fire slap with deep breaths.

"I'm looking forward to meeting him, Jim. Good to meet you, mate. Where are we headed?"

"We gonna pick Danny up at his hotel and head outta town up north to see the fabricator. Should be back in time to have a few beers and meet a few of the boys you'll be working with."

"Great, sounds good," Jack said.

They took his car along the highway a few miles. Tom and Jim chatted about the fabricator and how they both rated them from past work in the US. He pulled into a Marriott hotel and waiting at the entrance was a small, ginger-haired man with glasses. He was middle-aged but a lot younger-looking than those Jack had met previously, apart from Jon. He was dressed in grey slacks and blue short-sleeved shirt and carrying a leather zipped folder containing whatever he needed for his trip. Jim jumped out and shook his hand and the man climbed into the back of the large Buick with Jack. Tom remained sat in the front seat. He was the client and demanded respect. Lowly contractors and consultants sat in the back.

Danny introduced himself.

"Hi. I'm Danny. You must be Jack. I heard a lot of good things about you, Jack. I've no idea what you are here for and what the **** you are going to do but I'm not paying for you so hope we can get a few beers and enjoy ourselves on your budget. I've about spent my

****** team-building budget already on this big bastard."

He grabbed the back of Tom's shoulders and shook him. Well, the shake didn't move the leviathan but it was some form of bonding, Jack guessed.

"Well Danny, you better get your wallet out tonight, buddy, coz I got some big hitters coming to party," Tom interjected, laughing.

Danny turned to Jack, put his hands on his head and whispered, "I didn't get to mah beed till four this a.m. – on the piss with them in Bourbon Street." He then took his head in his hands. "Oh, mah heed. For ****'s sake I've got to stop doing this."

Jack was to find out that like the tiger in the children's book, '*The Tiger Who Came to Tea*' – he never did (stop doing it).

They headed up towards some Godforsaken swamp in the backwaters of Louisiana, Danny, Tom and Jim talking about things related to construction for the first time on his whole trip. Jack sat thinking maybe they needed some presentation to inform these great leaders of men of what his role really was. Or maybe, he just needed to wise up and realise his role was to get everyone pissed and laid. He stupidly began to think that he needed to talk to Jon... but oh no! he quickly realised his mistake. He then shivered at this stupidity and thought, *Let's get to Singapore first, maybe he'll be more empathetic in paradise. Best leave well alone and maybe Jon will go away.*

He and Danny managed to get a social conversation which was encouraging. Danny was Scottish and from Glasgow. He had worked in all the places Jack had in the UK and they both knew a few of the same people. So it was really pleasant for the estranged consultant to meet and to talk with someone who on first meeting seemed to have a similar sense of humour and on first impressions lived in the real world. He was wrong, of course.

Danny was Project Director of the main contractor who had secured the contract to engineer, procure, construct and commission the bits of steel and wires in the multi, multi billion project. No small task.

They talked quietly about all things past and respective backgrounds. They had indeed grown up in similar working-class families and areas and both moved through the industry to this eventual Nirvana, or Nemesis, time would tell which one. Jack asked him what the purpose of today's trip and visit was.

"Well for me it's to see if the fabricator has the capability in Asia to build the scope that they've bid. I'm also looking to see if they can meet any of the management criteria for best practice in HSE. Also I've been asked by our HR and our Corporate Social lads to see if they can manage in a multicultural environment. That might be why you've come down to look too? Your boss, Jon's big into that bullshit."

Jack didn't like to tell Danny that he was only there because Tom didn't want another grilling from Jon and he was probably a great excuse for them all to have another piss-up and the purported team build that he now knew he would be paying for. He was learning.

"Guess it should be of interest, Danny. I haven't been to see a fabricator in the South since visiting Lafayette and Morgan City ten years ago. Have they changed much?"

"I'm not sure, Jack. I haven't been to this one for sure," Danny replied and then whispering quietly, "but between you and me, I'm only going because our VP and your VP are friends of them. They pre-qualified before I came on board and have tendered, but I'm still not convinced we won't use existing, established Asian yards, mate. Been down here myself years ago running jobs, they are great guys and get the job done but expensive. But we need this built in Asia cheaper and times have changed with all the social, environmental and cultural shite things we have to ******* abide by. But I need to see if their senior management can meet our standards. They have a couple of their proposed Asian managers to meet us. I am definitely looking at their leadership in safety and also fairness and inclusiveness. I have to make sure they know how to employ and treat the Asians out there. I can't be ****** to get hauled back to Houston to have my arse slapped over any racial or sexual shite. I hope you can help with that, Jack... I'll buy the beers." And he then put his head in his hands. "My ******* heed hurts like **** today, mind. I had a few last night with the pipe line boys. God, it bloody hurts!"

Jack looked at Danny. His red face and 'heed' were glowing in the dark of the shaded window car. He did indeed look rough and he put his head in his hands and tried to doze off. It was a prelude to many, many other 'bad heed' mornings but Jack was yet to see the 'red heed' mornings that he ended up having to pick up the pieces after the habitual Danny meltdowns after a 'bad – and then the consequent – red head'.

After a few hours, they finally arrived at the town where the fabricator was based. They were told that they were to meet the owner and President at a hotel he owned first and have coffee and 'chew the fat' and would take his limo to his fab yard.

They did indeed meet the President for coffee. He was a charming, large-bodied elderly man. He looked and acted like Rhett Butler, the dapper Southern gentleman in *'Gone with the Wind.'* He was charming, polite and respectful. No jokes about the sexual orientation or deviances of Englishmen or if there was still open season on hunting them, just talk about the trip and purpose for visiting. He explained that they were in the process of buying an Asia yard and would send their best construction men to run it, hoping they could be successful in winning the small scope they had bid for.

Everyone climbed into his huge limo, which fitted everyone in the seats in the back. He offered drinks from his in cab bar but everyone declined as they were on full HSE alert and even if Danny was desperate to clear his bad heed, he was the boss and acted the part. They chatted about the project and his plans for his yard and generally killed the time as they drove through the backwaters of Louisiana.

Jack, in his innocence, looked out of the darkened windows and noted the swamps, rivers, jungles within which he speculated lived all known lethal carnivores and poisonous mini beasts, and wondered, *Why the hell are we going here?* There were plenty of Asian yards which he'd heard were located in a paradise of sandy beaches, warm seas, cold beer and thousands of beautiful girls.

As they finally drove up to the large gates of the yard, the President wound down his window. The searing heat hit Danny like a wave-of-searing-heat thing and he moaned, his head still hurting and he thought, *Oh, the wonders of air conditioning.*

From a small hut emerged a very small, elderly black guy. He rushed out of his hut, put on his worn baseball cap and ran towards the open limo window. He was bowing and when he saw the President began nodding his head as he approached the window and he ran to the gate and opened the large metal grilled doors to let the limo through. As the car slowly drove past the man, he took his cap off and held it to his chest and nodded to the President.

The President put his head a short way out of the window and said, 'Well thank you, George. Y'all have a nice day now."

George bowed his head and looked up with huge smile clearly delighted.

"Sure, sir, thank you sir, thank you kindly."

And he ran off to close the gate behind them. The President closed the window and turned to Danny and Jack looking pleased and proud.

"Government says we gotta hire n*****s... We got George," he said, smiling contentedly.

Jack looked at Danny and he looked at him.

"For ****'s sake," Danny whispered under his ginger moustache. Jack just turned his thumb down, gladiator style, hoping no one but Danny saw it.

The President took everyone into his huge office which was set some way off the large dirt and concrete covered fabrication yard. There were several steel structures, vessels and tanks in various phases of fabrication across the yard.

"Jim will take Danny and Tom on a tour of the yard soon. Bill, our HSE VP will come and sort you guys out with safety gear. Danny, you can meet Scott, the guy who'll be in charge of the yard. Everyone will report to him. He's my nephew so he is a true Southern kick-ass who'll make sure they do what we say. Jack, I thought you might like to meet the project manager who'll run the Asian project. We thought we better have an ethnic. He won't have much say, as Scott will run things, but he should be able to keep the natives happy. Guess that's your job too?"

Jack was about to attempt to correct him regarding his job and maybe explain the guiding principles of project management and cross-cultural leadership, but somehow he thought he would be wasting his time.

"OK sir, that should be very interesting," Jack replied, thinking, *I wonder what the poor 'ethnic' thinks of all this.*

Indeed Jack met him sat in his portable cabin at the far end of yard well out of the way of any management or human contact. He was of Indian extraction, it seemed, but had lived in the USA for many years. He was a graduate engineer who had worked for some of the large engineering contractors in small project management positions and had been 'head hunted' some time ago by the yard to target and bid for the massive amounts of work that was planned for Asian construction. Jack reflected that the yard they were looking at setting up was in China, not India, so he wasn't sure if the President had any geography knowledge or realised that his 'ethnic' choice may well be flawed.

Jack spent two hours with this individual and realised that he had found a person who needed some of his urgent counselling. Paranoia reigned, it seemed. He was a nervous, constantly twitching individual. He smoked incessantly and continually walked around and around outside of the portable cabin offices with his mobile to his ear. He had worn out a path around the offices in dust and mud. Jack's Springer Spaniel bird dog had done exactly the same in his garden back home. She was demented when she couldn't be out working and retrieving pheasants. The project manager was just as demented.

His paranoia was so apparent that he could not make a phone call in the office in case someone overheard him. His paranoia was, to some extent, rational, in that he told Jack that he had been taken off a small project on the yard as manager by Scott some weeks ago and he was certain he may get fired as no one spoke to him and they'd stuck him in his cabin miles from head office.

He doubted that he'd ever last to run the project and said that it was doomed anyway. Jack never knew how much that may be true until he interviewed him about the actual company and project they were bidding. After several interrupted attempts to talk to the tortured man as he ran out of the cabin and onto his mobile, pacing around his cabin continually, he eventually sat down in front of Jack.

"Tell me, why do you think it will go so wrong?" Jack enquired.

"I'll tell you, Jack, what's wrong," he said forcefully, and stood up and moved close to the white board. He took up a board marker pen and continued. He drew a box on the top of the board.

"He is the fab manager."

Ah, Jack thought. *He is going to explain the leadership and organisational structure. Good, a good place to begin.*

"He is a bastard," the demented man continued.

Before Jack could say anything, the paranoid Moghul continued, drawing another box and line.

"He reports to him, and he hates him," he explained with some satisfaction. He continued without stopping for breath, drawing another line from one to the other.

"Over here is the engineering manager. He's in New Orleans, and he hates this bastard. This is my construction manager. He is hated by him."

He continued to scribe another line on the chart.

"This is the proposed projects services manager. *I* hate him."

Then drawing one more line on the organisation chart and pointing to another box:

"He hates the whole project team."

So it continued. He then had to leave for the habitual cigarette and make a phone call and Jack watched as he paced around and around the office, phone at ear, smoke coming from mouth and ears and thought, *This guy will soon need a doctor.*

The project manager re-entered and picked up his marker. "Where was I?" he asked vacantly.

'In Dante's Inferno,' the intrepid consultant thought to say, but didn't. He just watched in awe at this modern-day paranoid Peter Drucker.

"Yes, here I was," he said, drawing another line from one box to another. "And this guy here, every bastard hates him."

Jack asked him to stop there. He knew now that he had the picture.

The 'Hate-o-gram' that the demented project manager had just drawn said it all. No trust, no clarity of roles, no respect and no leadership – but more than that, no fun. He decided it was cruel to continue as this tortured man may well burst an aorta or just froth at the mouth and die on him there and then over his empty desk. He thanked him and he phoned for someone to drive him back across the yard to civilisation.

They reassembled in the President's office. As Danny, Jim and Tom actually liked cranes, barges, wires, welding and big bits of steel, they seemed to have enjoyed their inspection and they chatted with the President and his senior team. All white, male, all Southern American and none with any experience of Asia or its many, many cultures, Jack thought. However, he was not consulted to make any comment as the rest talked about weld procedures and non-destructive testing. *Riveting,* he thought (sorry, not a pun), and no mention of management processes, communication plans and leadership; but who was he to butt in on construction talk? The holder of the piss-up budget, it seemed.

And after another boring hour talking about the magic of fillet welds, they left. Danny and Jim would present their findings to their proposals team but Tom was happy with the HSE for the client and that was really his only input as the contract was with Danny's company. Jack mentioned Paranoid Indian and his worries but was told by Jim, "Don't worry, he's only a sap! The man who'll run it is Scott, a good old ass-kicking, coon-ass construction man, that's all we need!"

Jack wondered if it was wise to mention his concerns to Jon but thought he'd ask Danny tonight over a beer in confidence what he thought first. They arrived back in New Orleans, curiously, just in time for Happy Hour.

And indeed it became Happy Eight Hours. They crawled along Bourbon Street enjoying the ubiquitous jazz music. Jack had never enjoyed jazz; his bearded, elderly friends thought him a philistine but what the hell? It was shit to him. More enjoyably for the Englishman they ended up in a cowboy bar and he had his first attempt to ride a mechanical bull. Everyone howled at the Brit being hurled off in a few seconds in a heap onto the floorboards. He reflected, *Just wait till I get you back home and see how you get on with the physical hell of good old British dominos or darts.*

They met a few of Tom's old colleagues and family. All of whom were as huge as him except a curious-looking man from the bayous who resembled the swamp rats who tried to kill Josey Wales in *The Outlaw Josey Wales'.* Tom introduced him as his cousin, Norman, and then put him into a friendly Japanese stranglehold and squeezed his neck until poor Norman's eyes popped.

"Norman is a real coon-ass from Thibodaux. Drove up here to see his baby cousin. He's never seen a Brit so I told him to come up and party, mind you he's never seen anyone but bayou folk. If he invites you down to see his folk make sure you got your banjo with you, boy! They might hog tie you naked over a log."

He howled with laughter and let Norman free from his slow asphyxiation. Danny and Jack took his hand and shook it, Danny, feeling his pulse to make sure he had not passed from this mortal coil.

"Hi Norman, pleased to meet you," Danny said.

Norman struggled to get his crushed voice box moving but whispered a hoarse greeting and rapidly drank a bottle of Bud that the Big Man gave him.

Danny and Jack drank more Tequila Sunrises than was good for them in each bar, which the locals all told them were a N'awlins speciality. In between worrying about banjos, being throttled by the Big Man's bonding routine, listening to screeching trumpets and trombones and being trampled to death by artificial bulls, Jack managed to talk with Danny, who seemed to pay the bill in every bar they went and then kept drinking and spending more and more.

"For ****'s sake, Jack, I've spent 747 dollars in that last bar. I could have bought a ******* 747 by now. I've pissed away the team-building budget just on the Big Man's ******* family already. I must stop doing this."

Jack was beginning to notice a trend with our intrepid project manager.

"Danny, what did you think of that fabrication yard today, mate?" he asked in a quieter moment in some bar that didn't have screeching jazz destroying his tympanic membranes.

"They know how to build shit, Jack, but I can't risk them over Asia with large modules without some track record. We may give them a small scope just to reduce the risk and to keep the boys back in Houston happy. I think they can handle that."

Jack nodded: "But what about the hell about 'we got George',

Danny, and that demented Indian project manager? Poor man is living in torture."

"Jack. We got a lot more to worry about than that, mate. This project's huge, the odd racist and 'paranoid wobbly' won't change the outcome. Anyway, I thought that's your job, to get us all as one team? You can start with this crazy fab yard lot and try to get then aligned with the 'wobbly' project manager. I do struggle with the *******s: wobbling their heads and those spots on their heed for ****'s sake. In Glasgow you only wobble your heed to throw a head-butt on someone and the red spot would only be the laser from the polis's rifle. Jack, you handle all that racism, sexism and culture shit for me, mate, and we'll get on great."

Then came a shout from across the room:

"Heh, Danny, this jug's empty, fill 'em up again, buddy!"

Tom was waving an empty gallon beer jug in his huge hand.

Danny moaned: "Oh ****! Go and get them in, Jack, put it on the tab. That'll make an Airbus I've bought now. I have to stop doing this, man."

Jack reflected that his time spent with Danny may well be more profitable than that with Paranoid Indian and his swamp inhabitants who probably were intractable. He felt that maybe despite his deep working-class, monochrome Glasgow roots, there was a multicultural leader in there somewhere: just had to keep him away from Indians until he'd culturally mellowed.

Tom suggested Danny and Jack jump in with him and Norman and head to a fish food restaurant for a late supper. The others would follow, he said. Norman had drunk a few bottles but didn't seem as drunk as the rest were. He said little but just looked amazed at the vibrant, multicultural, real world he obviously hardly saw. He seemed to Danny a normal and a well-mannered sensible man – fool...

They had only driven a few blocks when another car seemed to cut them up. Norman dropped the window and shouted some obscenity at the other driver and stuck his one finger up at the car. This seemed so out of character. Jack, feeling the effects of the drink and also remembering the incident in the hotel the night before, shuddered. Danny, more vociferous in drink, had to check him and voiced his concern from the back seat.

"Norman, you should be careful, man. What if he has a gun?"

Norman put his hand under the seat and pulled out a 0.357 Magnum, *Dirty Harry* style, which he could hardly hold up. He turned around, with his eyes blazing and stared now bulging out at the now frightened Brits.

"The mother****** better have a bigger one than this or he's a dead man; son of a bitch!"

Uhm! Jack thought. *Yet another raving lunatic.* This place may well be bad for his pension, simply because he may well not live to collect it. Gator Tom tried to alleviate their fears.

"Danny, calm down buddy. Norman's killed everything in known world, man or beast. He's a dead shot with handgun or rifle. You're safe with him, boy – let's go eat."

Jack sat back and looked at the back of Norman's head and listened as he now calmly hummed some quaint country song to himself, plainly in some other world to anyone normal, gun in one hand, wheel in the other, and he wondered if maybe it was time to have that talk with Jon about a quick exit back to civilisation.

They duly arrived at the restaurant without any fire fight or further trauma. The restaurant had tanks of all kinds of crustaceans, lobster, craw fish, shrimp and fish. Tom turned to Danny and Jack and explained the etiquette.

"You can choose which one you fancy and then take it outside and shoot it yourself."

Jack looked at Norman who was now twitching uncontrollably for no particular reason and wondered if Tom was joking. Norman's face twitched, his eyes bulged and finally he broke into a restrained laugh, which lasted for a microsecond, it seemed. This had been the only form of emotion he had observed, apart from the gun-induced maniacal behaviour.

Tom just guffawed and slapped his victim on the back, pushing him halfway into the unfortunate crustaceans. "Come on, buddy, let's eat."

Danny turned to Jack and whispered: "For ****'s sake they are all mad here, man."

Tom ordered two large round tables for everyone who was coming later and more beer for the four of them, and they sat at one of the tables. As Danny looked around he noticed that there were about three security guards prowling around the room, armed to the teeth with automatic rifles, handguns and wearing bulletproof vests. Now in Britain you didn't eat your dinner surrounded by the cast of 'Die Hard' so this was rather disturbing and he mentioned it to Tom.

"Danny, we are in a dangerous area of town, so best be careful. See that Chick Inn over the road there? Few months ago two ******* raided it as it was closing. They held the two counter girls up and took the takings. As they were leaving they just turned and shot the girls dead, for no good reason."

Danny looked shocked and said, "Dear God, that's terrible. Did they catch them?"

"Better than that, buddy, mah baby brother is a deputy here in N'awlins Police. They had been tipped off about the raid and him and five others were staked out waiting just over there next to where our car is. They were waiting for the ******* to come out and then arrest them, but when they saw them shoot them young ladies, well, they went a bit crazy. Baby brother put fifteen bullets into them and his buddies did the same. Over sixty bullets in both of them mother*******. Guess they won't be killing innocent people again."

Norman just nodded his head at the justice of it all and twitched in appreciation. Tom offered another beer. Jack looked through the window into the street and at the Chick Inn across the road and said a small prayer for all of them, but especially for him and Danny.

The rest of the night went without any trauma or gunshots and they finally hit the sack after saying goodbye to Norman who drove off into the night and Danny, who was dropped off at his hotel. Tom had decided he and Jack wouldn't get another red-eye flight to Houston but would meet Spinner's head man for the project who ran their Singapore operation but was home on leave. They were to meet him at the local drilling office in downtown New Orleans.

With a head that was throbbing, and after two visits to the toilet to vomit up the red-looking Tequila Sunrise remains in his aching stomach, Jack began to repeat Danny's mantra in his addled brain: 'I must stop doing...' They took a taxi to the office and were led into an office to meet Alf, the rig boss.

The meeting followed the same format as the others. Tom and Alf in full buddy mode chewing the fat about past encounters, drinking and girls, Jack sat waiting to talk about the 'bidness'. Tom broke off to say that Alf lived in Lafayette and loved hunting and was a friend of his cousin Norman.

"Alf and Norman go hunting down in the bayous when Alf's back. A jug or two of coon-ass whisky and they kin still shoot the right eye out of a raccoon from fifty yards. Alf, tell him about your last trip to Africa, buddy, with Spinner."

Alf stood up and walked around his office, smoking his cigar and pointing to photographs and to the wall of some stuffed extinct creatures he'd shot. He was a bit like Norman, not huge, but wiry and fit and quite young for the 'bidness'.

He walked over towards Jack, stubbed his cigar out on the ashtray on his desk.

"Jack, have you ever faced a Cape buffalo that charges at you from five metres from the bush?" he said, staring wildly at the poor man.

As he came from a small mining village where the likeliest wild animal to charge him was his wife or a rabid badger, this was a bit of a rhetorical question to the Englishman.

"If you ever face one," he continued after a long silence from the stupefied consultant, "make sure you have your 700 Nitro Express with you, turn and face him, don't shit yourself – and blow its brains out… I did."

He then didn't wait for any response but asked another rhetorical question. "Do you know what sound a buffalo makes when its his brains are blown all over the veldt?"

Jack shook his head in the negative with the sure fact he was going to find out what the unfortunate creature's last sounds were before it was turned into steak and fries.

The buffalo hunter then walked slowly towards his two visitors and slumped at their feet, his small body in a heap and said, "Harrumph. They slump on their knees like this and then say, 'Harrumph.'"

Well, Jack thought, *I am pleased I now know what the once magnificent animal's dying words would be. Harrumph,* and he decided that, yes, it was time to ask Jon if he could hurry to Singapore and start his work there before he too was sectioned for the asylum by the duly authorised medical officer.

And after a torturous interview with Jon the following morning in Houston, where all the life, enthusiasm and self-esteem were sucked out of him, he actually agreed Jack's efforts would be better suited to integrating and aligning the new teams that were now starting to be recruited to Singapore.

"I shall be joining you next week. I expect you will have reviewed Tom's execution plan and written your own up by then for review. Tomorrow I will meet with Tom and ensure he understands that I expect the plan by Friday. You can take it on the plane with you as good reading and you can do some staff work for once instead of roaming around drinking and carousing with the Neanderthals here. On projects, I can have no one who does not deliver or I will run them off."

Running off was what Jack did. He actually ran down the stairs to jump on the plane to the safety of home, and then to what he was told was a sexually liberated paradise. He left greased pigs, Cape buffalos, bayous and banjos and the 2nd amendment in Houston and N'awlins – well, so he thought.

CHAPTER THREE

Singapore

Father Bob

A few months later…

"Do you need any bodies?"

Jack stood back a little and reflected again that this was indeed a strange place with very strange people. He was definitely not studying anatomy or practicing necrophilia so why the hell would he need bodies? The person asking the question was an Australian man, Captain Abe, who owned The Outback Bar with his wife Dawn.

Jack became acquainted with The Outback Bar on Tanglin Road soon after arriving in Singapore and he was soon to realise that there were many strange people in The Outback, and Jack would find out they were as bizarre as the many people he had met in the past few months after his relocation to the Singapore project office with Gator Tom and the Iron Chancellor.

The Outback had reopened after a period where Dawn, the landlady and wife of Captain Abe, the other owner of the bar, had 'left in a hurry' back to Australia. Jack had met several people in this small island state who had 'left in a hurry' from their native lands, which made him surmise what they were 'hurrying away from'; he would find out as his life in Asia evolved.

Jack had taken a taxi from Changi Airport after returning from his first visit to Perth, Western Australia and the main office. He was desperate to get to the bar in time for a few beers before heading to his hotel.

Jack had quickly realised in his time in the Lion City that Singaporean taxi drivers are like all taxi drivers all over the globe. They never know where they are going. Jack found this curious given the fact they are taxi drivers. He began to speculate that this is because they operate the same fundamental economic and business principle that he was discovering in the oil 'bidness' that was that the longer they delay the journey, the more money they get.

He had also discovered that Singapore taxi drivers were a barometer of public opinion and culture, particularly regarding the difficulty of earning and keeping money. That evening he experienced yet another example of the hard facts of life in Asia and the difference between foreigners who earned mega bucks and the austerity that the local citizens had to live with. As they pulled into Tanglin Road, a Caucasian lady jogger ran out into the road without looking and the driver barked and swerved to miss her and he pulled up outside the pub. Jack, handing him his fare said, "Bloody hell, she was lucky, if she carries on like that she'll get herself killed."

"No worries, lah: it's all right for her but it'll be me who has to pay the fines!" the taxi driver growled back.

Jack shook his head and replied in the affirmative, "No worries, lah," and stepped down into the small cellar Outback bar and ordered cold Tiger beer from a beautiful-looking Asian girl behind the bar. A small stocky man with black moustache and hair was standing at the small bar, smoking and looking into an open briefcase on the bar and he greeted Jack amicably with a broad Australian accent.

"Gudday mate, good to see you again. You were with Shaun the other time weren't you?"

Jack turned to look at the man and nodded, he had indeed been in with Shaun, Ironman, the iconic Bostonian Irishman who was valiantly trying to sell Jack a whole Indonesian iron ore mountain and teak forest. Jack affirmed the Australian's query. "Aye, I was. Do you know Shaun?"

The small man chucked in response. "Know him? I bloody well

taught him – hah, hah, hah." The moustached man offered his hand over to Jack and said, "Captain Abe. This is my bar, mate. Have a beer with me."

He then shouted across to the lovely Asian barmaid. "Shah, get the lad a beer. What do you here, mate?"

Jack shook hands and introduced himself.

"I'm Jack. I'm working with the client on the Scorpio project. I'm just back from Aussie, just live up the road from here. Nice bar you have, Abe. "

Captain Abe's eyes lit up and he closed his briefcase, swallowed a large Tiger and took a long pull on his cigarette. He blew the smoke into the already toxic smoke-filled air, causing Jack to cough violently. Abe then asked the choking Englishman the strange question quoted earlier with a serious look on his face.

"Do you need any bodies?"

After a pause of a few seconds Jack realised that this wasn't any reference to Burke and Hare or any medical question at all and he was very relieved when he realised that it was the same perennial question, asked already by Harry the patron and his friends in that other weird place, The Sportsman's Bar, which he had frequented over the last few weeks. Night after night he was asked similar questions referencing the supply of live bodies; that is, working labour and technicians for the project.

Jack thought, *Another character in 'the bidness'*, and posed a question laconically but rhetorically, fully expecting the answer he got.

"I guess you can supply them, Abe?"

"Yeah, we can supply anything you like: welders, pipe fitters; you name it, we've got it," Abe confirmed, taking a slow draw of his cigarette and blowing the smoke in Jack's face.

"Oh, really?"

Jack gave him the bored, condescending answer he'd learnt from observing in the Singapore project office over two months the behaviour and communication style of the educated contracts manager, Steed, who could demean and demoralise a person with just two words. Jack was beginning to think Steed was a marvellous man, if you liked people who could humiliate a human being with just one stare.

But Captain Abe continued in an increasingly unbelievable sales mode.

"We can also supply you with a fabrication facility, tow boats, fit the turret, drill for oil, paint the tanks, sell you a yacht and carry out full frontal lobotomies on your contractor's quantity surveyors, supply iron ore from Ironman and white slaves from Borneo from the Commodore etc., etc."

Feeling he might be in the company of a master real contractor, his spirits picked up and Jack decided to humour him.

"What's the company called, Abe?" he asked, bored but slightly interested in this quixotic man.

Abe handed him a card from the briefcase which he perpetually carried attached to his wrist. He noticed it contained Abe's passport, many blue pills and a pen. He was soon to learn that the continual immolation of Abe's passports by his suspicious wife, the hidden stock of Viagra and also that this small battered piece of leather was his office, were the reasons that he never let this briefcase out of his sight.

The card said something like: *'Captain Abe's Pacific Trading Company'*.

Jack immediately thought of his days as a schoolboy reading R.M. Ballantyne's *'The Coral Island'* or *'Billy Bunter among The Cannibals'*. Coconuts and Copra, plantation owners in Raffles' long bar – it was difficult to imagine a *Captain Abe's Multidiscipline Oilfield Services Company*. So he asked where his company was based.

"Here," he answered proudly.

"What, actually here, this bar; this place?" the shocked consultant asked incredulously.

"Yeah: I'm linked to the internet and my intention is to move the whole bloody lot to Batam – and, Jack, that's where the future lies."

So this explained this amazing entrepreneur's business expansion plans. Listening to this was his wife standing at the end of the bar, a rather large, buxom lady with beautiful permed hair, flowery dress and extremely large bosom. She moved over to Jack carrying her Tiger beer, moving stately like a galleon across the ocean.

"Don't listen to the old bastard. It's not the business he wants over there. It's his ******* tart."

Jack was later to learn that evening therein laid the rub of the tale. Abe wanted to live in Batam, reduce his business costs, get closer to his markets, and Dawn wanted him to stay in Singapore. However, Abe had also, in a sea of Viagra and Bundaberg rum, fallen for a dusky maid of youthful age and Dawn, well aware of this, was not up for relocating the megalithic Captain Abe's corporation to the black hole island.

"I don't mind him screwing them," Dawn expounded later in the evening whilst finishing her fifteenth Tiger beer and pulling Jack into her huge bosom, in her soon to be familiar bonding routine. She was a big old friendly girl, our Dawn. Jack speculated that he saw Lord Lucan hidden in the expanse but was corrected by one of her barmaids; it was actually the local public health and environment inspector who had never found a way out after his last visit and Dawn's hug. "But, Jack, he's too ******* old to be living with them. I mean, he's been screwing them all over Asia. I've known that, it's what men do here."

Jack thought, *At last, a real contractor's wife's perspective.* He thought this would be tremendous feminine input material for any female consultants who read his Harvard Review. Or maybe *Cosmopolitan* might take on his story. Dawn completed her judgement of Abe's new romance.

"But it's up to him now; he's made his bed, now let the bastard lie in it."

Like all Australians, Dawn could use the expletive to its best.

During a night of feverous sales pitches from Abe and back-breaking hugs from Dawn, gallons of Tiger beer and intense smoke inhalation, Jack elucidated something about these two bizarre bar owners. They were both from Australasia and Dawn had opened a series of bars across the outback of Australia, and now had opened up a couple in Singapore.

They had had a turbulent life together and the latest marital bliss had been broken by Captain Abe's Batam expansion. Dawn told Jack that she would often remove his passport from his briefcase when he wasn't looking and burn it. This was her cunning plan to stop Abe from going to Batam Island, forty minutes away from Singapore. Batam was cheap to live in, and had many female attractions, which had lured many married men from the comfort of Singapore to the third world of Indonesia and the many young girls who were looking for someone to take them out of the extreme poverty they lived in.

Inevitably, Dawn's passport immolation ruse failed and Abe had secured many a duplicate one, possibly from Ironman, and consequently he left Dawn's ample bosom to set up his new company on the Black Isle. Indeed, Captain Abe followed Dawn's advice and relocated Captain Abe Pte Ltd and formed PT Captain Abe.

Abe had applied for more passports than Carlos the Jackal and each time he had to get a reference from his doctor, the Doc. It appeared the Doc was another character who helped keep the oil industry and contractors healthy and sane and Jack was looking forward to meeting him. Yet another crazy example for his research, he hoped. He was not to be disappointed.

Jim's businesses had made him a lot of money over the years and they had been a varied bunch of ventures. Fishing boats in Darwin, racing car driving, pubs across Australia, pubs in Singapore, marine engineering, yacht sales, and brokering; you name it, Captain Abe had done it. He was a marine captain and had sailed across the Oriental seas. He was a true East Indiaman, sailed and worked in some of the most beautiful areas of the South Pacific and China Seas and, like many sailors in the southern seas he was tied to the foam, also sadly, for Dawn, to the bougainvillea and the brown-skinned girls that inhabit this expanse of the globe.

"Jack," he said, smoking his thirtieth cigarette that evening and blowing the smoke Jack's way and making Jack muse that both that other sage and grand wizard of contracting, Father Bob, and Abe had nearly killed him off with bronchial pneumonia, "you can keep Europe. Who would want to live in the dark and cold, where women wear tights and woolly coats, for ****'s sake? But here, I love it, just love them all."

Jack reflected on Jim's past and his continuation of his wild life even in his late sixties. He certainly seemed to consume Tiger beer,

Bundaberg rum and cigarettes in vast quantities and surely couldn't keep this up. He asked him if life in Asia had always been so wild. Abe smiled and told him of the old days.

"In my good old sailing days my mates would go to Kalimantan. Take the big truck and chat up the girls in the bar to see if they fancied a ride for party, offer the dollars and wait for them to come to the truck. Then they'd drive off slowly and the bar girls would run after them. Ron would yell at Bobby to drive a bit faster until the girls used to straggle out a bit and until there was only two or three that could keep up with the truck. He'd then grab these front runners and haul them into the back and then everyone would head back to the ship for some fun."

"Seems a bit odd behaviour, Abe?" Jack asked. "Why not ask the three prettiest if they wanted to come and party with you all?"

"Oh, it was Ron's way of making sure the ones that came didn't have TB (Tuberculosis). The infected ones ran out of breath before the rest!"

Touché: Ingenuity, romance and innovation from real contractors from a bygone age.

The night drew on and the bar was filling up and Jack was starting to think about heading home when his attention was drawn to a bespectacled middle-aged Australian who was sat close by reading a book, smoking profusely. He was tall, very thin with baggy trousers hanging off his backside. He had a long, lank ponytail which hung to his backside and he wore sandals with no socks. Curious to know more about him, he asked Dawn, who had just swallowed a Tiger and given him another huge hug.

"He's a ****. He chases all my customers away. Thinks he knows everything. I've barred him loads, Jack, but he still keeps coming. Abe hates him but that's because he thinks he is harder, tougher and more clever than Abe. I just hate the bastard coz he loses me customers through his bloody arguments. We call him Bill the Argument."

Jack, again naively, thought maybe this guy was worth talking to as he was becoming worried about the continual bear hugs and Abe's nicotine-induced heart failure. So he did, and regretted it forever after.

Through a series of aggressive conversations Jack realised why no one had spoken to him in the hours he'd been in the bar. It seemed he designed such complex systems for banks and other organisations that he had the skills to control the security system of Bill Gates' mansions, disrupt the entire Singapore ERP traffic system and shut down the Mumbai Stock Exchange from his laptop, which Jack noted was by his side as he imbibed several Australian Victoria Beer, VB, 'stubbies'.

During this conversation over an hour Bill give a short lecture on the human rights record of Pol Pot; discussed how he shot a Vietcong sniper with a bow and arrow in the Mekong Delta and how he competed at the highest level at any known Australian sport. It appeared no one had done what Bill had done in his life.

He had won the Australian pool championships.

He had also won the heavyweight boxing championship of Australia and beaten everyone to a pulp in the Australian, South Vietnamese and American Boxing championships in "Nam'.

He rode to win the Australian dirt bike championships.

He was a champion free diver, and could dive farther than anyone in Adelaide and catch more abalones than any living seal, otter or sea mammal on David Attenborough's documentaries.

Jack was particularly unimpressed with his statement to him that he made more money in his business than Jack would ever make in his life!

'I am the only person in the whole of Hewlett Packard who knows what they're doing and I'm the only one who can program better than anyone in Bill Gates' two-bit company. The governments of three Asian countries relied on me for their IT infrastructure and call me personally, not my useless bosses or colleagues," the Australian wonder man confidently declared and took a large drink from his bottle of VB and he began again.

"Why do I dress like this?"

Jack looked at him, bored, getting tired by now. "No idea, Bill. Why?"

"Well, it's because I can," Bill answered, taking a large drink from his bottle of Australian beer.

His dress composed of baggy trousers, which like Father Bob's and Manju's, the Indian cook Jack had met, hung off his bony arse; a cheese cloth shirt, thongs, with dirty feet that needed Mary Magdalene to give them a bit of scrub up, and a long, greasy ponytail that reached down to his arse. His point was this:

"I am so good at what I do, I can tell anyone to **** off, and I do, and I wear what I like. I don't have to dress like you daft twats do."

Charming, Jack thought, looking at own his smart trousers and white, short-sleeved shirt which obviously didn't impress Bill.

"I see you get on with Abe and his Sheila. With useless mates like those I can see why you are unsuccessful."

Bill was obviously enjoying having someone to talk to. Jack realised that was why he sat at the end of the bar with a book on his own, as no sane person who actually knew him would wish to talk with him. Dawn was correct; he was an argumentative bastard.

Jack was about to take his beer and move back to the comfort of Dawn's bosom when Bill met his match. Amazingly, there was someone who was more argumentative than him. Into the bar walked a quite broad and tall, good-looking elderly man. He stood at the bar, his large frame and one dodgy eye wandering from person to person, a supercilious grin on his face with a large vodka tonic in his hand. Jack, becoming wiser to crazy inhabitants of The Outback wondered if he was in the presence of a master wind-up merchant or an absolute bastard. Time would tell. And it did.

Dawn shouted across to the newcomer: "Gudday Barry. Where the **** have you been all these weeks?"

"That's nothing to do with you, my dear, that's my business. But Dawn, you are looking lovely as usual, I've missed you darling," Barry charmingly corrected our buxom landlady and held his gin glass in his hand. He smiled and turned to lean on the bar. Dawn blushed; well it was hard to notice with the red face from a gallon of Tiger. Jack thought, *She loves a bit of flattery and this man knows how to give it,* as he was leering intently and chatting up the other barmaid, Shah, another beautiful Singaporean, within minutes of coming in.

"He's a bastard," Abe whispered to Jack on the other side to Dawn, a bit too loudly, as Barry raised his dodgy eye and just raised his glass to Abe, smiling.

"Who is he, Abe?" Jack asked, interested again in the peculiar interpersonal relationships he'd already discovered in this unique bar.

"He's a pommie bastard. Everyone calls him Belligerent Barry, he's so ******* rude and augmentative." Abe explained his dislike concisely.

"He's actually worse than Bill the Argument? Surely not, mate," Jack stuttered unbelievingly.

"Can't stand either of them but he's a pommie so he's got to be ******* worse," Abe said without consideration that Jack was also a 'pommie'.

Jack gave up on Abe and his pommie bashing and observed the new inmate. He kept looking around the bar, and given Abe's character reference, he thought his crooked eye must be scanning for victims. And sure enough, he was correct.

Barry focused on three Australian soldiers who were on R and R leave from Afghanistan and were quietly enjoying a drink in what they believed was friendly territory. Belligerent Barry decided to speak and shouted across the bar. "Heh, you Aussie bastards, did I tell you that you were thick, did I?"

Jack, expecting a mass brawl, moved away a bit from this new, not long for this world, Outback customer. The soldiers may not have understood his quite posh English accent, or maybe they took pity, as they just looked aggressively at him and turned to talk amongst themselves again. However, Bill the Argument, who had been sitting at the other end of bar with usual book in hand, pretending to read it, but in fact listening intently for a chance to get in with some unbelievable statement, divisive comment or plain lie to strike up a conversation and begin the inevitable argument, shouted across at Barry: "I'm Aussie and I definitely am not thick, mate."

"Yes, you are, you all are," said this new Tasmanian devil type character. The soldiers looked up, worryingly for Jack who wished he could dig a hole in the sand and crawl in.

"No, they may be but I'm not," said Bill. "I have a brain the size of a planet, not like the rest of the useless buggas in here, and I earn mega—"

But he was cut off by the person who Jack was rapidly beginning to think was insane or a suicide bomber on a death wish.

"I don't care about what you think or earn, and I don't give a **** about Australians."

He was looking scornfully through one eye that was half closed, his balding hair swept back, and supping the last of his vodka tonic and smiling lustfully and pointing his empty glass at the lovely Malay barmaid, Shah.

"A large one, my dear."

Taking his glass of gin and tonic from the lovely Shah, this nemesis of the Antipodes continued in aggressive fashion.

"Come on now, then, prove to me, prove to me, bet you can't, but prove to me," the Australian baiter repeated, without actually asking what to prove.

"Prove what, you pommie bastard?" asked Bill, surprisingly restrained.

"How clever you are, you thick ******!" shouted the new king of argument in The Outback.

Jack was beginning to think he was mad.

The soldiers stopped talking and stared over at the mad one, but also to Jack's dismay, seemed to stare menacingly at him, who had moved to distance himself from the lunatic. He thought, *This is no Oxford University debating society; someone is going to get hurt here.* Belligerent Barry at last asked his leading question.

"OK, OK, come on then, tell me, you Aussies, tell me. Where did the word 'kangaroo' come from? Come on then, you clever ******s, where and what does it mean?"

There was unfortunately no speaker in the chair at this world changing debate in The Outback that night and no Hansard or congressional record, but the facts were that Bill was stumped by the question, and so were the soldiers, whom Barry kept tormenting endlessly with the question until finally he told them the answer. This was the riveting fact that the first colonials to Australia, when they saw a kangaroo they asked the local aboriginals what it was. The aboriginals spoke no English and didn't understand so they answered,

"I don't know," which in their language was 'Kan-Ga-Roo' and the pommies thought they meant that was the beast's name.

He then went into another series of linguistic conundrums, quoting aboriginal and Papua New Guinea languages and culture, which of course the soldiers and the unfortunate Bill the Argument couldn't or wouldn't solve or answer. In the end the soldiers drank their beers and left. Jack was not sure whether they were exhausted by this new king of the Down Under speakers' corner or really were under orders not to batter non-civilians to death. He guessed the latter. After a recovery period, Bill carried on arguing but eventually he fell back into his book and Belligerent Barry arose as the new regent of obtuseness and provocation.

The evening wore on. Abe and Dawn had a huge argument over Abe's young female chum across in the jungle and who was paying the business relocation expenses to in the black hole island of Batam, and they ended up rolling around on the floor fighting. Jack was horrified but he noticed that no one seemed to bother. The barmaids kept smiling, taking money and Barry kept chatting them up. Bill was arguing with some Americans over how he and his Australian special forces were better than our American cousins and that they had reached the Mekong Delta before them but only after Bill had killed more VC than any known soldier with only his bow and arrow. Jack was told by Shah that this fighting was a nightly occurrence after a bottle or two of Bundaberg rum.

"Don't worry, our Doctor Jones stiches them up in the morning; normally, in the bar after a beer." Jack decided he had to meet the Doc.

As more VB stubbies went down Bill the Argument's throat he attempted to bond more and more with Jack. Jack started to see that maybe he had a good side, that most never saw, but after yet another personal insult, he decided that they never saw it because he had caused them to leave, throw punches at him or just stare disbelievingly at their glasses and wish they were somewhere else. He continued to socialise with Jack in his inimitable way, trying to be friendly with his one and only mate; he offered some advice to Jack.

"You should exercise more. You are my age and unfit."

"Bill, I swim a kilometre every day," Jack replied, getting bored and uninterested in this macho ritual.

"I swim six kilometres every day," Bill retorted.

He would, wouldn't he? Was all Jack could think. But as he didn't look as if he'd had a wash, he concluded that was also a lie. Bill stared at his friend without blinking and spoke:

"I can still kill you with one finger, mate, fit as butcher's dog."

He promptly went into a paroxysmal coughing fit, as the cigarette he habitually held to his mouth blew smoke into Jack's non-smoking face and he fell into a strange trance as his chest relaxed.

"You know, mate, I nearly died on Christmas Eve, 1972. I was shot by a Gook sniper in 'Nam. I was the best sniper and already killed more Gooks than anyone in the history of the Australian Army, but one got me Digger," and he proceeded to pull out what looked like American dog tags from his pocket. "You can you see the bullet mark? It would have gone straight through the heart."

He started to cry and tears welled up, as if he was remembering a life saved and a life gone by. His newfound friend put his arm around him and gave him a few words of comfort.

Bill looked up, took his comforter's hand and said: "You are a good un, mate. I like you. If I can help you I always will. I love my boy and my family; I never told many that before. I always miss them, you know. The Christmas Eve story always brings that day in 'Nam back to me and how I have thrown the life away that I was given that day all those years ago. Let's have another beer, mate."

That was the last time Jack saw Bill. He died some days after, coughing in another paroxysmal fit, he fell stone dead on the bedroom floor of his lovely partner's apartment.

As Jack sat in the bar a few days later, on hearing of Bill's demise he reflected on the evening he met him. Wouldn't it be great to think that for once the bullet story was true and that Bill was somewhere in heaven, playing a harp better than angel could ever do, VB in hand and a cigarette in mouth and asking St Peter if he knows why a kangaroo is called a kangaroo? He looked around at the many crazies in the bar and reflected on his first couple of months in this Paradise Island and how he'd met Father Bob in the first days in the project office, and Bob had started him on his quest to learn the secret that everyone seemed to know but him. He chuckled to himself as he recalled the first few weeks of work, beer and beautiful smiling girls and Father Bob's secret wisdom: "Stick with your fatha, bonny lad, and I'll show you how to bring gas ashore and make millions."

'Father Bob' had a propensity when drunk, which was most nights, to lecture people on the evils of Asia and to avoid the erotic ways of the Oriental ladies. He would often speak seriously through a haze of cigarette smoke and copious amounts of Tiger beer on how they should stick with him and listen to his wise ways, as he often said to anyone who looked younger than him, which was everyone. "You are still just a bairn."

Danny, on being lectured yet again through a smoke-filled bar room, decided that his own father may well have guided him similarly if he had been still alive, and Bob preached like any minister of the cloth, so he was named Father Bob, in sarcastic respect to both his paternal and his spiritual light.

Early in the first few weeks on the project they were sitting in the hawker centre in the Amari Hotel, Tanjong Pagar, having a lunch break after a hard morning in the office recovering from the excesses of the night before. Father Bob was poking at a plate of chicken rice and not eating any as usual, as he too had a tendency to Gator Tom's 'Bonanza ass' and he moaned:

"This food is shite. My arse is like a blood orange every day if I eat any of it. We need 'real bait' Danny, quick, or I'm gonna starve."

His despairing indictment of the local culture and cuisine was in response to eating like Gandhi for a couple of weeks. He was indeed very like Gandhi in his build but he was not on any moral fasting regime, it was the result of years of hard work, drink and huge quantities of nicotine which seemed to burn away every ounce of fat on his lean, supple body, and he habitually poured the whole crop of Western Virginia down anyone's long-suffering tracheas when he was lecturing them every night in his drunken state..

Bob had been looking for 'proper food' and living on Tiger beer and Marlboro cigarettes for some weeks. But he had heard of a bar in Orchard Road where in his words, 'they give you free real bait' ('bait' being a North East England word for food; real: meaning anything with mince or potatoes in it) and he was determined to find it and give up trying 'this foreign shit'.

Bob was going to be the construction manager for Batam Island, Indonesia and was waiting patiently to head the few miles across China Sea to that strange island. In the meantime with Gator Tom he was inputting on the design and constructability of the project. That was to stop the engineers designing something that could only be built using lasers, nuclear fission or nanoparticles. Father Bob wanted a steel thing he could build with a T square, slide rule and lump hammer.

Bob was a highly experienced construction man. He came from Tyneside, North East England. He was extremely thin, skeletal but above average height. He was bald with wire-framed glasses and middle-aged. Like Gator, he was also constantly writing construction execution plans and procedures for Jon. He worked for Danny but still had to suffer the daily interrogations from Jon on his execution plan, which Jon finally had to sign off as his client. This drove him to his nightly drink- and angst-driven preaching about senior management like Jon.

Danny, Jon and Gator Tom had all been mobilised to Singapore and Jack had begun the impossible task of trying to get Jon and Danny's management teams integrated and aligned to work as one, happy, loving bunch. Several team builds and many workshops, town hall meetings and one-to-one counselling sessions with plainly deranged people, and Jon's coaching on his execution plan had taken their toll on Jack. He had need of much beer after work. So despite Bob's cancer-inducing smoke and his religious sage-like lectures on evils of the Orient, it was a relief for him to walk out straight from the office with Bob and Danny to the drunken debauchery that was Duxton Road every night.

Bob also stayed in the same hotel as Jack whose only daily intake of solids was a room service burger at three or four in the morning. His burger was normally eaten after carrying Bob home under one arm. This was because Bob would wobble when he'd had several too many, and because the large storm drains held comfortably several of Father Bob's bulk, Jack tucked him under his arm like a rag doll to avoid the bag of bones falling in the drains. The drains emptied and washed out to the South China Sea, where he feared Father Bob would be caught by the hordes of small boat Indonesian fishermen and turned into nice chicken rice. Not that they would get much meat off his scrawny bones.

Bob continually smoked his cigarettes during the short haul to the hotel and in between he lectured his drunken colleague not to fall into evil ways or listen to management bullshit, but take his advice on all matters of the heart or mind.

All of them had never eaten lunch in the weeks they had arrived in Singapore, normally because Bob could not hold on to Kentucky chicken legs without throwing them at anyone with him or over his shoulder. Normally with Bob, food had to be taken after a beer. His motor neurones needed the Magic Molecule to fire properly, and as twitching was a problem some days with his bony arms, he had a propensity sometimes to throw his lunch around in the sober state they had to maintain at work. Also they couldn't drink at lunch as for some reason the 'bidness' had moved on from the old days and didn't like their staff getting pissed before 12 noon.

By early evening blood sugar was at a dangerous low and fist fights broke out in the engineering design office that Jon and Danny were now leading, and as none of the merry crew in these first few weeks were into 'working out' or yoga or sensibly eating before taking beer, they all left work in the evening and went straight into a bar near the office; the Here and Now.

This was so named because of a simple business principle. 'Here' you see your money: 'Now' you don't.' A basic fact, because as soon as anyone ordered a jug of Tiger beer, twenty-four Filipino 'hostesses' surrounded them and massaged their bodies and shoulders and generally eased the worries of a terrible day avoiding real work.

Unfortunately, Bob and his friends soon realised that this service was not free, gratis, and was not given because the bar owner was worried about the mental and occupational health of his customers and fellow residents in Duxton Road. The girls' attentions had to be paid for by the grateful customers with huge rounds of massively inflated prices for shots of dodgy tequila that the girls drank.

At the end of this Bacchanalian feast in Dante's Inferno of the Here and Now, the piper would have to pay the tune (a lot of mixed metaphors there, folks) and inevitably there would be a major dispute about the bill. As no one had any idea how many drinks, how many

Filipinos, or what antics of the clientele's perversions were being charged for, it was a no-win contest for the Chinese money man who served them.

Bob speculated every night in his lectures to Jack on their long and winding path home that the majority of these funds ended up in the hands of the effusive, smiling barman of the bar. He was certain that this humble bar man was nothing of the sort, he was a Peoples' Republic of China investment banker. So, in his opinion, unwittingly all were contributing successfully to the growth of China, the yuan and the budget surpluses of the western world. When Bob was told that this may be a coincidence and that he was just a normal Triad gangster, he adamantly proposed that the rise in the profits of the Here and Now and the GDP of China were far to coincidental and it was far too like the Grassy Knoll for him – and the Chinese are inscrutable as you know.

They all argued about the bill every night, abusing the smiling barman loudly, but always paid the smiling Chinese Rothschild his Singapore dollars, which he no doubt rapidly converted to yuan. Danny of course, would vow never to go back – but unlike the Tiger Who Came to Tea, he always did.

Richie was the large Australian Commissioning and Operations manager, he was the one who took the project from Gator Tom if it ever finished and made it work. He was massive as well, had played Rugby for Australia, been a doorman in many violent backwaters of his native northern territories and ran a whole 200 square miles of a cattle farm there. His favourite pastime in his home town of Katherine was wrestling bulls, leaping from four-wheel drive trucks onto them to wrestle them to the ground.

He frequented the bar every night and he spent vast amounts of his and Danny's team-building budget there. Due to his continued habit of beer and unlimited Filipino girls, Bob speculated that he had actually bought the bar twice over, plus several homes in the Philippines for the friendly girls.

Jack had survived these early days on Chinese green tea at work, twenty pints of Tiger and free peanuts in the bar plus the Mujahedeen served burger: Father Bob didn't. Jack had much excess fat to help but Bob was seven stone (please work it out in kilos yourself but basically he made Gandhi look like a Sumo wrestler) and that was with his twenty Marlboro and butane lighter in his pocket) so he really needed solid food to keep his ribs from sticking together and his trousers falling off his ass yet again. It was touch and go whether he would survive malnutrition until they found 'real bait' to eat.

One night Father Bob and Danny were in Then and Now and Father Bob said: "Danny, let's tilt out of here. Gator and the Aussie look like they are here for the long-term and Jack is too busy talking management bullshit with Jon. He's got a funny comic down the backside of his trousers and getting his arse smacked again by the German bastard. I've told him time and again don't talk to the mad bugger. Just listen to me, boss, Danny, I don't want you ending up getting carried away again by those lasses over there surrounding Gator and Richie and spending your team-building budget yet again, boss. Stick with me and we'll go somewhere safe."

As they strolled along the rapidly drying, rain-soaked Singapore streets, the humidity and heat making it uncomfortable to walk more than a few bars, they headed into a nearby bar which was Bob's favourite bar, Jo Jo Mahoney's. This was mercifully free of the team-building budget busting Filipino bar girls and had a wonderful female rock singer with an amazing range of voice and songs.

Night after night in this bar Bob had blown noxious smoke in Danny's face and lectured him on the need for chastity and the potential to lose one's gonads from the wife. But his favourite subject was about him – the best construction manager on the planet, and his ability to get gas ashore and also the fabulous secret of this business – that was that only a chosen few knew the secret and esoteric art of real contracting.

"Bonny Lad, listen to me, I'll tell you one day how all of this works out here and how to get oil ashore without having to worry again about your mortgage, your wife or that crazy Jorman client."

He continued after swallowing another half a pint of Tiger and smoking yet another Marlboro. "Just listen, watch me and keep your mouth shut and I'll show the way."

Danny was uninterested in this secret, as he was obsessed with his team-building budget spend and ensuring the Aussie and big Tom were happy, and therefore keeping his client relationship score high and convincing his bosses in Houston and Perth that he was normal and that most importantly he was on schedule. So they both drank until the early hours till Danny, realising his head would hurt yet again, left for his condo, and Bob fell into a storm drain and was washed down to the hotel.

Jack, however, was so desperate to learn that he soon followed Bob and Danny every night and weekends in a search for real food and listened to Bob's lectures on the evils of the Orient and how to get gas ashore.

Mind you, Jack soon realised that Bob never ate anything.

He nibbled at the sides of anything put in front of him and pretended that he'd eaten it, then put his napkin over the remains and lit up yet another cigarette. One weekend Danny, Jack and Father Bob found a haven of real food as they managed to find Singapore's Little Venice, Boat Quay. They soon realised that an Anglo-Irish pub, The Penny Black, served cottage pie and chips. The ingredient closest to their hearts and to most of the Anglo-Celtic foreigners, was of course mince. Not the sweet, feminine stuff you put in mince pies at Christmas, not that steak tartar shit they serve uncooked in France with a raw egg on the bugger, where a good vet could bring both cow and the nascent chicken back to life; but fatty, bone gritty, nuked, ground beef, or whatever your country calls it, but to them it was ambrosia, especially with potatoes in any form and with thick Bisto gravy. Real bait at last, Bob was in heaven. Jack sat there and watched the joy on his two colleagues' faces and reflected on a theory he had been developing for some time on what drives the cross-cultural behaviours of those who work in foreign markets.

He first read *Real Men Don't Eat Quiche* sometime in the 1980s. In this milestone of literature, the main hypothesis was the preposition that:

"How could John Wayne have wiped out the whole American Indian nation and thousands of Japs at Iwa Jima on a diet of quiche and salad?"

The book goes on to prove the undeniable fact that he couldn't – and asserts the immutable law that Real Men definitely Do **NOT** Eat Quiche.

Since that day Jack had pondered on this Duke's law of nature and how it related to modern-day economics and business theory. This had become especially profound as he found himself drawn more and more within the multicultural offshore oil and gas industry and amongst those in banking, financial services and technological supply chains that surround it. They had budgets that were greater than most third world countries and satisfied the growing energy needs of a global economy. They rebuilt countries after the quest for freedom and democracy had run its inevitable military course. They raised billions of dollars from those rapacious financiers and bankers that would soon bugger up his and millions of others' pension funds and they provided employment for hundreds of thousands of contractors, particularly in the various ass ends of the known world.

And the answer came to him like a 'Nam flashback', that sultry, humid day over a glass of Tiger beer in The Penny Black, Singapore. He looked at Father Bob's happy face and remembering the arcane secret the surrogate priest alluded to every drunken night, he concluded that only 'Real Contractors' could do these things and, like 'The Duke' they certainly did not eat quiche. Jack's theory was:

REAL CONTRACTORS MUST EAT MINCE.

But he had yet to be included in Bob's secret so he just sat there and enjoyed his cottage pie and chips and wondered if he had discovered a world-shattering management theory or was just pissed again.

He also began to realise that most of the people he'd met in Asia up to now had no intention of giving up their current luxurious expatriate existence, and most he had met had managed to avoid working for these megaliths of engineering anywhere near Godforsaken places, where, like 'The Duke', you had to avoid contact with the natives at all costs unless you had a Remington pump action shotgun with you. They did not work and eat in places that ended in 'stahn', or in Africa, or the Middle East or heaven forbid, Aberdeen – they worked (sorry, an oxymoron there) in Asia, in paradise.

He decided there and then that he would learn Father Bob's secret and study the cultural adaptive patterns that kept those employed in the oil-dominated rapacious financial businesses in paradise for as long as their wallets and gonads could stand it. The next week he found a secret temple of knowledge to help him his quest.

The three of them had heard of a bar that served free mince in vast quantities and on the following Saturday they found The Sportsman's bar, situated on Orchard Road, on the first floor of the Far East Shopping Centre. It was quite small and compact. A fluorescent St Andrew's cross, the Saltire (Scottish flag) and a Union Jack (British) were vividly displayed in the window. Danny was delighted and quickened his pace to almost run up the two flights of stairs. They entered the bar, to be surrounded by football (soccer to the uneducated of the world) images, pictures of players, managers, flags, scarves and shirts. It took the trained eye only a few seconds to recognise that ninety-odd per cent of these related to one club, Glasgow Rangers. And so their education on the religious divide that is Glasgow football began.

The bar is still there, changed since Father Bob's days but still a great place to enjoy Western and Singaporean hospitality with a flavour of Bonny Scotland without the monochrome football bias. Visit it and enjoy.

But first, what about the mince? Yes, lying in a large stainless steel catering container was a steaming pan of mince and onion, brown Bisto gravy smell wafting above the nicotine and beer and also a huge pan of mashed potatoes. It was mouth-watering to Danny and Bob as both were still suffering from Bonanza Ass.

They sat down and were greeted by a delightful brown-skinned, dark-eyed barmaid, Loraine, and as they ordered the ubiquitous Tiger beers she told them to tuck in as it was indeed free. So they dived in. Danny and Jack ate theirs, Father Bob pretended and put his napkin over it and lit yet another cigarette. Then the drinking began.

Because of the mince The Sportsman's became Jack and Father Bob's home, Danny joined them whenever he could get away from being tortured by Jon, or after pleading profusely to his bosses in Houston during late-night conference calls that the project progress and cost would soon be back on plan. The demented fool...

It was there that Jack was taken by a potential supplier to the project, who had given a presentation to the project team that morning. He was a strange and beguiling character, an American

Irishman from Boston whom Jack finally named Ironman after a few bizarre conversations. That night, Jack was in good form as Jon had left for Houston and he had had a few days of freedom and he was hungry.

"What's on the menu today, Shaun?"

Shaun turned, smiling, and Jack noticed he had a warm and friendly baby face with deep blue sparkling eyes. He said with his soft American accent. "Mince."

He continued after a pause. "Harry only has one menu, mince and more mince."

"Aye, I noticed," Jack said, laughing at this clever bit of wit.

"How'd you get into this business, Shaun?" Jack asked, taking a sup of the cold Tiger that Loraine had placed on his table.

Shaun's face lit up and he did look like an angel with his baby face and sparkling eyes. He launched straight into his pièce de résistance and the story Jack was later to see many times again repeated with unsuspecting captives of Ironman.

"I'm mainly into the resource business. I am really only the agent for the Thai manufacturer. My actual real business is in Indonesia. I have a project to mine a mountain of iron ore there and deforest the rainforest around it. It has more iron in it than the whole of Australia and the Chinese are desperate to get their hands on it. I am on friendly terms with one the generals for past favours and they have given me the rights to the iron ore mountain and a vast area of hardwood forest to chop down and sell. Here, take a look at the concession."

The folder he held up was a picture portfolio of his iron mountain, lovely pristine forests full of the teak trees he hoped to soon wipe out and ship to his buyers across Asia. He also had a sample analysis report from a Bangkok laboratory in Thai writing which purported to show that this sample had more iron it than in Haley's comet. From in his briefcase he took a glass jar with a sample of the ore which he claimed had been sourced from the mountain.

"Have you any links to anyone in your oil company who could confirm the analysis, Jack? I'll see you are well rewarded for your help when we start shipping it to the Chinese."

It was early in Jack's life caged in the menagerie that was Asia, so he was naïve and pleased to solidify his new friendship with this lovely American man and answered in the positive.

"I can certainly try to find someone. If not, I know chemical suppliers who would help us for sure."

"Cheers Jack, I have contacts with all the generals and politicians, buddy. I earned them years before. Want to see?"

Surprisingly he had pictures of himself with the generals and the then President.

Jack took the photo album and looked at the picture and sure enough it looked genuine.

"How did you get to know them, Shaun?"

Shaun moved a bit closer, looked at Harry who was standing at the bar scowling and whispered: "Let's say I helped them take power. I can't say much more, Jack. Do you know what I mean?"

Well, Jack thought, *I haven't a clue what he means but what the hell? This is Asia… and one more madman would not go amiss on the project.*

Shaun continued. "They gave me a concession for my help to mine the mountain and chop down the rainforests. I'm going to sell it before the Chinese end up taking the lot. Bastards are already stripping the world clean. They will eat their way through the world too." He was not too fond of the Chinese global market expansion, Jack thought.

Encouraged by this mercurial man's tales, he and Jack drank a few more Tigers and Jack found out that he lived in Bangkok and often travelled to Singapore and other Asian financial centres to meet friends and seek investment for his forest and iron mountain projects. He seemed more interested in this than the bits of pots and pans vessels his company in Thailand were attempting to sell to the project. Indeed, as the drinking continued Shaun launched into another sale pitch even more bizarre.

"Jack, have you met Digger yet?"

"No. Who's he?"

"He is the guy you will be getting all the earth-moving equipment from for the civil work in Australia. Great buddy of mine. You'll meet him for sure as he lives in Bangkok. He runs Asia and his dad runs the Australian end. Let me know and I'll fix up a meet. We can meet here, Bangkok and Jakarta or even Yangon. He's expanding like me into Myanmar."

Jack checked Shaun with his response.

"I'm sorry, Shaun, but I have nothing to do with that or to be honest anything much to do with buying anything. I only am consulting on the project, mate."

Shaun continued, seemingly unstoppable.

"That's no problem, buddy. I just want to buy some digging machines to help chop the teak down and mine the iron. The problem is I need to get a letter of credit for squillions of dollars. I need some investors to help. I reckon you can help. If you want to put some in yourself, I can make you a few million."

Jack looked at Shaun and thought, *Why I am having this conversation? I have no idea how to get a squillion-dollar letter of credit on some dodgy Thai bank and thought I certainly don't have the bank account to risk any of my money.* He decided to appease the smiling, likeable man.

"Shaun, I really don't have that sort of money, mate. And I know nowt about letters of credit but send me some stuff through and I'll have a look at it."

He decided to change track and asked: "What about the politics of destroying rainforests? Surely the politicians and army wouldn't want to rape their whole country?"

"They don't give a ****, Jack. They have been doing it with the Chinese for ages. But I do care, buddy. I am going to employ an environmental team and replant the area with soft wood to help the local people. I am also committed to save the orang-utans there, so looking for someone to help with that. Do you know anyone?"

Jack was surprised at this for it appeared that Ironman had a conscience and also that this was a bonus as his daughter was looking for a job at the time and she loved the environment and animals. He asked Shaun if she could help in any way and Shaun offered her a job there and then. Before they could go much further, Ironman's Danish business partner from Thailand phoned and his short period of mega deals was cut short as he was dragged out to meet someone more solvent than Jack to convince to hand over squillions of hard-earned currency.

He left with a promise that he would employ Jack's daughter as an Environmental Manager saving the poor creatures whose habitat he was about to destroy. Jack was pleased that he had met a good new friend and that his daughter may soon have a very interesting and profitable job, and as the genial man left he said so to Harry the owner, a sour-faced Glaswegian who had only two loves, Glasgow Rangers and Sharon, his Borneo head-hunter wife. Harry was standing at the bar scowling as usual.

"Fae ****'s sake are yeah daft in the heed? He's a con man, always has been. He's been coming to Singapore selling that iron all around toon for years, yeah daft loon, yeah, and he's a Fenian. I canna stand them bastards and you should nae be talking to the likes of them in here."

So began Jack's lectures into Glasgow's religious history and his life with Ironman and his squillion-dollar projects and also his life with Harry and his Glasgow culture. Harry was of course yet another enigma in this new world and his dislike of all things Roman Catholic and the green and white hoops of Celtic Football Club were to raise themselves many times in the following weeks and months of late-night and weekend drinking during Jack's initial research into this mad house.

But it was on a Sunday a few weeks later that he met Billy, an old friend of Father Bob's and Ralph, all from Newcastle upon Tyne, in The Sportsman's, who enlightened him as no one but the Lord Buddha probably had been.

Father Bob had taken finally pity on him when Jack asked yet again if he'd tell him about real contracting and Bob said: "Let's go to The Sportsman's, Jack, I'm meeting Billy and Ralph there. Billy and Ralph will tell yeah all about that stuff, man. I taught them years ago, man, even taught them how to be draughtsmen. Stick with me, son, and you'll lorn the secret."

So, desperate to learn more he walked down Orchard Road from the MRT station with Father Bob to meet this icon of real contracting.

Sundays were different and fun in Sportsman's. Harry used to change his menu for the strangers and locals who turned up – chicken curry, sausages (cholesterol wrapped in pig intestines), Scotch pie (cholesterol in wrapped in cholesterol) and sometimes a marvellous treat, haggis (sheep's intestines and cholesterol), oh the joy of Scottish haute cuisine, you may say and wonder why Glasgow is still the heart attack capital of the whole world. And the lovely Filipino, Amy, would sing like a nightingale.

Billy was funny. He was a small, bespectacled, rotund man with an engaging laugh and visage. He'd been real contracting for years and was extremely good at his job but he had a great ability to talk work interspersed with colloquial stories. He told Jack and Bob, as they settled into a day and night of Tiger and mince, of his hobby which was keeping owls, and that he once interviewed a young piping engineer in Newcastle with a tawny owl sat on Billy's shoulder. Billy kept asking the owl what he thought of what the guy had said in the interview in answer to his questions.

"Whoo!" the owl always replied.

And Billy turned to the owl then pointed at the kid and said: "This bugger, you stupid bird."

The young boy got the job and but he never forgot his first 'real contractor' interview with the owl.

Billy continued. During the breeding season his eagle owl was always horny. Given the fact that in Tyneside, UK, there weren't too many of these massive and splendid carnivores to mate with, it used to attack his wife's head. She'd scream to get it off as it bumped and thrashed around in her latest permanent waved coiffure.

"Bob," he chuckled, "with the owl's feathers displayed in full mating ritual sitting on her perm, she used to look just like Cochise in the High Chaparral."

As the day drew on Billy's tales of real contracting expanded, Father Bob had heard most of them but Jack was keen to learn more but the secret was never revealed and the laughter continued.

"Heh, Jack," Billy shouted across the circular bar table above the sounds of Amy's singing, "you'll never guess who I bumped into today at the opticians?"

"Who was that, Bill?" Jack shouted, very innocently.

"Everybody!" was his answer, said with a resounding laugh from all the drunken maniacs sat around.

Ralph was more reserved. Bob, with a wink in his eye, told Jack he had been a terribly dysfunctional problem child and also deluded man as he'd been born in Newcastle but supported Sunderland football team, their fierce rivals.

"He's like yeah, bonny lad, he canna be reet in the heed, son."

Jack laughed but thought, this is nothing to do with which local football team you supported, there weren't many he'd met so far out here in Singapore who were 'reet in the heed'. Jack asked Ralph what he was doing there as last time he had heard of him he was in the Middle East working on a project. Ralph being a quiet man, Billy answered for him.

"Jack, he left that months ago, it was managed by the Vice President's son. It was a disaster. He was called Broken Arrow."

"Why?" Jack asked naively.

"No bloody good and can't be fired!" he retorted with a resounding chuckle.

"He was so bad, Jack, if he were any more stupid he'd have to be watered twice a week."

Everyone laughed and Jack tried to continue with his conversation with Ralph, hoping for some sense out of the mirth and asked him what was doing here in Singapore.

"I'm on a job in the ship repair docks in Singapore," Ralph replied.

Jack, still naïve in this business asked, "How is the job going?"

"It's going great... it's really *****d. Best job I've been on in years, bonny lad," Ralph answered, smiling widely, clearly delighted and for once his voice excited.

Jack looked puzzled as everyone drank a few more slurps from their beers. Father Bob nodded knowingly in agreement with Ralph's wise words. Jack decided to stick to his own reasoning and logic and asked what he thought was a sensible question.

"But Ralph, if it's *****d then what's so great about it?"

All of the assembled looked at Jack as if he'd passed the port the wrong way again, shaking their heads in disgust. Ralph just smiled and continued his revelation.

"The job is totally *****d, mate, every job in this business is, but here it's a real bonus as Asia is great, not like ******* Saudi Arabia – here, beer, football, everywhere, and lovely lasses who look like movie stars and wear hardly anything. Over there, Jack, it was hell, nee beer, nee football on telly, nee lasses except those in full stealth bomber dress, for ****'s sake it's paradise here…"

He continued:

"Mind you, bonny lad, it'll tek Jesus to raise this ****** from the deed. I'm hoping to get another torkey and an Easter egg oot of this one."

Jack thought about this for a few seconds and then translated in his own head and it began to dawn on him the simplicity of it all. For non-Geordies (Tynesiders) and normal people, this is the management explanation from Ralph's statement:

"The project is totally over budget and is massively behind schedule. It will never meet the planned schedule for delivery in August. No one cares. Outwith a total change of management, contract and working behaviour or divine intervention, I am expecting to work and stay in this sexual paradise until Christmas and almost certainly I'll get to Easter."

Jack kept his own interpretation to himself but everyone laughed again at the concise and colloquial way Ralph had described the plight of the project. Sharon, Harry's wife from Borneo, was puzzled, however, as the references to turkeys and Easter eggs were not in her lexicon and asked a very pertinent question to normal people.

"What does he mean, Bob?"

Father Bob explained in his own inimitable way. He told Sharon that Ralph's metaphor of getting 'a torkey' related to a long-gone tradition when benevolent companies used to give their employers a turkey for Christmas. If you remember Scrooge, on his epiphany of kindness, bought one for Bob Cratchit and Tiny Tim in Charles Dickens' *A Christmas Carol*. Ralph was expecting the project to last at least till he could get his metaphorical turkey but he really expected to be given an Easter egg as well.

Sharon, being of sound financial mind and judgement cottoned on immediately, that this again meant Billy and his mates would be around for at least six months longer and hence would spend all their hard-earned, day-rated money in her bar. She smiled that big smile she always did when luring you into yet another round of Tiger but this time she offered to buy a round. She knew proper punters when she saw them!

Jack turned to Ralph and asked him what the company were doing about it all. Ralph explained, his happiness breaking his normally dour, weather-beaten face.

"They fired the project manager. They hired me and another hundred contractors six months ago. They are hiring another two hundred this week. They have put our day rate up to fifteen hundred US dollars and given us a loyalty bonus if we'll stay to the end, which is now already six months late. They have no chance of it working, it's *****d. It's bloody great, man. Here, sup up and have another Tiger."

Jack just looked at Ralph as he drank his beer and turned to Sharon to order another round. With his management consultancy head and his mission from the Iron Chancellor to deliver his project on time, on budget, that works, and not injure anyone, he was feeling uncomfortable with this logic and potential futility of it all. He turned to Father Bob and the old sage just winked at him through his wire glasses, he nodded his head to Billy and Ralph and whispered to Jack, his new apprentice in the magic art of real contracting.

"See son, just listen and lorn, we'll get you through this and you'll kna all aboot how it works soon. Let's stop taarking work. Get the football on, Harry."

And sure enough, Harry put a football match on the telly and everyone forgot work and enjoyed the evening. However, Jack couldn't stop thinking about what Ralph had said. Everyone was delighted the job was in a mess and even the project manager had been sacked. Failure seemed to please them all. Already he realised that he really couldn't rely on Father Bob to tell everything as Bob was trapped in keeping secret whatever syndrome was driving the behaviours that rewarded failure. Jack would always be the apprentice to his surrogate father and this knowledge was his power. It would require more covert work. So he decided that night he would lead a double life, one of a professional communications consultant, the other of a covert investigator of all things bizarre, crazy and insane...

Over the next few weeks his theory began to form and crystallise.

Everyone seemed happy and the craic was always fun, beautiful girls and smiling people everywhere and life easy going but he began to realise much to his surprise that very little debate was held on 'the value of the yuan' or hydrostatic dynamics in oilfield reservoirs, or, his own tome: *Process Piping for Softies*. It was always a debate on how long the projects could last before these bastions of the industry had to give up this fantasy world that 'real contracting' had brought them.

This was the unerring question on everyone's mind. On meeting any new acquaintance, it was always, "What job have you got?", or, "What project are you on?" and the ubiquitous question, "How long have you got?"

Night after night as people came into the bar, it was like giving news of a terminal illness when they said the job or project could be ending soon. Mass hysteria would break out: lemmings in the Tundra would hurl themselves off cliffs into rivers, they would be kissed by the barmaids a thousand times, vast quantities of Tiger beer would be ordered and Harry's face would look as cold as a Clydeside winter, as he realised another customer was doomed to return to the hell of real work. And probably back home to the wife.

Jack slowly began to realise there was a paradigm of behaviour here; a paradise paradigm.

'Everyone who is living in bliss will utilise their collective skills and experience to prolong the experience.'

Jack considered his theory most days and drunken nights and grew enlightened through this cultural abyss that he had found himself in. He began to question the rationality of it all. He recalled one of his favourite books – the classic, *Catch 22*.

In this wonderful book by Joseph Heller, the key player, Yossarian, understandably worried about his longevity flying bombing missions in the Second World War, asked, 'if he could be discharged on the grounds of insanity'. He was told by the doctor that: 'Only a sane man would realise it was madness to carry on flying missions' therefore QED, 'he must be sane not insane' – voila, c'est Catch 22.

Jack was starting to form his own secret theory, a new Catch 22.147 recurring, which became clear one humid evening sat staring through the Sportsman's window at the thousands of folk walking up and down Orchard Road. It was a simple Catch 3.21 recurring:

'One must be sane to join with and frequent with people who were comfortable, happy and secure working in banks, companies, and on projects where billion dollar losses were commonplace for their employers, yet they all drove Ferrari's and holidayed in Bali: Only an insane man would question the morality of this.'

He decided to persevere and learn more about his revelation but thought he may well have to start carrying a Taser or mace as most of his research subjects should really be restrained or on tranquillisers. Very soon in The Outback Bar and the project sites across Asia he would meet more strange people where he wished he had brought Buffalo Alf and his Nitro Express with him. Tasers and mace would have no effect.

CHAPTER FOUR

Singapore

Captain Abe

A few weeks have passed…

After his first couple of meetings with Captain Abe and his belligerent patrons he returned night after night to The Outback for his research project, and one night as he sat reflecting on Bill the Argument's death and watching Captain Abe drink another gallon of Bundaberg rum and inhale the whole Asian supply of the British American Tobacco company, a huge man entered the bar. He was tall and had an extremely large beer gut, with a shaven skinhead. You would be forgiven if you thought he was a Nazi Party henchman or UKIP MP but he was in fact a corporate banker. No difference between them all, one might say, and some would agree with you. He was leading the bank's financial audit team that had been in the project office with Jack and the team for a few weeks. Jack had got to know and like him and it had been a nightly ritual for them both to drink copious amounts of Tiger in Dawn and Jim's madhouse. Jack was hoping to gain an experienced financial person's input on his emerging theory of the industry.

He was Australian and called Marc and lived and worked in Australia as Asia Pacific VP of Risk Management. Over the few weeks he had known Marc, Jack realised that he took great delight in denying loans to ailing businesses, closing down a whole third world country overdraft facility and putting millions on the brink of starvation, and ruthlessly destroying any entrepreneur's dream of becoming the next Bill Gates.

Apart from these tendencies to genocide, Jack observed that he could be an extremely kind and generous man but with a tendency to extreme violence. As witnessed the night before when an obnoxious Norwegian had pestered Marc's lovely wife who was with him at the time and Jack was nearly hit by an unsuspecting Scandahooligan flying through the air in a crumpled heap into the corner after a swing of the huge arm.

"Alors!" his lovely long-suffering French wife whispered into Jack's ear. "He'll now want to stand on his throat and squash it. Stop him, please, vite mon chéri!"

Traits Jack thought he no doubt picked up in the board rooms of banks all over the world as he rushed and picked the bloody mess up and threw it out of the bar just before the size 12 boot came down onto the windpipe. It was obviously the big man's speciality when annoyed.

During nightly beers Jack came to understand that the big man's wife had had some serious mental trauma in her past, but it didn't take a genius to realise it could have been partly a consequence of marriage to Big Marc. Due to her continued mental anxiety, she had been referred to a therapist in Sydney and this lady doctor had recommended that Big Marc attend their sessions. This was after she had been put into a catatonic state, lying curled up in a corner of the room one long day whilst the big man was at the office. It was revealed that the trigger to this latest need for therapy was yet again the big man's behaviour, for remonstrating with her for the heinous crime of forgetting to put his orange juice on the table before he went to work. The latest therapist in the hospital wanted to get Big Marc to understand that his temper and actions could, like smoking, seriously harm his wife's health.

The female shrink asked the big man: "After having a tantrum about the orange juice, Marc, what should you have done?"

"I don't know, gone to work?" he replied, not really understanding what was wrong with his behaviour in the first case. The shrink corrected him.

"No, Marc – before that."

"Don't know. Got myself some apple juice?" he said frustratedly.

"No. Before that," she went on doggedly.

"I'm *****d if I know! Kissed the stupid cow?"

Thus Big Marc confirmed the shrink's hypothesis that his poor wife's problems were probably caused by her husband's behaviour, but she continued to counsel the financial wizard.

Triumphantly, she announced: "No, Marc, you should have hugged her."

"I don't do that," said the big man. "I'm a banker."

It appeared that the shrink gave up with these sessions and thankfully Marc's wife recovered from her illness. Well, for a while.

Mark's wife did worry, however, when she tried to get advice from the Singapore Mental Health Line about Marc's problem with his teddy bear. Her call was answered by a recorded voice advising her of the following:

Welcome to the Singapore Mental Health Hotline.

If you are obsessive compulsive – press 1 repeatedly.

If you are co-dependant – ask someone to press 2 for you.

If you have a multiple personality – Press 1, 3, 4, 6 and 7.

If you are paranoid – we know who you are and what you want, don't press anything and we'll send someone to get you.

If you are delusional – Press 7 and we'll transfer your call to mothership.

If you are schizophrenic – press 8 listen carefully and a small voice will tell you what to do.

If you are depressive – it doesn't matter which key you press, no one will answer you.

If you are dyslexic – press 69, 69, 69.

If you have a nervous disorder – wait till the beep, after the beep wait for the beep.

If you have short-term memory loss – press 9. After a while press 9 again.

And if you have low self-esteem – it doesn't matter which key you press, no one will answer you.

They didn't have a button for Marc's particular disorder.

It was still early evening in the bar and the customers were different to those Jack was used to later in the evening from whom he gained a wealth of information for his research. And finally he met the one elusive man he had been told about and had sought: the Doc.

The Doc was normally lunchtime, Saturdays and very early evenings man after finishing his surgery at tea time. The surgery was located above the bar. Jack had not been in the bar those times during these early days. Tonight the Doc was a bit later than usual to wind his way home. Abe introduced Jack and Marc to the famous man.

Doctor Jones was a small, thin-faced, spectacled older man. He wore the ubiquitous smart trousers and short-sleeved open shirt that most South East professionals wore, out with bankers and financiers who all seemed to wear suits. During the initial pleasantries Jack deduced from his accent that he was from Wales. He asked the doctor if he'd known Abe and Dawn long.

The Doc took a drink from his bottle of Crown lager and shouted out at no one in particular.

"For ****'s sake I've known those two buggers twenty years. What I ever did to get them as patients I'll never bloody know!"

He drank from the bottle again, plainly excited, and shouted again: "I keep that bugger alive you know," and pointed his bottle at Jim, "but with what he drinks and smokes and his bloody blood pressure he should be dead."

The Doc continued: "I am bloody baffled by the man. He's nearly seventy and he wants me to supply him Viagra and steroids to help him shag his way around the bloody jungles of Batam."

He pointed his bottle again and he howled to his surrounding audience: "He smokes more than anyone I know and his arteries should be solid bloody cholesterol with the pies the bugger eats, and don't get me on about the Bundaberg. I tell you he should be dead!"

Jack mused that this was indeed strange that this medic was actually distraught that his patient hadn't passed this mortal coil. *Yet another one in this zoo*, he thought.

Abe just laughed raucously at the Doc's woes and his prognosis on Abe's life expectancy. Totally unworried about his clinical diagnosis, he took another drink of Tiger and draw of his cigarette and added: "Tell them about when you first met us, Doc."

The Doc told them both that he had first met this medical marvel and Dawn thirty years before when Abe and Dawn had entered his surgery carrying a box. Abe placed a box on the desk and asked the Doc to examine its contents.

"I could smell something wasn't quite right and when I opened the thing there was a severed monkey's head. 'What the hell do you want me to do with this?' I asked the mad bugger. He told me it had bitten his son and he thought it had rabies," the Doc shouted insanely, drinking from his Crown lager.

The Doc ordered another bottle and continued: "'What the bloody hell am I going to do with it?' I screamed at the bugger. I was terrified and dropped the seeping head back into its box."

He shook his head as if the memory was too much.

"'Can you find out if it's got the rabies, Doc?' the crazy bastard asked me. He said his bitten lad was out in the back and his wound looked bad."

Through a series of expletives, howls and bottles of Crown lager the Doc told of how Abe's lad had been bitten.

Captain Abe's son had been bitten in New Guinea. Knowing the risk of rabies was high in this jungle outpost of Captain Abe's Trading Empire, Abe had tracked down the offending animal, killed it, and decapitated it. Note; business men were men those days; no power dressing, mobile phones as extensions of your penis or representing the sword for the warrior leader types among today's modern boardrooms. Captain Abe had an actual sword and took to hunting his enemies through real jungles full of actual predators, cannibals and man eaters.

The Doc continued and was ranting as he swallowed his Crown and explained his next actions.

"The daft bugga had packed the head in a box with ice and they had jumped a plane to fly to Singapore to find a decent doctor. How the hell they got it through Changi customs I'll never know. For

****'s sake, the head must have smelled like the floor of Dawn's Outback pub. I examined the lad, gave him some antibiotics as I didn't have rabies vaccines in those days at hand and they were very dangerous to give, and only should be given if you really had no way of examining the animal who had bitten the person or if you really knew it was rabid. So I told the mad bastards to leave and go to their apartment and I took the bloody thing down to the pathology laboratory at Gleneagles Hospital."

Our Welsh CSI mimic took the erstwhile rabid head down to the pathology department of the local hospital, where they tried to open up the cranium to observe the brain and take samples. He had been employed in the path lab many moons before and was respected enough to be allowed to get on with it. However, when the administration realised it was a smuggled monkey's head from New Guinea, he had to work fast before he was duly escorted off to Changi Jail himself. This was Singapore after all, and you were jailed and hit with large sticks those days for dropping chewing gum on the pavement. Even the medical profession were not exempt from this discipline.

"After three days in the equatorial heat it was just a soup, a soup of brains, blood and pus."

He delighted in telling them this pathological fact.

"I took a sample and we plated it off and waited for the rabies tests to come back."

He had calmed now, the Crown beer dimming the memory of it all a bit.

"The boy was OK in the end but those mad bastards have been my patients ever since."

And swallowing another large gulp of lager, he howled to anyone in range of his Welsh ranting.

"What the hell did I ever do to deserve them? And their bloody kids!"

He was raving again.

The Doc reluctantly took his leave after this tale, rushing out of the bar door swearing profusely and shaking his head at a phone call he had received. Jack and Marc were told by Dawn it was almost certainly from his Singaporean wife who she said tried daily to track him down in his peripatetic hostelries and get him either back to his surgery or home.

They all drank until late and Jack and Marc walked back up the Ho Chi Minh trail wondering what was next. The next day they found out…

CHAPTER FIVE

Singapore

The Doc

The next day…

Gator Tom, the big Louisiana man, was sitting in his office on Anson Road and Marc was talking to him about project money things. The big man seemed distracted and Marc asked him what the problem was.

"It's mah ass, Marc: I've had the Bonanza Ass for three days. Marc, what do you think is wrong with mah ass?"

"Maybe it's the Tiger and the peanut diet," Marc suggested.

This was probably a good cause of his anal problem as the big man when he first arrived in the Singapore office from Houston lived exclusively on Tiger beer (sometimes Jack Daniels as a dessert) and groundnuts in their shells, provided free by the Filipino-inhabited bars in which he perpetually lived after work. No one had ever seen him eat anything else. He never ate breakfast, lunch or dinner. He was a huge bear of a man, so Tiger and peanuts must be as nutritious even though it might induce haemorrhoids or a fungal infection of the ass every now again.

"Let's go and see an expert," Marc said encouragingly, remembering the previous night's medical lectures, and he took him to meet the Doc in his peripatetic surgery in The Outback Bar.

Luckily the Doc was ensconced in his usual place at the bar and Marc introduced Tom to him and the Doc continued in the same ranting as the night before, pointing at Jim and Dawn and anyone who was there.

"I'm used to treating Americans. They are more compliant than these bloody English and Australian patients I have. Piss pots, the lot of them. They never take any bloody notice of me. They all should be dead!"

He calmed, took another drink and spoke to Tom and Marc.

"Did I tell you that I have the American Medal of Honour on my surgery wall? I was given it for services in the Vietnam War. I used to look after the American military that were on rest and recuperation here in Singapore. I am a specialist in sexually transmitted diseases and I was awarded the medal for keeping the soldiers with the clap on the battle front."

He laughed and continued his recollection.

"I used to have a clinic in Geylang, the red light area those days and now, and treated hundreds of you bloody Yanks. I was so used to the same local girls coming in that I could recognise them by their private parts… hah, hah, hah." Everyone within earshot smiled along with his maniacal laughing.

He kept them all engaged with his stories of his clinic in Geylang. It seemed that he kept the local Triad gangsters' girls in top form and working and the main godfather was very appreciative of this and offered the Doc free samples anytime, which he never took. He also offered to help anyone 'sleep with the fishes' that may upset the Doc or refused to pay his fees. As the Doc's patients included some of the most important and wealthy families in Singapore, Hong Kong and also some VIPs from the Indonesian Government, he was very careful never to speak out of turn to Mr Corleone Chang in case he set his ninjas on his more sensitive source of earnings.

However, the Doc's latest sexually transmitted disease clinic of repute was not in Geylang, but was of course The Outback Bar and he continued to amaze Tom and Big Marc with his behaviour. To Dawn and Abe it was just normal of course.

They were talking about sexually related things, and the Doc was ranting about how he was the city state's expert in phosphodiesterase inhibitors and their use in sexual impotence. That is, he was being asked to prescribe more and more Viagra and Cialis to his 'piss pot' patients. The Doc was complaining that his Saturday and Sunday afternoon consulting sessions in the bar were now spoilt by having to advise someone who had had a difficulty with performance the night before with a take away from the Four Floors of Whores. He ranted that this performance issue of course had nothing to do with the twelve hours on the drink or that the 'girl' was not quite what the customer had been expecting, as can easily happen with 'take aways' from the Four Floors. As most of these customers of The Outback were looking for a prescription for Viagra, the Doc would have to explain to them, often very forcibly, that he wouldn't prescribe unless he could examine them professionally in his real surgery and rule out high blood pressure and cardiovascular disease.

Belligerent Barry entered the hostelry and took his place at the bar ogling Shah. Belligerent Barry must have overheard the Doc and picked up on the Viagra discussion and must have thought the great medic could help him with his extracurricular night-time activities.

"Doc, I have been getting problems lately with a hard on. I fancy giving that Viagra a try. But my Doc thinks it would be a bad idea because of my high blood pressure as the stroke which caused my droopy eye might happen again and top me this time."

The Doc stared up at the large man squinting in the neon light gloom and smoke-filled air.

"Of course you can use it," said the sexual medical expert in his usual acerbic way, "just make sure you don't get too excited. Just use it with your wife."

And he burst into infectious insane laughter and everyone joined him in his black humour. He left Big Marc and Tom to go over to have a word with the argumentative lothario and advise him to come to his surgery for cardiovascular tests before he'd ever treat him. Tom asked Abe if the Doc was married and Abe and Dawn explained the Welsh Hippocrates' trials and tribulations with his loving partner.

They heard that the Doc's wife and receptionist was a lovely Singaporean lady who kept a perpetual watch on his visits to The Outback and when she realised he'd been missing for too long, would unerringly ring him just as he was really enjoying a Crown lager over a hard-earned lunch break and then drag him out of the bar. The basis of this action from the lovely Rose was not related to his health or mental state in mixing with the inmates of The Outback, but purely financial. She was Asian, and particularly for the Chinese race, money and the accumulation of such was a prime driver in life. The basic Adam Smith mentality of Rose was that the Doc's consultation fees in his real surgery, diligently and gratefully collected by her, were much greater than his one bottle of Crown ale that grateful patients would buy him in his peripatetic surgery in The Outback for services rendered.

The good doctor lived in a perpetual state of penury because of this peripatetic life caring for his errant Outback flock during his lunch break, night times and weekends. His wife was the only one who could ensure that he spent enough time in his real surgery to pay their bills.

He never seemed too grateful to his long-suffering partner for her endeavours to save his bank balance, or the beta cells of his liver. He would hide behind much bigger men, and in the case of Dawn, ladies, when she was seen peering through the beer- and nicotine-stained glass door.

Rose became very adept at guerrilla warfare and would confuse his camouflage activities by going around to the back door and catching him cowering under Dawn's huge bosom or behind Big Marc's beer gut. To evade this military manoeuvre on his long-suffering wife's part, the itinerant medic had found bolt holes in bars that she never knew were within striking distance of the surgery, but she'd be relentless and call him regularly in an attempt to track him down and get him back to his more lucrative patients.

The Doc would swear and cuss every time his mobile rang and it showed on the display screen that it was his beloved's number. He'd rant and rave that she never left him alone to enjoy his small pleasure and the little free time he had from a life of trial administering his care to the lost and lonely, and he'd run out to the street, away from the usual bar music, to answer the phone and pretend he was shopping or between house calls.

Captain Abe told them that once he had made a major mistake in securing a new mobile phone for him. Abe said he had returned to the bar after earning money with his real, compliant patients in his real surgery and was delighted that he had bought a new phone from Singtel.

"It's got GPS; I can always know where I am, even when I'm pissed," he exclaimed excitedly.

"Didn't you get Rose one also and linked to this one?" Abe enquired. "Isn't that a bit dangerous if she's also got GPS and they are linked to locate each other?"

"For God's sake, man, ring Arun and let's get the bugga disabled, quick."

He quickly realised that this phone was a great threat to his regular free time libation period.

Arun it seems was a great friend of Abe and Dawn and luckily a patient of the caring Doc. Abe explained that Arun had very few bodily organs left, having lost a few due to excessive alcohol consumption over his short life. He was a wonderful Indian lad, with a great sense of humour who actually was an IT guy who could do great things and very modest, unlike Bill the Argument was. Abe liked him.

Arun's role in life, and his payment to the doctor for keeping him alive every day, was to ensure that the Doc's wife couldn't trace him using modern handheld communications technologies. For this service he received free consultations, medicines and the necessary medical certificates for his many days off work on the piss with the folks in The Outback, all of this medical care free, gratis and unknown to Rose as it was normally dispensed in the bar. This is a great example of symbiosis for biologists and young students who are reading this. Here two species benefit individually from each other's participation in transferring needs between themselves.

As Abe finished his biopic of the Doc to Marc and Tom, the Doc finished off with a shouting match with Belligerent Barry which the four bystanders heard; it seemed to be over some interpretation of James Joyce's epic novel *Ulysses*.

"What's that about, Abe?" Big Marc asked.

Abe answered: "The Doc is an expert in most things, mate. Literature, philosophy, science, you name it, he is the ******* best.

That pommie bastard Barry thinks he knows something about literature. He reckons he's a Master or something in languages or some shite like that. But I think he just loves winding the Doc up just for the argument. Told you all, he's a ****."

The Doc came back to his potential new patient fuming and howling at no one in particular.

"That English bastard said that *Ulysses* was shite. Shite for ****'s sake!" He drank a long pull on his bottle of Crown lager and calmed a bit. "I told the thick bastard he couldn't even read *Ulysses* if he had a brain transplant. He can stick his bloody Viagra up his arse as far as I care."

Gator Tom laughed and jokingly interjected: "Heh Doc, that's where I stick my Viagra. It works quicker!"

The big American then slapped the Doc on his bony back in friendship, knocking him and his bottle halfway across the bar, and asked him for his anal diagnosis.

"Doc, what do you think is wrong with mah ass?"

The Doc screamed at him: "For ****'s sake I can't examine your arse here. I'm pissed and it's not professional. Come to my surgery tomorrow. Here's my card."

And the Doc, calming down a bit more, handed him his card from his wallet. He added precautionary advice prior to their morning consultation.

"Looking at the amount of beer you've drank in the short time you've been in here I bet you are like all these other piss-pot patients I have in here."

He pointed around the room, but particularly to Captain Abe.

"See that old bugger. I keep him alive, you know. Have done for forty bloody years. Look at his blood pressure, it's ****** normal. Bloody normal I tell you."

And turning back to the Gator Tom he finished his tantrum shaking his head, clearly upset he'd kept Abe alive.

"He defies medical science."

He continued his rant with his new American patient.

"So I guess I'll have to prescribe you the same medicine as these piss pots to keep you drinking and fornicating. They all want antibiotics they can drink with. None of the piss pots will listen to me and stop drinking, so I have to prescribe Outback-friendly antibiotics. I suppose you'll want them too?"

The Big Man, smiling, answered in the affirmative and offered the Doc yet another bottle of Crown lager which despite his advice to his patients in the bar to abstain from all forms of the magic molecule, he swallowed with gusto!

A Singaporean man and complete stranger to Tom and Big Marc shouted across the bar when he heard the Doc talking about beer friendly antibiotics, "Heh lah, Doc, do you have anything for raging hangovers?"

The Doc lifted his bottle high and screamed: "Of course! I am the world's expert on hangovers," and drinking a large slurp he continued, "I bloody well should be; I've been having them for sixty years... Ha... ha... ha."

He fell about the bar howling with laughter which was heard by Rose, his lovely Singaporean wife outside on the street, who then saw him through the smoky haze of The Outback glass door and shuffled her small body past the two giants of the oil industry to confront her errant fee earner and husband. The Doc raved on to Big Marc and the crowd:

"Oh bloody hell, I tell you she could find me in the jungles of Borneo. She can smell Crown lager a mile away. It's her bloody birthday too."

Big Marc offered the lovely Rose a glass of Dawn's best Australian plonk red for her birthday which she accepted and sat down at the bar near Dawn, who embraced her in her huge bosom hug, clearly pissed again.

"Happy birthday my dear," Dawn muttered, raising her glass of Tiger and shouting across the crowded bar, "many happy returns!"

"I bloody well hope not!" screamed the Welsh Hippocrates to everyone in the bar, laughing and cackling himself into his usual apoplexy. Rose just smiled, as enigmatically as the Mona Lisa herself.

Abe explained to the two big men that this talk was all a charade and a black sense of humour from the great man. They were a great loving couple who celebrated fifty years of marriage a few years ago. They had a wonderful extended Singaporean family and the Doc would be lost without her, or so Abe and all his friends told him. He would say otherwise!

Abe explained that despite his continual complaining that he had been able to keep him alive and he was by far and away the best doctor he had the pleasure of being treated by. A pragmatist, with so much experience and knowledge of medicine, and more importantly, patients, than anyone in medicine he had ever met. He was a true professional, loved by all his patients with a sincere desire to help those in need of his tender care. He even missed many of his surgery-free Saturday afternoon sessions with his deranged patients in the bar to attend and study at postgraduate medical seminars – missing Tiger beer for medical knowledge? Surely this was a true sacrifice, from a true professional.

In days when doctors refuse to carry out house calls, this man at the age of seventy-six was still constantly attending his patients day and night in their homes, without charging the normal excessive fees of other doctors. It was just part of his normal service and dedication.

He was a man whose military and medical career had spanned the Cold War, the independence of Singapore and the opening of Dawn's first Outback bar. A Welshman through and through, Captain Abe believed the only person in Singapore to have Welsh as his nationality on his Permanent Resident's pass. He refused to leave the office for six hours until they did it. He had told Abe that he kept shouting at the confused girls at the Ministry of Manpower.

"I'm not bloody British. I am Welsh." He then explained more. "I even got a map and showed them where Wales was. Swore in Welsh at them to prove we didn't speak English all the time. They finally gave up arguing with me after six hours of howling at them."

Proves what a stubborn race the Welsh are, you may say.

And he finally cured the Big Man's ass.

The Doc met Gator Tom the next day when both had sobered up and after Tom had trodden the lonely path up the Ho Chi Minh trail after many hours in The Outback to be confronted by his darling ninja Asian wife who leapt at him from her hiding place in a Bayan tree. At this consultation, the Doc's financial problems were solved overnight.

This was because Gator was so grateful for his Bonanza Ass cure that he switched his whole family to the Doc. The fact was that the number of his children was huge, and that as most of this multicultural progeny had inherited his genes they were consequently very large, therefore they consumed vast quantities of medicines. In addition, the big man constantly needed pharmaceuticals to ease the problems of his extracurricular lifestyle and diet, which led to a propensity for various infections and gastrointestinal problems. Thus, the Doc made millions out of treating a cornucopia of illnesses from this avuncular American and his progeny.

During his consultation with Tom the following morning the Doc explained his perpetual dilemma and his torturous path to balance his love of beer and the craic and his need for coin of the realm.

"You see Tom, working with such a bunch of debauched and deranged patients from that bar doesn't always pay well. I have to balance the real work of consulting in this surgery for real, compliant, paying patients, with consulting and treating in my free time, the detritus of society and dregs and piss pots who are my totally non-compliant patients – like you, probably."

Marvellous patient respect and care, Tom thought.

"Let's take your blood pressure, Tom."

The Doc asked him to raise the long-sleeved white shirt which the American always wore and cuffed his arm and took the reading.

"For God's sake, it's normal. You're like that Australian bastard Jim, Tiger beer must keep you all alive!"

Tom looked worried at his healer's amazement that he was actually well and healthy. He remembered the night before, that the man did seem to get angry that his bar patients could have survived so long, especially Jim. He seemed a lot of the time to be well disappointed they hadn't tripped this mortal coil. Tom found this somewhat disconcerting, given he was his doctor and the Hippocratic Oath and its dedication to saving patients' lives and all that. However, ever the pragmatist and unafraid of most things in life, especially gators, Tom rationalised that, despite his rebukes and fits of rage and dementia at his piss-pot patient lifestyles, which curiously paralleled his own, the doctor still tried valiantly to help keep them all on this earth and inevitable trail of tears. The Doc continued to 'consult' with Tom.

"I had another of you piss pots in here the other day. The big South African guy, Hansie; he runs your shipping or something?"

"Yeah: great guy," Tom confirmed.

The Doc shouted: "Great guy! He's never out of the bloody Outback," and throwing a sheet of paper at Tom he exclaimed, "look at the results of his medical. They are all bloody normal. Bloody normal I tell you. The amount he drinks he should be dead!"

Tom picked up the results and noticed that unlike some of his there were no red values anywhere. He thought to try to calm the apoplectic medic.

"Heh, Doc. He does eat a lot of fish."

The Doc grabbed the results off him and bawled at him: "Fish! bloody fish! He smokes eighty a day for bloody hell's sake. He could smoke a whole bloody salmon with that lot. Look at his blood pressure. It's normal! He's like that bloody Australian piss head Abe. They both live on Tiger beer and cigarettes and they are both bloody normal. It's not fair!"

Tom sat looking at the esteemed doctor and wondered if he could do with a Tiger himself to calm the angst, and he was about to offer to take him downstairs to The Outback but the Doc closed the consultation quickly.

"Take this prescription to the pharmacist in the Four Floors of Whores. I know she has these antibiotics. They are the Outback-friendly ones so you can drink what you like. All you bastards never listen to me, do you? You all carry on your piss-pot lives and take no notice of me so just take these and come back if your arse doesn't stop burning."

Tom went back to office with his new alcohol-friendly tablets and what he hoped would be a Bonanza-free ass. Gator reflected on his time in The Outback and with the Doc. The Doc appeared to keep the players in the 'bidness' and the surrounding feeder chains working in paradise in his own parochial Welsh way; unwittingly he continued with his kindness and skill to maintain some of his patients' ability to stay in an endless cycle of money, booze and sex, interposed with short periods of actual work. The Welsh magician was trapped in the matrix, such a wonderful carer and giver, a great man, and Tom had a strong feeling he'd be back to get a lot more help from the Welsh mystic healer later in this parable.

CHAPTER SIX

Western Australia

Digger

Time moves on...

Jack sat in front of his boss and potential nemesis and listened to the latest instructions:

"You will go to Australia and you will try to sort out those people. I want to be sure they understand what we are going to achieve. If they don't listen you will write a report and I will go down and run them off. They are much like Americans: the minds of amoebae. In Germany we unified with similar Cro-Magnons evolved from the East, and look what's happened to us. Because of the Belgiums and Italians we now have to work with and listen to the French – the French! Mien Gott!" And don't get me on about the Greeks."

Jon shook his head and dismissed his tortured consultant.

Jack took his instructions, deciding that life would be much easier if he followed his leader's directions. Life here was becoming too good to challenge Jon who he conceded had much more experience than he had anyway and sadly, despite a certain xenophobia, was often very correct. Why get upset? Just live the dream.

He duly flew off from Changi airport to the Far Shore; his second trip into the strange and distinctly foreign land from Singapore and its pleasures. He was greeted in the office by the Environmental

Manager for the project who was valiantly trying to keep the liberal and caring hordes of legislators, politicians and normal people happy with the plans to dig up their beautiful oceans and rainforests. She was a very engaging indigenous woman who had studied and worked long and hard to find a niche in life that would give her a career which helped her native Australian people and environment, yet she could rise in the ranks of a very male-dominated industry. She greeted him warmly.

"Gudday, Jack. I'm Naomi. I hear you are here to help with our Cultural Awareness and Indigenous Heritage programs?"

"Yeah Naomi: along with a few other things. Jon wants me to look at how all things are going here early days. Dredging, civil works, relationships with the contractors and how we can build teams to make it all go better, looking forward to working with you, dear."

Naomi looked aghast and shocked and angrily said: "Please don't call me 'dear'. I am not a bloody furry animal, your bloody deer."

"I'm sorry, just an affectionate term where I come from. Please excuse me," said Jack apologetically.

Naomi didn't relent:

"I don't give a **** where you come from. Here you use that sexist term and I'll report you to HR."

Jack just decided to concede and said: "Can we just move on, Naomi? I've said I'm sorry."

"OK but be careful how you talk. You pommies seem to think you still rule the ****** world."

Jack reflected on his life in Singapore and that the female gender were much more passively friendly and obliging in all ways of the real contractor but also that he should tread carefully in this new world. They went down to the coffee shop complexes below the huge office block that the project had rented. Jack had pondered last time he was there why most meetings were held in these coffee shops in the sun rather than the expensive rented air-conditioned meeting rooms, but after a nice Americano and a croissant in the warm morning sunshine, he thought, why the hell not?

Naomi told him about the environmental problems. It seemed there were several similar projects in the Australian resource companies' portfolios at the time and needless to say, there were a few Australians who had issues with what they saw as ripping up the Australian farming belt and dredging huge traits of Barrier Reef, Aboriginal homelands, crocodile-infested swamps, pristine coastline, and wiping out dugongs, dolphins and small marsupials, maybe sucking the water tables dry and also deforesting ancient rainforest. But obviously, the project and the other companies and government agencies and authorities had diligently and expensively approved the projects through extensive research, testing and approvals processes and also legislation and parliament approval.

Jack was in full appreciation of the environmental efforts and listened intently but he had also heard of a major difference with operating in Australia rather than some of the less regulated countries. He had been told in The Outback and in the Singapore office of ways that less regulated countries had the approval stamps made long before any public fuss and the non-free press would report how better off the people will be by getting all this foreign investment money in house rentals, food, bars, sex industry, slave trading etc., etc., and everyone would be happy – except the dugongs, of course.

Naomi told him that in Australia this is not the case. It is a democracy and for some strange reason the people actually expected to be told the truth and have a say in their future. Weird stuff and certainly not good news for resource companies who need to dig up large tracts of the people's livelihoods, ancient homelands or holiday destinations and sell the proceeds to the Chinese at vast profits. Jack thought about Jon's mission, that it was good project and business sense to invest in environmental, cultural excellence and social and partner integration. But he was wary of talking about it to Naomi in case he made a politically incorrect boo-boo and was reported to HR.

Naomi took her leave of Jack and he decided that he'd had enough of dugongs, aboriginal artefacts, small mammals and coral reefs and in good 'real contractor' behaviour he claimed jet lag and went back to his hotel. He had arranged to meet Digger, the man who Ironman had told him was supplying all the 'digging machines' that would soon wipe out all the poor creatures that Naomi was trying to protect.

He had a nice nap and walked down the road to the pub where he was meeting Digger and on entering he was greeted by a younger, attractive, blond-haired, slightly balding man with wet damp hair brushed across his head. He was sat at the bar, glass of Bundaberg rum and Coke in his hand, chatting to an attractive young girl. He wore a coloured batik shirt and white trousers and he held out his hand.

"Hello mate, I'm Digger."

"Hi, I'm Jack. Great to see you, mate."

They enjoyed a drink or two and talked about their respective lives and work for a short time. Digger told Jack that he was from Sydney and had been sent over to the UK for his education as his father had emigrated from his home in the east end of London and wished his son to have an English education. He attended Marlborough Public School and had been in Asia many years running the heavy plant earth-digging business his father had created in the Australian mining fields, and now expanding into Asia. He was mainly involved in the Asian business but hoped to get some work in the fabrication sites across Asia from the project. He lived in Bangkok but had recently moved to another apartment in Pattaya and was engaged to a young lady from Myanmar. Jack asked how he'd liked school in the UK.

"Loved it, Jack… had a great time but sport was hard. I could do the rugby but the cross-country runs were lethal. One lad died on a race against 'Do the Boy's School'. We think they left him in a ditch; exhausted. Wasn't for me."

He finished off his rum and Coke and ordered another, smiling profusely to the lovely barmaid.

"But it was British university that did for me, matey," he said after stroking the girl's hand as she passed him his glass and not really looking at Jack but the pretty Aussie girl.

Jack was beginning to think Digger wasn't too bothered about talking about yellow digging machines or iron ore mountains and he posed a pertinent question: "Why was that, Digger?"

"University wasn't for me, Jack, couldn't get up out of bed for lectures or get out of the pub to do assignments and the young student fillies were just too hot. Bloody hell, man, what was a boy supposed to do? And maths really wasn't my strength."

He took a sip of his favourite tipple.

"So Dad brought me back home, and gave me a deputy MD job in one of his factories in Queensland. I was given an office next to his, as he was running down the hours he spent at work."

Jack guessed the rest of the management team and workers really appreciated this meteoric career rise from our erstwhile Donald Trump.

"Problem was I had this older filly in tow from the local pub, rampant she was, especially when we got squiffy. We'd be at it, Jack, all night. She loved my whip and mask and other toys. I'd be whacked and getting up early was never my strong point, you know."

Jack listened in awe of this story about his early education into business life and his struggles with real work after a life in public school and an undoubtedly depraved sexual teenage life. Obviously he had not been able to manage his own time and learn and work without constant supervision or his dad threatening to take his sex toys away.

He continued, glass of rum in hand and cigarette in another, sleek, wet, brushed back blond hair shining in the bar light.

"I'd have to get up early, about nine thirty, was a bloody nightmare after college. Some days when Dad had flown up from Sydney I'd have to show willing and get up earlier and race into the office in my little MG Midget sports car and put my foot down, Jack, and I'd race to get in before him."

Another drink, a draw on his cigarette, a lean forward and he went on.

"I'd get there before him, race up the back stairs into the executive suite where only my office and his were, open my door and get sat at the desk with papers spread out. Just in time, as Dad, would open the door and say good morning and go off into his, next door. As you can imagine, I was buggered, up early (note: it was 10 a.m. by now), a night with the filly and the grog and every day a near miss with Dad. It fair knocked me back. So I had to have a little nap to get over it all."

As you do, Jack thought, memories of Danny and his office and his sore heeds.

"The good news was that my dad was the only one who was allowed to open the door without my permission. The bad news was he didn't knock. So I used to lie down behind the door with my feet against the door and go to sleep."

"Why was that, mate?" Jack asked, as Digger drew another cigarette and blew it into the air.

"It's obvious. If Dad opened the door I'd sit up quickly and put my hands behind my head and do sit ups, pretending I was exercising." And he smiled at Jack and finished off his rum. "Bloody marvellous," he said and ordered everyone another round of drinks and lined the barmaid's pockets yet again.

Jack stood looking at this icon of hard work and perversity and remembered his conversation with another 'entrepreneur' and son of a self-made man he'd met in Duxton Road when he first arrived in Singapore, a man he had named Brad the Bottle. Brad, who had his own bottle-making business in Singapore and also liked drinking the fluid contents of the wine bottles he made most nights (hence the name), told Jack of another novel work behaviour.

Brad, who appeared to be a lovely man, had been in Asia many years and he told Jack the story of his father who had started the first bottle-making business in the UK in Yorkshire. It seems that one day a rather large man with a shaven head, camel hair coat and carrying nothing but two huge hands like plates of meat arrived at the company reception.

He handed his card over, grunting: "I've come to see the boss. He's a bit late with paying one of my clients."

The diminutive receptionist asked him to be seated and after reading his card, decided that she would hand it personally to Brad's dad. She entered the boss's office and handed the card to the founder of this great bottle enterprise.

She stood back in amazement when the normally placid entrepreneur grabbed his coat, briefcase and car keys and hurriedly left the building by the back staircase. The card had seemingly given him a shock and he decided discretion was the better part of valour.

Brad chuckled and told him the card had only two statements on it.

TERMINAL SOLUTIONS Ltd.

"We Don't **** About."

Both of them considered that this was one of the best pieces of effective marketing literature they'd ever heard of – Brad's father paid the bill the next day.

Jack smiled as he remembered Digger's own work anecdote and also Digger's calisthenics with the wooden door, and thought they were great examples for his business case model of self-made entrepreneurship. He was broken out of his management theorising by an extraordinary statement from Digger.

He spoke softly, holding his ubiquitous glass of rum and Coke in one hand and cigarette in the other.

"Jack, when you come to see us in Bangkok or Pattaya, would you like to come to my house and watch me and Angel and my old girlfriend in bed? I'll put on a BBQ and cook you some real Aussie beef to keep your spirits up, mate."

Certainly, it wasn't normally what the astonished Englishman's friends and acquaintances at home came out with at dinner so he decided that perhaps digging holes with yellow machines wasn't as boring as he thought and maybe he should take time to find out a lot more of this man and how he could educate him into Burmese and Western cultural integration. Then he remembered Gator Tom's advice about the ninja and a propensity to remove gonads whilst you sleep, and thought martial fidelity may well be safer and turned down the offer. But Digger's response floored him in his naivety of all things multisexual.

"No worries, mate. But when you get to Thailand you'll think different, mate. All girls there like each other better than men. It's their culture. I love it, me. My Angel often treats herself to one or two as a treat for me too. In fact it was my birthday day before I left our distribution office and apartment in Pattaya to come here for this meeting with your lot. She took me to a bar on Walking Street and watched a girl band singing for a while. Angel loved the two Sheilas in the band and asked me to pay them for her to play with and I could watch; real birthday treat for me."

Jack felt he should say something.

"Did you enjoy it, Digger?"

Digger stroked his sleek hair and said: "Not really. We went back to the house but I was knackered, mate, been working all day and the grog made me squiffy and I was hungry so I wasn't up for it really. So Angel and the girls went to bed and I cooked myself a rack of ribs and a steak and watched Michael Jackson in concert on video."

Jack guessed that Angel enjoyed his birthday present more than he did. The lounge lizard seemed to go into deep thought and depression as he recalled his lost birthday present, and started up a deep conversation with the pretty Asian bar maid about his armoury of sex toys. Jack sat back on a stool in awe of the man.

Suddenly Digger perked up and leaving his newfound conquest he turned to Jack and said: "Bloody hell, I just remembered I left the whip and the mask on my bed in Bangkok."

Jack, surprised that that would worry him given his wife's sexual liberation asked: "What's the problem with that, Digger?"

"It's my mother, she's staying with us this week and she always tidies up my room. Last time she threw away my two packing cases of antique porn videos. Bloody woman! I'll just go outside and phone Angel to see if she can move the whip and mask just in case. I've had them since school and they are my favourites."

And he left the bar, his cell phone in his hand. Jack just sat back, took another beer off the lovely Asian girl and waited for the great man to return.

On his return, Digger ordered another round of drinks and one for his new true love behind the bar and took a huge calculator from his back pocket. He put his head in his hands. He woefully explained his dilemma, swallowing another glass and lighting up another cigarette.

"I had to take a call out there from one of my biggest suppliers. They want me to pay a hundred thousand immediately but I haven't got it. But, I am owed fifty grand from my customers, so if I can get that in I can pay the suppliers what I owe them."

"I'm not sure how you can do that, mate. Fifty from a hundred will leave fifty still to pay," Jack helpfully corrected the unfortunate lounge lizard's gargantuan maths challenge.

"Oh shit," Digger wailed and took another sup of rum and Coke, took the calculator and began pushing the buttons; this seemed to be his only office equipment, apart from his mobile. Jack thought he was a lot like Gator Tom in his minimalistic approach to working tools; the mobile and calculator being the only equipment Digger's Asia Pacific megalithic empire owned. He began the momentous math challenge on the calculator of taking fifty from a hundred.

This took five minutes of pressing different buttons until he asked the barmaid to do it. A good English public school education never did anyone any harm, Jack pondered, and after watching his mental gymnastics with the sales ledger and calculator, he guessed algorithms and string theory were not meant for our Digger and that his short time at university studying the vagaries of algebra had certainly not helped him.

"Oh, shit," Digger repeated with his hands to head when he saw the negative answer, and then he took a long sip of his rum and Coke which seemed to calm him and he looked up at Jack.

"I'll have to talk to them, Jack. I'll be all right, they like me and I'll sort them out."

He put the mobile down, ordered more drinks and bought all the barmaids a drink, never another thought for the glitch in the accounts, and continued with his courtship of the starry-eyed Asian girl who was enraptured by the great man's tales of corporate raiding, his father's sheep farming in New South Wales and the various perversions he could offer. He even took time to show Jack another picture of his wife Angel and a lovely Philippine singer in his bed with the offer of a ménage à quatre next time Jack was in Thailand.

As Digger continued his onslaught on the bar girls, Jack pondered the great businessman's dilemma. It seemed obvious that his father expected him to show some degree of business provenance and an auditable set of accounts and Digger had to front this Asian side. This was apparently proving difficult for the lovely lad because frankly work appeared difficult for him and he sought to avoid it, because it seemed his natural aptitude was not in double entry book keeping or supply chain management in the heavy plant business, but was to be found in his profound and proficient work in swallowing Bundaberg rum, smoking cigarettes and romancing delightful ladies in his company. But he obviously had some business ability as he had won the contract from the main contractor to dig up the Australian rainforest.

Jack enjoyed his evening with Digger and liked the man's company. He had never met anyone quite like him and Asia was becoming stranger by the minute. He left him ensconced with his lady friends to return to the hotel.

He said his farewell to his new acquaintance.

"Will I see you in the morning, Digger, in the office?"

Digger put his arm around Jack and gave him a big hug, the gallons of fermented molasses taking their toll, and stammered: "Been great night mate, loved the craic mate. Let's do it again tomorrow night. Same time, same place eh? Why don't you stop and we'll take these girls down town, the night's still young, man, and then I've got a few lamb chops in the fridge to barby... We can eat , get squiffy, enjoy the girls' company and be happy, matey."

Jack gave him a gentle pat and turned down the offer.

"Sorry Digger, not my scene, but I really have to get to bed, got a few meetings and interviews tomorrow. I thought you were meeting our boys on the civil and dredging work?"

Digger looked crestfallen.

"Oh shit, don't remind me. The buggers have scheduled the meeting for one thirty p.m. I'll have to get up early. It's a lot easier in Bangkok, matey: Tomorrow get yourself finished up as soon as you can and we'll party."

And he gave Jack another drunken hug and went back to his wooing. Jack left and he strolled the short walk to his hotel. He passed the office as he walked and wondered what Teutonic Jon would make of the likeable, but intractable civil plant supplier if he ever met him. He made a mental note to do all in his power to make sure that meeting wouldn't happen. He liked Digger too much.

CHAPTER SEVEN

Western Australia

The Watermouse

The next day...

Jack woke early, breakfasted and walked to the office. He was greeted by the HR lady manager who took him for a coffee again in one of the bistro coffee houses at the base of the office. It was a delightfully warm and sunny morning and a great way to start work; do nothing but drink coffee. Jack was beginning to warm to Australia and its al fresco way of working.

But he had forgotten the golden rule that he had learned the day before, don't say anything remotely personal or be affectionate to any female, or indeed male. So after a long talk about the weather, the trip, the visit schedule, he forgot the golden rule and in general chatter about their respective careers and life he asked the HR lady if she was married. He was immediately chastised and the lady warned him yet again.

"That is a personal question. You have no right to ask anyone in this organisation about their relationships and it is very poor behaviour from someone who purports to come here to tell us how to behave. If you continue like this I will have to interview you officially and discipline you. I'm sure Jon would be thinking to run you off."

Well, Jack thought, *this isn't going too well.* But he did have an inner chuckle at the thought of Jon meeting this lady and her trying to chastise him. He kept quiet, apologised and they went upstairs to the Engineering and Operations floor and 20th floor, where he was given a visitor desk and the HR lady asked if he would drop her a photocopy of his passport and flight details and she'd ensure he was booked on the plane home, and she also gave him some mind bogglingly boring HR travel procedure to read and copy. *Marvellous,* Jack thought. *They want me home already.*

He looked around the huge open-plan office at all the people working at their stations and eventually found a large photocopier. When he looked at the photocopier it resembled the NASA space program command centre in *Apollo 11* and was beyond his limited IT skills. So he asked a lady engineer sat next to it who was diligently trawling the web for nice holiday locations if she could help.

She looked away from her next vacation and glowered and angrily shouted at him: "Who do you think I am? Your ******* secretary! If you don't go away I'll report you to HR for inappropriate sexist behaviour."

Jack shuffled off, deciding he better try to find some Aussie male company before he was hauled before HR and the law courts for sexual perversion. Needless to say, he later found that Human Resource departments in Australia were larger than the Engineering departments.

He soon spotted Richie, the operations manager whom he knew from nights of drunken pleasure in the Then and Now and felt surely he could relax in his company. Sure enough Richie was happy to take him back downstairs to the al fresco coffee meeting rooms to kill some time before his next meeting and talk to him about how the project was going.

Richie was another huge man with a varied background of running large projects, in charge of offshore oil and gas producing platforms, fighting bulls, shearing sheep, street fighting and playing rugby. There wasn't much he hadn't done. He was in fact a very good and talented engineer and he asked Jack what experience he had in running engineering departments. Jack told him the truth.

"I've none, mate. This is the first time I've been on a project as big as this, I'm not an engineer. I'm here to help with the team and communication."

Richie laughed out loud and asked: "So you know **** all about engineers and how it all works then, mate?"

"I'm ready to learn, Richie. What's so different about managing engineers?" Richie burst out laughing again.

"They are all ****** crazy, that's the problem, and if you don't understand about what their real purpose is then you're *****d, mate. You drink with Father Bob don't you? Sound fella, that... good construction man. Listen to him and learn – he knows his stuff. Has he not told you the secret then?"

Jack was staggered. He didn't think Father Bob and this avuncular crazy Aussie both had some secret formula or mission to run projects. He thought this was too good an opportunity to learn. They were both sober for once so he may well remember what he learnt.

Richie sat drinking his coffee in the shade of the sun and Jack learned all about 'real' engineering that beautifully warm, relaxing Australian morning.

Richie explained a few simple rules about engineers in jokes and fables. He started with a few facts:

"To the optimist, the glass is half full. To the pessimist, the glass is half empty. To the engineer, the glass is twice as big as it needs to be. And normal people believe if it isn't broke don't fix it. Engineers believe if it ain't broke, it doesn't have enough features yet.

"You'll like this one, Jack," the big operations manager continued. "A client engineer was taking a break from when he heard a frog calling out him, 'Please, if you kiss me I'll turn into a beautiful princess for you.'

"The engineer bent over and picked the frog up and put it in his pocket. Returning to his office, he began to work on the drawings when the frog spoke from inside his pocket. 'Please, if you kiss me and turn me into a princess again I will stay with you for a week.'

"The engineer picked the desperate amphibian out of his pocket, smiled warmly at it and promptly but it in his pocket. The frog, desperate by now, croaked from inside the pocket, 'If you kiss me and I turn into the sexy, beautiful princess I was, I'll stay with you and let you make passionate love to me and explore your wildest passions.'

"The engineer picked the frog out again, smiled knowingly and put it back in. The frog finally groaned from inside his pocket tomb: 'Look, I'm a beautiful princess. I'll let you do anything that you've dreamed of in your wildest passionate dreams. Why won't you kiss me?'

"The engineer said: 'Look, I'm an engineer. I don't have time for girlfriends but a talking frog, that's cool.'"

Richie laughed at his anecdotes but then got serious when he began to explain the benefits of being a client engineer rather than a contractor engineer.

"As you can see, Jack, being a client isn't too stressful. Mind you I've never worked as hard as I do now with that crazy German boss. Strewth, he is hard bloody work. He never ******* gives up… plans, procedures, documents and he wants them on time. He doesn't realise that that is not what we are here for. We are here to make sure that **** all is done on time. Does he not know that? The cruel bastard."

Ah, Jack thought, *now we are getting to the crux of it all.*

Richie continued.

"Does he not know that writing execution plans, procedures and test plans takes months of hard day rate earned dollars even though we have the last ones kept on our remote hard drives and all we are doing is transcribing bits of data across and copying and pasting? The art is to look busy and professional and generate enough plans, specifications and procedures to justify your existence because when some deluded contractor bites our hand off to take the punitive lump-sum contract at a ridiculous price and unachievable schedule, you will spend the next four years rejecting the revisions of the documents that the contractor also spends years writing to match the requirements of your documents."

Jack was astounded by the simplicity of it.

"You can use any excuse to delay the acceptance of the contractor's plans and procedures, none of which matters in real life as no one ever reads or follows them anyway, especially construction managers. Great excuses are grammar, spelling, syntax, formatting, etc.; the list is endless to the real client who is a master at this. Of course the more experienced real clients never use excuses like technical and engineering reasons for rejecting these plans and procedures, this will give the ******* greedy contracts managers and lawyers reasons to claim extraordinary sums for change of design and give them a get-out-of-jail extension of time to the insanity of accepting a ridiculously impossible schedule in the first place."

Richie took a drink of coffee and smiled across the table at Jack and continued his lecture on real clients.

"Real clients use mundane, implausible and inane reasons for rejecting plans and procedures like prose, spelling and sometimes the best one, lack of rhyme. And once the construction is underway and you arrive on site in your much bigger car and office than the contractor, you can spend days and days requesting the contractor to attend your progress meetings, where you can berate them on their lack of performance and request more statistics, plans, key performance indicators and reject every change order for the cocked up design you were responsible for, increasing the financial burden on the contractor, elongating the schedule and of course tormenting the demented contractor's project manager."

Jack thought of Danny and the Paranoid Indian and could relate to how clients could torment and derange them. Richie followed on to his conclusions.

"Client project managers like to torture their opposite number as it shows they are managing their stakeholder's money well and even if the project is years off schedule and looking to cost more than Trump's Mexican wall or the Trident missile program, you can be seen to have fulfilled your role as a client and survive to gain another round of day rate increases and loyalty bonus."

He looked pleased with himself and decided to sum it all up.

"So, if I summarise the role of client engineers – 'client engineers change things not to make the facility safer to operate, more productive or prolong asset life; they change things to ensure the job is delayed long enough for them to secure a more lucrative position after their flawed engineering is finished. They then are employed to fix their mistakes and operate the facility. They stay forever doing this but only if the location has unlimited sex, drink and cheap houses to buy their girlfriends.'"

Richie howled with laughter and slapped Jack on the back.

"Well, don't tell Jon that or he'll run us all off for sure."

Jack was not sure if this was reality or just a bit of storytelling from a master storyteller. He would learn the shocking truth later.

Richie decided they could stay another half an hour so he purchased another two coffees and moved on to describe the lowly contractor engineers.

"Jack, you really should know by now that real contractor's engineers know that we client engineers like to change things so they always design something with an obvious fault in it, obvious only to client engineers. This means that the client will change it and you can then charge him an extortionate amount of money for implementing the change during construction. There is always a hell of a fuss made about these changes and change management procedures are the contract manager's only tool to control these egotistical maniacs. In my experience with change management procedures there is only one constant: they change as the project progresses. My theory is; the rate of change of change management procedures is directly proportional to the number of client engineers on the project provided the engineering man-hours are constant. Everyone gets hung up about a few multimillion US dollars of changes and the contract managers do battle, drawing in all of their cohorts and legal experts when the flanking manoeuvre has already been played with Sun Zhu precision. Napoleon, eat your heart out: these buggers don't march on their stomachs, they march with signed time sheets for another week of engineering change that no one but they can understand."

He laughed and asked: "Surely you've seen this in the Singapore office, mate?"

Jack sadly had not realised that all of Danny's men were following this paradigm and humbly had to admit it. Richie continued his lecture.

"You see, engineering changes mean much more time to fix the thing, delaying the inevitable demobbing of thousands of draughtsmen, piping engineers, electricians etc. for months, and hopefully, for those who live in this paradise for years. It is the main role of the contracting company's engineering manager to extend the life of his men. Engineering man-hour histograms never reduce in response with the classic progress S-curve. They are constant, right up to the end when they are transferred to the commissioning and operations budgets."

He sat back in his chair and took a phone call on his cell phone and when he finished he explained some more.

"You know Brian, don't you mate? You've been on the piss many times with us in the Then and Now. Didn't you know Danny has him shadowing me every night, man?"

Jack thought about it and it dawned on him. The conversations he'd had with Brian and with Danny now made more sense. Brian was the contracting company's engineering manager. He was a soft spoken, highly experienced and dedicated to the company. Sadly, Jack had heard that in trying to keep up with the drinking and nocturnal bar habits of Gator Tom and Big Richie, who Jack now assumed he had to shadow as his clients, he had donated all of his life's savings to the lucky, hardworking Filipino girls and the smiling and now much richer owner of the Here and Now.

Richie explained.

"Danny even told him he could sleep with us to ensure our engineers sign off every engineering change the first time they see it and before Lord Paul, the contracts manager got his hands on it and knocked it back. The daft Jock told him to never let the engineering man hours get larger. He had to keep the man-hours within the S-curve budget and then Danny thinks he can finish this project on time and on budget and get a huge bonus. All project managers are deluded, of course. Brian is *****d because of this and it's been disastrous on his wealth, health and marriage."

Richie laughed, not particularly bothered about Brian's well-being, and kept on with his revelations on real engineering.

"Danny's objective is unachievable, just like the schedule, the budget and the manpower histogram, the engineering man hours have just kept on growing in a constant linear progression. The only things to shrink are Brian's wallet, expense account, marriage and health."

He laughed again and joked.

"And Gator Tom, has grown even larger on his diet of ground nuts and Tiger beer, provided every night by Brian's expense account and my Filipino friends in the bar are getting even more prettier and building more houses. It's magic, mate, being the client."

It seemed to Jack that everyone but he knew that this was an impossible task that Danny had given Brian, to keep the man hours on target and preserve Brian's tenure on the project, and also keep the whole project team in paradise for years. So the astute project team kept inviting their demented ginger-haired leader into 'the matrix' that was Here and Now every night. Constantly pissed, confused and surrounded by grateful Filipinos and his devoted team blissfully unaware of the impending explosion in man hours and inevitable delay. Jack had heard him only three nights ago cry out in some form of belated prayer to the God of project directors for help.

"For God's sake, I'm another six hundred bucks down again. I have got tits in my ears, hands down my pants and ate nothing but bloody peanuts and it's only eight o'clock."

Danny then raved dementedly, yet again to no one in particular, holding his ginger head in his hands.

"Why do I do this?"

Cue the comment from Richie who was yet again in full Filipino courtship mode.

"Heh, don't worry, Danny, just set 'em up again, this one's too quiet. Think she'll need a few more tequilas to loosen her up."

And sure enough our erstwhile project director would start again with the laconic statement, his personal mantra, to no one in particular.

"I must stop doing this."

Richie told Jack that these secret laws were inviolate and that he was the only one who could handle the super egos of the lead client engineers but he was only delaying the inevitable of a futile freeze of change. And Richie was correct as Danny had frozen the design weeks ago and that was supposed to stop all changes after this date. No one believed a word and true to form, after more 'ch-ch-ch-changes' than David Bowie could stutter, Lord Paul, the contracts manager, entered Richie's office to show him yet another twenty-four change notices, a daily occurrence, which he had promptly rejected like all the others previously.

Lord Paul pretended to be concerned and furious about yet another few million on the costs and a few more weeks of delay but he knew that the last people to leave the project were those in contracts management who keep knocking back the changes and then argue about it for months after the super brains that designed it and caused the changes had left for an even more lucrative contract.

Richie explained to Jack that Lord Paul and Steed, Danny's contract's manager, would be the only ones left who knew anything about the reason for the change, and would spend months in splendid isolation in luxurious lawyers' offices, arguing about them. All of this time the people who caused the changes, the engineers, would be working offshore, one week at work and three weeks off in a sexual paradise, earning US$2,000 a day, attempting to fix the very changes they made years ago.

Jack thought this was masterful teamwork when you think about it; maybe his short time on the project had achieved a cohesive effective team.

Richie finished his soliloquy with a final truism.

"Only project managers worry about these things, because only they get fired. They do not want change. They have a pathological hatred of those who initiate it. This is why they are demented."

They both went back upstairs to the engineering office. Richie said he'd join Jack with Digger after work in the bar. He had to go now and do some work. Jack reflected that it was nearly midday and very little had been done up to now but he was a lot clearer on how real projects worked!

Luckily for his continued employment he met another male at his next interview. He too was an environmental and political expert and he had been tasked with explaining to Jack the ins and outs of such riveting documents and procedures as the Environment Impact Assessment and the Social and Housing Conditions Assessment. He was a polite, mild mannered, shy individual. A highly educated biologist and scientist originally and he was part of a team of environmental scientists who were planning and managing the Civil and Dredging works. His name was Doug, soon to be renamed Watermouse.

After an initial hello and introduction Doug said that as it was nearly lunch they may as well head downstairs yet again to the al fresco meeting place and have refreshments, and indeed they did. They talked over a nice pizza and curiously, a glass of wine. Australia was the only place Jack had been to where the office allowed self-policing of small amounts of alcohol. Very civilised, he thought, he was beginning to like Australia and Australians – well, the men. And indeed Doug confirmed his worst fears about Australian females.

Doug had worked in Asia before and he was amazed that the contractors back in his Aussie homeland were for some reason happy working for less money, without the attractions of sexual gymnasts and compliant females to keep them company. Indeed, he explained that Australian woman could be extremely non-compliant when it came to male instructions here, and whilst they may well be sexual gymnasts, they tend to keep that to themselves or with their partners.

Doug confirmed Jack's fears and sympathised with his three faux pas with the ladies previously, and potential incarceration in the HR dungeons. He confirmed that all Australian women have partners. They do not have husbands, and heaven forbid you ask about their personal life. It also seemed that Australian male partners were not for protection or love, as most of the woman could well look after themselves. Doug sadly and morosely claimed that the rampant Aussie Barry McKenzie male was a long-lost cause there.

He warned Jack that the males were indeed rampant and aggressive but mainly to themselves, through frustration and gender confusion, but they know who the boss is in any heterosexual relationship. This was mainly hidden from the rest of the world where the paradigm is that Aussie backpacking, sunburnt, fit, charming young males run amok with the local womenfolk during their world tours. In Australia, they know their place, hence the sowing of wild oats in Europe and Asia.

Doug with a small tear in his eye leaned across the table out of hearing of the hordes of HR ladies eating their salads and drinking their latte coffee and whispered: "For God's sake, at one time the country was run by a woman, three states were run by women, some companies actually led by women. They even have a women's group here who advises the boss. It's a fact that they do not have a 'bloke group'."

Jack pondered: no real man would be comfortable with this and obviously it was why most had left to happier climes where leadership is proportional to Swiss bank balances, not intellect. It was possible that Australia was not for real contractors. He suggested this to Doug and asked what had happened to the old ways of the macho male and gallons of piss being drunk while fighting crocodiles. Doug said all wasn't lost as this week it was Schoolies' Week and he explained to Jack the marvellous cultural festival of the passing of age of Australian youth.

He spoke excitedly of something that he felt kept the Australian dream alive. At seventeen years old the youth leave school and they all descend on the Gold Coast and spend a whole week on the piss. Parents drive up to refill the hotel and motel freezers with booze to keep them topped up. Not a cultural visit to Rome, Florence, Paris, a week the in Rockies with buddies hunting, fishing and rock climbing, or two years' National Service getting beaten with sticks in the armed forces like most Asian and some European countries, but a drug- and drink-ravaged week of binging and sexual cavorting.

The media encourage this, and Schoolies' Week, where the elite of Australian education and future leaders of the free world drink themselves into oblivion, is the prime-time promotion of Australian culture. Jack quietly chuckled to himself and thought that well known Australian cultural attaché, Sir Les Patterson, would be proud.

They both finally began to talk about work. Jack looked at his watch and again smiled to himself. Digger may well be getting up now for his arduous meeting.

It seemed that Doug was one of a group of harassed scientists that resembled a leper colony in the office. This group was the environmental dredging team. They were lepers and pariahs because they were constantly put on notice to quit.

Doug explained that this was normal behaviour from project services managers. This project services manager seemingly believed, as he did with anyone but himself or his team, that environmentalists were worthless and added no value. Jack was to see this trait was prevalent in all project services characters, this is the way of all staff project services managers; they hate contractors and they hate cost. They also hate wasting company money on people who might care about other things than money, like indigenous races, poor people and cuddly things like koalas or dolphins.

Doug said that this increasingly paranoid group of scientists were concerned that they may well be being watched and their e-mails monitored for being too close to environmental groups or regulators and their like-minded friends in related agencies or the media.

The project services manager had reinforced this paranoia with a statement in the monthly management meeting on risk assessment. His lesson for leaders in huge, sensitive environmental projects was simple:

'Never employ anyone who has worked before in environmental study or shows any past history of caring for the environment or people: this is called a project risk.'

Doug was becoming quite apoplectic despite his mild personality and he said: "There is also another solution, of course: don't employ accountants and number crunchers in positions of power, who know nothing of environmental management, PhD theses, and scientific logic and the cost consequences of upsetting the tree huggers who controlled through one vote the Australian Federal Parliament."

Hence this was the need in Australia for approvals and the inevitable need for environmental teams and subsequently major cost additions which were sent to torment the already tormented project services manager. This explained his irascible cost control man's return to deranged behaviour whenever he saw this fine educated bunch of academic geniuses.

Doug moved on to tell Jack of how the team had named him Watermouse. It was because he had had to study the poor creature, or its real name, the False Water Rat, and he was now the world's expert on this mythical creature. He had to study and try to track this endearing critter down in the swamps and jungles of the island where the project would eventually go, allowing the company to sell liquid gas to the Chinese barman from the Here and Now; now masquerading as the commercial manager of a large Chinese oil and gas conglomerate.

He said it was well known that this mammalian rodent creature doesn't actually exist and was now probably extinct. However, it was supposed to have been spotted in the swamps on the island, and in true compliance with the company's corporate and sustainable development values, the Watermouse had to spend night after night avoiding crocodiles, sharks, malaria-ridden mosquitoes, and black water fever trying to find the elusive creature. This was to make sure that Digger's bulldozers and chainsaws that were about to start buzzing like the huge mosquitoes didn't wipe out the world's only mammalian rodent-like unicorn.

Needless to say, the Watermouse didn't find anything on the coral island but he did get more paranoid with the fact that he was sent to certain death, and cleverly off the payroll by the clever project services' manager, every night to find a mythical creature. He wasn't too happy also in his paranoid delusional thinking that the company may well have a bug planted on his bedroom table lamp or that his garbage may be being collected by the CIA.

Doug told Jack that he had actually been employed to track another small creature that could not be allowed by environmental legislation people to be squashed under the bulldozers. This was a pebble mound mouse (for those biologically minded, *Pseudomys chapmani*).

It was also complicated because this rodent, which it appeared was not as mythical as the water mouse, lived on the land where the first governor of that state had lived. This was further complicated because that other Australian regulatory discipline, cultural heritage, was involved to protect indigenous people's ancient sites and also yet more complicated, expensive and time consuming procedures were imposed to ensure indigenous people were not offended or compromised. This potentially slowed down the piping men.

"Jack, it seemed the pipeline passed through the old property of the governor and as he held the first licence to legally shoot aboriginals, the bosses expected the pipeline contractors to dig up thousands of old aboriginal bones. That, coupled with the bloody mouse, stopped the trench digging for weeks. I was abused and treated like shit by the contractors for not giving in and letting them just carry on. It was bloody dangerous, mate."

Aye, Jack thought, *yet another few billion dollars on an already late project.* "Did you find any bones or mice?" he asked.

"Nah, we were miles from anywhere and the contractors said they would just carry on digging and filling behind before any 'abos or mice huggers' could come to see what they had turned over. They threatened with burying me as well if I found any mice!"

He looked terrified still after all the years.

"The head superintendent was from Darwin, and he said that the governor must have made some serious money outta shooting abos, as he being the governor could have put a bounty on them of five dollars a body and as he would have been the only licensee, would have made himself a fortune. Bloody animals, that lot from Northern Territories, mate."

Ah! Jack thought. *Even in the face of rampant genocide and ethnic cleansing, our Antipodean real contractors saw some good business coming out of it.* But he speculated that we will never know how many unfortunate trespassers (a matter of 1880s legal opinion) are buried under the land, as there are many flat mice and a pipe carrying gas to the thriving billions in China hiding that legacy.

They finished lunch with yet another coffee and Watermouse asked who Jack was meeting next. Jack said it was the site construction manager, Pieter.

Watermouse looked shocked and nervous. He uttered: "Be careful for God's sake, he is a maniac. He wants to sack all of us. He thinks we and the dredging boys are spies of the government or part of some liberal NGO conspiracy. I think he has a screw loose, mate. He's never been to site, we think. He just sits in his office with three laptops, emailing everyone. He tells everyone he is the company president's mate; fought with him in 'Nam or some jungle hell somewhere in some Godforsaken third-world hellhole. He hounded poor Bill for months, Bill was sure he was followed home at nights and his phone was tapped. Bill was our dredging and dugong protection expert. He got so sick with worry that he just got up one day from his desk and left. Pieter and the project services manager had long faces for days as they wanted to fire him themselves. Pieter nearly had an apoplexy when he spotted Bill's name still on the desk a week afterwards, as he thought he may well still be there in the cupboard under the stairs and being paid."

Jack looked unbelievingly at Doug.

Doug noticed the look and said: "Jack, honestly we are all under some form of surveillance. I think Pieter may be CIA or Australian secret service. He never does any bloody construction, just plots with the project services manager to sack us all."

Jack shrugged his shoulders, comfortable in the knowledge that up to now he'd met so many crazies on the project in in the bars surrounding it that one more couldn't be too bad. He was wrong of course.

"Why do you have three laptops, Pieter?"

Jack had settled into Pieter's office. He noted that there was no laissez-faire meeting and trip downstairs to the café au lait offices. Here he was made to sit on a small chair in front of a huge desk with no refreshment offered. The sunlight glaring through the windows onto his face with Pieter sat back staring at him, peering at him intensively as if trying to read his thoughts.

Pieter stared at him motionless for what seemed an eternity and suddenly he spoke.

"One is to e-mail my men on the project and keep their asses working. One is a direct line to the Perth management. One is to the president of the company, who personally sent me here to fix this mess."

He stared at Jack intensely.

"You see, Jack, I am not really just a construction manager, I am bigger than that, been sent over here to sort out the management and spy on all they do and report to the president. I've built bigger things than this in the military and for the company and the president knows I'll sort this one out and wants me to keep it all between him and me. There is something that isn't quite right about the tree huggers on this project."

Jack stated something quite obvious to him.

"Pieter, you've been here a few months and nothing much has changed except the team seem demotivated with the personal attacks. I hear the dredging team and environmental group have done a great job getting the EIA through and have already had their execution plan agreed by Jon and corporate. Admittedly after Jon asked them to rewrite it six times, but that's Jon for you. But the real point is that that you should be off managing the remote Asian fabrication sites, not sitting here, mate. Why do you worry so much about the guys and their environmental friends?"

Pieter looked over the open lids of his laptops and put down his rimmed circular glasses. He was well over six feet and thin boned, very chic and despite his Dutch ethnicity, an American lover, very Clint Eastwood-like. At that time he was well over seventy years old and wore traditional cowboy checked shirts and jeans every day just like Clint, but always American Redwing rigger boots, and never site overalls. He glared at Jack for some minutes in deathly silence and then hammered the desk with his fist and howled at Jack.

"Goddamn, I'm not gonna tell you that! My work is secret; my life here is no different to when I was in the military. I've been taken prisoner undercover by the Indonesians, and I've been shot undercover working for the Yanks, and don't ask me about Central Africa, I'd have to kill you if I tell you more. They send some young, jumped-up bastard to question me! I don't have to listen to you."

He stared at his prey for another long silence and began again.

"I think you had better interview the others and let me know what they say about me but keep it short and sharp, your report, I only read one-page reports. I will be on the phone to Houston tonight; so you better be aware of that."

Jack decided that it was more fruitful to leave this conversation and surrealist interview and left to talk with the VP of HSE, Robin, who briefed him about the veracity and the reality of Pieter's claims. It appeared that he was thought of in good light by the president, because of his past performance in delivering projects in hostile environments by military means.

Robin said the problem was that here in Australia, stuck in an office, he seemed to be obsessed with security, covert NGO activity and potential dissident environmentalists who sought to stop the eventual deforestation and plunder of the Australian natural world.

Robin explained: "Jack, we have spent over one billion dollars to get our EIA approved and to ensure we have every 'I' dotted and every 'T'' crossed with central, state and regional Government and all the NGO's, cultural heritage and environmental groups known to man. We do not need the secret service in our office to make sure we all do our jobs mate. Can you not just get Jon to send him to an Asian site and let him spy on the buggers up there?"

Jack pondered for a few moments on his past months on this project.

"I guess I can ask the question, Robin. But by God he is some angry dude for sure. But my little experience on this job is that these old warriors have long tentacles into corporate, mate. There is a lot of loyalty to what they must have achieved in the past. I'm sure once he gets back into the jungle and onto site he'll forget about the 'commie tree huggers' and do what he's good at."

Robin nodded but looked anxious.

"Jack, wish that were the case, mate. He has brought another guy in from the States to work with me for a month. He is ex-Special Forces and is part of our 'security audit team'. He seems to know **** all about HSE but a hell of a lot about surveillance and killing people. You need to meet him. Are you going for a beer after work? If you are we all go to the pub next door at five thirty, I'll bring him along. It'll scare the dredging boys but they are getting used to worrying by now. I'll take you down to see the dredging boys now if you want, for half an hour, and then we can head downstairs for a coffee and then off to the pub. "

Jack was pleased to be with someone sane and clearly into the Australian way of sun, coffee and good company rather than waterboarding, white noise and nail pulling. As they walked towards the open-plan area for the dredging boys, Jack noticed the project service manager passed them on his way to his work station and when he saw the dredging lepers he shook his head walking past them, and shouted across the whole office. "Have you not gone yet?"

Robin looked worried, whispering with his hand to his mouth.

"The poor bastards are in constant fear of their contracts being terminated or not renewed. Last week Pieter and him told them, the poor buggers, that their budget was cut and they were being moved to a cupboard under the stairs with just a microscope and a fishing net as tools! I think we'll give them a miss today Jack, we might be targeted as well if we are seen with them. You can meet them in the pub. Let's go and have a coffee."

At 5.30 p.m. Jack and Robin went to the pub next door. Sat at the bar was Digger, hair wet and brushed back, Batik shirt, white trousers. He looked as if he had just got out of bed and the shower.

He was romancing another bar girl, this time she looked Vietnamese, with a large Bundy and Coke in his hand. He greeted them warmly: "Gudday Jack; what are you drinking?"

"VB beer please, Digger. Digger, this is Robin."

After the pleasantries they settled on a bar stool next to Digger and Jack asked him how his day had gone.

"Tough Jack, bloody tough; that Richie and his mates strike a hard bargain. It fair knocked me back, all the thinking and recalculating. I had to go back to the hotel after half an hour and luckily I had asked the filly from last night to come to the room to help me with some administration. She's doing maths at university so she helped me with the figures."

He took a drink of his rum and stroked his hair back and continued his tale of hard work.

"She sent a fax to my dad with the new numbers. He'll ring me tonight. Nice girl. Didn't screw her of course, don't do that these days now I'm engaged, unless Angel is in bed with me and fancies a filly herself. She will just help me when I'm in town with my admin. We were both so tired that we lay down and took a nap each: just made the pub in time."

Jack looked incredulous at Digger. Did he really think that he believed him? Stop thinking, it wasn't his problem and he was starting to learn that Digger was, well... Digger, so it probably was true.

The Watermouse came in with four of his mates from the dredging team. They all took beer and started to socialise with each other. Jack learnt of the many ways to dredge vast holes in the coral reefs and sea and how to protect small furry creatures, sea grasses, dugongs and many other species of our Lord's creation. They mentioned many times their suspicion that they were not long for this corporate world and that another few billion dollars would be needed to ensure these critters and vegetation were not annihilated by the huge suction machines supplied from Big Hansie, but they were too scared to tell anyone in case the project services manager and Pieter fired them.

The project services manager had broken down into an apoplectic fit that afternoon when they had presented their new budget. They all thought he had died as his bald head went red, sweat teemed out of him and he collapsed onto the desk. Until he recovered, then screaming and cursing he ripped up the spreadsheet with their new cost budget in front of them all. He ran into Pieter's office, where they locked the door. Pieter bashed his three laptops like Beethoven playing his sixth symphony. Who he was communicating with they didn't know but they feared the worst.

Jack was becoming very sorry for these poor scientists and wondered if Jon would have any sympathy if he discussed their plight, but then he remembered Tony the document controller and thought maybe it was wise to let this run its course. Guiltily, he thought he was bottling this, but he'd never met a dugong so why worry too much about them?

Robin introduced the tall, wiry gentleman who came into the bar as the American HSE security man, or potential CIA operative; it was hard to tell. He whispered to Jack and the others. The dredgers were stunned into silence, drinking beer fast and talking about sport, diving, cooking, anything but dredging.

They had all moved from the bar to take up a few tables, leaving Digger in full lounge lizard mode with his lovely barmaid. Jack noticed that a lady who had been standing close to them with white headphones in her ears had moved with them and sat herself uncomfortably on a small stool right beside them again.

Jack mischievously whispered to the Watermouse: "Doug, that lady has been listening to everything we say and has done for the last hour."

"What makes you think that?" Doug asked, looking around very suspiciously.

"She has a set of earphones in her ears and a phone but when we say anything related to the company, she turns around or her face changes in recognition. She is not plugged into the phone, my friend, but it is a microphone."

Jack explained this carefully, but really casting a line to see what fun he could raise from this paranoid David Attenborough who was frowning and trying not to look at the lady who sat next to him, earphones still in her ears.

However, Jack's joking became real when he went to get more beer at the bar and the head barman said to him, "Do you know that woman is watching and listening to you?"

Jack was taken aback but he had been suspicious as to why she had moved when they did. The paranoia was catching, it seems, and Jack said: "Is that so? I thought she was suspicious, but surely you should stop the woman coming in here?"

The barman succinctly explained: "No, it's a free society."

Again, Australian democracy in action, Jack thought. In Singapore, she would either have been the secret police or if she wasn't, she would have been whisked off to Changi Jail in seconds and beaten with sticks. *Ah, the joy of a liberal society,* he thought.

"Well, if you don't kick her out, we'll stop spending vast quantities of money on your shit beer," he advised the barman, not very diplomatically.

"Please yourself, you pommie bastard," the barman spurted out of the corner of his mouth and walked away. *Oh well, the warmth of the Australian landlord,* Jack thought. Not long now and back to Filipino, Thai and Indonesian bar girls, who had no knowledge of the prison ships and exile for stealing loaves of bread, but only warm smiles and a spine like an elastic band.

This Mata Hari continued to sit there listening intently. Jack mentioned his conversation with the pommie basher to Robin and he suggested it was possible she was just looking for a story from the gossip and loose lips of those working on a very socially sensitive project, the story might appear in the press. If not, he said, she was Pieter's accomplice and was a company spy. He then said he'd check with the CIA man and see if he'd slip up.

So he asked their security man quite clearly and forcefully: "Is this woman a spy in your vast security experience, mate?"

The killing machine looked casually at Robin and said without blinking or showing any emotion: "She's definitely not one of ours."

At which statement the Watermouse spat out his beer and whispered to Jack: "Strewth: 'not one of ours'. That means the bastards must have them here. I knew it, I knew it."

He promptly drank up and ran out of the building, quickly followed by the dredging outcasts.

The only one of the team left was a tall, well-built, fit Australian man who had been introduced to Jack as The Paranoid Android. They had named him that because every word, every e-mail, every reorganisation was a company plot and he was indeed like Marvin from *The Hitch Hiker's Guide to the Galaxy*. He had a brain the size of a planet but was living in corporate misery with his paranoid corporate political lot.

This wonderful example of paranoia was highly intelligent and very experienced in all aspects of government legislation and approvals, politics and communication, but he spent his days and nights keeping his long-suffering wife awake explaining the law of Venetian City State politics, Borgia assassination attempts, Kennedy conspiracy theories all linked to the company's new organisation or any communications from management above him or heaven forbid, the Project Management Office.

The Paranoid Android, being of far superior intellect to any of the mortals he worked with (and less gullible), remained. He actually quizzed the lady on her reasons for her interest in them all but he refused to tell what he found out and left soon after, head in hands, phone on his ear and long-suffering wife getting ready with her ear plugs and Valium tablet.

Jack and Robin went to another bar where Big Richie had joined Digger. Richie with a petite young girl sat on his lap who he introduced as his sister, was laughing as usual. The night ended up in a similar way to the previous. Digger racing out to take his phone calls and coming back flustered and trying to press his calculator which the bar girl sorted for him, and everyone drinking far too much. Jack and Robin refused the invite again to go downtown to see the fillies and eat BBQ chops at 3 a.m. at Digger's hotel.

As Jack took a Singapore Airlines flight back to the paradise of Singapore, he sat drinking a cold Tiger and thought how he would like to bring the long-suffering dredging team and the Paranoid Android to Singapore eventually, and the paradise regions of the world. The only form of anxiety they would have there would be the usual: that is, how long the project would last and could they survive another night of Tiger beer, chicken rice and calisthenics!

He also reflected on Australia. The natives there are not hostile; they don't eat you or kidnap you, they just bash you (but maybe that's because he was a pommie). The girls there seemed to prefer good-looking, healthy young men and seemed not to prefer middle-aged, fat, balding German paedophiles, Scandinavian alcoholics and American Vietnam War-damaged sociopaths, which was a puzzle.

With high taxes, lower day rates and salaries, returns are not on par with more 'normal' countries. In such places as Australia the projects should have been running well, on schedule and on budget, according to his budding hypothesis, as anyone with any sense would want to get out quick. But he couldn't see these being much different to any other projects in nicer, sexually liberated climes, as the staff and contractors seemed to be quite comfortable that the job may be late and they were happy to be here.

He guessed this was because most had their families here, and people actually wanted to live in this lucky country and bring their offspring up here. So they forgo the divorce-threatening behaviours of the paradise regions.

He supposed there must be benefits, if you can avoid the water, rivers, the bush, the toilet – funnel web spiders scared him more than great whites; guess it's something to do with nether regions hanging down and hairy backed, big fanged – urgh!

Also if you could avoid the bars and especially televised Australian sport (Goebbels could not have done a better job when he mobilised the Teutonic masses at Nuremberg to march on Poland than biased Australian sports commentators do at reporting Australian prowess in sport). Then he had to admit the place wasn't too bad to settle down into and this is why these people actually wanted to stay here, for their family's future and not their own sexual perversions. He took a glass of Chablis from a beautiful smiling, compassionate Malay airhostess who massaged his aching shoulders, ate a nice chicken satay and decided – some people are very strange.

CHAPTER EIGHT

Batam Island, Indonesia

Emmet

Some months later...

After months of engineering design in Singapore the first project actually began constructing big steel things on Batam Island, Indonesia. Father Bob was sent over to lead this work along with many others. Gator Tom joined him on a visiting basis from Singapore.

They quickly found that there were contractors still living in Batam Island, just over the water from Singapore, who hadn't been heard of at home, or by any living member of the free world, for thirty years. As they scanned across the 'people' in the bars in Batam, Gator was sure he was back in Tombstone – any moment Doc Holliday would stop coughing and shoot some Clanton in the back in front of you. These they both decided were some of the finest real contractors they had met.

Most had come to work for the large fabrication yards, where they built big steel things or they lifted big steel things off barges, and never went back. Unlimited young girls, excessive cheap drink, isolation from normal human behaviour and a general lack of interference by anyone but their immediate boss, who was generally living rough in the bush with some post-adolescent schoolgirls, led them to decide they liked this lifestyle.

Father Bob in his British way was sure that undoubtedly it must have been like this when the colonial powers ruled the world and the globe was indeed coloured red. However, this was the 21st century and they didn't have to fight the natives anymore; just entertain them and buy them a house.

The vitriolic Welsh subcontracts manager on the project, who had the nature of a Jack Russell terrier to anyone who he was in dispute with, had put roots down in Batam and was trying to improve the image, and he and Father Bob were in The Jungle Bar in that latter-day Sodom and Gomorrah town, Nagoya:

"She's twenty, I tell you.'"

This was about a very teenage-looking girl who was sitting on a Batam old face's knee. He looked not unlike Hagar the Horrible without teeth.

Bob soon realised that people got lost on Batam and many had never returned to their homes far away in the USA, UK, Scandinavia or Australia. One day Bob realised one famous Briton was still there.

Father Bob found Lord Lucan.

Lord Lucan was a famous English aristocrat who allegedly killed his maid and then fled the country over twenty years ago. The British press periodically would report that he had been found, in France, Argentina or America. There were many sightings but no one had heard of him since his rapid exit from the green and pleasant land, until now.

He was in Batam, Bob was sure; he was running The Bistro Bar. Bob and Tom were amazed to meet this famous man on entering this fine establishment. Standing erect as only an ex-guardsman could, full coiffured moustache and immaculate Queen's English accent; there he was: a little greyer but definitely him.

He denied it, of course, but Bob knew for sure. Why didn't he shop him to the *News of the World* or *Daily Herald?* Well what harm had he done to them? He was probably just misunderstood, not a real homicidal maniac, like their last project manager. They both decided that he'd served his sentence out here in the hell that was Batam; plus he gave them free beer to keep them quiet.

The intrepid construction men realised that there were many strange people on this island, who like Harry of The Sportsman's and Dawn of the Down Under, 'had left in a hurry' from their previous locations. Batam was a black hole that many fell into; even Father Bob, to whom Tom posed the statement that he thought Bob had turned native lost in the space time warp that was Batam, responded with his usual wit, "Ah, Tom, bonny lad, there are many black holes over here."

He said this with a knowing smile, and indeed Tom soon found out that he was right and his lectures all those months ago on the temptations of the East seemed to have been forgotten by him on this paradise isle.

They soon found out that bars in Batam centre, Nagoya town, are full of 'characters' and it was difficult to find one that didn't have some sort of black hole in it. Stephen Hawking could have found many event horizons here but his wheelchair would struggle to navigate the huge pot holes that made up the road system in the town and he may well have ended up being trapped in one of these wormholes like Father Bob's American construction superintendent, Martin the Oblate Spheroid.

Martin, of large spherical shape, was strolling along a few weeks after Bob and Tom arrived, taking in the night air and as he did often, was seeking a lecture on the second law of thermodynamics and event horizons in black holes in a bar down the road, The Ore House, when he fell into one of these chasms. He, being rather small and very rotund, very like a dung beetle, could not get out of the storm drain and his little round body was stuck upside down, legs and arms in air. He called for help but no one came to his aid, there being no light or traffic, other than the odd Ojak scooter running bar girls home from their dalliances in hotels.

Given each one of these holes had a propensity to house much human detritus and most of the known vermin in Asia – he found the missing Australian watermouse in this sewer – and as Martin had a wallet and an expensive watch sticking out on his chubby arm, he was indeed in a dangerous position. He remained there for some time, slowly losing his sanity and his libido for black hole lectures, his voice becoming weaker and his strength waning by the minute as he struggled valiantly to wiggle and squeeze his oblate body up from the chasm and the chance of imminent bubonic plague.

Coincidently, his cries were heard by Father Bob, who was strolling along heading for a bar and some evening entertainment. Peering down, he saw his employee upside down, little chubby arms and legs twitching and covered in various toxic wastes. He thought about just leaving him there and pretending he hadn't seen or heard him. He knew this would have been a good laugh and would be great craic in the bar when he arrived – as you may gather, another expert in managing human endeavour and how to motivate people. But he realised that it would not look good on his health and safety statistics, and thus eventual huge bonus, if one of his employees had died stuck in a septic tank and mugged of all his possessions by the rapacious natives, so he tried valiantly to pull him out.

In the end he gave up. His slight Gandhi figure was not meant for hauling a seventeen-stone totally round globule of lard from holes, so he phoned for Big Gator to come from the bar.

It took many efforts to prise the unfortunate spheroid from the hostile black hole and when he finally got out he was covered in mud, crap and various other things that can't be discussed in a family story. His boss strolled off to his night's entertainment and Martin crawled back to the hotel to reflect on night life in Batam and road safety, and realised it's safer to stay in the hotel and watch The Big Bang Theory on TV than research black holes in Nagoya.

Father Bob sat at the bar with the Big Man and Richie, who was visiting the site, and they laughed at the plight of the spheroid.

Richie, who had worked Batam many times nodded knowingly, smiled and said: "Aye, you always have to be careful not to end in a Bule trap."

He explained that Bule was the local slang Indonesian word for foreigners. All three laughed at the thought of these drains purposely designed and placed in the path of drunken foreigners to trap and rob them of their valuables.

Night after night during those first few weeks the two construction men and Richie, when he was there, trawled the bars of Nagoya. The only two bars they really found without extracurricular activities were the subtly named The Red Cock In – note the missing second 'n' – and Wallabies. These were relatively free of the omnipresent dusky maidens. Bars like Lucy's OAR House, The Jungle, The Ice Pub, PP Bananas, etc. were throwbacks to the American wild west without spittoons; you just used the floor and not only for spitting on. They found that The Rose bar had its own double bed, which saved on transporting your new true love to one's room and paying hotel bills.

Richie's marine operations manager Jimmy got involved on the bed with some Asian gymnastics. Jimmy was sometimes prone to paranoia and this increased exponentially with his ardour and he was sure someone was watching him from within the only other item in the room, a locked wardrobe. He left his lady *in extremis* and proceeded to try to bash the door down and ultimately bash the unlucky voyeur to near death, as was his wont when paranoid. Unable to get the door open, he ran downstairs and picked up a large meat cleaver and ran back up and began hacking the lock and door with the cleaver. Finally, he forced the door open and the wardrobe, being a little unstable, fell on top of him, emptying its contents of lots of bottles of cheap ladies' perfume and toiletries. The missing voyeur was only a figment of his usual mania. It took him several showers and a few days to stop smelling like a Turkish brothel.

Before his marriage and settling down to a life of wedding bliss at home and torturing subcontractors at work, the Jack Russell Welsh subcontracts manager was an expert on these places, as he had been on Duxton Road in Singapore prior to being sent to Batam.

At the time Father Bob took over, he was doing what he did best; waging genocide, torture and war on the Fabricator and he would seek his relaxation in Bob and Tom's company. He pointed out his skill in accountancy in The Jungle bar.

"I tell you, Bob; they're cheaper if you take three. Let's run and get them before they get taken!"

Forever protecting the company's budget, like a true quantity surveyor he believed in discount and a pound of flesh even in his personal matters.

Bob chastised him.

"Bonny lad, have you nivva hord the story of the two bulls: the old bull and the young bull. I'll tell yer: the young bull spots a herd of cows and shouts to his dad, 'Heh, Dad, let's run down and screw one those cows!' The old bull turns and says, 'No, son; let's walk down and screw them all.'"

Father Bob blew out a puff of cigarette smoke and finished lesson number two hundred and twenty-two. "Listen to ya fatha, stay away from the girls and I'll tell yer how to get gas ashore and what this business is all aboot."

But the Welshman was too excited for Bob's sermons and forgetting the three girls he stammered about a five foot, brown-skinned, black-haired girl playing pool.

"Look, I tell you, she looks like Maria Sharapova."

Bob blew another cigarette into the air with his bony hand and rebuked the horny contracts man yet again.

"Look, mate, the only thing she has in common with a Russian tennis player is that she plays with balls."

And indeed Bob was right again because they all did. Their game of pool in the next bar, The Ice Pub, was accompanied by several of these 'coaches' assisting them to position their cues by adjusting their centre of gravity with one hand caressing their testicles.

They had both checked into the hotel for the initial first construction. This was the hotel of choice for the project teams as it was the only one with any working fire alarms or deluge systems. The others had been checked by HSE and found that the deluge system water nozzles had no pipes connected to them!

Tom would stay there periodically as he had all the other sites to cover; Bob was there until he could find himself a house. Those who had gone native had houses or flats somewhere in the bush, from where they would be driven in to the nightlife by subcontractor-employed Indonesian drivers who worked extremely long hours and could keep their mouths shut, at least to the westerners, about the exploits of certain perverted contractors which were well known to the Indonesian population.

They found that the hotel was a good hotel. It was comfortable and had all the amenities they required. It even delivered room service condoms, which both thought innovative and good for the HSE part of the project. It was managed by the enigmatic and effervescent Emmet, an Irishman who, like many people they had met in Asia already, had to 'leave the country in a hurry'. He had had been in Batam for more years than Lord Lucan, it seemed. He was famous like Lord Lucan. He was a marvellous man because he invented the Emmet Pie.

This pie was unique for Father Bob and also for Danny the demented project manager when he planned to visit, this was because the meat had not been minced; it was still in solid lumps of steak form. You could buy these pies in all the bars in Batam as Emmet had a thriving side line selling them outside the hotel. Richie said they were like good old Aussie pies and best eaten with fries in the early morning, in bed after gallons of Bintang beer. Father Bob ate little and Gator just ate ground nuts as he did in Singapore but sometimes he'd stray from his diet and his favourite was the Emmet Burger. Again Emmet had developed the recipe, and it was made from mince so all were back in the comfort zone with this source of solids.

Emmet told Tom that he had been a chartered accountant in a previous life, and therefore he was not too skilled in brand management. But he followed the McDonald's marketing strategy of branding everything 'Mc', so everything he invented was the Emmet something.

Bob and Tom soon realised that so it was with sex. The Emmet Screw, the Emmet Dick, etc. After work each night he'd greet them as they got out of their car.

"Top of the evening to you boys: Putri, get the boys two Bintang on my tab and I'll have one too. Come on, let's sit down and have a craic."

The three of them would sit down in the lounge and Emmet would discuss continually, and did every night, his sex life with them. After many nights of this and when Father Bob had heard enough about his huge sexual organ and with whom and where he put it, he would politely make his excuse that he needed to meet someone and retire upstairs to get changed.

Tom stayed, swallowing gallons of Bintang, and swopped stories with Emmet every night, as he had similar war tales to tell of past projects and both of them headed off into the night, mimicking the old rugby song, Eskimo Nell style:

'Tom with his 6 gun strapped to his leg and Emmet with his prick in his hand.'

The tales got more extreme as the weeks went on. And so did the lack of sleep. Sleep was impossible in the hotel unless you were comatose with Bintang beer. This was simply because every room was full of wannabe Emmets, or maybe Emmet was in every room next to you. The sound of sexual cavorting, shrieks of fake Indonesian orgasms, incessant flushing of toilets and showers as the evening and morning's bodily waste products were disposed of, filled the night air.

Father Bob decided to move out and sadly, he soon went native, like most other construction managers there, and found a house in the jungle. He lived in the same kampong as Captain Abe, both wearing sarongs and sandals after work, smoking themselves eventually into the dedicated and caring arms of the Doc. He advised Abe on how to run his Captain Abe trading empire most nights and the dangers of the ways of the East. Abe took little notice!

Tom and Father Bob would sit at breakfast before Bob left for his kampong in the jungle, Tom nibbling at eating beef, bacon and beans, Bob smoking with a coffee, and they would watch their own staff leaving for the work site, and also the Japanese and Singaporean businessmen as they were closely followed by dozens of wet-haired little Indonesian girls who all had a tell-tale condom packet impression on the ass pocket of their tight jeans, cell phone in their hands and who neatly jumped their little tight backsides onto an OJAK, one of the millions of small motorbikes that act as taxis and are the backbone of Asia's transport system.

The ubiquitous motorbikes were the only form of transport for the millions who lived there and the contractors had an on-going bet on who could find the most people on an OJAK; one guy from Jakarta won. He spotted a driver with helmet, a wife with baby in arms, young son and a goat (no helmets). The project HSE man could never understand the sense in having a law that the driver must wear a helmet (loose term for most helmets were just tin hats) and his young family, and pet goat, can sit with him totally unprotected. This was Asia, he was constantly told.

Emmet was proud of his hotel, particularly when Richie was checking out after his initial stay with Father Bob and Gator, the Big Man.

Lia, the lovely receptionist, was diligently removing non-expense items from his bill and any incriminating evidence that his partner may see. She took off the room service supplied condoms and turning to Richie she asked, "Did you use the mini bar, sir?"

A common question in many hotels, but in Batam it could have different meanings. But the beautiful receptionist didn't expect the following answer from our colleague, the large Australian from the billabong.

"Strewth! No. I think I might have sat on it a few times, though."

Later Emmet confirmed to Tom and Bob at his nightly sex teach in that the mini bar had been torn off the wall and virtually destroyed as a result of these gymnastics with his new Indonesian partner, a very petite lady from Sumatra. There would be no charge for this though; all in a night's work and Emmet was a great at client relationships and keeping secrets. Yes, Emmet ran a sound hotel.

Back in work, Father Bob got settled into recruiting and leading his team and torturing the fabrication yard's project manager. This particular construction yard had been in Batam for nearly thirty years. It had excellent facilities and the Indonesian workforce was as good as anywhere in the world. The island needed the yard to keep going. It employed at its peak over 10,000 men and supported through its schooling and health care the families of these friendly, hardworking people. It was run by Marlon Brando.

Batam was Brando's Island, just like Brando in Tahiti, or more accurately, the part he played in *Apocalypse Now*. He would stake out the perimeter of his fiefdom by placing heads on sticks. This is my kingdom; all who enter here abandon hope. Brando would take the virtual heads from unsuspecting clients and stake them out around the yard. This was backed up by the sure knowledge that the Indonesian police, navy and army would ensure any client who didn't pay their due monies would never get off the island as the navy would blockade the harbour and the project manager would be incarcerated in a very hot and humid jail cell, and the project team would be refused exit visas.

Father Bob understood this as he was a real contractor par excellence, but many clients did not understand Bob's wisdom and his lesson that he would tell anyone who listen, that is:

'In Indonesia to work is to live. Not to work is to die, so anyone who interferes with this simple paradigm risks some form of action from the people or the authorities. If a company employs thousands of people who depend on that company to live, then you should not behave in any way that might affect the viability of that company or harm the management who employ the people: A symbiosis and cultural alignment in harmony.'

So Father Bob in his ancient wisdom and with the skill of his craft nurtured and manipulated Brando.

Brando had worked on Batam for many years; he had brought his family up there and was extremely proud of his company achievements, the island and the people, and rightly so. He was surrounded by contractors from every oilfield and drilling location in the world. Men who'd pioneered the West Coast of Africa, Alaska, the North Sea, and Tasmanian Shelf and on and on. These men had built some really big steel things over the years and knew their business.

And Lord, could they drink. Bob and Tom frequented the clubhouse some nights before meeting Emmet and hearing his tales of fornication and it was like something from a Stephen King novel. The star ship *Enterprise* didn't carry the variety of extra-terrestrials that would inhabit the bar after work. The Star Wars bar had nothing on this one.

Cheap booze, excessive unregulated sexual activity, little food, general isolation from haute coiffure and the latest Parisian fashion houses, did little for the demeanour of our Indonesian tigers.

On Tom's first visit he thought that he had strayed into a seventies party that had gone badly wrong, with some really bad shit being taken by the participants. He had another 'Nam flashback'; he was back in his college days and hallucinating on acid or something. But no, these were subcontractors.

He was puzzled and asked Father Bob for more wisdom. "Bob, why are they are all like this, man?"

Bob looked at him through a cloud of Marlboro smoke, took a long drink of his Bintang and revealed to Tom an epiphany. "Bonny lad, these are real contractors. They understand like you and me the secret. Who would ever want to leave this place, man? See Beauregard over there, he's been here twenty years, married to a nineteen-year-old now. There's Dwayne, back in coon ass land he'd be married to an eighty-year-old. Here he has three that he lives with all under twenty-five. And the whiskey, bourbon, vodka, Tom, you name it, is ten dollars a bottle in this clubhouse."

He took another draw on his cigarette and smiled at the big man.

"The company even built its own whorehouse and employed its own venereal disease doctor. The guys were supplied with their own antibiotics and creams and only if they needed a shot would they have to get the doctor out. They treat the local girls as well." He laughed, his small face twisted and continued. "I guess they are proud of the company's sustainable development programme and record of community and support."

Tom nodded in appreciation. Taking a large swig of his cheap Jack Daniels and Coke he smiled and said: "Hell, Bob, this contracting is some life, buddy."

Father Bob smiled in return.

"Sure is, Tom, even Mother Theresa would have turned native here."

Dwayne was a rough-looking, wispy-bearded, grey-skinned and grey-haired man and he walked over to talk with them both.

"Hi Tom. Howdy Bob. How y'all getting on here now?"

"Pretty fine Dwayne, some clubhouse y'all got," said Tom.

Dwayne scratched his bony ass and agreed. "Yeah: it's something special, man. Y'all fancy coming hunting with us Saturday afternoon?"

Tom perked up and cheerily answered that he'd love to. Father Bob declined. He had too much work to do.

"What y'all hunt here, Dwayne?" Tom asked.

"There's a few wild hog, the odd lizard, if we're lucky might get to shoot a monkey or two. I'll pick you up at the hotel," Dwayne answered.

"Sure, man, let's go hunting. You hunt back home, Dwayne?"

"Sure do, man. I shoot wild hogs mainly. I love to hunt them with my buddies' dogs. They corner the critter, I roll up in my truck and then blow the bastards' brains out with my Colt 45. Great sport, man."

Father Bob sat back and looked at the brave hunter whose eyes were popping out of their bony sockets in some form of feverish madness and thought, *Not much sport in that, bonny lad.* He preferred flying racing pigeons.

Dwayne continued excitedly: "I also go for elk. I'm a fully paid-up member of the Rocky Mountain Elk Foundation. Let me get you some pictures and maybe you'll donate, buddy."

He left and came back from his truck with a couple of leaflets which he handed out to Tom and Bob. Tom looked interested; Bob just ordered another beer and scanned the leaflet.

It seemed Dwayne's purpose in life was to raise money for the Rocky Mountain Elk Foundation and this was the mission statement of that august society.

The mission of the Elk Foundation is to ensure the future of elk, other wildlife and their habitat. In support of this mission the Elk Foundation is committed to:

- *Conserving, restoring and enhancing natural habitats;*

- *Promoting the sound management of wild, free-ranging elk, which may be hunted* **or otherwise enjoyed***;*

- *Fostering cooperation among federal, state and private organizations and individuals in wildlife management and habitat conservation; and*

- *Educating members and the public about habitat conservation, the value of hunting, hunting ethics and wildlife management.*

Dwayne left to go and get a picture album to show them more killing fields. Bob pulled on Tom's arm.

"Bonny lad, clearly the cause of supporting the survival of the Rocky Mountain elk so that Dwayne and his fellow lunatics could roam the hills freely and kill and maim them at will, is not what Jon's sustainability programme execution plan was all about. Also, buddy, I worry about what Dwayne might be doing in the lonely hills and backwoods with the statement **'or otherwise enjoying them',"** Father Bob sarcastically said to Tom and they both laughed and waited for him to arrive back.

Dwayne came back and showed pictures of slaughtered elk and pigs minus their brains. His favourite though was a slideshow of his African kills hanging from piano wire, post the 'Valkyrie' plot to assassinate Hitler – von Witzlelben style. A poor zebra that he'd shot was a real attraction to Gator, the big man.

"Heh, Dwayne. My new wife loves wearing pretty furs and things when she comes back to the US. Next time you shoot one of them zeebrahs will you skin it and I'll have it made into a coat?"

"No problems, Tom. Here, look at this impala. I chopped its hind leg and brought it through Changi Airport last month. It's in mah freezer. After the hunting Saturday we'll BBQ the son of a bitch. Bob, you want to eat some?"

Bob declined.

Dwayne continued with thoughts on hunting and also on courting Batam style.

"You know the girls out here are not much bigger than those impala. Ah guess most weigh only as much a field-dressed deer when neyked."

Father Bob shook his head in despair at this courtship routine despite his longevity and his time in Asia and subsequent desensitisation to shock at some weirdos' awful behaviours; he thought maybe these people should be exterminated like the poor animals they chased.

The laughter at this insanity brought a couple of Dwayne's buddies over to join them and they asked what the fun was about.

"We're just discussing the company's sustainable development program; we gotta protect the wildlife here, human and non-human," Father Bob joked.

Dwayne broke in again. "Well that's a pity coz last night we must have broken a few sustainable rules, buddy. Last night driving back to the bush from work, we ran over a black cat. Brett got out and saw a cat curled up in a ball, it must have been badly injured. So I took a baseball bat," Bob thought, *As you would normally do*, "and beat the mother over the head to put it out of its misery. I threw into the bush nearby. And damn me, didn't this disturb another ******* black cat which flew out of the bush. But this was the one we'd actually hit with the truck, it was limping badly from the accident and the other mother must have just been sleeping by the road."

"Moral: it is dangerous to sleep by the roadside in Batam," Bob concurred and laughed with them all.

But he turned to Tom and whispered, "For ****'s sake keep these crazies away from our HSE man and Teutonic Jon. These Batam ******s have killed more things than Agent Orange."

Tom smiled, and then remembered that the long arm of the Australian environmental man reached far.

"Bob, we both got to meet that AQUIS man form Aussie tomorrow, buddy. Sure hope he doesn't want to talk to Dwayne and his buddies. Waste of mah and your time, buddy. Last time I shipped modules to Australia the mothers had us crawling around site looking for ants with a magnifying glass. We spent weeks cleaning the seagull shit off the barges, man."

It appeared that the Australian environmental team had a long reach. Oil companies build lots of big steel things like Lego bricks that they ship to Australia on barges and stick together in the blazing heat, swamps, red dust of the Beautiful Country, and finally make liquid gas to sell yet again to the Chinese.

They build them overseas because it is cheap; no unions to disrupt and delay the work and, as everyone hoped, no environmental persons like the Watermouse and his mates to slow up the project or cost money. Sadly for all involved on this and other Australian projects that transport big steel things into the far shore, the Australian regulator has a long reach, and it is not possible to ignore environmental legislation and pressure groups even in places as 'liberal' with their environmental and foreign corrupt practices acts as Batam. Indeed, each Australian project is controlled by AQUIS, the Australian Quarantine and Inspection Service rules and regulations. As any visitor to Australia knows, they enforce these rules rigorously at points of entry.

The TV programme 'Border Security' shows what happens if you try to bring in the odd tiger penis, Granny Smith apple, couple of kilos of dried chickens' feet or soil on your golf shoes. Unlike Singapore you are not hit with sticks in Changi Jail but can get severe financial penalties and lose your Granny Smith apple. So it is with big steel things that may harbour foreign beasties and plants. They are sent back or kept on their barges at millions of dollars a day until highly paid Australian unionised labour clean every last piece of seagull droppings off the steel — and heaven forbid that you import a live beastie.

AQIS procedures and inspectors are added to the cost of these projects, much to the consternation of project services managers and also construction managers, who are not known for their patience and love of anything that stops them from building steel things. Hence Gator's consternation with the inspectors he had to meet the next day. He continued with his tale of woe.

"On that last project in 'Nam, we spent days and months cleaning the damn modules and barges, put up quarantine areas, eliminated all critters on the site and in the sea and nuked every plant and bug we could find. We thought we had cracked the whole thing. Then the day of sail away, the VP Asia Pacific came with all the Houston top brass. Red flew in too, first visit to 'Nam since his days there. I was worried about the man in case he had any flashbacks but as usual he was tough as his snake-skin boots; a good old boy, Red. Anyway we all stood on the quay with trumpets and band playing as Big Hansie's ship towed the barge away with the first module on. It shone brighter than the South China Sea, the thing was so clean. Then as it moved away from the quay and into the bay and finally off my hands, a ****** monkey climbed up to the top of the module and started ripping the celebration banner up we'd placed on the top deck. Where the **** it had come from no one knew but the ****** had hidden on there somewhere. The mother actually looked as if it was waving at us!"

He took a large drink and poured a Jack Daniels from his bottle on the bar, the memory too much for him. Father Bob laughed till his tears flowed.

"Heh, Bob, it wasn't funny, man. The VP nearly had a coronary and Red was snatching and twitching, he musta flashed back a bit, because he screamed for a M16 rifle to shoot the ******. I just told the boss of the Fabricator to stop Big Hansie towing and bring the

****** back."

"What did you do with the monkey, mate?" Bob asked, still laughing.

Tom was laughing now and he playfully patted Father Bob on the back, breaking his spinal cord. "We couldn't find the son of a bitch. It vanished. Where it came from or where it went, no one knew. The Gooks were mental trying to find it. They were in and out of all the pipe racks, the equipment rooms the barge tanks, searching the docks and the sea, but no sign of thing."

"Let's hope that Dwayne and his lads have exterminated our simian friends at the weekend hunt by the time the AQUIS man gets here, bonny lad," Bob stammered, still coughing and spluttering from the broken back.

So it was the next day in the Batam yard, after a long lecture from the AQUIS man on the rules and regulations, Tom and Father Bob escorted him on a site tour.

After a good thirty minutes of walking in the tropical heat and humidity with full protective equipment on, everyone was sweating and hoping they could avoid long delays out there if the inspector found anything amiss. They came to an open packing case with a large piece of equipment from a German manufacturer. The Australian AQIS man inspected the equipment and case and noticed a small frog quietly croaking away, not far from the equipment and case.

In his excitement and passion, as this was the first beast he had seen on the fabrication yard, out with the American construction men, Gator and Dwayne, he promptly put a stop on all activities until he identified whether the frog was German or Indonesian.

He carefully collected the potentially Teutonic amphibian and told everyone he wanted an exclusion zone around the equipment and area while he searched the internet to identify the species.

For some reason he had determined that if it was Indonesian, then many may well have sneaked into the big steel things. If it was German then he took it on his conscience and the company environmental policy that he could not allow the Indonesian indigenous species of frogs to be infiltrated by a German invader.

"Why not?" Father Bob whispered to Gator. "The Frogs had allowed German invaders in twice before."

The environment man was worried about past amphibian invasions to Australia, that is, the cane toad, which has taken over vast stretches of his land and is subject to interesting Australian sports pastimes of how to extinguish life from this most prolific breeder.

Unfortunately the frog was difficult to identify, it could have been Indonesian or German, accordingly to our David Attenborough. He was an ex-fireman from Queensland, and not as highly experienced or qualified on the Linnaean Taxonomic System as the PhD holder The Watermouse, so they were not convinced of his ability to identify the evolutionary origin or classify bio species – put out sugar cane field fires, yes – but phylogeny? No.

He decided to close the area down, and began putting up exclusion area tape around the container and said he'd call the environmental team in from Perth. He also instructed Dwayne to search the ponds next door to collect frogs so he could compare with the German frog.

Dwayne was twitching nervously and Father Bob saw his right hand moving up and down his hip, looking for his forty-five calibre weapon, Bob assumed. When he realised he had no weapon, as unlike the Philippines, guns were for some strange reason not allowed on site, he lost the plot and screamed at the AQUIS man.

"This company is on one million dollars a day liquidated damages for every day these steel things sit in this Godforsaken, place you son of a bitch. Nothing and no one will stop mah men building and moving steel things, certainly not a ******* bull frog."

He stormed across the exclusion line, pulling the multicoloured tape out of the way and ranted at the AQIS man.

"Goddamn, you have stopped mah job, because of a ******* bull frog. Are you a ******* idiot and or a tree hugger, some liberal Democrat lover, you goddamned aboriginal son of a bitch?"

Ah, Bob thought, *here we go again, the wonders of a Louisiana education and twenty years living native with little exposure to corporate social responsibility, or civilisation on the black isle of Batam.*

"Where's the goddamned frog, you son of a bitch?"

The environmentalist held his cardboard contamination box that he had diligently carried around the site hoping to collect some unfortunate insect or beastie to inspect and hopefully stop the job. Now he had succeeded. He placed it on the ground and quietly said, "I'm sorry but it's the rules, got to make sure we don't contaminate here or back home. I'm not sure if it's from here or Germany."

Our Dixieland American construction guru looked down at the box, looked at the AQIS man, lifted his size 12, Red Wing rigger boots and stamped on the box, which totally squashed the box and unfortunate frog.

"It dohn't matter now where it's from: Y'all git back to work, you mother******s!"

Thus was ended the great frog debate and the career of the AQUIS man. He wisely left before the Batam police arrested him for walking on the pavement or wearing a loud shirt, charged him millions of rupiah to get out of jail and revoked his work permit. In Batam, even the police knew construction managers ruled, not amphibians.

Tom and Bob had seen off the AQUIS man and headed back to the hotel for a well-earned Bintang. They were greeted as usual by an ebullient Emmet, who ordered them their beers, sat down with them in the lounge bar and began to tell them about his latest fling with his new partner from Sumatra, using the mini bar technique that Richie had perfected.

Bored with tales of his immense phallus and where it ended up, Father Bob interrupted him. "Emmet, we had a bit of a laugh ourselves today, mate. Tell him about the German frog, Tom."

And Tom did.

This amused Emmet who moved away from tales of bodily function to one of further innovation and recycling sustainability on the black island. He told them that he had spoken with the night shift manager for the site in The Ore House on Saturday night. It seems the metal recyclers had secured their mates' fishing boat and had sneaked up to the wharf where the big thing that he was building was moored.

They had a colleague in crime (or business: one man's thief is another man's environmental activist) working on the site and he had access to the large copper wire cables that were coiled on drums. He had dropped one end of the cable over the wharf, into the sea and onto the boat.

They had fastened the cable to the boat and their boat had pulled away into the middle of the bay and anchored as a fishing skiff. They then proceeded to pull the cable from the reel onto the boat, their colleague in crime feeding the cable from the reel into the sea. Now these recycling adventurers were practical men and not into the Archimedes theory of displacement and had not calculated that insulated copper cable of high voltage also had an armoured coating, a lot heavier than copper. So the law of specific gravity passed them by and after a few more pulls of cable onto the boat it promptly started sinking, and as it was a continuous line to the cable reel, they couldn't offload it quickly and it dragged the boat under. The site manager was alerted to their plight by their screams and shouts and promptly called out the security to assist. The boat sank and they ended up in the water but were rescued by the yard's safety boat.

Father Bob loved the story and made it into one more mini lecture and lesson for big American Tom on his visit to the Black Isle.

"Bonny lad, this is a lesson in crime or recycling, it doesn't matter which, that's the beauty of real contracting. Stick with ya fatha and I'll lorn ya the rules."

CHAPTER NINE

Northern China

Steed

Some weeks later after Batam…

"Let's choose one at random and run him off, then see what the rest do."

This was the solution that the Iron Chancellor, Jon, the oil company project director, was proposing to the client project executive team in order to resolve a small industrial relations dispute within the team in China. This had occurred in the shipyard where the project was building more steel things which actually floated.

Jon was a highly intelligent man, a great visionary, with sound knowledge and had a tenacity of his native Rottweilers to get the right answer and was 100% behind delivering the project for his company, for the client government and ensuring that the contractor made money. This was unusual for an oil company project manager for they also understood well the secret of real contracting.

To this end, he insisted on a team that was focused on delivering joint goals that balanced the conflict between the client's schedule and cost and the contractor's profit. All worked hard to do this, and to everyone's surprise he was right, it seemed to be working, though not everyone remained convinced. Of course not, why should they? This novel strategy might shorten their time in this sexually liberated paradise and their eventual huge pension fund or Rolls or yacht like Lord Paul had achieved. It just wasn't proper contracting.

Jon's statement was one of novel employee relations management. Stephen Covey would be in wonder at the Iron Chancellor, but then again the Iron Chancellor was always novel in his approach to human relations management. His HR management skills were honed on working with the intellect and management behaviours that he himself upheld.

He struggled with non-delivery and would challenge individuals to intellectual duels and argument, mainly to get a more robust plan or document out: other times, just for fun. He followed the Duke of Wellington's approach to HR management.

"I will keep on flogging them until morale improves."

Steed, the main contractor's contract's manager told him during a separate meeting that his reference to 'running off' people in China was a storm in a teacup. He couldn't believe that contractors who were working in China would have any intention of upsetting the applecart and losing huge day rates and a life in an oriental sexual wonderland. They had changed from Father Bob's days on Tyneside, where they actually went on strike in his Press Fabrication at Howden yard for damp salt cellars. Here it was important to stay as long as possible.

Steed was sitting with Jon discussing money when he told him this. Steed and John got on surprisingly well. This was because after a motivating interview with either they had a habit of leaving individuals quivering like amoebae, self-respect obliterated forever. They had a mutual respect for each other's superior intellect. Jon had grown to like and appreciate Steed through a series of observations and meetings. He appreciated how Steed could destroy people with one-line retorts and concise rational argument.

"Oh, really? You couldn't co-ordinate your cigar to your mouth," said Steed to a member of Jon's client team, when he told him he had been given a co-ordination role. Jon appreciated this because he ran the person off not long after as he also observed that Steed had been correct. Jon bore no grudge or maliciousness; he was just practical and focussed on delivering what he was paid to deliver and expected everyone else to do the same. Much like Steed:

Steed continued his staff appraisal for Jon: in the presence of another unfortunate one of Jon's team when he was informed this person would be handling things from now on.

"Oh really? He couldn't handle his luggage."

Jon soon realised that Steed had been correct and in a rare moment of reconciliation he sent the object of Steed's comment to work in Batam, which was like sending him to be lost forever but at least he kept earning mega bucks and could enjoy the pleasures of the jungle island. However, when Steed came across him on the Black Isle, he being unforgiving and lacking in any form of human emotion, he told him in a meeting:

"You are as useless as a three-legged cat trying to bury its shit on a frozen pond."

Our humiliated unfortunate left not long after this appraisal on his own accord.

Steed was also an important player in cultural alignment and ecumenicalism in all its forms — as he didn't believe in any of it. When asked if he'd like to participate in most activities meant to spread team spirit and multicultural understanding, his predictable answer was always: "I'd rather not."

This was also Steed's polished English reply for most things that he found irrelevant to the task ahead or his immense mind. He struggled to align and integrate with anything but the contract articles and common law and from attempting to extort large quantities of money from Jon's team through extortionate claims and variations. Jon admired such people.

Steed was perfect with his contract management technique which was the 'bland, could be interpreted as anything statement', but really is: 'Don't be so stupid, you ignorant person.' His habitual retort put the opposition into a catatonic state. This retort was simply, his classic statement: "Oh, really?"

"Oh, really?" was Steed's answer to anything he believed was inane or untrue.

Jon decided that if Steed thought the dispute they were discussing was a storm in a teacup that he should go with Danny, Steed's boss, up to China. He called Danny into his office.

"You will go to China and sort that bunch out. Steed and Lord Paul will go with you as I wish him and Steed to clear up any contract ambiguities with those Chinese imbeciles. You may wish to use Steed to advise you on how to manage your men, as plainly you have let them run wild. Phone me when you have sorted it, if you can't I will come up and run one of them off at random as I still believe that will work."

Steed looked at Jon over the top of his half-moon spectacles and said: "Oh really?"

Danny just went redder in the heed but was learning to keep his powder dry with Jon. There were more important battles to fight.

Paul was Steed's opposite number contracts manager in the oil company. He was called Lord Paul, so called because of his current day rate earnings on the project and because he owned a Rolls Royce. It was rumoured that the large yacht seen at St Tropez, France, by a colleague that was called '*Change Order*' with its small dingy towed behind called '*Original Contract*', was Lord Paul's.

Lord Paul had developed a healthy respect for Steed over the last few months. He had learnt by having to pay out several claims and variations to contract in response to Steed's unique advocacy.

So all three were sent on a mission from Jon, like Lord Elgin during the opium wars, to sort out China, and took an early morning flight from Changi.

The errant men the Iron Chancellor was about to run off, were working in North East China. They arrived in a quite modern Chinese town but typically drab in places with more than its share of soulless concrete housing and office blocks. But compared with many other ex-communist towns around the world it was very habitable and the surrounding countryside and coast attractive. The local Chinese were proud of their city and in the face of their past history, they had done well to make it a place for western foreigners to work and play. It was freezing in the winter and bloody hot in the summer.

The hours of work on site and the offices there were long, mainly because Black Bob, the Scottish Presbyterian site manager, had grown up with a Victorian approach to his staff, as he did in most places this iconic construction man and engineer worked. He had a

Danny like mantra:

"Work hard and don't play at all, it'll make you go blind."

Nevertheless, the project boys loved it up there. Why? This was simple, same rules as before. It was a sexual paradise; the natives didn't want to behead you or give you the Chinese water torture. They wanted you to buy them a bar and/or apartment and take them out of the drab world they'd lived in since Mao did the first sponsored walk.

The merry men earned lots of money too and food and drink was cheap. And like everywhere else in Asia, male looks didn't matter too much either, the beautiful young Chinese girls all followed the same Robert Redford principle as everywhere else: big wallet, massage and marriage.

Danny had been many times but it was Lord Paul and Steed's first time so they checked into a lovely Shangri La hotel and made for the surrounding bars. Danny, in his usual naivety, promised them a great night and but would be heading home early as he had a big day the next day.

In Maggie's bar, Danny had asked Lord Paul where had he been lately, as he'd been missing for several nights from the Here and Now bar on his nightly 'team building' visits. The owner had been complaining that his takings were down.

Lord Paul replied in his polished Queen's English: "Danny, I've been in hospital for a few weeks. I had operations on my hands."

Given his propensity to initially reject any claim, change order that crossed his well-polished desk, Danny responded sarcastically with: "Was that to prise money out of them, Paul?"

"No, Danny," was his cutting response. "I'd shaken hands with Steed and lost my fingers."

Danny was beginning to listen to Jack during his teach-ins in The Sportsman's bar and he was beginning to understand that this was the way with the contract persons; they were of course the artisans of real contracting. Always the first located in paradise, as they are employed to write the original contract and always the last to leave, as they settle the huge claims and penalties arising from everyone working in paradise on huge day rates and bonuses paid to those workers and management who allowed the project to fail. Marvellous stuff, if you can get it.

Danny, who had several degrees in using spanners, wiring plugs etc., now told aspiring engineers to become quantity surveyors and contract lawyers. They may seem like boring degrees and professions, but you can enjoy the art of destroying people's careers, lives, confidence and finances and earn mega bucks in the process. Either those jobs or maybe they could inflict the same damage as a banker, like Big Marc.

Soon into the bar came big Richie, escorted by his latest partner, a lovely slim Chinese girl, long black hair, tight jeans and tee-shirt, whom he introduced to the assembled intelligentsia.

"Gudday guys, this is Rose. She's from Mongolia. She's a scientist, she says."

Danny pondered this statement. *I didn't think Rose would have been a common name in Mongolia, and not many nuclear scientists in these bars, but what the hell: this is Asia.*

Richie shouted across the bar to Maggie, the surrogate Mongolian owner: "Get the beers in for the boys Maggie and send a few girls over to, it's too quiet in here."

"Oh, ****!" Danny exclaimed to Steed. "Here we go again, another 747. For ****'s sake, when will it end!"

And sure enough, two hours later, surrounded by lovely Mongolian scientists, he was several hundred yuan down to Maggie, who was now masquerading as the wife of the Chinese barman in the Here and Now and Danny was lamenting his familiar song to Steed.

"Tits in my ears again, bills everywhere, I must stop doing this!"

"Oh really," Steed retorted, staring over his half-rimmed glasses and twisting his face, bored and uninterested in his boss's perpetual self-inflicted plight.

Big Richie was sat at the bar with his Mongolian Einstein on his lap while she was fondling his nether regions. Danny, remembering his nuclear physics momentarily thought she may be searching for his boron rods.

Richie looked up from his String Theory antics and looked at

Danny with a glow on his face.

"Danny, despite all this fun, I want to retire at fifty."

To Steed, who was listening looking extremely bored with the conversations and the antics, it was plain this guy had not aged too well, to say the least. As they said in Britain: 'He must have had a hard newspaper round as a kid.'

"For ****'s sake, how old are you now, man?" Steed shouted, waking up and visibly surprised at the statement. He peered over his half lens glasses, face contorted as if in another gurning competition.

"I'm forty-two!" Richie exclaimed alarmingly, and a little offended, expecting a positive reinforcement message on his retirement at the early age of fifty.

Steed, looking sardonically over his half-moon glasses and turning away disdainfully from the broken unfortunate man uttered his classic: "Oh, really?"

Richie was initially little upset, but thinking he'd joke with the impassive Englishman, he tried to bond with Steed.

"It's a hard life out here, mate. Moving from site to site, living in digs, girls everywhere. I never get home to the wife and kids back in Oz for months."

"Oh really? Then why do you stay?" the polished voice retorted, not particularly interested in the answer.

Richie, thinking he now had the edge, smiled.

"This is my wife here. When I wake up she gives me a blow job and then runs the shower for me while she goes into the kitchen and makes my sandwiches and snacks for work. When I come home she greets me at the door, takes me to the shower, washes me and gives me and a blow job. She then gives me a full body massage to ease the pressure of doing very little in the site office all day. She then comes out with me to the pub, where she is now and keeps quiet while I have fun with my mates. Once we have had a few beers I will take her home and have sex."

And looking smugly at Steed he said: "Wouldn't you like that?"

Steed turned away twisting his face with pain.

"I'd rather not."

They left the bar to be surrounded by the orphan children that are sent out to beg for money of foreigners. Sadly they get beaten if they don't achieve their targets. But most of the contractors would give something to stop the beatings if not to feed the poor waifs. Some were made of sterner stuff.

One of them, a young girl, pulled at Steed's immaculately pressed trousers looking up with her deep and big oval brown eyes, pleadingly at the great man, who brushed the hand away with distain and twisting his face into several contortions, he shouted – "**** off!"

Richie, clearly astonished and still not appreciating Steed's resolute behaviour, chastised him.

"Come on, mate, the poor bugger's trying to earn a few cents, man. Just give her a dollar or two."

"I'd rather not."

And he walked to next bar. Steed was wise to the ways of the Chinese child exploiting gangsters and his heart like all contracts managers was refined in a furnace fuelled by contract articles and extensions of time, not compassion.

They entered Alice's bar, run by Alice; Maggie's Bar, by Maggie; Guns and Roses by Rose and so on, Danny realised that this place was a bit like Emmet's branding philosophy of his pies and burgers and sexual organ, everyone was a somebody's bar. But they were accommodating hosts with even more accommodating staff. Most of the bars were owned in part by guys on the project or other contractors who had come for a project and stayed in a perpetual world of night-time frolics, cheap noodles and dodgy DVDs to watch.

Bar games were popular in these bars. The Tumbling Tower game was the favourite in Alice's bar, where the 'barmaids' would join in with you to see how high the tower could be built, inserting one brick at a time, until someone knocked down the tower and lost.

Danny asked Steed if he'd like to play and got the usual response.

"I'd rather not."

Steed sat down to think about what he'd rather do. So Danny played with Lord Paul. Lord Paul won the Olympian contest. Danny's partner then promptly grasped his hand and thrust it down her panties, making the poor man leap out of his seat and to the door – the silver medal. Lord Paul rapidly drank his beer and left. He didn't want to see what the gold medal was.

The next day Black Bob picked them all up from the Shangri La and took them to site. Danny sat in the back, his head sore and red as yet again he'd stayed out with Big Richie and his girlfriends until the early hours before stumbling into his bed, forgetting his pledge to go home early, and was in no great mood.

Bob told them that the main reason for the problems Jon was concerned about was that two groups were just not getting on. One was the Indian engineers and the other a bunch of expatriate, mainly Scottish piping engineers.

"Jon sent that entertainments guy, Jack somebody, up two days ago to look at what could be done. **** knows what he can do. I've just sent him out to site to talk to the Chinese every day; it'll stop him interfering with us. Juan, Jon's site rep, has kept him pissed every night as he's useless and clueless too. Brian came up to see if he can sort them but he can't."

Danny came to life.

"I'll sort the ******s. Get Brian to get them into a room for 10 a.m. and get Jack out of bed and in the office. Jon will run us all off if we don't use the English ******** and he's got a huge team piss-up budget so let's see if he's any use before Jon runs him off and we lose the beer money."

Bob turned from the front seat to face his boss.

"OK Danny, I'll get it done. Oh, you and I have to go to lunch today with the shipyard boss and the leader of the local Communist Party. It'll be a drunken one, boss, so we'll not be coming back to site."

"Oh, ****! Not another banquet. I can't keep doing this for ****'s sake. I need ghost busters to eat that Chinese shite. And the ******* tens of toasts to each of our penile functions, and that ******* Mao Tai for ****'s sake, they serve it in ceramic bottles as it melts ******* glass. It ****s up mah heed every time."

He turned to his aristocratic contracts executioner.

"Steed, would you like to go instead?"

He got the predictable response.

"I'd rather not."

Danny met Jack in his office on site.

"Hi Danny: I thought Jon had told you I was heading up here?"

"Aye, he did but I didn't think we'd have to sort out this lot. Mah heed hurts, Jack. I think I need a nap. Close the office door, mate, and pretend that you are and me are talking and working; write something on the flip chart every now and then. I'll turn my back to the door and doze off for a while."

And so he did. Jack spent forty minutes pretending to be in intense debate with the ginger man, while Danny's men, needing to talk to their leader, peered through the glass panel in the door and Jack put his hand up and patted his watch to say come back later.

Eventually, Jack shook his patient awake, who moaned immediately.

"Oh ****, ah divn't feel much better, Jack. I need a curry puff."

Jack anticipated his need for the food of the Gods and had ordered several of the fried cholesterol specials, and these seemed to help the red heed somewhat. They got down to the task at hand.

Jack counselled the demented, ginger-haired, Scots project manager on what his problems were with his piping team and they decided it was time to facilitate a solution to the issue. He began to counsel his ginger friend on how to behave within the meeting.

"Do not get the 'red heed' again; it doesn't work within the Asian culture. It'll only make them clam up and we'll get nowhere. They are pretty upset about the swearing and crude behaviour of the expats to them within meetings and the office. Let's try to be reserved in this one. Give the Indians some respect."

He gave this expensive advice, because Danny's 'red heed' (a propensity to go bright red to match his hair and look like a crazed Mel Gibson) in full anger and hurling Celtic expletives had caused many a strange reaction from the melting pot of races up to now. He was after all supposed to be the boss, the patriarch, and Asians especially respected hierarchy and age, particularly the Japanese contingent.

He continued with his coaching.

"Also, I know you're biased at the moment. Try to be fair and equitable at the beginning."

He knew that his patient had struggled with Indians and their behaviours in his past life. He was then still very culturally conservative, not as he was to become a convert and icon to multicultural management, and now he was evolving in his ability to accommodate those of a different world than Glasgow.

Jack continued with his advice and coaching.

"Practise the active listening that you preach. Allow me to open up a dialogue, explore what the issues are and do not predicate the outcome."

"OK, let's do it then," Danny said, striding into the meeting.

The Indian managers were at one side, and curiously enough, though it probably isn't a significant correlation with behaviour, our Glaswegian piping protagonist and the unfortunate shrinking Brian, the engineering manager, who had to manage this latest Indian mutiny were on the other. Jack could see that he felt like a siege of Cawnpore was about to descend upon him and he may end up in the infamous Black Hole.

Jack welcomed them all and turned to write a few rules of behaviour on the flip chart. However, Danny couldn't wait; his heed was growing redder because he was thinking about Jack's advice on real contracting. He knew his evolving theories on the ways to delay projects in paradise, namely, that he was facing another schedule delay, cunningly concocted by his piping expatriate contractors, who were more expert than the commissioning group at this tactic. He started screaming in his heavy Glaswegian accent at everyone.

"Before Jack starts, I want to tell you ******s, if you can't ******* agree how to work together after this, I'm going to fire one of you *****, and I don't ******* care less who. It will be at ******* random!"

Yes, cultural alignment consultancy can be difficult in a madhouse.

They left the meeting and Jack resolved to discuss and feedback the meeting with Danny over a beer, as it seemed the only way to get through to him when the red heed was in full flow.

Danny left for yet another banquet with Black Bob. Danny, being the head man, had to be entertained lavishly by his subcontractor, the shipyard. It was protocol. It was Chinese 'face' and you had to eat 'the foreign shit' as he so eloquently told anyone when inviting them to help him suffer the meals.

The problem for Danny and most normal human beings was that there was a difference between the more spicy exotic food in South East Asia and the Chinese seafood served here, and that was the simple fact that in this place it was invariably alive when you ate it.

In any sane person's experience, invertebrate animals from the lower evolutionary scale were not meant to be eaten by anything but fish. Even sea anemones, jellyfish, sea slugs, sea urchins and sea cucumbers are pretty well untouched by the predators with which they cohabit in the ecosystems off the Northern Chinese coast. Even fish don't eat them, yet they take pride of place on a seafood banquet menu in China.

The only way to eat these things is to be in an alcoholic stupor. Even the Chinese know this. So every banquet was a Bacchanalian feast of constant toasts to each other's senior management, contract relationship and penile erectile function, so that by the time you got to eat the animals without backbones you had lost your lower brain functions of sight, taste and smell. Luckily an ability to vomit was the last to go just before loss of bowel control. The language differences could cause serious problems at these orgies of platitudes and self-mutilation.

Danny faced the table and looked aghast at the array of creatures he had to eat, and indeed, he would need *Ghostbusters*.

"How you like?" the head shipyard man asked Danny with a heavy Chinese accent. Danny slowly chewed a live marine invertebrate, trying not to be sick and hiding the look of horror on his face.

"They are a bit rubbery," he replied, smiling through the disgust, hoping not to lose face with his Asian host.

He remembered that Jack had coached him that he had to give 'face' at all times.

His host's face gleamed and he exclaimed excitedly:

"Lubberly! Hah, pliss have all of mine."

The head man was plainly overjoyed and emptied the whole bowl onto Danny's plate, insisting that he ate all of his favourite live marine invertebrates as a special favour from him. Danny's red face turned white as he loyally chewed through his 'lubberly' molluscs.

He had pride of place between the two head people. Curiously the head communist was a woman, which was most unusual, to have senior female company in a hierarchal male-dominated business. However, she didn't speak English so Danny didn't have much difficulty culturally aligning with her. His site manager, Black Bob, was seated directly opposite Danny, diameter to diameter.

The talk was very formal and lots of Mao Tai slipped down all throats. This horrible stuff and smelt like the solvent Danny used to buy from the local garage to burn other people's Guy Fawkes' night bonfires down. They were served an assortment of delicacies, which Danny, with his conservative Scottish taste just nibbled at, grimacing under his ginger moustache and saying the odd 'lubberly,' to approving nods of heads, and more mao tai added to his cup. Then the pièce de résistance was brought out and placed lovingly in front of Danny. It was a huge lobster, with the shell of its tail removed. He took one look at it and turned the table to the left, trying to mouth something to Bob across the diameter of the table.

Bob couldn't make out what he was miming but watched as each subsequent diner pulled large portions of the flesh off the lobster's tail, grunting with pleasure and making approving comments in Chinese, as they ate the glistening meat, and then turning the table one more turn. As the lobster came nearer and face-on to him, Bob looked up again to Danny and he was miming furiously trying to catch his eye.

As the lobster faced him, Bob realised what Danny was still miming.

"For ****'s sake, it's still alive, man."

As the unfortunate crustacean came to rest at his place Bob noticed its eyes were moving like a terrified shit house rat from side to side and its little feelers and mouth parts were moving up and down in some pleading gesture of, 'Help get me back to my family and the *Little Mermaid.'* Like his fellow Scot and fussy colleague, Bob turned down the chance of a nice piece of the blue-white, glistening, poor living thing's tail, and like the port, passed it to the left and watched as it was completely devoured alive by the time it reached Danny again. They no doubt lost face, but more importantly remained hungry. They left for the hotel and stopped off at McDonald's for a burger. American cuisine culture won again that day.

As everyone settled into a night of nuclear fusion and debauchery in Maggie's bar again, Danny asked Jack what he should do if he had to suffer another 'shite foreign meal' and Jack gave him some Father Bob advice and a new lesson:

'Always lie about your diet and allergy to certain types of foreign food to foreigners. Never ever eat invertebrates.'

Danny thought this sound advice.

Danny moved on the real work.

"How did today go, Jack, on site after our meeting? I thought it went well, mate."

"Well Danny, let's see how they take your advice. I'm sure they know the intent is to get them all working as a team."

Danny looked puzzled and said: "But the wobblies don't drink! How can we get them in the team?"

Jack thought for a second maybe he should explain cultural and social things to the bemused Scotsman but bottled it again as it was getting just too hard.

"Leave that up to me, Danny. I'll sort it."

Jack had decided to leave the hard counselling stuff and enjoy the evening. Danny, feeling pleased with his self and still pissed after many bottles of mao tai at his banquet, asked Jack how Jon was.

"Well Danny, I spoke with him and he was pleased with the progress we made at resolving the industrial dispute. He was a bit disappointed that our site representative in Dalian had allowed it to happen, and I was instructed to motivate him to better things next time. He told me, 'Juan needs something firmly planted on his nuts, put the fear of God into him. Hell, he's only Mexican!'"

Jack smiled and Danny, possibly in agreement with Jon's management instructions, laughed and said: "That'll motivate the dago to better things!"

"Sadly, the motivational theories of Maslow and Hertzberg are not held high up in the Iron Chancellor's lexicon. It seems nor are cultural alignment and appreciation of other nationals a great priority, especially the Spanish speaking nations. He is very clear with roles and responsibilities on his project is our Jon – cultural and team stuff? – he's clear, that was my job!" Jack said, grinning.

Steed turned to Danny and gave his opinion on the subject.

"Jon is quite correct. Juan is of no use. He even tried to tell me today how to estimate cost. The man is a fool. I corrected him."

Steed then walked away to talk to Lord Paul about money and yachts. Jack whispered to Danny that Steed had actually really upset the mild-mannered and likeable Juan.

"I had to counsel him and stop him phoning Jon. He didn't know that Jon would probably have run him off and hired Steed instead of him! I've got the email exchange in my pocket: thought you'd have a giggle at it. First Juan sent this e-mail to Steed who'd questioned the Client's method of estimating costs."

He handed a piece of paper to Danny and he began reading Juan's e-mail:

I realize you copied me on the distribution for information purposes, which I do appreciate. However for the avoidance of doubt and for the sake of clarity I think I have to comment on the following:-

Quote

Another industry convention can reasonably get to $24.3 SINCE WHEN IS FACTORING BY 60% A CONVENTION?

Unquote

Perhaps the estimating technique used to arrive at the value stated in Andrew's note has been over simplified to the point that it has been misinterpreted.

The technique or method is sometimes referred to as the "SIX TENTHS RULE," due to the most commonly used factor being the ratio of physical size or throughput between one "project' and another being raised to the power of 0.6 (zero point six). This scaling factor is applied to the known cost of Project 1 to derive an estimated cost of Project 2.

This technique is more correctly referred to as Algorithmic Method or Parametric Cost Estimating and can be described as:

Algorithmic Methods

The use of mathematical formulas to make estimates. The formulas are derived from research and histoDawnl data and use inputs that relate to physical characteristics, performance characteristics, functional characteristics, productivity factors, and other known cost driver attributes. Parametric models are considered algorithmic models.

Parametric Cost Estimating

A cost estimating methodology using statistical relationships between historical costs and other program variables such as system physical or performance characteristics, contractor output measures, and manpower loading. An estimating technique that employs one or more cost estimating relationships (CERs) for the measurement of costs associated with the development, manufacture, and/or modification of a specified end item based on its technical, physical, or other characteristics.

A parametric cost estimate is one that uses cost estimating relationships (CERs) and associated mathematical algorithms (or logic) to establish cost estimates. Parametric techniques are a credible cost estimating methodology that can provide accurate and supportable contractor estimates, lower cost proposal processes, and more cost-effective estimating systems. I hope this helps.

Danny threw the e-mail back.

"For ****'s sake, Jack, he's sick in the heed."

"Well Danny, you may well be correct for he's asked Jon for compassionate leave after receiving Steed's reply."

Danny laughed.

"He's no miss."

No flowers from him or from Steed then, Jack thought.

Danny asked: "What was that Steed's reply?"

Jack gave him Steed's e-mail. It was just one line:

"And I thought you just guessed it…."

Danny chuckled loudly, his red face getting redder, and shouted across to Brian, who was entertaining yet again and surrounded by Big Richie and the Scottish piping engineers and many Mongolian scientists who could well have been examining them for radioactivity in their groins. "Get the beers in, Brian. I have to go home soon, got an early start on site tomorrow."

But he never did.

CHAPTER TEN

Bangkok, Thailand

Jungle Jim

Next year…

The project had a large contract with a supplier in Thailand of many steel pots and pans, long tubes and spherical things that boiled and froze gas that came from offshore. It had gone into the inevitable delay and Jon was determined to get it back on track.

"You will fly to Bangkok and spend time with those imbeciles Danny has managing that place. If you have any problems with our people there you will call me and I will fly up and run them off. Please go and do some work for once. And keep out of the bars and clubs and no girls. Thailand is a septic tank and you have no willpower like me. You will fly tomorrow. Do not come back until we are back on schedule. Goodbye."

So Jack was instructed and motivated to head out of his very comfortable life in Singapore to the hell of Thailand. He chuckled to himself as he left Jon's torture chamber, remembering his last couple of visits to the land of smiles. 'Keep away from the bars and clubs and no girls.' There was nothing else in Thailand!

He arranged the flights, hotels and the meetings with the team up there and he also phoned around to see who was in town. He was pleased to know that a few of the 'regular Outback boys' and his newfound acquaintances would be up in Bangkok and also in Pattaya, so he arranged a few meets and beers. He did not tell Jon.

He had a weekend spare before visiting the company making the pots and pans so he decided to visit Digger who had given him an open invitation. He visited him in his new Thai retreat in Pattaya.

Digger continued to run his business when in town from his small rented office and apartment there and from bars in town. Digger arranged to put him into a small boutique hotel that he recommended rather than the grand ones that Jack could have booked through the company, and told Jack he'd meet him there at 10.30 a.m. when he arrived from Bangkok.

Jack arrived at the hotel to see Digger ensconced at the bar with a lovely Thai lady sitting on his lap. He had the usual wet, brushed-back blond hair, white trousers and Batik shirt.

Digger greeted Jack warmly.

"Hi matey, hope the drive was OK. Let's have a drink. What do you like?"

Jack took his hand, shook it and asked for a Singha beer.

"Marvellous, Jack." Digger took the beer from the lady who had left his lap and opened one from the ice Hesky behind the bar and handed it to Jack. "This is Pia, the owner. Well, her husband is, but he's away working in Africa for next three weeks on one of your projects. He's from your neck of the woods I think. She's a lovely girl and will help you get settled in once we've had a few beers. Come here, Pia, and let me show Jack your panties."

*Oh ****,* Jack thought. Here we go again, and it's only 11 a.m.

"It's all right, Digger. I'd rather she showed me my room, mate."

"No worries. There's plenty time. Now Pia, come on now, onto my knee." And she did, but this time not sitting but bent over his knee and he lifted her very short skirt and showed off her tiny black thong.

"Lovely matey, isn't it? She's gorgeous. She likes a spank too."

And taking his hand he gently spanked the land lady while she giggled and laughed. Jack, shaking his head looked at the man, who seemed to be in complete peace and contemplation, almost transcendental. No thought that this obtuse behaviour was nothing but normal for a Saturday morning. He took a drink and realised that Jon had been correct; he really should have avoided the place.

After moving his stuff into his neat, comfortable room they drank a few more and Digger said he'd take Jack to the tennis club. He drove without worrying about the several rum and Cokes in him and when they arrived, Jack looked on in amazement. It was rather surreal – to see a picture postcard green from middle England or South Australia, surrounded by a rather large Thai woman sat washing her pants in a tub next to the tennis balls and on the other side a Thai man sawing wood from a shack he'd built against the clubhouse wall. He then stripped off naked and washed his body from a rainwater barrel. Jack thought, not the sort of surroundings and cultural scenes one would expect at the lawn tennis club in Wimbledon, Melbourne, Roland Garros or Flushing Meadows. Even more surreal was the welcome Digger gave him again.

He introduced him to the young, pretty Thai landlady by bending her over his knees again, lifting her skirt and spanking her gently. Again, this is not what you'd expect in pleasant Melbourne society. This was even more bizarre because this time her English husband who unlike the last landlady's was not stuck in some armed camp in Africa watching steel get welded, was sitting in a wheelchair. It seemed he had suffered a stroke and was unable to move or say much, he just stared, face contorted, trying to remonstrate at Digger's unique greeting modus operandi; or so Jack thought. Then the poor man gestured to the Thai bar lady and it seemed she could understand his mutterings and she started opening a bottle of beer. It appeared he was not upset with Digger's greeting but offering to buy Jack a drink.

Marvellous, he thought. What sort of place is this that a disabled guy would find it normal that his wife was being spanked half naked by his best customer, and his first thoughts were to buy his latest customer a drink? A sharing and inclusive culture, he thought, one more for the Harvard review.

The day and night went on in much the same way; Digger seemed to have a host of lovely ladies who were perfectly happy to show off their panties and get a light spanking and Jack was perfectly happy taking behavioural research notes and observing Digger in his worship and meditation. Digger finally made his excuse and said he had to go back and see Angel and host a BBQ for her family. Jack went back to his hotel and the next day he flew to Bangkok, Digger promising to meet him on Monday evening in his favourite bar.

After Monday visiting the supplier of the boiling pots, Jack was driven back to his hotel in Bangkok and strolled out to meet a few old friends in Taffy's bar in Washington Square. He had also arranged to meet Shaun, Ironman, as well as Digger. Big Marc was also in town that week auditing the supplier and doing some banking stuff with the Thai subsidiary of the company. So he anticipated a week or so of decent evenings and the weekend.

Ironman, he had learnt over a few drunken sessions in Singapore and Jakarta, was even more of an enigma than most he'd met. He seemed to have such a chequered past, which was a maze of Danish shipping magnates, Indian urea sales, South African wine, CIA, DEA, FBI, Indonesian Generals, Taiwanese squillionaire steel mill owners and of course, contracting in American oil and gas companies. He was perpetually trying to get investment for his 'projects', so that he could dig up iron ore, sell teak and replant vegetables to feed the starving masses of the area that, because of Ironman's deforestation, would then have had no trees for shelter or food to hunt and gather, or indeed white rhinos or orang-tangs for Jack's daughter to save.

Ironman's colleague and partner in enterprise in Taffy's bar in Bangkok was another American Irishman from New York, Jungle Jim. Jungle Jim, if you believed him, or Ironman, was an ex-FBI, ex-IRA quartermaster, or ex-whatever and was an expert in building roads in the jungles of Asia. These roads were not the multi-lane concrete and asphalt highways familiar to us but were dust tracks covered with a magical substance formula known only to Jungle Jim that miraculously stuck the dust together to form quick laid, cheap and usable roads. A veritable gold mine of a business, as Ironman kept telling Jack. The product Jim called T-Flex.

Jungle Jim, however, never seemed to have any money, and never really seemed to be in the jungle, just Taffy's bar and The Outback when visiting Singapore and trying to drum up road-building contracts with Ironman.

He smoked cigarettes profusely and should have used the tar he coughed up from his lungs when he stood next to anyone at the bar in his formula. He also drank much beer and whisky. He was an elderly man and not really very well, it seemed, and certainly didn't look like he was ready for creating pathways through the Malaysian jungle.

Jack soon came to realise that Ironman (or more accurately Ironman's lovely and charming Thai working wife) was funding his road-building enterprise. Ironman said that as he was a mate from past life (which life, or which personality, no one ever found out) he couldn't see him stuck in the house without cigarettes and a beer so he had bought him his little pleasures in life as very often over the years Jungle Jim apparently had little income.

Ironman, when he had funds, was a very generous person to many people and also extremely charitable though his church and mission links. Misunderstood by many, but like most out in Asia, he was trying to keep solvent, bring up a family and hopefully one day to make that squillion. He also was hoping the Jungle Jim's formula could one day be turned into money through a vast road-building empire across Malaysia and the jungles of Asia.

Wonder of wonders, a few weeks before Jack's visit to Bangkok Jack had asked Ironman in The Outback one Saturday where Jungle Jim was these days, and Shaun said he was in the jungle, the Malaysian jungle to be exact. He was laying roads in palm oil plantations. Seemingly, Ironman had secured a contract with the Sultan of Johor to plough a furrow and lay a road across the whole of his vast estates of palm oil and rubber plantations. Jungle Jim was leading a team of local natives in laying the T-Flex with his lawnmower-type applicator up and down the jungle pathways.

Now, everyone in The Outback looked a bit aghast at this fabulous story, especially Captain Abe and Dawn, who had heard them all before. Ironman as usual got upset at those who questioned the veracity of this story and the physical improbability of Jungle Jim, elderly, unfit, coughing his guts up, pushing T-Flex laying machines through the steaming tropical jungles.

But in the spirit of friendship, and the fact that Ironman was paying the bill, all decided to beg to differ on Ironman's latest attempt at global dominance in the road-laying business.

It was a huge coincidence that Jungle Jim arrived back in Paddy's bar the evening of Jack's visit before Shaun arrived. As described his enforced absence was attributed by Ironman in The Outback some weeks before to his Herculean efforts in the jungles of Malaysia, laying roads with his wonder product.

Jim looked a broken man. His already bulbous red nose was protruding across his face, red, oozing, burnt to the cartilage. His brow was dark brown and cracked. He had lost many kilos and he looked drained. He came to the bar and asked if Taffy wouldn't mind buying him a drink as he was waiting for Ironman to settle with him for the work he had just done in Malaysia. He was expecting about US$5,000 and was feeling very happy with himself.

He explained to all that he had indeed been laying a road, though not the hundreds of kilometres and squillion-dollar contract that Shaun had told about, but a small test of his wonder product in a palm oil plantation. It had been a tough time for the impecunious and elderly man and he had pushed his lawnmower up and down a jungle track for days on end with his Malay labourers, eating little, with no funds for food or drink as Ironman had supplied basic living expenses to the poor man. But he was looking forward a gallon of beer and a pack of Marlboro and his pay check.

Ironman duly arrived and they went off into a quiet corner to talk business and divide what everyone thought were the spoils of Jungle Jim's labours. A massive argument arose with shouting and temper, with the bulk of Taffy stepping in to separate the warring entrepreneurs. Jim exited the bar, hurling expletives at his erstwhile mate and partner in the road-laying business, no money having exchanged hands.

Jack sat with Ironman and asked him what the hell that was all about.

"Jack, I can't understand people like Jim. I help them with their business. I use all my contacts with the generals and sultans to get his T-Flex going. I get him a contract and he starts wanting to fight with me."

Jack asked him: "Why did you fall out?"

"It was over his share of the deal. My dearest manages the accounts, as you know." (His wife, being Asian from a wealthy interracial Thai/Burmese family who made a well-known ointment to soothe aches and pains was well educated and worked in a Bangkok multinational bank, and she was super-efficient at money counting and saving it from the likes of Jim and the other bar reprobates, as Ironman knew to his cost.)

He continued.

"Anyway, she has been adding up every beer and pack of cigarettes I have bought Jim over the last years, plus taxi fares and the odd chicken rice here and there that I bought him and the expenses to get him to the jungle and has deducted the total from the share of the money we were paid by the sultan."

Oh dear, Jack thought. *Here lies the rub,* he feared.

"Have a look, Jack, here's the account."

He handed over an A4 sheet. It appeared that they were paid US$20,000 for the road (not the squillions, it seems). The cost of product plus lawnmower and expenses for Jim's mud hut in the jungle and labourers were about US$10,000 making a nice profit of US$10,000. It seems the deal between the two was 50/50 split, so it looked to Jack that Jungle Jim should have received the 5k he was expecting for his toil and sweat in the jungle.

"Problem is, my darling girl has deducted the booze and cigarettes that I've bought him over the years and the interest and administration costs on the money plus my own management fee and he owes us two hundred US dollars."

Dear God, Jack thought, *poor Jim.* He assumed, and anyone would, that buying your mate beer and tabs when he was down on his luck wouldn't go to a debit account on a balance sheet for future pay back. But with Ironman's very cost-conscious financial wizard wife it obviously did.

Ironman couldn't see at all how Jim had got upset and gone mental and he was aggrieved when a few told him that maybe Jim's reaction was understandable. He left, shaking his head, misunderstood again, and went off to drink his profits somewhere else more user friendly.

Those in the bar that evening who knew the irascible American shook their heads at the entrepreneur's latest financial misadventure but after a few more beers, they couldn't stop laughing at the thought of Jungle Jim ploughing his furrow, pushing his lawnmower thing up the jungle track, sweat streaming off him, mosquitoes biting his arse, sun burning his huge nose while Ironman sat on a bar stool in the bar in Washington Square counting his newfound wealth. It was a great partnership and a business broken in two but with the personalities involved, inevitable.

Months later when Jack was in the bar again he was told by Taffy that Jungle Jim appeared back in the bar angry, broken but still sure of his wonder product and sometime after, he was looking for sponsors and investors to fund him on his new venture. He had been over to Indonesia, where a huge sink hole had opened off Java and was spewing out millions of tonnes of lava and mud.

This was destroying vast areas of pristine environment and the Indonesian government were at a loss for what to do. Jungle Jim had convinced some shady government people that his road-building product could be poured into the seething mass of the sink hole and would block it up like a kitchen sink full of Polyfilla.

He was certain this would make him the millionaire he should have been. He found no takers for his scheme in the bar that day. Digger nearly put his hand in his pocket but wisely didn't and many others all kept their hands very much in their long pockets; not even a beer, never mind thousands of dollars in investment.

Jungle Jim was not seen again. Whether he fell into the sink hole with his lawnmower and sticky product or made millions remained a mystery. Digger said he had spoken to him moons later in Bangkok and he told him he had made his million and saved the Indonesian Coral Sea and the planet and he handed Jack the American road builder's phone number. Given the amazing life of those in that bar, and Jim's ingenuity and hard work, no one would be surprised if Jungle Jim finally did make it; but he would never get a penny out of Ironman's lovely wife, that's for sure.

Big Marc arrived just as Jungle Jim and Ironman exited. He had had a tough day closing down the Thai economy and bankrupting the project's supplier of wires and plugs. So he was happy.

He came in with Hansie, the project's supplier of barges, module transport ships and all things marine. He was a Dutchman but brought up in South Africa so his political correctness was a little bit unpolished, as was his tact. He had little time for any race but his own. All Africans were kaffirs; all Norwegians snow kaffirs; Arabs, sand kaffirs; and his particular venom was left for anyone of Indian extraction – curry kaffirs.

He could drink copious amounts and was always claiming after a long shift offshore on his barge that he had a thirst like a 'mine kaffir'. The Doc in Singapore was forever in apoplexy at his smoking and drinking and his healthy blood tests but here in Bangkok he was free to do and say what he liked.

He and Big Marc settled down on their own at the end of the bar, saying they'd join the rest later, obviously with something to talk about. Digger was by now on another bottle of Bundaberg, which he had specially ordered in for him, and sat looking more morose than normal but still chatting to the barmaid with tales of his many mechanical sexual devices. Jack just sat taking in the atmosphere and wondering where Shaun had gone now to spend Jungle Jim's road-building profits, and if he would finally get his letter of credit for the iron mine off anyone in the next bar.

Big Marc told Hansie that he was enjoying his new flat in Sydney. He liked the place and he lived on the beach by the sea and was in cultural and spiritual harmony with the creatures that inhabited it, that is, great white sharks. He had settled down into a normal routine: Marc working, destroying entrepreneurs' dreams, bankrupting millions of Aussies and making millions in bonuses and still getting pissed and stepping on unsuspecting victims' throats; his wife sitting in doors, catatonic, getting more and more neurotic about the orange juice and also the blue-tongued lizards that lived in the garden. However, felt he had to tell someone that evening that they had spilt up a couple of times over the last couple of months and that he struggled to understand why she should want to leave such a loving husband. Hansie agreed with him that indeed it was strange. He had similar tendencies to Big Marc, with reference to compassion or empathy. Marc told him that he was happy though that she had left his two cats each time. This cheered him up tremendously, as he only loved only two things, an inanimate stuffed toy bear that he carried everywhere with him and his pussies.

He attempted reconciliation with his estranged wife. Amazingly, she had returned to the marital home. Her return had conditions, however; one that he would personally get psychological counselling, which surprisingly, he duly had. He had spent most of his annual bonus on this, whilst his wife also took counsel from the same psychiatrist.

His counsellor had helped him realise that he had a Mr Angry inside him which manifested itself in extreme violence to males or lack of compassion for his wife's illness and behaviour or indeed his customers. Thousands of dollars to tell him that, Hansie thought. Everyone knew he was a sociopath, for ****'s sake. He worked as a banker, for God's sake; it wasn't difficult to suss that. The Doc would have diagnosed that for the price of a Crown beer.

Anyway, for Marc this was a major turning point in his life and sitting on the bar stool in Bangkok he showed Hansie his 'Cuddle Cards'. These were business cards with teddy bears cuddling each other that the counsellor had given him. He was instructed to give one of these to anyone who provoked him or when he felt an aggressive turn coming on for any reason. Rather than batter the unfortunate person, or bank customer, to death with his size 12 brogues, he had to hand out pictures of his teddy bear.

Hansie was not impressed. In his world, like Marc's, it was normal to batter people half to death when they got on your tits; especially anyone who may have a hint of kaffir in them – that is, anyone not from Afrikaans heritage.

"Marc, that's bullshit man; that card wouldn't stop an Afrikaner from the Veldt, boy. I should know, I've been kicked from end of the Transvaal to another every rugby match there and after in the bars. I think that shrink is taking the piss, man. How much have you spent on the ******?"

"Hansie, I didn't believe a word, mate. None of the shit, but it seems to have worked, man. Hear me out, mate."

And he confessed.

"I actually saw Mr Angry go."

He continued showing some emotion.

"In my mind he was very real, and I got to know him over all those counselling sessions and in my own time. I could see him in my mind and he became a friend, and then one day he just turned around to me and waved goodbye. I knew then that he had gone forever and I was changed forever."

As Marc had shown as much emotion in public as a great white shark and was not one for giving a guy an even break, unless it was his legs or his company's balance sheet, even such a sceptic and hard man like Hansie was truly pleased that Marc had come to reconcile his differences with Mr Angry and that could only be good news for him and his relationship with his tortured wife: and he told him so. However, Marc revealed otherwise.

"Couple weeks ago she suggested she would leave again. I went to see Rudi the psychiatrist again and he persuaded me to come back for a few more sessions and meet with her. But he told me that he'd been counselling her on her own a lot more lately."

He drank a whole glass of Chang beer and ordered two more for him and his friend.

"He seems to be spending a lot of time with her, Hansie. They are both ******* Frogs so who knows but it's cost me thousands as well."

"I'd be spending time with your lass, Marc, the body she's got, mate. And I'd take the thousands of dollars too as a ******* bonus. Get wised up, man. He's probably screwing her and hoping for your next bonus cheque," Hansie said, not being very tactful as usual and doing little to reassure the angst of the big man.

Big Marc drank another schooner of beer, scratched his huge head, put his Teddy Bear Cuddle Card in his wallet and looked at Hansie. He thought deeply for a while, his furrowed brow frowned and then he whispered through his shark-like mouth: "If that is really the case, then Mr Angry will come back and he'll visit Rudi again, but this time he'll be carrying a welder's hammer!"

Hansie knew he meant it and was delighted his mate had come back to the fold and away from Cuddle Cards and compassion for other human beings.

"Come on Marc, cheer up, mate. Let's go and see the daft pommie kaffir Jack and Digger. Digger looks more miserable than you, mate. He needs a laugh."

So they joined the rest at the other end of the bar and Marc, feeling suitably refreshed after his positive counselling session with the big Boer, ordered them all beers. He looked down at Digger who was looking into his cell phone as if it had just bitten him, and asked him why he was so sad.

Digger looked up and said: "It's Angel, Marc, she's all upset with me."

"Never mind, sup another rum and you'll be over it, mate," Marc said as sympathetically as he could, not really caring too much about Digger's latest emotional tiff but trying to be sociable with his very likeable and friendly mate.

"But, Marc, read this please. Tell me what I should do," he pleaded, handing him his phone.

He looked at the message on Angel's phone and it was a threatening text message from some guy. It was demanding that she pay this guy back the dollars she had taken from him some time ago or he would come and beat her up and take it. Digger had phoned the local police and reported it to them. Angel had gone ballistic with him and threatened to leave him.

"Why would she be upset that you phoned the police? It's a serious threat out here, mate. They kill you for **** all," Marc asked, rather puzzled.

"That's the problem, Marc. I don't know why she is upset," Digger whined and then holding back the tears filling his eyes he hung his head even lower – just like Eeyore in '*Winnie the Pooh.*'

Hansie had been standing quietly aside and listening to this. He looked down at the grieving lounge lizard with his hardened, weather-beaten face grimacing in disbelief. In his best Afrikaans booming voice, he shouted: "Brace up, boy. Be a man. She's a bloody whore. What did you expect?"

This counsel from the Oprah Winfrey of Bangkok on the past habits, or not, of his future wife strangely did not help stop the tears flowing. The Afrikaans, satisfied that he had made a man of Digger, turned away again, uninterested in his recovery or the outcome of his wise words. Marc poured him yet another rum and Coke and took his last 'Cuddle Card' from his vast wallet and placed it in the poor lad's hand and softly whispered in his ear: "Have another drink, mate. It will make you feel better."

And indeed after a few more drinks Digger did indeed feet much better and showed Marc and Hansie pictures of the latest ménage a trois – Digger fully ensconced with his favourite mask and carrying his whip.

The evening wore on with little talk about yellow digging machines, supply boats, letters of credit or cross-cultural communication. Talk was difficult anyway because of the bar girls clawing at genitals and stroking hair and massaging shoulders. In Thailand, like in the Four Floors of Whores in Singapore, it was difficult to know what sex is what. Dwayne's method of 'examining them like a hog' was not de rigour anywhere else, thank God, but the Black Isle, Batam. Doing a *'Crocodile Dundee'* that is, grabbing a potential female partner by the crotch to see if there was anything there that shouldn't be, didn't work so much as many lady men had their gonads removed.

Jack was still learning about this strange place, and was not very comfortable with the hermaphrodite nature of ladies, men or both in one body, and was even more educated when Hansie introduced a friend of his who came into the bar later. Hansie waved at a tall, good-looking black man who entered with a beautiful Asian girl on his arm.

"Heh, Nick, come over here and join us. You back in town long?"

The man smiled and came over and shook Hansie's hand, who then introduced everyone at the bar.

Nick then answered Hansie with soft West Coast American accent.

"Yeah Hansie, I'm back, sure am. Just five days, mind, and taking Angie out tonight for a nice dinner after here. Then back to Switzerland and head office."

He sat at the bar and with his lovely lady sat on his lap stroking his chest. Everyone looked at her in awe as she was a real beautiful, sexy girl. Nick ordered everyone a round of drinks and they all started talking and drinking about life. Nick explained to Marc, Digger and Jack that he was a VP and main board executive who had run Asia Pacific but now lived in Switzerland, but he kept his house in Bangkok and his new wife here, who was sat on his lap.

Digger was delighted to have a female to talk to rather than talk about work or male things like football, rugby, and baseball and went into his usual courtship routine, despite her marriage vows to Nick. After thirty minutes or so Digger asked Nick a leading question out of the blue.

"Nick, Angie is gorgeous, mate, but she tells me she's a lady boy. Strewth, she's the best boy I've ever seen, mate. I've fancied getting myself one to join Angel and me; would you recommend one, mate? Or maybe we could share?"

Nick laughed and replied as if this was just a normal conversation.

"No, buddy, Angie is my wife. I love her and she loves me. We are not up for sharing. Maybe the other two I have in Hong Kong. I'll bring them down next month. Now, they are hot... and they keep me on my toes, son. I think we'll have some fun then."

Jack shook his head and asked Marc if this was usual behaviour up here. Marc just growled that of course it was. "Get a life, mate." The evening wore on and Jack, feeling the effects of the drink thought he'd try to understand why such a good-looking successful man would marry a lady boy when he had the pick of any beautiful girl in Asia, or with his looks and wealth, probably the world. Nick explained the simplicity of it all.

"Most nights in the bar you will go home if your wife calls you or picks you up, and have a boring night sat by the television or listening to boring couples talk shit around a dinner table."

Jack looked at him and reluctantly nodded. Jack knew in Singapore as his family were living with him now that he had a witching hour when the drinking and fun with 'mates' came to an unwelcome and untimely end.

Nick continued.

"When you have been dragged home I will stay here with Angie and drink more beer. Then we will go to the footie bar and we will watch English soccer, a great priority as she loves it and I now have grown to like it. I guess your wife won't take you out to watch football or even let you watch it at home?"

Uncomfortably Jack nodded. After a few early evening beers in the bar he would be tucked up in bed or babysitting or listening to other couples' endless talk over dinner about lazy maids, the price of champagne brunches, holidays in Bali, etc., etc.

"You see, that's why I married a man; she actually likes drinking and sport more than me and I never get any grief about turning out with the boys. She is just like a man, one of you lot, in the bar she is one of the boys; but afterwards I can take her home and screw her. Why didn't you do the same?

Indeed, why not...?

The next day Jack headed off to continue Jon's mission to find out why the contractor and fabricator were not able to work with each other to resolve the fact that that the project was six months late and costs had escalated to those of the debt of Goldman Sachs. Jack was asked again to look at aligning the warring parties. The protagonists of both sides came up with novel new ways to surprise and educate him about managing teams and process control on projects.

During an interview with the fabricator's corporate project manager from head office in Bangkok, Jack began to understand some of the brilliant ploys and games real expatriate contractors could employ to sustain their life in sexual and financial heaven.

"Khun Jack, I am sick of having Danny shouting at me with his red head to get my Farang supervision out onto the site and effective. We have tried everything. I've sacked the construction manager, recruited four guys Danny's construction manager recommended, increased the day rates and added a loyalty bonus."

Jack sat listening to the demented senior Thai manager and remembered Father Bob's nod and wink and Ralph's revelation in The Sportsman's about his own project manager who did just that: all to no avail.

"So to be honest, Kuhn Jack, I've just got tough with them. Every time I visit they are sat in their portable cabins or main office so I gave them a minimum of six hours walking outside on the site. Anyone who didn't I would fire. And last week I did. Only two of them I kept."

Jack pondered before asking another question.

"Well, Khun Chai, I guess you have to start to make changes as obviously it hasn't been working in the past. How's it gone since?"

"Well, as you can see progress is the same, below target. But that's probably because you have introduced more changes to the scope; as you have done ever since the job started."

Here we go, Jack thought, Khun Chai was going into contractual defensive mode and blaming their client, which was normal and understandable but wouldn't solve the progress and productivity problem.

"Khun Chai, Jon wants me to see if we can change behaviour and get everyone working to the same progress goal but keep the contractual negotiations offline. I'm heading back to site and I'll try to see what the background conversations are and what is stopping them working effectively. Are you OK and will you support my recommendations? Danny is in full support. If we can't find an answer I'm afraid Jon is coming up and I'm sure we all don't want that."

Khun Chai looked shocked at the thought of the Iron Chancellor arriving and, for an Asian, showed some visible emotion, stuttering out and waving his hands at Jack.

"No, no, let's keep Jon in Singapore. Last time he came I had to stop my Australian construction manager using his car driver and bodyguard to shoot him after the monthly meeting. There is still a hundred thousand baht contract on his head. You go down to site, my friend, and if you need me phone me and I'll come and fix things."

Jack was pleased that he may well have some support from the Thai company but by now he realised that money mattered more than team spirit and that in Thailand life was cheap if you interfered with their acquisition of money or offended their culture. He would have to tread carefully.

On site he met the two remaining, lucky site supervisors. He observed they spent most of the day in their offices working hard, reading the internet, discussing their day rates and next leave period to Bali or Hawaii or generally staring into the wilderness that was the empty site.

The site was empty because the big steel things hadn't been built, of course. He was realising that this was classic real contracting that Father Bob kept secret; hope the job is so late that you don't even have to leave the office, as there is no steel to bother inspecting or men to manage.

Jack could see there was an ambiguity here with Khun Chai's instructions to work harder on site yet clearly they spent more time on their computers. But being diplomatic, he tried to get the answer through tact.

"Guys, I heard from Khun Chai that he has asked you all to be on site six hours a day. How's that working and why did he sack the others?"

The large built, older American piping man answered first.

"Boy, have you been out there? It's forty degrees and ninety-five per cent humidity. No mother****** in their right mind is going to walk around all day in that."

The younger, tall, thin Dutchman butted in.

"Even the Thais don't work in the sun. Look over there under the two thirty-metre columns, the painters are all asleep and it's not even lunchtime. Man, this place is heaven out of here but on site it's ******* hell, man."

Jack nodded empathetically but pursued his investigation.

"Yeah, it's the same in Indonesia. I've no idea how they work through Ramadan with no food intake all day. But obviously Khun Chai must have seen that you are all not out? He sacked two of you last week. Why did he keep you?"

They both looked surreptitiously at each other and must have decided that Jack was in with the arcane secret society as they explained the simple way they had deceived Khun Chai. The American smiled and drew close to Jack and opened his desk drawer. He took out a large bottle of sunscreen and told him the simple way they had survived the Thai's cull.

"The other two were both young guys; Brits. They hadn't been out here long keen and were a bit stupid. They decided to get out and do what the man said. They covered themselves in this factor two hundred sunscreen to stop the burning too. I said to Rudi here, 'That dawg don't hunt, boy, let the daft bastards go out like that every day. I know a better way.' So Rudi and I followed them every day but we didn't use sunscreen, I put baby oil on our faces so they fried."

Rudi laughed and interjected: "Yeah, Bobby is a wise old fox as you Brits say."

Jack was curious and asked an obvious question.

"Why did you want to fry your faces? What good was that?"

Bobby laughed and slapped Rudi's back.

"Ah can see you ain't been out here long either. Are all you Brits rookies?"

Jack just smiled and sat waiting for the answer.

"It's simple, man: when that Thai boss man came for the weekly site meeting he saw the two Brits had white faces and that Rudi and I had bright red sunburnt ones. Progress was of course as shit as usual so he lost his temper and sacked the two who he thought had sat in the office all day. And when he went back to Bangkok and we went back to normal behaviour sat in here."

The two survivors laughed and shuffled a few more documents on their desk and looked at their computer screens for the latest share prices for their investment portfolios, and Jack decided that maybe he should move on to talk to some others.

During his general discussions across the site and warring parties he elucidated certain clues to the fact that most there seemed in blissful harmony with the chaos around them. Maybe it was the fact that extracurricular life in Thailand was more of a priority and pleasure than twelve hours working on a construction site in the blazing heat. No more so than his afternoon post-lunch talk with Danny's Japanese site manager on the job who seemed less passionate and worried about bits of steel and wires, than he was about the staff and contractors' bodily wastes and ablutions. He showed Jack around the site and the offices and was delighted to explain his adherence to the company's health a safety policy and his staff's wellbeing.

He was so proud of his response when being told that there was a huge turd in the toilet that had not been flushed away by the unfortunate toilet user, he went into apoplexy. Therefore, he promptly e-mailed the whole project team to threaten them with instant dismissal if they failed to flush their bodily wastes away to the already sewage-full waters of the once pristine Gulf of Thailand. However, being professional and committed to the company project management system, he developed his own management procedure in consultation with the HSE and quality departments for the effective and safe flushing of turds down the toilet. This was posted above all toilets on the site. This was its content:

TOILET OPERATORS MANUAL

Enter the stall and appraise the situation.

1a. Adequate paper for the task at hand?

YES – Skip the next step

NO – Move to another stall and report the outage.

1b. Toilet and seat clean?

YAE – Skip the next 2 steps

NO – Wipe and/or flush as appropriate.

Vow never to do the same thing to others.

2. Do I need to sit on the seat?

YES – Sit and be comfortable.

Skip the next 2 steps.

NO – Raise seat the seat.

Aim carefully.

3. When finished, clean yourself and the area as needed.

4. Flush by holding the button down until the water stops flowing.

5a. Review the results for completeness.

5b. Does the bowl only contain clean water?

NO – Return to step 4.

YES – Exit and don't forget to zip.

Jack considered this a brilliant piece of project process control design that would make a huge impact on the project's HSE record and also Thailand's overworked and redundant sewage system. He wished he had thought of that and he could have spent a whole week designing and producing that and impressed Jon with his staff work for once.

He decided that maybe it was time to go back to Digger, Ironman, Big Marc and the bar, spend a couple more days of freedom in this 'Thighland' paradise before having to face Jon back in Singapore with the bad news later.

CHAPTER ELEVEN

Singapore

Kneecap Dara

Sometime in year one...

"I'm on a bender, Jack."

Jack received the usual greeting above from Kneecap Dara on entering The Outback Bar one Saturday afternoon after returning from Thailand. After this greeting, he asked this genial Irishman, for no particular reason but to start him off talking: "Have you not been commissioning today, Dara?"

"Nah, Oi got pissed last night. The job's nearly finished. So now Oi'm on a bender."

Kneecap said this as he pulled out of his pocket and examined a series of credit card receipts and then asked with a blank look on his face: "Jack, what toime did I leave you last noit?"

"Oh, I think about five fifty p.m., Dara."

"For feck's sake, Oi've got a receipt from The Four Floors at 3 a.m.," he exclaimed as he pulled a receipt from the pile. "Oi can't remember a thing. But Oi think there was still one in me bed when Oi left."

He then cried out laconically, failing to remember whom or what he had taken home that early morning: "Feck it, Jack, let's have another bender!"

And so it was with Kneecap. It seemed that he was on a constant bender. He had never seemed to work that much in the months Jack had known him. He was a real contractor.

He told people that he was a commissioning manager and that he worked on similar projects to Jack's all over the world. Jack had found out what commissioning was some months before and was beginning to learn the art, so he asked him a few pertinent questions like, did he colour in piping and instrumentation drawings (P and IDs) all day?

"What the feck is a P and ID?" the genial Irishman answered.

Now, as this seems to be an engineering drawing that demonstrates how a system works and is essential to commission facilities, or so Jack was told, that is, it enables commissioning people to press buttons that make the thing work, he began to wonder about KD's commissioning qualifications which were a lot different to Jack's project's own precious cherubs he had met in the office project.

Unlike Kneecap, the project's own commissioning engineers were perfect examples of real contractors. There were many of them on the project since the early days and many years before there was any facility to commission. This seemed odd to Jack when he first arrived.

He was told by the long-suffering, but then still naïve project manager, Danny, that this was a master stroke.

"I've never had so many commissioning guys that started so early. This is the best planned commissioning job I've ever been on."

And so it was. The intrepid commissioning men would take the P and IDs once they'd been produced and signed off by the super ego design engineers and then proceed to colour the various lines with different coloured marker pens. Curious to know why, Jack asked Jim, the wily old Scottish commissioning manager, what were they doing.

"Aye, they're breaking the systems down into subsystems. Essential, Jack, when we actually start commissioning," he replied with an air of superiority.

"And when will you start doing the work, Jim?" Jack asked, again very naively, for this was early on in his education.

"Not till construction's finished, and that'll be years late, always is, so we'll probably start one year after those construction fools think it will be mechanically complete."

He said this so confidently that it worried Jack, for he was still naïve and still believed that despite hearing Ralph's secret, everyone's purpose in life should be to bring the project in on time without hurting anyone. However, Jim seemed delighted that it would be a year late and he would be proven correct. Jack was astonished this date was well past the scheduled start for commissioning.

"So what will you do till then, Jim?"

"What we're doing now. We are colouring in and planning the job," Jim said triumphantly.

Now Jack worked it out that they had something like 300 P and IDs and had six or seven of Jim's cohorts to colour them. So that was fifty each, for say 600 days; that meant they were colouring 0.08 of a drawing per day. He timed how long it took his four-year-old and his playgroup to follow the whole set of lines with their crayons and they finished in three weeks. He also spotted that the valves were the wrong way around, unlike the engineers.

Everyone was in awe of these men. Except Jon, of course, who tortured them incessantly to provide him with a plan. But Jim was more wily than a fox who had been appointed Professor of Cunning at Harvard University, and he managed to even fool Jon that they were worth their enormous day rates and he even recruited more to colour in the multiple revisions of the drawings that Brian's wily Scottish piping engineers had changed to ensure that their Scottish mates in commissioning could join up the dots. Everyone was happy, except Danny of course who got more demented and Brian, whose man hour S-curves just got bigger and bigger.

These icons dressed immaculately, worked hard all day at crayoning and colouring and played unbelievably hard at night, but only in the nice areas of South East Asia, never in the remote hell holes where the gallant construction managers were passionately actually building steel things. As these were where the knobs and buttons for these demi gods to press and see if the big steel things worked actually were, Jack was surprised they never went there.

He was told by those in the know that to this day they had never set foot on any of their construction sites or the facilities. And when asked why did they never go and actually commission anything, Jim's epilogue was always the same, a bit like Danny's Here and Now mantra: "We're planning the next one."

Indeed, Jim did just that. He moved his little team of haute coiffured engineers to another of the company's projects and spent four years colouring in drawings again – and yet again, he never left the office or the bars and never set foot on the facility he was supposed to commission. A master, if not the Master – you should be in awe of this man.

However, Kneecap was in blissful ignorance of the crème de la crème of real commissioning. Jack asked him how could he be a commissioning manager and seemingly not read a drawing. He explained as he was well on his way to another bender, "Oh, Jack, Oi can read the manual and Oi can kick arse, that's all that's needed."

Indeed, he may well have been right, maybe that's all that was needed. Even Danny began to realise that his well-planned job was indeed well planned, for his commissioning team's pension funds, not necessarily for his liquidated damages avoidance.

Certainly, Kneecap was never seemed to be there on his jobs to press buttons or anything. He was on his perpetual bender. In fact, Kneecap never seemed to stay anywhere more than a few weeks or months.

He would tell most in the bar that he'd worked here, there and everywhere all across the world. Alaska, Greenland, Brazil, Amsterdam, the USA, in fact it was hard to think of anywhere he hadn't been. Being a true conspiracy theorist, Jack was highly suspicious of why this mercurial Irishman moved around so much and often at a moment's notice.

One day Jack suggested he leave his favoured Outback bar and come with him to The Sportsman's for some mince to eat. He agreed. They entered together, smiling and laughing over Dara's latest battle with his Indian fellas but Kneecap soon lost the smile as he observed the various British imperialist icons hung around the walls. He visibly shrank a few inches, hunched his back and tried to bury his head in his shoulders.

He stopped in his tracks and whispered to Jack: "For feck's sake, Jack, where have you brought me? I can't stay here; it's hell on earth and they'll kill me for feck's sake."

He was looking around the walls at the Union Jack flags, pictures of the Queen, Charles and Diana standing together in that famous wedding picture where they try to make him look six foot six and she is what was once politically correct to say, a dwarf, and Harry was glowering at him through the smoke as if he already knew his ethnic and religious origin. He tried not to look at any of his bête noires on the walls and kept his head down but Harry kept looking over at him. Jack realised that this was not healthy for his lovely Irish friend so told him to go and sit over by the window and he'd order the beers.

'Let's just go," Dara said.

"No, we can't do that," Jack replied. "Harry's clocked us, man. He can tell an unbeliever from twenty paces, let's just brave it out."

Jack went over to the table as far away from Harry and the pictures of the British Monarchy as he could.

Harry greeted him as he went to the lovely Loraine to ask for two Tigers. "You OK, big man? Who's your mate? I haven't seen him with you afor noo."

"Oh, he's visiting from Brazil."

Dara did have a tan after his latest commissioning trip to wherever he was hiding.

"Thought I saw him in the Floors the other night fighting with some Indians?" Harry said, scowling.

"Nah, Harry. He just arrived; works for Petrobras."

Jack moved to head over to the table and Harry grabbed his arm and never missing an opportunity, in full body shop mode said: "Does he need any pipe fitters, son?"

"Nah, Harry. He's in banking."

Jack moved towards Dara through the crowd and Harry just stood staring over, scowling and looking thoughtful. He could spot 'Fenians' a mile off.

This Jack knew well as he had been in the bar one day when a Scotsman came in. There was just Harry and Jack; Loraine had gone to the bathroom. The delighted man tried hold a conversation about how great it was to be in a Scottish bar. He'd travelled from Glasgow on holiday and been told about the bar and was ecstatic talking about the tartan kilt stall and all the football shirts hanging there. Harry just grunted and kept talking to Jack, watching the man, not asking if he wanted a drink either. The man spotted the one non-Rangers shirt hung on the walls from Partick Thistle and said that he supported them, clearly hoping to enjoy his time in the Auld Country bar. He asked for a beer. Harry ignored him and went on talking. He looked aghast and asked again. Harry just turned away.

"**** you," the dejected Scotsman said, and walked out.

Jack turned to Harry and asked why you didn't serve him.

"He was Celtic," he replied with a snarl.

"No he wasn't, Harry, he was Partick," the astonished Englishman said, shaking his head.

"All Fenians when they come in here say they are Partick, when they are really Celtic. I know more than yeah English will ever do about Glasgow, son."

So Jack feared that Kneecap may not get his beer. The good news was that Loraine had already brought it over so Jack sat down and both tried to drink up hurriedly.

Jack noticed that Dara was looking into a mirror but there was no reflection, and was reminded that the way to know a vampire was to make them look into a mirror as they don't leave a reflection. He thought Harry must have his own Fenian vampire mirror and ways of identifying the origin and religion of his customers!

Kneecap never went back…

Indeed, after a few encounters he did reveal his secret. He told Jack one night in Down Under after several beers that he came from County Donegal and had been recruited into the IRA briefly in his teens and had been asked to take part in a kneecap of someone for drug dealing. He got very tearful that balmy evening in Singapore and was very remorseful of this and on more reflective nights said he had given up to follow his chosen global peripatetic career of reading Mechano Set manuals and kicking arse. Many who knew him briefly in his frequent visits to the Doc's bar surgery often wondered what other secrets this mercurial man had. He certainly didn't like to stay anywhere long, that was for sure. So it was that one day he packed his bag again, never said goodbye to anyone and was gone.

A few months later The Commodore was in great form in the Down Under one Saturday. Strangely Steed was enjoying the banter and the tales of these stalwarts he had befriended over the last eighteen months since beginning his mission to bankrupt the subcontractors and suppliers on the project and stop Lord Paul gaining a new turbocharged Bentley. Big Marc was also in attendance and discussing with Steed the best way to liquidate the fabricator in the Philippines who had become particularly troublesome to him. The Commodore was uninterested in any of this as it was beneath his aristocratic self.

The Commodore was a regular visitor to Singapore as he sailed his own and the yachts of other people between his home in Hong Kong and the lovely tropical islands of Singapore, Langkawi and Kho Samui and Phucket. He drank in The Outback as he had known Dawn for many years. He had left England one day 'in a hurry' on his yacht and ended up in Asia of course.

He was tall, handsome, weather beaten with a full head of brown hair, very articulate and very experienced in the ways of the world. His naval career and life as a captain of merchant ships had made him forceful and stern when not enamoured with people or their behaviours. He could be pompous and aloof if bored and in company of lesser mortals.

There was an aristocratic air to the Commodore and he was distantly related to the Duke of Rutland, he said. He always managed to abuse Arun, the Indian IT man, when in town, not intentionally as the old matelot liked Arun a lot, but with no compassion or conscience in most of his observations on all things lower than his social standing.

As Big Marc talked balance sheets and liquidity ratios the Commodore was recalling to the rest of the inmates of The Outback the time when he ran a cargo ship out of Bombay. He recalled.

"I used to whip the bastards into the cargo holds with my bull whip. Lazy bastards, they were just as skinny and idle as you, Arun."

Arun, who was stood at the bar drinking his daily bottle of vodka which seemed to keep his only remaining internal organ ticking, just smiled at the weather-beaten matelot. Long ago he'd given up trying to integrate into this culturally correct disaster area which was The Outback.

The Commodore looked and acted like Harry Flashman, the renowned bully and rake from George MacDonald Fraser novels. The Commodore would have made a great actor in a movie of the book *Flashman in Great Game*. He may well have revelled in carousing with Indian slave girls and whipping punkah wallahs and tying mutineers to gun barrels. Poor Arun just drank his beer and played his awful music on the CD player and got on with life.

The Commodore when visiting Singapore always ended in The Outback. Most liked and respected him and he gave sound, but hard advice to many in their introspective days. He was never scared of telling anyone how it is. This Saturday afternoon he was holding fort and telling the Doc's bar patients about his days on the high seas as a Sea Captain, and how to manage lesser mortals.

Hansie was there, as usual with cigarette and girl in hand and his blond locks flowing in the nicotine-filled room, and he agreed with his treatment of curry kaffirs but was interested in how the Commodore had kept his crew free of anti-social diseases on his long voyages.

The Commodore, who was a contemporary of the Doc in medical matters, in that for many years before meeting his lovely Chinese wife, as an oceangoing ship's captain, he had to dish out the medication to the matelots who had caught the time-honoured marine diseases. He knew a lot about tetracyclines, penicillins and sulphonamides and he told the big Boer of his need to give all three for the 'Black Crab'. This was the dreaded sailor's hat trick of syphilis, NSU and crabs (pubic lice).

"Hansie, I could eradicate the Black Crab from most of the lads but the stewards kept giving it back to themselves. I was injecting so many, at one time I could recognise my sailing chums by their backsides."

Hansie nodded in appreciation of his dilemma.

Captain Abe just whispered to Ironman: "The pommie bastard's a sand shoe sailor for ****'s sake. I sailed more big ships than he ever did. Talks shite: just a sand shoe yachtsman."

Abe and the Commodore had many heated discussions over the size of each other's marine prowess; it was a man thing.

This talk of yachts promoted Ironman to change the subject away from sexually acquired disease to business.

"Commodore, this new yacht you are building. Would you like to build it out of teak? I have a load coming out of Sumatra next month."

The Commodore looked down his straight Roman nose and his weathered, lined brow and twisted his face at the American entrepreneur and gave him his usual straight-talking answer: "Of course ******* not! Are you insane?"

The Commodore was built of sterner stuff than Ironman's other consumers of his imaginary teak forest and would have none of it, but he was prepared to show Ironman what his latest hull design could do and invited him to cruise with him to Langkawi from Singapore.

"Great," Shaun said, "can we fish?"

"Yes," said the marine marvel, "we'll put rods out of the back, stock up with Tiger and rum and have a great time for a few days."

"Is there enough room? Where will I sleep, Commodore?" Shaun asked.

"With the boat boy of course; I do sometimes," the aged matelot replied confidently.

Shaun never went.

The Commodore was always a source of amazing naval stories and after many years on the high seas before he settled down and became a landlocked family man, he was a fountain of knowledge of the propensity of sailors to relax after a few months of sexual deprivation. It seemed to his friends in the bar that there were very few things in nature that the Commodore had not sought some form of solace in his early career after a period of sexual inactivity on the ocean wave. Mind you, given his comments on boiler stokers, and, 'until you'd had one, you never knew what life in the Navy was about', they doubted he went long without slaking his libido on board the ocean.

Buffalo Alf had returned to Singapore from an offshore visit to his drilling rigs off the coast of Sumatra and he interrupted the Commodore's discussion on sexual depravity with his own experiences in Africa. This was when he mentioned how the African Matabele were thought to be fond of their opposite gender or the bovine friends they herded.

"You bloody numbskull!" the Commodore shouted. He could be rather boorish sometimes. He continued and interrupted Buffalo Alf and the rest of Doc's patients' riveting talk on sexual behaviour between consenting adults.

"Unless you have had a goose, you know nothing about pleasure!"

This stopped the conversation dead.

Buffalo Alf asked the great man in what way one should enjoy a goose.

'Only one way, you fool, it has no teeth and a long neck. Use your primitive brain."

He was smiling with a hint of humour but the audience never ate pâté de foie gras again.

The great marine man continued: "The only man, woman or beast I regret coupling with all those years ago was an Eskimo. Smelt like fish. I sent the bosun out to bring a few on board when we docked in Northern Canada. We had to hose them down with the ship's hogger and I'd order the deck crew to scrub them with carbolic soap before I could even attempt it. Mind you, after two months in the frozen Arctic you'd do the same."

Well, Ironman thought, *maybe not*. He guessed that the Commodore was another hopeless romantic.

Then out of the blue, Kneecap Dara the jovial Irishman exclaimed: "Oi used to live with one!"

He smiled affectionately, interrupting this multicultural and multispecies dissertation on the relative merits of the female of the animal species; mind you, they were only assuming the goose was female, not a gander. The Commodore never confessed to what gender.

Kneecap continued: "Oi stayed in an igloo, for a few months."

All who were listened just looked aghast at this amazing man's latest revelation. The Irishman continued and stated emphatically: "Oi actually liked my Eskimo girl. Oi thought she was all right."

They all looked at the Commodore's gnarled and twisted face and looked back at Kneecap unbelievingly and interjected in his own inimitable way: "You would, you ignorant Irish twit."

"Oi nearly stayed and married her, but Oi had to move on," Kneecap continued, ignoring the Commodore's attempt at Anglo-Irish reconciliation.

He had to move on: the priceless mantra, from an endearing character.

That same day he had just turned up again after a few months' absence. He had phoned Captain Abe at tea time the day before with the usual greeting.

"Oi'm on a bender. Where the feck are you?'"

And when the good Australian entrepreneur entered his bar there was Kneecap, as if he'd never been away, ensconced in The Outback, mortal drunk yet again.

"Oi flew overnight from LA. Oi flew first-class this time. Oi pissed off all the posh passengers coz Oi was on a bender. Oi couldn't be fecked to go to work today so Oi'm in here, pissed."

And so he was.

So pissed that he couldn't remember again where he'd been. He was sporting a black eye and a cut across his eyelid. Abe had called the Doc down from his real surgery to treat the Celtic casualty.

"Oi'm on a bender and oi was drunk last noit, Doc. Took some Thai girl from the Four Floors and when she stripped off Oi didn't loike what Oi saw. Oi mean she didn't have balls or anything but Oi didn't loike it. You know what Oi mean?"

As the Doc had not experienced this close encounter of the lady boy kind, but didn't want to extend the story any longer than necessary, for Kneecap could go on when he was on a bender, he just nodded in response.

"Well, Oi told her to feck off."

"Phew, close encounter then, Dara," Abe butted in and stated sympathetically, hoping he could get on with talking about Australian Rules football or something less disturbing than unknown gender to the rampant Australian male mind.

"No, coz Oi fell asleep, didn't Oi."

"Oh dear, she took your wallet then?" Abe sympathetically asked.

"No, Abe, Oi'd already hidden me valuables in the safe."

Fearing what was worse than him losing his valuables, and hoping he'd been right about the unfortunate girl's appendages, Abe asked:

"So what happened then?"

"Oi woke up nearly drowning, for Jesus' sake. She'd turned all the taps on and blocked the sink holes. Oi nearly drowned on the fecking ninth floor of the bloody hotel!" he continued lamenting.

A woman or lady man scorned can be a dangerous beast.

The Doc was listening to this in amusement and remarked that, as the unfortunate lady appeared to have doubtful sex organs for the female species, she could easily have been one of his partner's first sex change clinical trialists. It appeared that fifty years ago it took some considerable time and a few unfortunate sex change patients before he and his surgical partner got the technique to the level of success it is now.

"Oi think I really pissed off two Indian fellas last night, Abe. Don't know where Oi was but I didn't get in till foive a.m. What toime did Oi leave you?" Déjà vu, Kneecap style.

The Doc examined and treated his eye at the bar, and after receiving a beer in payment from the genial Irishman, he shook his head, bemused yet again that Darwin's theory of evolution was proven correct; a naturally selected species of drunken maniacs inhabited this microcosm of the world. He took several more Crown lagers from a grateful Kneecap and was yet again dragged screaming from the bar by his spouse before Kneecap carried on his bender and the inevitable nightly show down with 'them Indian fellas'.

The next day, the Commodore, who had sailed a client's yacht from Hong Kong to Singapore that week and in a rare show of kindness to his fellow man, invited Hansie, the big man's girl at the time Siti, and Jack to visit his client's yacht which was moored in the

Republic of Singapore Yacht Club. This was going to be an afternoon of pleasure on the yacht's luxurious aft deck, drinking Tiger beer after the earlier Sunday morning session.

Hansie, also in a rare act of kindness, had asked the Commodore if Kneecap could come with them. Surprisingly, the Commodore had said yes and he left the bar early to sort out everything prior to the rest arriving after a few more beers.

As he left he said: "Remember to pick up Jack at the ferry terminal in your taxi. He arrives from Batam at one forty-five."

Siti confirmed she would stay sober enough to remind the two men who were well on the way to drinking their eighth Tiger beer each. They ordered a five-man taxi and headed off to pick up Jack at the Harbour front terminal and then head along the AYE expressway to Singapore Yacht Club.

Jack wondered as he sat in the five-man taxi on the way what the patrons of such a fine establishment and the yachtsmen who had moored their multimillion boats there would think of this motley crew on the piss next to them.

A diminutive ex-IRA man, who couldn't speak one sentence without a verb, noun and adjective and sometimes an adverb derived from the verb – to ****.

Also with a huge, smoking, beer guzzling, more expletive using than Kneecap, politically incorrect Boer.

A dusky, large-breasted, half naked Malay girl with a body carrying beautiful looks to do die for, and most of it showing or being stroked passionately by the big lad.

And also a Greek God, with a body like a temple.

What he didn't expect was the phone call from the Commodore.

"Jack, is that daft Irish bugger with you?" he asked excitedly.

"Aye. What's up?"

"Get rid of the man, quick! Dump him on the street."

"I'm not doing that, man, he's a mate. What's wrong?"

"For ****'s sake, Prince Edward is here, you have to show your passport to get in. They'll never let that Irish bugger near the place and we'll get bloody arrested as accomplices. Dump the bugger."

Jack had to think quickly. Difficult, you may think after years of research in this place and the habitual several cold Tiger beers already in the system from the Batam ferry, but he turned around and asked the hapless Irish mythical engineer: "Dara, did you remember to bring your passport with you?"

"Oi brought one of them."

"One!" Jack exclaimed astonished, but thinking he may have the answer. "Which one? Have you got many?"

"Moi New Zealand one, I think," he said, pulling out a passport that plainly wasn't a European-style passport.

"Marvellous," said Jack and spoke back into the phone to the Commodore.

"Commodore, he's got his Kiwi passport, that'll be fine."

"Fine! Fine! How the bloody hell is that fine? How many passports has the bloody man got? He'll have us in Changi Jail, by God. Dump him, dump the bugger!"

"Calm down, Commodore, we'll be OK. We'll just let Siti smile at them and push her tits through the window, they'll let us in. They always do with Siti," Jack replied, confident in the dusky, sexy lady friend's ability to distract even the most homophylic of men.

Her partner, Big Hansie, nodded his huge head of blond locks knowingly and compliantly, in agreement that this would be a good strategy. Ah, the wonders of pair bonding, respect for your partner and true love. Let's hope there were no women MI5 security there though, he thought.

Indeed, he calmed the irate and anxious Commodore down and they managed to fly through security without a hitch. This was a worry when you think that the umpteenth heir to the British throne and the Commonwealth was within a few metres of Kneecap, a rabid anti-monarchist, an Anglophobe Boer, a Muslim from Indonesia and an ex-member of the Workers' Revolutionary Party. Jack guessed they took one look at the Tiger beer cans and Siti's beautiful assets and realised these maniacs were no threat.

A great day was had by all. Kneecap was on his best behaviour.

He had to be because the Commodore had threatened: "To keel haul you, you Irish bastard, if you get us thrown out of this club."

Which was enough to keep Kneecap on his bender until they retired to The Outback yet again and he went off into the night to find those 'Indian fellas for a fight again'. And so it continued, until he left Singapore yet again without a word to anyone.

CHAPTER TWELVE

Jakarta, Indonesia

T Squared

Early in the project...

"Bob, have you ever seen Crocodile?"

T Squared asked Bob the above question out of the blue, one quiet night in a bar in Jakarta.

"No, I don't believe I have," Father Bob replied. He continued and asked inquisitively and somewhat naively, "What is it?"

"It's a movie about someone screwing a crocodile. Would you like to see it?" he enquired of Bob with glee in his brown eyes, raising a small gin and tonic to his olive-toned face.

Father Bob remembered what Steed would have said and quickly advised him:

"I'd rather not."

So began another conversation in Jack's long quest for the arcane secret of real contracting in the crazy world he inhabited. He was with Father Bob and listened to his Geordie mentor speaking with Tricky Tuan, or T Squared as the subcontractor had named him after watching him and his own quality manager skipping out of the Bat Cave in Jakarta, hand in hand, singing, '*Got to pick a pocket or two*,' à la Fagin and the Artful Dodger in '*Oliver*'.

Jack and Father Bob had been sent to Jakarta by the Iron Chancellor to assess the subcontractor's management systems and attempt to get a construction execution plan from them. As Jack stood at the bar drinking his umpteenth Bintang beer and inhaling the toxic fumes of Father Bob's twentieth Marlboro, he smiled himself as he heard T Squared's astounding revelation about interspecies relationships and remembered Jon's last words to him.

"You will take that unintelligible man Geordie Bob with you to try to get some sense of how these construction morons hope to build our steel thing. You know nothing of construction so you will need an expert. I cannot go myself so that Northern idiot will have to do. Try to keep him and you sober. I expect you to forward me an execution plan and a quality management system from those incompetent dotards before you return or I may run both you off. Jakarta is a septic tank so you will not go into bars and spend all your time with the perverts and girls that live in them as you appear to do most nights. I will keep your partner in crime, that American imbecile Tom, here writing his latest revised execution plan so you will have no excuse for your bad behaviour. Close the door as you leave."

Jack was smiling as he recalled it was Tom who had told him about the Bat Cave.

"Jack, when that son of a bitch sends you to Jakarta make sure you go to the Bat Cave. There's more pussy in there than the whole of Singapore. It's a man's bar, boy, lots of my buddies drink in there, tell them I sent you and they'll look after you. Goddamn, I wish I was going with you, sat here writing this shit all day for the kraut... what I'd give for a greased pig and a jug of sour mash."

Yes, Jack thought as he watched the hordes of little dark haired Indonesian bar girls swarm around T squared and his companions, Tom was correct, but he sure wasn't going to tell the Iron Chancellor he'd been there. Better pay cash for the drinks, no company credit card receipts on his expenses for certain. He was learning.

T Squared was big in the world of quality consulting in Asia and was visiting Jakarta as an independent expert with his own consultancy company to advise some less eminent quality people in a large Indonesian/Vietnamese prawn farm food company when he was introduced to the intrepid pair of Jon's ambassadors in the Bat Cave bar.

T squared was a very approachable Vietnamese gentleman, who, when he shook hands with Father Bob for the first time, it felt as if he'd just taken his watch, his wallet and his left kidney to sell on the open market. When Bob collapsed with renal failure later that evening and couldn't pay for the dialysis, he realised he had.

The client's quality manager (QM), whispered in Bob's ear worshipfully.

"He can get you deported in a blink, or several years in Changi Jail. You need photographs of the project manager and sheep? No problems, T Squared can fix that."

T Squared was the QM's hero, he was an icon to the QM, and he was striving to emulate the great man.

They were both quality professionals, that famous breed that has its finger in every pie; procurement, engineering, fabrication, management, etc. You can't do anything in the industry without a procedure that has been approved by the 'quality' department.

Father Bob had explained all about 'Quality' to Jack during the flight and the early evenings drinking through the usual haze of smoke.

"Bonny lad, most quality departments interfere with everything and have more fingers in more pies than Little Jack Horner, and if you dig deep enough you'll come out with something more bizarre than just a plum. This is because real contractors know that every project needs a quality department, not to ensure the client gets a beautiful new shining lump of steel and wires that actually works, but to create as much delay as possible. People strive to become quality managers or inspectors; it's a lifetime ticket to that new Ferrari."

Bob took a large drink of his Bintang and continued: "Listen to your fatha, son, I can tell you more about quality than that Jorman twat. Even if you move on from Quality, when you realise that you know sweet FA about 6 Sigma, and have spent the last twenty years earning huge day rates on jobs where despite your undoubted prowess at procedures and inspections the quality is still shit, you can turn to that other essential function, document control. Here you can see your career out employing a host of beautiful girls to do the work."

He smiled at Jack with the knowing smile that meant only he knew the real secrets of the job and industry and continued his lecture and yet another lesson.

"You see, as in all forms of human endeavour where brain power is needed and workers need to actually know how to use office equipment, IT systems, procedures and process complex information, girls are the only ones who can do this efficiently. Of course you could employ ugly ones and you probably do so in areas of the world where the normal dress is a bed sheet that covers every square inch of skin like a stealth bomber, or they are clad head to foot in the skin of a yak or they wear Burberry mackintoshes and tartan kilts and eat porridge constantly. But real projects and real document control managers are located where their employees are amazingly attractive and are proud to wear little or no clothing, which highlights their attractiveness. They do not fear the Arctic winds, the wrath of a fundamental religious maniac or the lesbian human resource manager. They know it makes sense to keep in favour with the boss, because they will be the last ones to store the million documents and drawings for which Ironman's Indonesian rainforest was destroyed to record and log the heroic efforts of the project team."

Father Bob lit another Marlboro and put his arm around Jack, looked around to make sure no one was listening and he concluded his epic on Quality and Document Control.

"Jack, ultimately only the project services manager, document control manager and his document control girls will survive the project services manager's genocide and ethnic cleansing as a project closes out. This will normally be some two years after the oil, gas or gold, iron ore is flowing and the arbitration court case is finished from which legal process the contract managers will have earned their second Rolls Royce and another yacht named, *Liquidated Damage*.

You see, document controllers are the last to store away the record of this remarkable feat of human intellect over the elements of nature. They are the survivors. It is Darwinian in its simplicity. The survival of the fittest because of one simple fact:

They Are The Only Ones Who Know How To Use The Photocopier!

Bob smiled and gave Jack some of the best advice he'd had in his career.

"Bonny lad, here's another lesson from ya fatha: '*Girls do all the work on real contracts. And a pretty one costs no more than an ugly one.*'"

Jack nodded in appreciation of this knowledge, comfortable that Father Bob must trust him to share this profound and secret philosophy with him. He was getting to believe that one day he may become a real contractor and Father Bob may well adopt him and let him join the closed ranks of his fellow practitioners.

As Bob went off to the toilet, and as he staggered through the massed ranks of partially clothed girls, his bony body being fondled affectionately by the girls and complimented on how he was such a 'big boy', Jack reflected on his experiences up to now and he realised some simple facts of contracting life. If he had to counsel anyone on career choice he would urge those who were not quantity surveyors, contracts managers, materials and safety engineers, if you can't be a document controller, then train to be a quality inspector.

He realised that inspectors are like auditors, they have to find faults or why would you need them? And as a consequence of finding faults, you need them to confirm the fault has been fixed, and then keep paying them to repeat this process ad nauseam.

On this project there were over 200 inspectors on the job at one time, a virtual real inspectors' body supply company's dream ticket. You provide inspectors at extortionate cost per day and their whole purpose in life is to find faults and instruct them to be repaired and then inspect them again, find a new fault and so on. That will extend their time on the job while the unfortunate client waits for his new toy to roll out of the production line.

Jack waited for Father Bob to return, his aching bony parts having been suitably eased on his tortuous walk back through the throng of feline masseuses, and in a moment of real contracting vision, he made his own paradigm declaration and sought to gain the great man's approval.

"Bob, while you've been away I have come to a conclusion which I think you'll approve of."

Bob took a long draw on his thirtieth cigarette and blew the smoke into Jack's face and said, "Aye, what's that bonny lad?"

Jack made his declaration, coughing through the smoke, but with a look of glee on his face as he knew he was getting to understand the 'bidness' at last.

"The time a project is delayed is directly proportional to the number of quality inspectors that are employed."

Father Bob smiled affectionately and nodded.

"Aye son, you're starting to learn from ya fatha. We might make a real contractor out of yeah yet."

The subcontractor's quality manager had brought T Squared along to the bar as he also had fixed up a meeting with Mr X, the owner of a certification company allied to the client government's certification agency where part of the project was being built. This was, in a true corporate compliance way, not really how it should be, Jack thought, but T Squared knew the man very well and also the quality manager thought he could help ensure the wheels of certification were oiled enough to ensure the project was not delayed.

Jack had considered the whole process of certification weird. All of these big steel and concrete structures need to be approved and certified by someone other than the 'Quality' Departments of either those building it, or those that buy it. Why? Well, Jack had asked that question many times in the past. He failed to see why companies whose intellectual know-how and management capabilities could put a man on the moon, build the Hoover Dam, find, extract and process oil and gas from beneath 300 metres of the world's most hostile seas, move it across deserts, seas and mountains, turn it into complex organic molecules – need a guy with a welder's certificate to tell them they've done it right – but they do.

Of course it is all part of the same principle that he would finally write about and publish in the learned business journals. These inspection and certification companies make millions, so do their employees. Large engineering contractors do not: particularly where the final approval is held with government-owned agencies in, shall we say less controlled countries.

Most of South East Asia was not regulated as rigorously as the West – Singapore a shining exception – and many colourful characters played a part in certifying this particular project. Mr X was one of them.

Jack had remembered the Iron Chancellor's statement on certification directed to his own quality manager during a grilling and torture session in Singapore.

"We will require approvals to be granted on a continuous basis with the proper documentation, government seals and stamps. We don't want to have to wait until the end and delay the start-up of our project. You will manage this process with those third-party agents and ensure the government provide these approvals at each stage of the approval process. You will meet all of our compliance and AFCPA rules, if you don't I will run you off."

Jack reflected on this motivating speech and worried that maybe meeting these third parties in a dodgy Jakarta bar was probably not as compliant as Jon probably meant. Nor was having T squared 'mediate' the process probably correct practice, but what the hell? This is Asia, he was constantly told by those in the know.

All five of them went off to a quieter end of the bar. T Squared had paid the girls sums of money not to bother them, it appeared.

Father Bob turned to Jack as they walked to the spot and said: "Check your wallet, son, that wobbly may well have used your dollars to pay off the lasses."

Jack duly did and patted his back pocket, but of course it had gone along with his left kidney.

Feeling important at last, Jack reiterated an edited version of Jon's edict to the assembled team in the bar.

"We will require approvals to be granted on a continuous basis with the proper documentation, government seals and stamps. We don't want to have to wait until the end and delay the start-up of our project. You will meet all of our compliance and FCPA rules."

Mr X's face lit up as if he'd just received a visit from Santa and he stammered out excitedly: "You want stamps? Stamps! Oh yes, I can have the right ones made now, very quickly and give them to you to stamp the documents yourselves."

Jack choked on his Bintang. T Squared nodded and added: "I can have them made in Vietnam. It will save a few dollars which we can all use any way we want."

Mr X and T Squared shook each other's hands in appreciation of the great quality man's prowess in stamp making and collecting. Jack remained speechless, his youth and naivety showing through in the face of such renowned experts in certification. Father Bob, who saw

Jack's pain and innocence, came in with a timely intervention.

"Bonny lads, we don't quite work that way. My friends, I like you, and I am sure you will deliver the stamps, but I'll never trust you enough to let you do it."

So it was that the quality manager was not run off and ISO 9002 and American Foreign Corrupt Practices Act (AFCPA) remained intact, and the Iron Chancellor's will was done.

Nevertheless, Mr X was 'in' with the government, so it was agreed that the quality manager would come over and talk in more detail, without T Squared in attendance, with Mr X on other things than stamps, and the QM kept on making trips to the capitol with his bag full of procedures and returning with the correct stamps.

As the evening wore on T Squared invited the two project men to visit him in Vietnam, where he said he could help with the usual delay by customs approvals, certification and general government interference of the project's small fabrication project that was about to begin in Vung Tau. Jack agreed that he'd talk to his boss, well his boss would tell him, if he could visit and help with these problems. Bob just stayed quiet; he had no desire to leave Batam where he was beginning to feel like a native.

They then settled down to enjoy the evening. The subcontractor's quality manager was an American called Brad. After several beers he relaxed more and was delighted that Bob was living in Batam and he delighted in sharing his own experiences of the black hole island.

"What airline are you flying back, boys?"

"Garuda," Bob replied.

"Dear God, Bob, does your boss not like you, buddy?"

Brad whispered this out of hearing of Mr X who was now surrounded by many bar girls, with T squared holding court buying them all drinks and new houses with Jack's purloined wallet. He explained his concern.

"They have improved a lot, buddy, over the years, but once I took a flight from Jakarta to Singapore and I noticed that the pilot and his co-pilot had left the cockpit to talk to a stewardess and take a drink of coffee. The plane must be on autopilot, I thought. Suddenly the plane humped as it hit a small amount of turbulence, the cockpit door slammed shut and the pilot went back to return to the flight deck. Problem was, he couldn't open the door. I sat in absolute terror as the airline staff began pulling and banging on the door, jabbering away excitedly in increasingly loud Bahasa. Unable to force the door, they began running down the plane searching for items that could prise it open. After several minutes of bending spoons, knives, forks etc. they must have realised that they needed something bigger.

By this time everyone on board knew of their plight and panic was setting. I said a prayer of or two I was sure this was the time to meet my maker when I saw an airline staff man running down the plane's aisle with an axe. He hurled himself at the door like a Tasmanian devil, hammering and chopping, bits of the door flying all over first-class, terrified passengers. Finally, the lock gave way and the door opened and in rushed the pilots, Changi airport in the distance. Yes, buddy, it can be dangerous out there in Indonesia."

Father Bob was unaffected by this story as he had no fear of airplanes, as he had travelled more miles than any living construction man and he topped the story with one of his own.

"Bonny lad, I once phoned Singapore Airlines several years ago from my site in Malaysia to enquire if I could buy their used aircraft tyres to use as fenders for my barges. I was told, 'We sell them to an Indonesian airline.'"

The night wore on and as usual Jack forgot his boss's instructions to stay free of bars and girls that inhabited them, but this time he had to look after his surrogate father and make sure he did not wobble down a storm drain or end up taken hostage by the Islamic terrorists that were very active at the time. God knows (well, Allah knows) what they would have thought of Bob's lectures on real contracting. He would have converted them, Jack thought, to the only other deity that real contractors worshipped – tax paid huge day rates. So Jack carried Bob back to their rooms above the Cave, leaving T Squared, Mr X and Brad to spend his wallet on the girls and sell his kidney on the open market in Vietnam.

It was very much to his surprise that on his return to Singapore, without any axe needed to chop down the cockpit door this time, that the Iron Chancellor actually agreed that he could go to Vietnam, but not to meet T Squared, as Jack had wisely failed to mention the Asian gentleman and his stamp collecting, but to try to get an organisation pulled together for the small construction project in Vung Tau.

"You will go to Vietnam and stay there until you can give me a sensible organisation and execution plan. As usual Danny's rabble is mismanaging these people and Steed is trying to claim it's our fault. I will tell them the facts of life today at the progress meeting that, on projects I pay them to manage, not to mismanage, if they refuse to do what I pay them for I will run them off and employ a contractor who will. We must all work as a happy, integrated team and you will ensure we do. You will go and help them while I crucify and torture them here. Close the door as you leave please."

CHAPTER THIRTEEN

Vietnam, Vung Tau

Radar Red

A month after Jakarta...

Before flying off to Vung Tau Jack spent the weekend in The Sportsman's with Danny trying to counsel him on how not to lose the 'red heed' with the Iron Chancellor while he was away.

This was Danny's favourite place in the world; it had football, Tiger beer, good whiskey and mince. It also had a Partick Thistle football shirt on the wall, so he felt at home.

It also did not have Jon, the Iron Chancellor, so it was his refuge, his personal sanctuary. Jack was his shoulder to cry on and to counsel in the days when the woes of project management made him more deranged than usual.

It was here that Jack, from his revelations with nights of drunken research with Father Bob, Harry and all his cult followers, offered his profound advice and lessons on project management that had worried Danny constantly, but he being a logical engineering man could only accept that it was true.

'When a project is going badly wrong it is an immutable fact that only the project management gets fired. The only way to get out of the mess is to hire more real contractors, pay them extortionate money by the day and extend the schedule.'

Jack had explained that everyone knows this except management and that project managers live with an impossible task. They are given by estimators and contract managers a schedule and budget that are impossible to achieve. The only way they can make any money for their company is to screw the client, yet they are held accountable for maintaining a sustainable client relationship. If this relationship sours, the company might lose the billions of revenue in those softer contracting areas where the same client is extracting billions of dollars of easier earned profit and the same contractor is being paid extortionate amounts of money by the client for building these big things.

That is, in countries where unelected corrupt governments are putting up the money or the US is rebuilding another war-devastated country and paying their tame mega contractors vast quantities of taxpayers' money to rebuild it.

So if the unfortunate project manager makes money in other areas of the world where profit is hard to earn by pissing off such clients, they are fired. It is a constant problem. Churchill once said that 'Russia was a mystery wrapped in an enigma.' Project management is no different.

Mainly, however, they are demented, misunderstood creatures.

Danny in a true symbiotic relationship helped Jack survive the long hours of work and extra hours' research in the bar, mainly by being with him most of the time. You see, like all Glaswegians, Danny liked a dram or two, or in his case a beer or two; the whisky bottle was reserved for after conference calls with Houston corporate management and to get the corporate financial audit teams pissed.

He liked football immensely and The Sportsman's Bar was welcome relief to the Filipino-haunted, Chinese money-exchanging bars he'd originally frequent. It was a relief for the wallet and for the project's team-building budget. The constant flow of funds from his wallet to the glasses of Gator Tom and Richie and in support of Brian in his attempts to control the engineering man hours had always made him sad and cost him mega bucks, and also added considerably to the barman's currency exchange business, the Filipino housing boom and to the eventual global domination of the Chinese economy.

Of course the reality that Father Bob could have told him why this happened and that this was just a logical consequence of real contracting was hidden from him. He suffered from a Dualist personality; he was either extremely happy or extremely sad, or maybe mad, and it doesn't matter for this story which.

He was happy when drinking and eating (even when he paid the bill; he was too pissed normally to care) and very sad when the effects of the Magic Molecule were wearing off, which was normally about 10 a.m. Jack was his comforter and advisor during these sad times. He always advised his lovely, overworked and very efficient PA not to book appointments during this period and certainly not to let safety engineers, material engineers, or Indian piping engineers or insulation managers meet him.

Danny particularly hated safety engineers and material engineers. He was always trying to fire them. His lovely assistant Beautiful Cloud had to stop him many times from physically attacking them on those mornings when his hangover from the Here and Now Matrix was too much for him and his ginger heed was throbbing.

Father Bob being particularly astute in studying the artists of real contracting probably wasn't wrong when he gave Jack another lesson on the secret art.

'Safety engineering and metallurgy are the subjects that real contractors should study at college. You will never have to work again unless your project manager is a sociopathic Scotsman.'

Danny also hated all things to do with insulation and painting. In one meeting of his loyal project team where Jack had to facilitate a positive outcome over a huge potential claim over faulty application of insulation, he made the statement in the presence of his insulation manager and insulation engineer: "I hate insulators more than I hate safety engineers. Insulation is run by ****** morons."

Yes, the demented man was adopting a humanistic approach to his management style, Jack thought. He was learning from that great motivator of men, his client, the Iron Chancellor. Subtlety and compassion had not touched these two great men, innocent virgins in a land ruled now by human resources and political correctness. They were both a challenge to Jack's skills as a leadership and communications consultant and a great source of material for his next PhD.

As they drank in The Sportsman's and Danny was talking irrationally about an early night again, Jack remembered that only a few weeks ago and after a particularly difficult corporate audit on his lack of progress and the subsequent early morning drinking session after his corporate bosses in Houston had mangled him, Danny had entered Jack's office yet again and sat down head in hands and whined like a modern-day Jeremiah.

"Mah heed, Jack, me ******* heed. It hurts. Four o'clock I got back to bed. Was great when I got to work, had me curry puff and now it hurts like hell. Oh, mah heed."

This was always the case, the Danny Paradigm. Come to the bar after work, threaten to come home early, have one more, and then with no willpower at all, be dragged off by his team into the Matrix which was Anywhere, a transvestite-run night club in Tanglin Shopping Centre. Another 757 later and a 4 a.m. finish, he'd roll into his bed, be up at seven and in the office by 7.30 a.m. He'd eat the usual curry puffs for breakfast, he'd be great, until the witching hour stuck and his heed felt like a thousand of Buffalo Alf's African bison were running through it.

Danny was an unusual Glaswegian in that he actually liked other football teams; also unusual in that he supported Partick Thistle. Someone has to. Being a Scotsman, you might think that's a strange comment but it is true. You see ninety-odd per cent of Glaswegians only watch two teams, either Glasgow Rangers or Glasgow Celtic, never both.

They do not actually like watching football played by anyone else. They don't actually like watching their own team. It's like going to church when you were a kid; you had to go because that's what your parents made you do. So it is in the sectarian society of Glasgow; from conception, supporters of either team were destined to go either to Celtic Park or Ibrox stadiums; Celtic Park if you were Catholic and Ibrox if you were Protestant, blue/orange or green, Tricolour or Union Jack, you didn't have to like it but by God you'd better support it.

The rivalry between Celtic and Rangers had nothing to do with football, it was to do with living and working in The Dear Green

Place that was Glasgow, European City of Culture, where the old religious divides between Scottish Protestants who made up the majority of Ulster's early population and the Catholic Irish who migrated to Scotland, were manifested through support of two football teams in Scotland. This was pure hatred in some cases and in a few old-school dinosaurs, pure bigotry. This has changed over the years in The Dear Green Place as you will be told in these enlightened times by many of each tribe, and thank whoever's God for that.

In Singapore, there were many great people of both Hun (Rangers) and Timm (Celtic) who could mix together without resorting to cut-throat razors at dawn. So it was in The Sportsman's. The only colours in there were orange and blue and the only flags the Union Jack or Saltire. This was Glasgow Rangers territory and Harry was true blue. The bar was home to the Rangers supporters of Asia and the David Cooper Memorial Society for which Harry and Sharon frequently raised money. It was also the home to the St Andrew's Society and raised several thousand dollars for the Singapore breast cancer charity. Often visited by 'dignitaries' from Ibrox and Glasgow, it was an oasis for all peripatetic Rangers fans travelling in Asia on business or pleasure.

Harry, who owned the bar, had left Glasgow many years before.

"I left in a hurry, son."

This was the only thing he had told Jack about his past life. As with Dawn, Emmet, Lord Lucan, the Commodore, Ironman and a few others in Asia, many of these characters seemed to Jack to have 'left in hurry' their last place of abode. One of Harry's best friends was one of the leading criminal barristers in Scotland and came to The Sportsman's every year for Burns Night, where he fondly liked to greet the assembled guests of Harry with: "It's good to see so many old clients in the room."

With this de facto evidence, you can reflect on Harry's past life.

Harry was what you would call a character. He was a wealth of information on real contracting, sociology, history, poetry, criminology and the past bigotries of Glasgow. Jack learned a lot about life in late-night conversations with Harry. These conversations would sometimes take place to the sound of a flute and the melodic thump of the Lambeg drum, the sound of Orangemen on a march down a Glasgow or a Belfast street as like-minded patrons would take up the tune of *The Sash* or some other subtle homely Orange tune. Most non-Scots felt strangely out of place on these occasions – and sometimes very confused. Danny was used to it all having been weaned on this in the tough Glasgow streets he had lived prior to becoming one those tortured human beings, a project manager.

Jack wasn't so well educated in the ways of Glasgow and after a few hours of listening to Danny's trials and tribulations that evening of how he'd tried to convince yet another corporate audit team that he was on schedule and budget, he decided to leave Danny talking to a fellow Scotsman and talk to Harry at the bar. Harry was talkative for once.

"Hallo son. I see Danny's getting pissed again. Does he need any pipe fitters, son? I've got a mate over there who has just arrived from Brunei. He's looking for a start. See Jimmy over there, son?"

Harry pointed to a very drunken man who had just staggered across the room towards the door to go to the toilets which were outside and next to the Chinese antiques shop.

"Aye Harry, is he another pipe fitter, mate?" Jack asked, not particularly bothered if he was or wasn't.

"No son, he's a scaffolder, but I can write his CV to look like he's a ******* mechanical engineer if Danny wants him. He's one of the boys. You know what I mean?"

Harry winked and nodded as if Jack was now a fully paid-up real contractor. In fact after several late nights, Saturdays and Sundays of these discussions with Harry and his friends, Jack had finally been allowed to know the inner workings of The Sportsman's and its true meaning and worth to the many real contractors who inhabited it.

It was probably after the fifteenth handshake from most of the patrons that Jack realised that almost all had either tried to examine his metacarpal tendons for damage or were examining his wrist for a scaphoid fracture. He was curious to know why there were so many men skilled in orthopaedic surgery – he knew of course that some broke legs for a living in Glasgow or Belfast but he wasn't sure that they were supposed to reset them! So he had asked Harry, who had winked that knowing wink that he used when he was about to begin another Harvard Business School lecture on William of Orange or Thomas Paine's *The Rights of Man* and finally Jack was introduced to an esoteric world of Robbie Burns and Freemasonry.

Harry was a Mason, proud of it, displayed it proudly with his symbolic ring and other regalia in the bar. Jack realised that the industry was well founded on craftsmen of all disciplines and many were on The Square. Many of Harry's patrons were members of the Singapore Lodge or lodges across the world and it was a natural occurrence to meet more than the average share whilst imbibing Tiger by the gallon in what was their peripatetic temple, The Sportsman's Bar.

Harry continued trying to sell his bodies to Jack for a few more minutes. Jack, bored but with an ability to look interested in anyone's conversation, especially when a hint of disinterest probably meant he would be found floating in the Singapore River with a sgian-dubh in his side or hanging like an Italian banker under a bridge over the river, nodded in appreciation of Harry's wealth of talent.

Jack was never more astounded than when he learned that the supply of skilled labour was the most important element of any project. How did he learn this unassailable fact? He was told it by every real contractor he had met in the first year; particularly those who had part shares in companies that supplied this labour or had a brother or uncle who was 'the best piping engineer to come out of Perth'.

The place he met these people was The Sportsman's or The Outback.

Initially he had learnt of this art in The Sportsman's and Harry was the man who knew them all. Body shopping, or supplying skilled personnel, involved the company which supplies the bodies, either employing them and passing them on to their client, typically for a fee, or the client employs them and pays a finder's fee. Either way, this business transaction follows all the laws of real contracting. Harry had explained this in two simple lessons to Jack one drunken November night whilst the patrons played homely marching tunes to the sound of the flute. "Son, the business is simple."

The longer the bodies are on the client's books the more the body shop company makes; the greater the loss to the engineering contractor.

Harry then took a sup of his gin and tonic and revealed his next lesson:

'And that means that the only people to make money out of a real contract are the companies that supply the engineering contractor with real contractors and of course the employees themselves.'

Harry looked pleased at revealing this secret to his new member. Well, as pleased as he could with his cold, gloomy visage that always looked as if he was about to carve his name on your forehead with his 'chib'.

Jack contributed to this sacred business commandment with his own conclusion.

"So Harry, I guess...

'That everyone is hoping for a delay as this will mean more bodies for a longer period. The bodies are delighted and so is the company that supplies them; only the project manager is sad.'"

Harry of course knew this, as did probably thirty different characters Jack had met who said they had men they could supply at the drop of a spanner or hard hat. This was all well and good, Jack would say, sorry, but he didn't employ anyone and stony silence followed. This was an almost nightly occurrence over copious Tiger and mince for months until the penny eventually dropped, hence Harry's attempt that night to persuade Jack to get Danny to contribute his get-rich scheme.

Poor Danny did employ people but he was always quick to point out that the contracts were always placed by the shadowy resource management group and he would have to kill himself if he revealed their telephone number. This was run by Peter, a sadistic Welsh project services manager (are there any others?) who enjoyed negotiating terms and conditions of employment with the masses and where ever possible ensuring that they never got what their line managers had naively promised them.

The Iron Chancellor's project services opposite number, Ted, had a pathological hatred of the main contractor and his own real contractors bordering on the insane, but liked Peter, and in general displayed similar traits to Peter, except he would shout and swear very loudly at anyone or thing, male or female, to make his point. Peter had been brought up in a different contract managerial style, more the silent assassin.

The client's project services manager had been brought up in South Africa where Tere'Blanch and Pik Botha were revered as leading strategic thinkers and politically correct management was still in its infancy. Like Peter, Ted was constantly trying to get rid of his own consultants and real contractors.

He was in a rage most of the time he saw any of them.

"What the **** are you doing here?" he greeted The Ferret, a real contractor electrician who had bought his own yacht and parked it in Phuket harbour next to Lord Paul's on the proceeds of his day rates. "I thought we'd got rid of you ages ago?"

The Iron Chancellor, overhearing this friendly greeting chastised him for seemingly letting the cat out of the bag.

"Sshh, he doesn't know yet."

Ted worked hard and he did look after those he cared for. Curiously enough for someone who seemed to have a sociopathic distrust of all contractors and their potential to extend the contract, he was always proud to say that he would be the last one to leave the project. Maybe in Ted and all project services managers is found the grand masters of real contracting after all.

The lads were getting rowdy in the bar and one of them, a tall Scotsman from Aberdeen, decided it was time for some marching music and he took out his flute (as you do) and started playing. They all joined in, singing their various Orange songs, however, when the flute player turned to the Scottish National Anthem, *'Flower of Scotland'*, Harry stopped dead selling bodies to Jack and turned to the large Scotsman and shouted in a snarling Glaswegian accent: "Stop playing that Jacobean shit!"

Which the man quickly and obliging did, and went back into the dulcet tones of The Sash.

Harry turned to Jack and quietly said in that menacing Glaswegian drawl: "******* Jacobean bastards."

Now this surprised our naïve Englishman as he thought all Scotsmen loved the ode to beating the English at Bannockburn. Not, however, Harry and The True Blues that inhabited that place. Harry explained his history seminar further.

"Robert the Bruce was a Catholic and Bonnie Prince Charlie was a

215

puff, a Catholic and he was born in Rome. That is nae our national anthem."

And he pointed at the large picture of the Queen above the bar and the Union Jack above it proudly proclaiming: "Our anthem is *'God Save the Queen'* and that's our flag."

Jack looked at the men singing their songs through the smoky haze of a packed bar and realised he had learned yet one cultural alignment lesson.

'If you sing songs that relate to great moments and men of Scottish history, make sure you know who you're singing with.'

But Jack was confused. Well, so would anybody. He tried to rationalise these profound tenants of Scottish culture and see some rational sense in it all. He surmised that the real national anthem is, to many of our Scottish Rangers loyalists, *'God Save the Queen'*, and the country flag is the Union Jack. They are British. Just as the Irish Tricolour is the flag to our Celtic hosts and they are Scottish.

Luckily, Jack thought normal people in Singapore had only to drink with these people. Paranoid schizophrenia was not what he'd signed up for during his extracurricular enjoyment. But every now and then, some normal people may have to work with Scottish people and then it is only sensible to try to align with their culture or face a Glasgow kiss or razor across your chops. He proposed to write a bit of friendly advice in his next cultural alignment seminar, they could take it or not, but if not, avoid attending Ibrox stadium wearing your crucifix and singing quaint Irish folk songs, and avoid Celtic Park with a bowler hat, sash and drum.

Jack was to become hypnotically drawn into the conversations over many a night and gradually gained a Master's in The Religious History of Great Britain and Ireland and learned something very profound, that was that whilst they might hate each other, they still didn't like the English. This was strangely reassuring, because like Pavlov's Dog, he'd been conditioned to believe this was a universal constant and it was comforting to know that despite their own bigoted, psychopathic dislike of each other – they hated the English more!

Danny came over to avoid the attentions of one of Harry's potential pipe fitters and joined in the conversation. Harry was delighted to invite the great man to his next Burns Supper the following week. Danny decided to take a table for Harry's lovely wife Sharon's breast cancer charity and talk moved towards Burns. What Jack was not aware of, until Harry's late night lectures, was Robbie Burns' Masonic roots, and he'd certainly never been to a Burns Supper so the thought intrigued him.

Robert Burns was an alcoholic, a rake and philanderer, suffering from venereal disease. If he hadn't been a poet he might well have been a real contractor or literary critic. His poetry is indecipherable to most and also for many others but his pen produced some of the most endearing verses and songs in literature; *Old Lang Syne* for one. His birthday is a reason (do they really need one?) for Scots the world over to get rat arsed and listen to even more rat-arsed Scots quote Burns at them all night. Purgatory for some and heaven for others, you make your own choice.

The conversation was interrupted when into the bar came a huge man, plainly well sizzled. As he entered he stripped off a Glasgow Celtic football top and waved it at the assembled masses. Earlier in the evening there had been a Glasgow Rangers versus Glasgow Celtic Derby match, something that resembles a Palestine vs. Israel kickboxing match, and clearly this man was enjoying the Celtic win. His huge stripped body was emblazoned with Celtic and Irish regalia tattoos; shamrocks, Tricolours etc. Draped around his neck were enough gold crucifixes to have converted the whole of the Inca nation. He proceeded to shake hands with everyone and abuse Harry and any other Hun he came across. Curiously, no one was offended; there was no attempt at physical violence. The size of him and mad look in his eyes seemed to put most off. This went on for some time until he fell off his stool, mortal drunk, and split his head open and lay there bleeding profusely.

Danny, who was standing drinking with Harry, had observed this behaviour with an air of disdain, and whispered to him: "Are you nay going to help him?"

"**** him! The Fenian bastard," Harry snarled out of the side of his mouth.

Sharon and the girls helped him up and mopped up the blood with a dirty beer towel. Danny whispered to Jack that her nursing skills in the jungles of Borneo had come in useful. They placed the big man on a stool and poured him another Tiger beer to ease the pain and hopefully kill the tetanus or rabies acquired from the bar towel.

Surprisingly, given his outburst, Harry went to him and began to talk and laugh with him. Both of Harry's guests were confused again. Danny asked Sharon: "I thought Harry wouldn't care about him, he's a Tim (Celtic supporter)."

"Nah," she said, "he's his best friend from home, Big Tam, and they love each other."

So they were introduced to male bonding Glasgow style and to Big Tam the Tim, and got very drunk in his company as he told tales of football and days gone by in the Auld Country, and they left even more confused over the cultural divide that was Scotland. Jack would soon meet Big Tam again and in different circumstances.

Not everyone in the bar was involved in this sectarian rivalry. There were plenty of normal football fans, like Danny, and from all over the world many others, Americans, Aussies, Dutch, Norwegians etc. who liked strange games like rugby, baseball, tennis, Australian rules, etc. The project team drank and socialised with most of them, the common thread being that all of them were praying, if they had a God, that their projects and expatriate life would perpetually overrun. Consequently, their life in the Rivendell of the third world would never end. Of course they were all delusional most of the time.

However, Danny was practical and conservative in most things that he did. He was from working-class stock, born and bred in the poverty of Glasgow. You were brought up to be hard. Work hard, play hard. Men were men, and women were mainly your mothers. You ate real food: 'not this foreign shit' as Danny often quoted from Father Bob's bible on eating in foreign places.

Nevertheless, even the most pragmatic of men would get confused when the world was not what it seemed. Not, with Harry's midnight seminars on 'the vagaries of 18th century Scottish political history' which he had grown up with, but with transsexuality, which he hadn't grown up with.

He was always approached on Orchard Road when walking home to his Scott's Road apartment by homosexuals and lady boys, or transvestites to you. These 'girls' were almost indistinguishable from real girls. It was just the Adam's apple, which some have surgery to remove, or their height which sometimes gave them away. As we know, trying a *'Crocodile Dundee'* – that is, grabbing their balls on being introduced – didn't work that well with those who had those appendages surgically removed as well. Dwayne the psychotic pervert from Batam swore that the only way to tell was to examine their teeth and their feet. He had a charming courtship routine as you can imagine.

Danny was more traditional. Four hours earlier on entering the bar that night he had exclaimed excitedly: "A Chinese poof," a transsexual, homosexual or just someone different, "just asked me if I wanted a blow job. I told him tae **** right off. He then followed me and asked me if I wanted his phone number. I think he had liked me talking dirty tae him, for ****'s sake."

This was a regular occurrence and most assumed it was his ginger hair they were attracted to, as he was short, wiry, with a broken nose and teeth, no Brad Pitt, and it was clarified by the Robert Redford principle, even 'poofs' can spot a big wallet from a little one.

Harry's bar was then, and maybe still is, unlike some of the other Asian bars, as the girls in it were not 'bar working girls' trying to earn money for selling inflated-price drinks for their rapacious owners. The bar staff were delightful, hardworking local nationalities and the clientele were polite and respectful to them. On very few occasions rude and aggressive patrons were dealt with by Sharon, Harry's charming wife. Sharon was from Borneo, and if life has taught you anything, it's that you do not mess with people who shrink heads for a living and are married to alleged Glaswegian mobsters who have access to Perry Mason as their personal brief.

Sadly, some people are not as educated in life and you can find their shrunken heads on Brando's sticks outside the fabrication yard in Batam or Sharon's condo.

Sharon was a lovely woman and it had never ceased to amaze the project boys to listen to her speak with a clipped Glasgow accent. There are plenty of oriental ladies in Glasgow who speak Glaswegian, they are mainly in Chinese and Indian takeaways, but very few who could also speak in Iban and Mandarin and knew the intricacies of how to preserve and shrink the heads of your enemies.

She helped many through some difficult times normally when the reactive depression struck as a result of yet another night of Tiger and mince, endless depressive flute music, Orange lodge marching tunes, and Big Jim, the chanter, singing *'Glasgow belongs tae me'* long into the humid night.

The night ended in its usual trip across Scott's Road to the Kentucky Fried Chicken and Jack bought a take away of fried chicken and chips. As Jack had an early morning Singapore Airlines flight to Ho Chi Minh City and onward to his mission from the Iron Chancellor to align the warring tribes in Vung Tau, he went home with his usual supper. Danny, his willpower destroyed by the last Tiger beer, walked with a Tamm the Tim and a few other lost souls to Anywhere's to continue the session and the usual 'sore heed' on the morning.

The next day, after arriving at the international airport, Jack took the boat from Ho Chi Minh down the Saigon River and sat crowded in with the locals looking out of his obscure, clouded window at river level at the mangrove and jungle that crowded the river banks, and thought of how this must have been so intimidating to Red and his fellow Marines not so long ago. But today Jack was more worried about the lack of lifebelts or restricted access to escape the claustrophobic narrow tube which seemed like a death trap to him.

He took up residence in that very French-looking town, Vung Tau, south of Saigon. After a few days of visiting the construction site and main project office he had begun to realise that Vung Tau was very like Batam, but with more class, and because of the French influence, definitely more haute cuisine and culture. The bars were cleaner, just as cheap and seemingly, according to all in the know, the girls were cheaper. Certainly getting a hair cut was an interesting experience!

The main bar he frequented was McCallam's at the Song Hong Hotel. It was owned by, guess who? ...McCallam.

He was a large, somewhat aggressive when drunk (which was often), Irish man. His bar however, was kept free of the many girls that worked every other bar in town, so that one could drink and socialise without having your body stroked constantly.

The reason for this was that McCallam owned most of the other bars and therefore took his share of the extracurricular activities of his customers there. His bar in the hotel was kept for his own lady and those customers who would bring their wives and girlfriends in when they visited Vung Tau.

Most of these ladies lived in complete ignorance that outside of McCallam's, the place was a veritable Sodom and Gomorrah with a bit of Caligula's Rome thrown in. They were delighted their hard-working, lonely men folk were so looked after in good old Irish style and whiled away their evenings singing Irish folk and rebel songs, served by respectable Asian ladies who were as innocent as the young Brooke Shields.

Jack began to like Vung Tau as a town, as it was very French-like, without the French. It was sad that Gary Glitter made it so famous. This famous British paedophile, once famous for songs such as '*Do you want to be in my gang?*' established himself here and ended up in jail for having sex with an underage girl. He was finally extradited to Britain.

The problems were quite difficult to sort at site so Jack was kept there for some weeks by the Iron Chancellor and he was met by Red who had flown over from Houston to Singapore and then on to Vietnam for a corporate peer group audit of the whole project's construction sites. He had decided that given the findings on the Vietnam project he and the Big Man, Gator Tom should relive their 'Nam days and see if they could help solve the problems.

The quality department was mainly responsible for the peer group and government teams whilst the project services managers dealt with the money side. Peer groups were teams of company 'experts' who were assembled from around the world to audit different phases of the job. They were a nuisance to the esteemed leaders as they disrupted the otherwise efficient working of the team and they might have come up with bad news about cost and schedule. The Iron Chancellor was particularly unimpressed when he heard they were descending upon his project.

"People on peer groups are no use for anything else, that's why they are on them. Does he have any experience?" he asked of one member.

"Yes, he's been in the job twenty years," a colleague replied.

"Well, he can't be of much use or else he would have been promoted by now."

This was the Teutonic leader's final confident statement on that issue.

The job of the quality department was to get them stoned every night and lost in the black holes of Batam, the Philippines, Thailand, Korea, Vietnam, China, Australia and Singapore. And make sure they had pictures of them in errant behaviour.

Of course the quality manager had been taught by the iconic T Squared for many years and was an expert at this, and consequently Danny or Jon never got a bad report. The quality genius provided his own reports, but these included only the police records, photographs and zoological veterinary bill statements!

Danny's purpose in life was to get a good audit from both the money men and the quality team. He spent a lot of the 'team building' budget on this task. He was good at it. He bought many 747s, Filipino houses for Richie's girlfriends and his like and Gator several hundred sacks of groundnuts, but it always provoked the same response in the morning when he came to sleep in Jack's office with his red heed hurting after another successful and positive audit feedback session.

"I must stop doing this."

Red and Tom enjoyed the first night in McCallam's and the next day Red and Tom met Jack in the project office allocated to them.

Jack could understand the respect that people in Houston had for Red's presence, as he had stature and an air of maturity and natural leadership. He could see physically and behaviourally why he had built a reputation as a strong leader and hard man.

He had been a military man and was used to discipline and orders being followed. He also normally recruited a team of company men who also had the same philosophy, work ethic and successful experience. In many places this work ethic, process and leadership had built big steel things efficiently and to company standards. Here the audit had revealed that the supplier was plainly intransigent to any change from their contractual obligations, as it was not in their contractual advantage to do so as they faced a multitude of engineering changes which they would argue caused the delay; and so had the usual impasse and subsequent dysfunctional schedule and cost for all parties.

Jack's recovery strategy was supported by Red and the also supplier, and it was to align both teams, remove the apparent barriers to trust and dysfunction, and get an integrated team to deliver.

The schedule had of course been revised many times to rev 3.142 recurring, helping the delivery pressure on the integrated team.

Red had showed his reflective moments for sure during the site meetings with him and the previous evening's social chat, and showed he cared deeply about his company and his team as indeed did Tom. Particularly his time in Vietnam had had a profound impact on him.

Red was a very perceptive and disciplined man and expected the same from his troops. During the short time Jack had known him he was very piercing in his questioning or statements and had a habit of leaning his head towards anyone and turning one wide eye directly into their own eyes, staring them down for a period of several seconds, awaiting their response. It was unsettling but got results as it obviously made people think carefully about what they told him. He expected and got the truth, but Jack soon realised that he also used this one-eyed staring in moments of reflection on life.

As they talked in the office that morning he revealed his struggle to convince the Iron Chancellor and the corporate HR department that he was correct in his management plans and style. He was very professional and accurate in his method and knowledge of how to run a construction site and took personal offense if this was questioned by those without his own experience.

Jack tried to console him that things would get better and they now had a plan and he would try to upwardly manage the Iron Chancellor, despite the absolute impossibility of that task.

Red was in reflective mode looking out of the window at many hundreds of large bits of steel and pipes on the yard and watching the painters sleeping yet again under the modules, when suddenly he snapped his head up, set his one eye upon Jack and said: "Jack, I can hear a chopper."

Dear me, Jack thought, *he's really gone now, and we are back in 'Nam' again.* He pondered as he watched Red, ears pricked and one eye staring at him and thought, *It must be awful to have those memories.*

Red stared away from Jack and Tom and pointed his staring eye at the window.

"Can you hear it, boys? I think it's a Cobra." Both Jack and Tom could hear nothing but the gentle snoring of the painters under the modules and that of the English contracts manager asleep next door.

"No, sir, I can't hear a thing," Tom answered confidently. He was thinking maybe it was time to have another long talk as an old friend with him about giving up this arduous contracting life for a well-deserved break.

"Yup… It's heading this way, come here and listen."

Oh well, let's humour him, Jack thought and got out of his chair and came to the window. Tom kept seated and drummed his huge hands on the desk.

They listened in the silence for some time and then gradually they heard a distinct whirling noise in the distance which got louder as they waited. Red pointed to a small dot.

"There, boys, look over the sea, it's coming in low."

He turned to stare fixedly at Jack with his one eye.

"It's just like I used to do to surprise the VC. I used to wait till I could see the whites of their eyes, and then," he paused for a few seconds staring through his monocular eye, "I'd let them have it, bang, bang, bang!"

He raised his voice in the staccato *blat, blat, blat* of a machine gun and continued staring at Jack through the one eye waiting for a response. Jack remained silent as it was obvious it pained him to talk about this. Red relented with the ocular inquisition, turned his head and pointed.

"Can you see it now?"

And sure enough, over the sea and heading to the yard was the plain sight of a helicopter, a chopper, getting louder and nearer. Hopefully, Jack thought, not fully armed as Red's had been.

Jack was reminded at this moment of Radar O'Reilly in that superb book, movie and TV series 'MASH', where he was always the first to hear the choppers coming in with the wounded to the hospital. From then on, Red would be Radar Red to him.

The chopper was a private one, not military, hired by the fabricator's owners to bring clients in. Radar Red looked very reflectively at it when it landed and Tom told Jack after Red had left to walk the site that he guessed the sight and sound of military 'choppers' still reminded him of his personal hell.

He returned to the Asian war again that evening when they were sitting overlooking the sea at a local restaurant. A beautiful spot and they were sat low down over a sparkling China Sea, talking about work as usual, and they stopped to look at the view, which all remarked was in fine form that hot and sultry starry evening. Radar again went into his reflective mood and put his one eye next to Jack's eyes, and after a delay of two to three seconds, which seemed an eternity to Jack and anyone else under Radar's scrutiny, and he spoke softly.

"I used to fly in low over water just like that, buddy. Hedgehopping across trees and paddy fields, across water as bright and shining as this, no more than five feet above it. Then suddenly we'd be onto the VC. They never saw or heard us coming."

He stared and fell silent for a few seconds and continued: "Then, *bang, bang, bang,* I'd shoot them all. Or they would shoot us. I lost a lot of great buddies that way."

He pointed his monocular stare alternatively at Jack and Tom and waited for a response. Tom just nodded in recognition and said: "A long time ago, Red. I guess very long time ago, my buddy. Let's have another drink to all our lost buddies."

Red looked at them in his expectant way for a moment and turned away to gaze at the water again for some time and then quietly he whispered to no one but himself: "It never leaves you. It never does."

And they drank late into the night and talked of happy times.

Red left to travel off to the site in China and carry on his corporate audit work. Tom stayed for a few more days helping Jack with his attempts to persuade the stubborn site management from all sides to come to the table and give up the conflict. Tom enjoyed his stay in Vung Tau and managed to drink most of the bars dry of Jack Daniels, made McCallum another million and bought several new houses for the lovely Vietnamese girls who hung off his huge body each evening. Jack realised after he'd left that he could not remember him eating anything during his entire visit, only groundnuts nuts yet again. Tom remains a true nutritional mystery to the World Health Organisation to this day.

T Squared phoned Jack. How he knew where he was, God only knows. But he had influence in many places, that is for sure; the zoo where that crocodile came from for one.

"Hello, Jack. It's me, T Squared, where are you?"

Jack replied to this surprise call: "I'm in Vung Tau, trying to sort this site out. Where are you?"

"I'm in Ho Chi Minh. Want to earn a million?" he asked, nonchalantly.

"Wouldn't mind, T Squared, but how?"

The Asian quality magician whispered in his quiet, Vietnamese voice: "Come up and see me, I can't talk on the phone."

And indeed Jack did go up to see him, that next weekend when he was due to meet someone in government for hopefully a bit more politically and ethically correct business purposes. T squared was consulting and developing a quality management system for a Vietnamese company and lived with a couple of mixed ethnicity Asian types, who he had supplied from his own company to his new company, charging his new company for the same employees he crammed into his three-bedroom apartment. He was charging the same employees many dollars to use his company-supplied apartment.

Jack thought he never stopped – this was a grand post master in quality management and stamp collecting for sure.

They went out for dinner to a Vietnamese home-brewed beer and eating house. Excellent beer, and it was cheap as chips but T Squared had ordered the Vietnamese version of Dalian's invertebrates. These actually had mammalian or reptilian backbones, but worryingly, these were very small back bones. Jack ate what was put in front of him. His comparative anatomical knowledge was limited. He came from a family that mined and poached the lands of an esteemed aristocrat and he had eaten most birds and mammals, but the vertebrates arrayed on their plates, after sucking the miniscule amount of meat that masqueraded as protein from them, were not of any species known to David Attenborough.

T Squared seemed to enjoy it and so did the very quiet and sincere Vietnamese that he'd brought along to meet with them. After a few glasses more of the excellent home-brewed beer, it was revealed that this man was indeed another Mr X, who could give as many stamps as the project may want and he could facilitate it so that they could provide as many body shops and quality people as they could find to the whole of the Vietnamese economy.

Jack was reminded of the many body shops in The Sportsman's, Down Under and other bars and also his Asian friends, with their version of this approval philately and thought, maybe it's time to make that million. However, one shake of T Squared's hand and the loss of his final kidney and strangely, the poorly fitting and worn suit of the 'money man', made him a little bit concerned that maybe a better, safer and more financially compliant way to earn money would be to finish the project and sell his business theories to Harvard Business School.

QED, he finally ended his days drinking Tiger beer in The Outback, talking to Ironman about potential squillion-dollar deals and poor as a church mouse. And T Squared is probably on his own yacht like Lord Paul and the Ferret in Phuket marina, eating rodent vertebrae and watching *Crocodile* with Digger and the Oblate Spheroid in attendance.

But probably it was a good decision by the poor consultant... for once.

And the next week it was in Vietnam that Jack met again Macadam.

Willy or Wullie Macadam was another ginger-headed Scotsman (there's only six million in Scotland and twenty million outside). He was a friend of Tam the Tim, despite Macadam being more Orange than a Cadbury's Chocolate Orange or Good King Billy himself. He was the head Mason, and head of the Orange Lodge in Glasgow. He and Harry had fallen out; over what, remained a mystery.

Macadam was a character and he assembled a few expats in Belly's bar (aptly named from the Australian owner's ample figure) to celebrate the Dutch protestant King Billy, the Duke of Orange's victory over the Scottish Catholic king of England at the Battle of Boyne in Ireland (Jack was even more confused than ever over this piece of history and why they wanted to celebrate it). But this was 12th July, and Jack was told forcefully that Orange men march.

Macadam decided that Jack, as he was there anyway, could be a token Orange man for the day and could march through Vung Tau with his mates and end at McCallam's bar – and so they did.

This was much to the amazement of the locals. This day they did not have their orange sashes and bowler hat, or the Lambeg drum, they just sang their songs and played the flute. Jack dodged into bars on the way, trying not to be associated with these lunatics, but couldn't escape as they dragged him out screaming each time. '*The Sash*' had never been heard by the astonished Vietnamese and Jack doubted whether it would again.

As they ended up paralytic in McCallam's bar they retold the tales of old marches. The squad had actually marched down an Indonesian village one day fully sashed and bowler hatted with drums and flutes aloud. One can now understand why the North Vietnamese kicked out the foreigners all those years ago and maybe you may still wonder why they didn't, that fine day in Vung Tau on July 12th.

A few days after the Orange March Jack travelled again in Ho Chi Minh visiting the regional corporate offices of the fabricator to discuss his plans for solving the disputes and conflicts on site when coincidently he bumped into Tam the Tim in the reception. This time instead of being stripped to the waist, heed wrapped in a bloody beer towel and looking like he was about to join the cast of '*BraveHeart*,' he was as immaculately dressed as Steed. An amazing transformation and he was waiting to enter the offices, with an expensive Savile Row looking suit, leather briefcase and huge smile.

Jack greeted him with a wary nod: "Hallo, mate."

'Heh, big man, gud tae see ya agin," growled Tam, moving solidly towards the consultant. "Ah didna know that yeah wor working here, big fella?" he said, shaking Jack's hand in a firm bone-crunching grip.

"Aye," Jack said, trying to feel the blood return to his fingers, "I didn't know you were in the business?" The pain from his crushed hand eased somewhat.

"Aye," he explained. "My name's Tam and whit's yours, my brother?"

Big Tam was actually head honcho of a globally recognised certification company. Big Tam could speak Mandarin, or at least sing it when pissed, and he was a repository of knowledge about Asia and the industry. Like Harry, the big man had grown up in Scotland and he was subject to the usual sectarian rules. As a Catholic he was vehemently Celtic but was friends with many Rangers supporters. He was just liked by many. Jack asked him about the person he was visiting today, whom they both knew to be rather obnoxious and conceited.

"Big man, if you had an elephant, he'd have a ******* cage to put it in," was his reply about this type of person. "Let's have a beer tonight, big man. I know a few good bars. Lots of lads like us... know what I mean?" and he tapped his huge head as if Jack should know what he meant. Jack didn't know, but he was now used to the strange secret behaviours of real contractors, especially the Scottish ones, so he agreed to the meet.

During the evening's entertainment, which consisted of lots of drunken Scotsmen getting even more pissed, little food and lots of girls hanging off large men, Jack found out that Tam knew of T Squared and many other quality managers and knew many 'colourful' characters across Asia, and that he moved in similar essential stamp-collecting avenues. They were all in awe of the big Scotsman, so Tam, Jack guessed, must have been a post master general.

Tam knew of all the legitimate ways to gain 'stamps' and was on best terms with ministers, presidents and Mr X. He told Jack he would expand upon these many stories but he was under the Official Secrets Act and T Squared knew where he lived and he still has the photographs of that crocodile!

Jack finally returned to Singapore and faced the inquisition from his Teutonic boss. As the site had now returned to meeting the revised 3.142 schedule, his boss was pleasantly pleased for once. Jack took the few usual, and masterly blows to his self-esteem with dignity, and also the satisfaction that he had lasted three years now and the Iron Chancellor had not run him off... yet.

CHAPTER FOURTEEN

Singapore

The Iron Chancellor

The third year...

Gator Tom looked at Lee the Boxer and both could read each other's mind. Only in The Outback could you have a failed assassination plot and be taught how to kill a Cape buffalo and cook an African elephant's trunk.

Buffalo Alf was visiting again, and Tom had invited him out with some of his American colleagues for the usual night of drink and debauchery. It seemed that Buffalo Alf had family who lived in Africa and needless to say he was not enamoured when he heard that a certain African dictatorial leader was being treated in a Singapore hospital. The Doc, who was on the edge of the company, had heard Alf's comments and shouted in his maniacal way: "That bastard, I hate him and all these bloody men in whitewash who let him and his like come here. I'd shoot the lot of the bastards."

His mention of the men in whitewash was a parody on the book '*The Men in White*', a history of the People's Action Party (PAP), and the ruling Singapore political party since independence in 1965. It was led from conception by Lew Kuan Yew from 1959 to 1990; his son became current prime minster after his resignation.

To continue; ominously in this case the Doc's ranting seemed to strike a chord in the American white hunter's African head and as he listened to the rant he had quietly been considering his plan, and he declared: "I'll strangle the bastard. All I need is to get close to him and I'll do it now."

The Doc, excited now and clearly building up to a crescendo of angst, shouted across the crowded room, too loudly for some of those who were locals, given the possibility of the Singapore secret police and microphones located next to them in Dawn's emporium.

"Let's go now. I can get us through the hospital and I can get you close and you can strangle the bastard."

They began to drink up their beer to head off on their mission, when it was suggested by a couple of the more enlightened patrons that given the chance of escape was nil, and that the noose awaited anyone here, especially if you were to show the government security to be inefficient, it would be sensible to have a couple more beers and think upon it some more.

This they decided was a wise cause of action and after two more Crown lagers the Doc was too pissed to bother and started arguing with Kjel the Norwegian about how, with his daily drinking habits and blood pressure, he should be dead.

Alf finished this session with a description of how to kill a Cape Buffalo, in similar manner to the way he described it to Jack a few years before, and also how to eat an elephant's trunk, which he reckoned was the most valued by the African tribes, and should always be donated free and gratis to the tribal chief. It is, in his opinion, delicious. He also explained that if you are faced with a charging bull elephant, make sure you have your 700 Nitro Express with you. All assured him they would keep one ready at all the time just in case.

For those budding Jamie Olivers out there, or in the case of the one female reader, the gorgeous Nigella Lawson, this is the recipe, according to Buffalo Alf.

ELEPHANTS TRUNK AUX CHAMPIGNONS

First: track and shoot an elephant, preferably with a 700 Nitro Express.

Second: *cut off the trunk with a handy pocket Swiss army knife or get one of the beaters to hack it off with his machete.*

Third: *take a pair of ordinary pliers, put your foot on the trunk and grab the mucous membrane inside one nostril and rive the membrane with all the blood and mucus out. Repeat with the other nostril.*

Fourth: *feed this to the raging mob of jackals that are surrounding you now to keep them from attacking you whilst you prepare the main delicacy.*

Fifth: *roast the trunk on a roaring bush fire for 30 minutes; take care to avoid stampeding wildebeests.*

Sixth: *peel off skin and enjoy with nice Chablis and a few buttered mushrooms.*

Most of them settled for chicken rice from the local hawker centre that evening.

Buffalo Alf also had a recipe for goat tripe curry which he gave out freely to the assembled lunatics in the bar that night. This was very timely and pertinent because Dawn had been given the frozen goat by a vendor who was exhibiting at an Aussie Food and Beverage Expo at Changi Expo Centre.

Dawn had been invited there by the two intrepid goat chop vendors as she had relieved them of most of their savings the night before in The Outback and they gave her three tickets in the hope she would come along with a couple of friends, and the visitors to their stand would buy enough to pay for their flight home to Melbourne.

Sadly for them, Dawn invited Arun the Indian IT man to go with her. As Arun never had much money in those days – well, not his own – the goat herders had to stay more nights at Dawn's emporium working as her new bar girls to pay for the mountains of free drink and food that their guests ate at the Expo and for the excessive and extortionate drinks she kept serving them again that night.

Dawn was given a free goat in exchange for the bill. This was chopped up at the bar sink by Buffalo Alf (no environmental health issues in The Outback, because the inspector was still hidden in Dawn's bosom) with his array of knives he kept in his coat: the killing one, the skinning one and the boning one, as one does. He gave a few of the local drunks some meat and also pieces of the tripe too.

Some took the bits of Billy Goat Gruff home to their delighted wives, with a recipe for cooking the tripe. Of course Buffalo Alf was an expert on the entrails of cloven-hoofed beasts, you may gather by now. Arun's lovely Indian mother tried to cook it and was evicted from her condo, for the smell was worse than an astronaut's underpants. Gator Tom threw his down a storm drain on the way home for the rats, hoping Father Bob or Martin the Oblate Spheroid wasn't lying in it. Everyone else gave up after boiling for only twenty minutes because the smell was obscene and horrendous.

Buffalo explained that if you ever have the need to eat goat tripe curry, you need to boil the tripe for six hours to soften the surrounding membranes of the smooth muscle and he duly cooked his curry. He had a full-blown cannibal cooking pot in his rented condo's garden, powered up by butane gas burners in which he cooked various exotic dishes of endangered species and their entrails. His neighbours had moved to California – the African veldt and its cuisine were not for them.

The next night Buffalo Alf brought the curry into the bar and those in Dawn's company all enjoyed the rewards of the African's cooking pot and the impecunious Australian goat herders' enforced generosity. All agreed it was indeed worth eating; not cooking, mind, but definitely worth getting your local African neighbour to knock you up a dish or two.

Alf had shot most species, and possibly *Homo sapiens* and the Batam experience had demonstrated to Jack that the whole meaning of sustainable development may not really have got through to most of those who work in the resource pillaging industries, especially with social and community impact and management.

He mentioned this to Jon one day, and that maybe it was time to realign the team to the cultural and sustainability goals they had originally taken time to work with them on. Jon was not impressed.

"You have already done that. I see no reason to take my staff away from doing staff work that is important to delivering this on time. Are you telling me you have failed in your job?"

"Eh… no… Jon," Jack stammered, thinking maybe here it was, the ticket home. "It's just that maybe everyone just needs a reminder and it will help to have some team building with them anyway. It's been a while since we did anything positive with the boys here in Singapore, Jon."

"If you wish to have an event to celebrate good staff work or progress I will endorse that. If you are confused over why you want to spend money on them for cultural awareness, sustainable development or reward for delivering results, then sit down and I will have to discuss with you why you are deviating from expected results and your execution plan. If you have no clear use on this project I will run you off."

Jack swallowed hard and quickly replied. "No, Jon, it's quite clear, I will take them all bowling and we can mix up the teams, even invite some locals with the expats to engender cross-cultural bonding. A few beers afterwards and everyone will be happy."

Jon looked at Jack for a few moments which seemed like an eternity and far worse than Radar Red's one-eyed stare.

"That will be acceptable. I will review your progress next Friday, please book the appointment in the system. Go and sort it and close the door behind you."

Jack walked out sweating; a close shave, another few weeks' grace hopefully.

In Singapore the project team were more interested in the human animals that they may harm, or more importantly may harm them, by living in these multicultural times.

They had started investing heavily in cultural awareness training in Singapore and the many other Asian offices and sites and with key suppliers across the globe at the beginning of the engineering phase; this had been one of Jack's many tasks allocated by Jon. This was to ensure they did not upset the locals too much and would leave a positive legacy in terms of cultural improvement.

The first seminars were run by the Singaporean corporate human resource director and his sadistic henchman, who made Igor from '*Young Frankenstein*' look like Mary Poppins. Everyone was told that they would be flogged within an inch of their lives, keelhauled and have their balls nailed to the Merlion (mythical half lion, half beast symbol of Singapore), if they so much as spat one piece of chewing gum on the pavement.

These Singaporeans informed everyone that in Batam, if they so much as fell asleep with a girl she'd have the whole medical team from the renal unit around and zap, gone in the blink of an eye: you'd wake up minus your right kidney, sold to the highest bidder in Jakarta (as T Squared had taken Father Bob's left kidney he was very worried about this one).

Anywhere in Malaysia was like the Bronx, Gaza or an IS-held region in Syria; just don't go near as an Anglo-Saxon type – and in the Philippines they would kidnap you for the price of a St Miguel; in Thailand all would end up sex slaves – and in China, Vietnam or Korea, heaven forbid they stepped out of line. Chinamen would torture them by feeding them invertebrates as food if they darkened their KTV lounges.

If the purpose of these lectures was to scare everyone into finishing the project on time and go home, leaving the next job to be done by local nationals, by which time most expats began suspect it was, it didn't really work. It didn't really have an effect because most real contractors had been to a lot worse places than this. Alaska, Port Moresby, Baghdad, Lagos, Darwin and of course Aberdeen or Middlesbrough come to mind. Those of you who have had the pleasure of working in these places will know that. The attached press cutting on the delights of Aberdeen may remind some of you of these cultural beauties. Remember, you have a choice!

Finally, The Mirror sent reporter Jenny Johnston to Aberdeen to test the claim, made in the British Journal of Psychiatry, that Aberdeen is the nation's most miserable city, where up to 20% of residents suffer from seasonal affective disorder (SAD).

One of the people she approached was a grey-coated man waiting for a bus. Did he think, she asked, that Aberdeen deserved its title as the most miserable place on earth? "F*** off," he replied.

The sadistic henchman told of the Changi Jail rattan cane and how it would take a backside to the bone with one stroke by men trained to hurt, causing impotence if it carried on to the nerves – a frightening thought for most of the rampant males. However, Singapore was softie contracting territory and a few minor skirmishes with the generally friendly locals was to be expected. Unlike Batam and elsewhere, where they were advised the jungle and a shallow grave beckoned the unaligned and culturally unaware.

Of course many of the contractors were intractable and were not really here for anything but the money: culture was a thing for people with time on their hands.

Steed the contracts manager was articulate and refined, yet some elements of the region's culture left him high and dry. Lion dances are remarkable events with colour, vibrancy and life and are held all over Chinese-inhabited Asia at the Lunar New Year period. Jack had invited him to a Lion dance on the first Chinese New Year, his reply the predictable: "I'd rather not."

Some, like the gun-toting endangered species killers had needed careful counselling when out and about in the region.

Gator was worried one day. Randy, his colleague, was off to Cambodia on holiday, the scene of his past war nightmares in the seventies. The night before he had left for Cambodia he had a rather aggressive moment for him as, being a client, he normally spent all day working hard asleep in his office but that night he attacked a supplier who had angered him (not chilled out enough, it seemed).

"Hell, Danny, I hope he don't have any flashbacks in Cambodia. He chased that supplier around Harry's Bar with his double-edged Gook knife last night," Tom remarked to Danny quietly over a Tiger and several bowls of empty peanuts for his dinner.

Luckily, Randy enjoyed his return to his own personal killing fields of South East Asia without incident and his double-edged Gook knife remained sheathed.

Jack had decided to include Randy in his cultural awareness seminars along with the Big Man very early in the project as he slowly became more aware of their military affection and laid-back behaviours.

The avuncular American Gator Tom was a man of habit. Most engineers are, but he only went to two bars, the Here and Now (which he was shortly to own) and The Country Jamboree. For his huge bear size he was a shy man. He'd walk nowhere. He never took public transport, only taxis and big ones at that. He liked to know who was around him. When during the early days of his assignment in Asia the world was still gripped in the aftermath of terrorist attacks across the globe and he was hard to miss. His huge head was a 'sniper's dream': a head like a medicine ball.

His colleague, Randy, of Gook knife fame, was lean and tall, an ex-Marine, 'Nam' veteran. He was much quieter than Gator as he originated from the West Coast and in many ways was typical of the place. He was a child of the sixties and seemed some days that he could still be there; he was definitely chilled out, that's for sure; whether he was hallucinating under psychedelics or he was remembering the sixties when on 'wacky baccy', it was hard to tell. He sat in his office most days with an unlit cigar in his mouth, just staring out into the wilderness that was the Singapore skyline.

One day Jack asked him: "What's the craic today, Randy? You look puzzled about something."

"Just remembering Woodstock, buddy, just chilling out," he replied.

He seemed not to do much else. However, as you may now understand, he was a real client and real work was for contractors.

He sometimes loosened up though, and one fine evening Randy and Gator Tom, Father Bob and Jack were drinking in a more refined establishment than usual, in the Amara Hotel bar. They both held a louder than necessary conversation, smoking huge Cuban cigars.

They were watching the American Air Force and Allies obliterate remote Islamic villages on CNN, in a bar full of local indigenous people, many wearing Muslim headgear.

"Whoa, sure did give those Ayrabs a good pasting," shouted Gator to no one in particular. His voice was as big as his body though and, given the native surroundings, it was a little too loud for Father Bob and Jack.

A few minutes later his colleague, Randy, seemed to be in a meditative state yet again and staring at the carnage erupting on the telly, staggered a bit side to the side, as if dizzy or disoriented.

"Whoa, just had a 'Nam flashback there, boy."

He uttered this with a glazed look on his face, and this confirmed the need to move on and the two English observers took Father Bob's whispered advice: "Jack, let's get the hell out of here son, those 'wobblies'," all non-Chinese to Father Bob; Malay, Indonesian, were Indian-looking folk, "look as if they are gonna kick our arses."

They slipped out of the side door whilst the Big Man continued to extol the virtues of Western Democracy via F16s and smart bombs and Randy began whooping with joy at the smell of the butane cigar lighter as he lit another Cuban monster, remembering the days gone by of *Apocalypse Now* and "the smell of napalm in the morning."

They smoked more in cigars than the local bar staff earned in a month, and their reflections on *Apocalypse Now* and George Bush's 'war on terror' may have left the Asian masses pretty well convinced that maybe the insurgent's style of democracy wasn't too bad after all.

Danny attended a few of these workshops but sadly he still struggled with the humanistic leadership that Jack preached. Danny secretly admired his client the Iron Chancellor and his compassionless management style, and some days he'd practise it. On one of the workshops when project services manager in Singapore, who only had one leg, told Danny of his difficulties in submitting a final presentation, the great Scott replied without pity: "Well, I wouldn't like to be in your shoes... uhm... well, shoe."

Steed was even more cynical at the workshop, having been pressganged at the risk of being run off by Jon, he was forced to attend.

"You are being very cynical, Steed," declared the highly paid and experienced consultant during a particularly interesting debate with Steed.

Our master of semantics and one-line assassination replied, "No, I'm not. I'm being sceptical."

The consultant gave up after this and all the attendees retired to the bar.

Jack gained courage and decided to describe to Jon some of the behavioural examples of his integrated team demonstrated above but was careful not to include his boss in examples. Jon had told Jack that he must listen to this new lesson in real contracting:

'Ensure you put the project team through Cultural Awareness programs. Do not miss out people from Louisiana, Oklahoma, Arkansas or Scotland.'

However, Gator Tom was a true professional at work, a highly experienced engineer and project manager and was both culturally and politically correct in all his work relationships. Curiously he never came out to play at weekends, as they were spent with his lovely wife and his kids. He only drank after work during the week. All came to realise that the bars after work were really extensions of places of work for almost all of team, as most nights they'd put to rights what should have been put to rights in work. People who they needed to talk to who had flown in from head offices, or came from the remote construction sites or suppliers and colleagues who had been tied up in endless progress meetings with clients were always available to catch after work. Those who had family stayed shorter hours and spent weekends with them, those who didn't stayed longer and spent the weekends free of the bar girls in bars like The Outback and The Sportsman's. Some of course preferred the multigender attractions of the other bars; they were a holistic bunch, for sure.

Bar meetings were of course much more pleasant than meetings in the office facing the Iron Chancellor and his demands for actual work, and heaven forbid, actual deliverables or facing the visiting bosses from Houston, London, Perth or Yokohama and trying to convince them everything was on schedule. This was probably because of the Tiger, groundnuts and also the lovely bar girls who made the conversation fly by faster.

Most looked at the girls as an essential part of the bar service and treated them with respect and enjoyed their less divorce-threating tactile behaviours and rewarded them in highly inflated drinks and tips, that was as far as it ever went, the Big Man included. However, back in the office Gator was a constant reminder of a novel approach to real work.

Jack came to understand the American icon mainly after comforting Danny's sore 'heed' with curry puffs early morning and then visiting the avuncular American with a couple of rice and dried fish nasi lemaks in an attempt to get him to eat anything but his groundnut supper. They always ended up on his lovely secretary's desk to share with the other local staff. Gator was of the *'Wall Street, Gordon Gecko'* paradigm that *'food was for wimps'*.

Also, Jack realised not for him were management plans, engineering drawings, spreadsheets or any form of non-liquid sustenance until he sorted his priorities out; hence his habitual shredding of the bar bills. He was an expert time manager and delegator.

The internal culture had been developed over three years as the team struggled through interminable lion dances, vegetarian buffets, lucky draws, moon cakes, Chinese banquets and Indonesian dancing.

However, a few examples of offline behaviour had promoted Jack's recent brave discussion with Jon. The irascible German had paved the way in political correctness and creating a human relations culture of his own but the week before in a project executive meeting he informed people that he had decided to 'out place' the forty-two-year-old (going on fifty) boss of one of the contractors.

"I am not happy with his performance. There's going to be a turkey shoot except there's only one turkey. He's old, fat, bald and Norwegian."

The human resource manager pointed out quickly to Jon that this was a classic politically incorrect statement that contained most of the things you can't get away with these days. "Think about it," he said. "Age-ism, size-ism, hair-ism, rac-ism."

Jon was not amused.

"Please do not interrupt me when I am talking. You are in HR and your job is solely to fill the forms in when I appoint someone and fill them in when I fire them. You will do nothing in between. Do you understand?"

This was followed almost immediately in the same meeting with another one on ageism.

When asked to approve a new contractor coming on board the team, the esteemed leader said: "He's dead."

"No, he isn't. He's my friend and he's only sixty-eight," his hopeful sponsor, the project services manager exclaimed.

"Well, he may as well be," was Jon's only comment.

The one-legged project service manager wept a little but being a solid and reliable company man he remained calm. And bravely he decided to broach another non-engineering or progress related subject, knowing from past terrors that human interest disinterested the great Prussian leader.

"Jon, we have placed travel restrictions on all project employees in South East Asia after the terrorist bombings there. A few of the non-staff contractors wish to play golf on Bintan Island. Will you sanction a variation to this and approve?"

Jon unerringly said: "It's all right if they go. If we lose them, they're only contractors."

This was the Sensei of motivation and political correctness, and probably no one else's answer, to that. The Iron Chancellor was a master of cultural alignment. And he decided in his wisdom to send Jack off to the Philippines to sort out a subproject which had gone somewhat offline.

"You will go to Manila on Monday. I expect you to return when you have got that rabble in line. If you fail I will have to go and terminate the project manager. I have run off the last project manager and sent that lunatic Dutch Pieter there as it's his equipment they are supposed to have built by now. Try to educate him, it's difficult, he's Dutch, but you are paid to do that. If you can't I will have to terminate you. Try to keep away from the bars in that denizen of debauchery of a place. I will monitor your activity and your expenses. Your activities in Vietnam, Bangkok and Jakarta I have noted in my journal and you have a tendency to spend too much time in bars. I thought you were intelligent, but obviously as you are from Northern England, you must not be. Send me your recovery plan by Wednesday. Goodbye and close the door, please."

CHAPTER FIFTEEN

Manila, Philippines

Passionate Pieter

Year three...

Sadly, Jack did end up in the bars. Where else could he solve the problems of real contracting? On the Sunday before he flew, as a farewell to Singapore bars and to say hello to Manila bars, he decided to relax in The Sportsman's as usual. There he met Big Pat again...

Jack had first met this megalith in The Sportsman's in the first year of the project. Every Sunday Jack liked a beer and had traditionally gone to the pub. Nothing new there, you may say. Sundays in Singapore were difficult for people like him, brought up where Sunday lunchtime was always the pub or working men's club until you were thrown out and your mother, and then, if you married a real man's proper wife, your wife, cooked you your Sunday dinner. You could then enjoy a snooze after a difficult day drinking with like-minded men all worrying about relegation from the Premier soccer league.

It was difficult in Singapore because most people were recovering from the extracurricular activities in the Four Floors and the like and normally had been drinking till daylight and then enjoying the pursuits of their labours. Few people carried out the tradition of going to the pub at opening time as they were still comatose from the night or morning before. That is, everyone except Big Pat, Jack and

Harry the Hun, who had to open up the bar.

Pat was always there before Jack, standing at the bar, his huge hand clutching a beer as if it were an egg cup. He always had his newspaper (not a broadsheet) folded on the bar, on top of which was his wallet and mobile phone. He looked intimidating. His shoulders and back were like the Great Dividing Range. It was his head that frightened most. Buffalo Alf would have had to use his 700 Nitro Express to knock this beast down.

His head had no ears; well, those that were left were just pulp. His forehead had lines etched into them like Les Gorges de Verdun and he didn't smile much. His head was of course shaven with a number one cut.

Jack was lonely though, with just him, this Goliath and Harry's dour and morose face and lectures on Scottish Masonry every Sunday, so he tried to get into some conversation, but all he got was a nod and a frown.

Until one day Harry asked him why he didn't talk to the big guy. Jack replied: "Coz I can't get an answer."

"Aye, he disna say much, the big yin, but I hear he's now got some work on your project in the Philippines I think? He might need some bodies off me, big man, so you should talk to him, son," Harry said.

Hum, Jack thought. *I'll toss a bit of raw meat at him and see if he doesn't tear my head off.* He had to be careful, because Harry may well have got it wrong and maybe he'd been turned down for the job. Maybe he was just waiting for the chance to beat the unsuspecting consultant to a pulp. He took a calculated gamble and reached for his Nitro Express and elephant trunk filleting machete and asked him if he worked on Scorpio.

The giant turned his huge head and glared menacingly through slits for eyes.

"Aye," he said.

Phew, Jack thought, handing the gun and knife back to Harry, who would have use for them back in Glasgow, he was sure. At last he had some form of bonding and interpersonal recognition from the normally silent giant.

"Aye, so do I. Do you fancy a pint?" he tentatively asked, as he was still frowning at Jack with a face that looked as if it could melt Super Duplex.

"Aye," he said, and swallowed his full glass in one swallow. *For ****'s sake,* Jack thought, *his oesophagus is as wide as his head.* And that was the start of a great friendship. Note, friendship, not conversation: It became apparent over the years that Big Pat says very little. "Aye," is a sign of major social bonding and if he stops responding in the positive, time to get the Nitro Express out or run. Like gorillas, his speed is fast over short distances so get out fast and keep going.

This was wise, Harry explained when the big man had left to go to the toilet, because the big man, whilst to his various families and friends has always been a gentle giant, was not always to some.

It seemed he had a run-in with Scandahooligans around the Four Floors of Whores in Orchard Towers the night before; it appeared that he was a bit xenophobic and Harry whispered: "Big yin, if you keep talking to him try at least to speak in a British accent of some sort. He doesn't like strangers, particularly Scandinavians. I heard that that **** off Danish shipping guy in the Football Bar of the Four Floors was offering to fight everyone and had frightened off a few. He saw the big man sitting alone at the end of the bar, newspaper, phone, and wallet on bar, minding his own business as usual, he walked over and told Pat he has going to kick his arse and kept on shouting at him. Pat said nothing, swallowed another pint in one go, stood up, turned around and headbutted the guy unconscious. They dragged the body out of the bar and left the Great Dane asleep for some time outside before the Chinese bouncers threw him down the stairs. Pat sat down, and the landlord asked him if he'd like a pint on the house. 'Aye,' was all he got in return, and Pat continued to watch the footie match in silence."

Harry continued and nodded in appreciation:

"He's a man of few words yeah'll find out soon, big man."

Pat came back from the toilet. Harry greeted him: "I hear you had some bother last night, big man?"

"Aye," Pat said. And surprisingly he added more words to form a full sentence. "Had some more down in Pasir Panjang too, mate."

"What was that all about, Pat?" Jack raised the courage to ask him.

"Bit of botha with some Kiwis," he growled.

In a process of monosyllabic words and very short sentences Jack got the gist of what had occurred. It seemed that seven Kiwi drillers on shore leave from an oil rig in Keppel Shipyard had been in the bar. They had upset a lady in the bar and Big Pat's mate had told them to stop it or else.

His mate was six foot four like him and was also a Millwall supporter, and those in the know with English football hooligans will know they are normally psychotic mass murderers. It appears the Kiwis, knowing numbers were on their side, surrounded Big Pat and his mate. Bad move, never corner an enraged rhinoceros; Buffalo Alf would tell you that, at least unless you had your Nitro Express with you.

The outcome was that six Kiwis were beaten to pulp and thrown out of the pub. The last and most annoying was left on the pool table, being battered senseless by Big Pat's immense fists whilst the owner, an Indonesian head-hunter, probably a relation of Sharon, Harry's wife from The Sportsman's, had broken a pool cue over another's head, and was using the sharp end to stab it into the unfortunate Antipodean's thigh.

Pat had returned to the scene on Sunday morning to help the owner wash the blood off the walls and ensure there was no return of the magnificent seven. Their rig boss did return, however, and apologised profusely for the trouble they had caused and paid the bar owner money to have the pool table's blood-soaked cloth replaced.

Jack nervously decided that maybe Pat was a wealth of social and psychological research for his paper on real contracting as he also appeared to be in the 'bidness', and as a fortunate coincidence, he worked as a subcontractor to the project's Philippines site. They agreed to meet up in Manila that week for more beer. Jack hoped he could get a few more sentences of conversation and hopefully they wouldn't meet many Scandinavians or Antipodeans.

Jack was sent to Manila by Jon to review why another of the subprojects was in construction delay and looking like cratering financially. Jack arrived at the international airport which, to be polite, was rather tired in its appearance with few mod cons, like cleanliness, efficiency, food and drink or working toilets, and he was glad to take a hotel-supplied limo to his hotel in Alabang district, Manila and some hopeful creature comforts.

He stayed there as he was meeting Big Marc and Aussie Richie in the Union Jack Tavern in Festival Mall for beer that evening. He was looking forward to visiting the Philippines as he had nothing but good experiences with the Philippine people he had met in Singapore and at work. He was soon to find out after two weeks there that whilst the Philippines was undoubtedly beautiful in places, it was also in many ways a mess. Given his experiences to follow, he really couldn't come to any other conclusion.

That first evening he met his project friends in the Union Jack Tavern. A great bar resembling The Sportsman's in that it had lots of soccer TV on in each bar and more importantly it offered mince and cholesterol in many, many ways, in mince pies , in shepherd's pie, in mince and tatties and also haggis, neeps and tatties. Also they had an Indian chef who cooked proper British Indian curries. And as a real bonus, all the girls wore amazingly short tartan skirts and were friendly and gorgeous. Jack thought he had died and gone to Heaven. A real contractor's paradise.

During the evening his financial friend, Big Marc, explained to him that things were not what they seemed here regarding normal financial practice and audit. He had been sent to check the accounts of the contractor for the project and he was astounded at the many and varied ways of accounting for their costs.

"But Jack, these seem mild compared to some. A good friend of mine in Manila who advises one of the richest (non-politician) men and corporations in the Philippines told me when they acquired a company recently the auditors asked them what should they do with the 500,000 pesos a month payment to the Maoist NPA Mafia, which was shown in the accounts, and that they were using this as legitimate tax-deductible expense. My friend advised that his president would either convert that to a franchise for one of his retail outlets for the leaders or he would fund a military base and use them as protection rather than the NPA. I was ******* amazed at the financial dexterity of this icon of corporate governance and innovative interpretation of regulatory financial controls."

Big Richie interrupted this conversation with his own interpretation of the Philippines' culture.

"Jack, you know there are the five Cs in Singapore?"

"Yes," Jack replied, "everything that Singaporeans strive for: Condominium, Credit Card, Cash, Car, Country Club."

"Correct, my pommie friend: But here in the Philippines, there are three Gs that describe the politics and people. Gold, Gooks, Guns."

Richie took a drink and started another cultural lecture.

"I have to say, in my experience that is not far wrong. It amazes me still that Filipinos whom I worked with, drank with and who kept many families of all races going as helpers to families outside of the country, seemed to come from such a place that was so at odds to the wonderful nature and hardworking dedication of those people. I know not all were like this and to be fair many, many people I've met in the country itself are lovely, hardworking and very clever people. But the poverty here is bad, the corruption sad, but mostly I am amazed at the violent behaviour here. I've not seen that prevalent in any Asian country I'd lived and worked in. And very few things work on time or to any plan, mate. You'll soon find that out when you head on site."

Jack thought this all a bit worrying given he was sat enjoying great beer, mince and tatties and served by smiling, beautiful, short-skirted, long-legged, olive-skinned girls. No hint of corruption, violence or indolence so he took in the comments and wondered what faced him on site.

But the next day there was a golf day planned for suppliers, contractors and the client so he was picked up by Richie and taken straight to the course early a.m. as dawn broke. He loved to hear the roosters crowing as they drove along miles of hutches where the thousands of fighting cocks were tied to the roof hutches, crowing out their macho cries. It seemed quite surreal. The next few days were even more so.

Jack turned up at 6.30 a.m. and was introduced to the three guys in his golf flight. Pieter was there also and they exchanged pleasantries and Pieter said he'd meet with him the next day to discuss why Jack was there and what they were going to do to help change the outcome of the project. As usual Jack didn't feel any warmth or affection for his help. Pieter pointed to the others in Jack's flight and explained who he would be playing with.

"You will be playing with a friend of mine, Rudi. He's from Rotterdam and a good guy. Enjoy the golf."

He headed off to tee off with his own team.

Jack walked over to the three guys he would be playing with and shook hands. He knew no one and they never asked him why he was there. Jack shook the hand of the person who he assumed was Rudi and offered pleasantries.

"Where are you from, mate?"

"Rotterdam," Rudi replied.

"What are you doing here?" Jack asked, as he had no idea who was playing that day, could have been anyone from anywhere, and he had yet to been seen near the site or office. Rudi explained as he swung his golf club in practice.

"I'm working on a big construction project here. I'm a piping superintendent for the managing contractor."

"Sounds canny," Jack replied. "What's it going like?"

"It's going great, man. It's absolutely ******! It was supposed to be finished in a few months' time. No way in hell, it's ******. I'll get another year out of this, maybe two. This place is heaven on earth, man, girls everywhere, cheap beer and the day rates are great. The job is a mess and it's ******* marvellous."

He was smiling ecstatically. Jack thought to himself, not too kindly, Soweto is heaven on earth compared to parts of Rotterdam he'd worked in the past but didn't say so. He was quite large! But he was correct; it was a paradise here for sure.

Rudi continued and pointed to a small, lean, well-dressed Filipino man.

"See that guy over there teeing off? Don't tell him anything what I told you, mate, he's the project director. The daft idiot thinks it's going to end soon."

Then, turning to Jack, swinging his club in practice, he asked: "What are you doing here?"

Jack pulled a driver out of his bag, pointed it at the project director teeing off and replied nonchalantly: "Oh, I work for him over there teeing off and I'm here to make sure you don't get another year."

He spluttered, apologised and pleaded to Jack not to tell anyone but Jack comforted him in the sure knowledge that he knew the craic already about real contracting, he needn't worry. Jack confided in him his secret research into the work of real contractors in paradise, which he could read soon, and that he was now one more statistic in an absolute proof that it was true.

The next day Jack began his interviews and due diligence on the project and after a couple of days he realised that this project apparently followed his emergent theory, in that there was an unlimited supply of young ladies and cheap booze, it had nice beaches and many places where you could go native and hide from ex-wives, police, debt collectors and irate, demented project managers. Many had. And the project there was, like the country, in a bit of a mess.

So when he was asked to assess the status and do a cold-eye review and produce his report to Jon on why the project was miles late and massively over budget (Steed and Lord Paul would argue for years that it was or it wasn't. For the purposes of this narrative, and to non-contractual people, it was as late as a ten-month pregnant lady when he arrived) he was really confident that this would be an easy assignment. This was because he had already written the report on the plane and also provided conclusions and a recovery plan.

To him it seemed the cause and effect was obvious; building steel structures on a paradise island? It had to be the same paradigm as he'd seen before and the conversation with Rudi at the golf course proved that. He hoped to spend some time pretending to be intelligent, innovative and with great insight to the ways of project management, teamwork and cross-cultural communication and integration but mainly, as the report was already written, enjoy the some of the less divorce-threatening pleasures of this purported Shangri La, beautiful diving, golf, decent food and lots of St Miguel light beer.

Sadly, after interviewing some of the leading players and protagonists in the debacle, he was told by all that no one wished to stay here, they wanted to get out, back to more compliant contracting areas of the world.

It seemed they were not enamoured with being held in armed camps masquerading as hotels and condominiums and surrounded by an on-going Mafia war over the lavish spoils that the rapacious natives were expecting to purloin from their project. Indeed, some people had already been shot over certain disputes over who had the rights to the various spare bits of the big steel things that were being built. The client thought they did. The Mafia thought they did. The police thought the highest bidder did.

Contrary to his theory that if the real contractors wanted out of here, the project should be on time and budget. Oh dear, he soon realised he had strayed into an environment that belied everything he had found out and written about and heaven forbid, he may have to work for a living in an area where the natives weren't so friendly and he may well be lunch. He may well need some personal protection and certainly he'd need psychological counselling after this assignment before facing the Iron Chancellor.

After a few days there one morning he reflected on his experience of construction managers in the car on the way to the site from the armed camp of his hotel as he passed in the crazy streets and hundreds of random pedestrians who walked in the dirt roads as there were no sidewalks. All the locals seemed in ignorance or complacency of the imminent risk to their lives of the multicoloured people's taxis (jeepneys), cars and motorbikes that crowded the streets. As most of the jeepneys had references to redemption through faith in Jesus Christ and the certainty of resurrection from the dead, he mused that the drivers must have a divine third-party insurance policy of far greater value that that offered by secular earthly underwriters.

As he observed the poverty and the fragility of life in these streets, he began to understand the need for empathetic management and cultural awareness of what drove and motivated the thousands of workers on the site he was visiting and how to change behaviours which were self-protective for both the workers and the management. These were basically the local national workers' motivation to earn money, keep their jobs and survive to feed their families, and the real contractors' – to stay there as long as possible. No one wanted it to end for completely different motivations but the end result was the same.

Managing this mix was not easy and particularly for the construction managers who were tasked to do it. He reflected that he had known many construction managers who imposed great company discipline on their teams and their subcontractors and suppliers. Some were 'real characters', that was he had observed in some certain differences with management style, maybe showing a little bit of eccentricity, or maybe they were just practising the construction manager way. He soon realised that Pieter was certainly eccentric and certainly had his unique way of managing his people and sites.

During the last week he had had several encounters with the Dutchman; most had ended up in fits of anger and emotion from the great man. As the days went on Jack came to the conclusion that everyone was terrified of this irascible man, even the biggest guys on the construction team and all races on the project. His reputation was legend, it seemed, and talking to men who had worked with him across the world in the unfriendly places like Chad, Nigeria, Iraq, and Aberdeen where Pieter had built large steel and concrete things very successfully, he was a construction god, but a sometimes a frightening one.

After Jack's leadership alignment workshop that he'd ran that week he was having a beer with Pieter. It had gone remarkably well and for the first time, people started to believe it may be possible to change the course of the project through alignment of all parties, collaboration and integration of the teams. These were soft, cuddly, human things which Pieter had violently disagreed with. Surprisingly, Pieter had been very supportive and helpful throughout the workshop day and showed great leadership and support for all that was proposed and developed through the day. Jack told him so over the beer and thanked him for his positive input but he also had to make a final statement.

"Pieter, you have been great today, buddy, but I believe that you are one of the angriest men I had ever had to deal with in my 'cuddly' consultancy world."

Pieter looked at him, twisting his old, weather-worn face in pain and he banged his first on the bar as he screamed: "Angry! I not angry, I'm passionate."

He stared menacingly at Jack for his reaction. Jack recovered quickly for he was getting used to the mania, smiled and said: "Pieter, you sure are passionate, my friend."

Pieter put his hand on the consultant's shoulder and got up to leave and as he turned his head back to him he smiled a knowing smile and said with surprising warmth: "Jack, I think we'll get on OK together. You keep on with the bullshit and I'll keep on with the passion."

And indeed they did. But from that day on he was Passionate Pieter to Jack.

He stayed on this assignment some time and worked with Passionate Pieter and grew to realise that he was very good at control and command. He was indeed passionate and Jack began to understand his passion was an honest, inherent need to achieve results and fulfil his role as the person accountable and responsible to his company to do that. Like all construction managers, he did not accept fabrication of the truth and searched for the truth through hard questions and took no prisoners. Despite this he didn't blame any of his staff but took the flak himself from his superiors like the strong leader he undoubtedly was, but still keeping everyone under control with his laptops and reporting back to his secret mentor in Houston or maybe Langley. Jack never found out where.

Jack grew to like and respect the 'passionate' Dutchman but his role was to lead the project away from conflict towards collaboration and to keep the protagonists from reverting to norm, not an easy task.

Jack also came to realise quite quickly that Pieter held his team to the same company standards of discipline that he had always held. Many struggled to adapt or endure this discipline, of course many were experienced real contractors and were not enamoured with a strong leadership focus on getting the job finished on time and their eventual return to the chaste, chill and austerity of home.

One day after the first couple of weeks the corporate HR team were coming into town to carry out an anti-bullying teach-in on company philosophy and procedure. Passionate Pieter's team were in good humour for once at the thought of this and spoke to Jack in quiet anticipation of the great Dutchman's reaction to the new politically correct way from the poor innocent girls from corporate HR.

Also they all wondered how his secretary, Maria, would respond to the HR teach-in, as she was the best witness of all to his 'passion'.

During his staff meetings in his office, or if he had taken a particularly difficult call from his boss or the PMO manager on progress and key performance indicators, he'd hammer his desk and howl through the open door at Maria.

"Maria! Maria! Where the hell are you? Get in here now!"

Maria would duly put down her noodles and rice and hurriedly pick up a pen and note pad and run through into the great man's office, the pen trembling in her hands.

"Yes, Sir Pieter, what can I do for you, sir?"

"Hell, man! Where the hell is Tim? Go get Tim. Tell him to get his ass in here now."

Poor Tim was the overworked and overburdened mild-mannered project controls man. His main role in life was to run into Passionate's office every time Maria came to pass on Pieter's order. He was always tasked with answering Pieter's questions on why the job was so in the shit. He was only two doors up but was always politely summoned by a quivering Maria and he ran down the five metres to the banshee's office and impending torture. This was much to the amusement of the administration local staff sat around and the project control staff he managed. Tim rarely had an accurate answer as he never had an updated schedule that meant anything factual, and was only of use to the waiting mass of litigation lawyers that were lining up to make millions out of Pieter and Tim's schedule woes.

He had a stammer under pressure and the constant, relentless, aggressive questioning from Passionate about progress, Key Performance Indicators (KPIs), manning levels and 'where is my fully resourced Rev 3.142 schedule?' often drove him to verge of breakdown.

"I've gi-gi-given you the answer," he'd stammer, with everyone outside the office listening to the latest Spanish Inquisition torture of Tim.

"Goddamn, what you've given me is bullshit. Get your ass back in there and batter those lazy ******s and get me a Rev 3.142 recurring now!"

"Yes sir!" Tim would shout and stamp his feet military drill style and walk out, his head a little more bowed each time.

After the ritual slaying of Tim, Passionate would holler through the door to the expectant Maria, who managed the constant supply of cigarettes he smoked constantly every day.

"Maria, where's my packet of Marlboro!"

Again, he was a living example of Father Bob syndrome. Only eat real bait, never foreign shit, smoke thousands of tonnes of tobacco a week and work fourteen hours a day, this kept them both lean, and in Passionate's case mean.

This episode would be repeated most days, with Tim being summoned by Maria from his relative haven of lies, statistics and dammed lies from his subcontractors which he juggled daily with his planners to try to provide Passionate with cohesive and sensible answers, and then running down to Passionate's den to be tortured and sent back with even more work to do.

The morning after the HR teach-in, Jack asked Dick, the American subcontract's manager: "How did it go?"

"Jack. It was good, even better when they showed a video of someone banging the desk and shouting and hollering at his staff. They stopped the video and asked everyone what they thought of this, and was this bullying? We all looked at Maria. She just smiled, turned nervously to look at Pieter who was looking uninterested at it all was staring into space wondering where his mythical revised 3.142 schedule was, and Maria continued to try and look as if she was busy writing."

After this feedback, Jack walked over to Maria's desk, where she was eating her usual plate of noodles, head down, not seeing him, and he banged his fist on the desk.

"Goddamn, Maria, where are my Marlboro!"

She dropped her fork, picked up her notebook and looked to jump up. Jack put his hand on her shoulder and quietly said: "I hear you enjoyed yesterday's seminar, my dear?"

"Yes, Sir Jack, very much," she answered, smiling knowingly, very relieved.

In fact, Passionate was actually very good with the local staff and with Maria. He never was anything but respectful, courteous and a bit of a father figure to them. But with his experienced real contractors, or engineers, who should have known better and didn't provide him with honest and clear facts and data, he tortured them. He was very well culturally aligned with the many nations who worked the site and ran a tight, safe, well-disciplined ship, and they held him in great respect. Jack pondered this and decided that again, cultural values are a matter of culture, not HR department rules. Even asylums have values.

Jack's research showed that Passionate's main record was in directly managing subcontract labour on contracts that paid for work done by contractors. They were used to being responsible for their destiny and in charge of directing men, equipment and materials to where their plan and schedule dictated. They worked on land that the client, mainly governments owned. Here, now, in the paradise world of contracting, they were managing engineers and suppliers of bits of large steel, vessels and wires who owned the construction yard and manufacturing plant and also controlled the routes for the iron and steel things to leave the country when built. In many cases they may well have owned the town and the local mob and the police were heavily linked to the financial success of such suppliers of steel things. It was their country and their rules.

Of course the main conclusion to all this, Jack reasoned, was that by building these things in low-cost paradise of seaside resorts, using expatriate management on massive tax-paid day rates, where girls were pretty and available, did not help the process. Passionate Pieter's obstacles were possibly insurmountable from that principle alone!

A lot of places Passionate had successfully built big things had been where everyone wanted to get out quick. Only he stayed in these horrible places willingly. In Africa he was leading a huge project where they lived in armed camps at night with little to do but eat, sleep and work. The natives were hostile; you may well have been the lunch there. Everyone wanted to get out quick, so the work went to schedule.

Passionate was so dedicated that he wouldn't take leave. One of his past employees, Texas E and I Wayne (whose years of working in armed camps with Passionate Pieter had turned him slightly strange) told Jack in the Union Jack Tavern one night that human resources had to send a rescue mission in a chopper to force him out and take his leave. He said that Passionate was last seen by his relieved workers physically restrained, in a safety net, raving and shouting orders and instructions to his deputy as he was hauled up very reluctantly on a wire into the chopper. A great legend in the industry whom you may well will meet in paradise one day.

Jack was interested in Tim professionally, and in a caring way, like a sick pet, after observing him get tortured three times a day by Passionate and still maintain a level of professionalism and motivation, he asked him his views of the project.

Tim's main gripe was of course that mind-boggling art of planning. Jack listened intently as he remembered Jon, his boss's last words to him as he had left Singapore on the need to get an accurate, fully resourced plan from Pieter and Tim.

"The contractor has done a great job on planning. We have done a piss-poor job. We need to plan our own activities so that I can hammer you all when you fail to meet them! Go and make sure you do not leave site until you have a plan from those numbskulls."

He knew that this was an impossible task but he would try and then come up with some excuse when he faced the wrath of Jon again.

Jack had long ago decided that planning was a black art and planners were a breed apart but they were masters of the esoteric art of real contracting. They conjure up histograms, bar charts, Gantt charts, S-curves, Key Performance Indicators, you name it, and they will provide it to the hapless project manager, who needs this data to demonstrate to corporate sponsors and the auditors that he is in control of the project. He is never in control of the project, the planners are. This is a simple law of contracting.

Imagine in a perfect world, that is outside of real contracting, where the planning department produce a plan that demonstrates when you will start and finish each activity and when you will finally finish the job. The project team then execute this to the plan and the job finishes on time and everyone is happy. What would happen to the planners? They would be redundant after producing this plan. Any computer-literate local graduate on S$3,000 per month can input the progress data each month to show the delighted project manager that he is on schedule. Of course as you will know by now, this would be against all the rules of real contracting.

Firstly, like client engineers, it is never in the planner's interest to provide any deliverables or especially a plan that does not need constant revision. So they work diligently with like-minded engineering and construction engineers to develop unrealistic norms that give massively underestimated man-hours and time periods for tasks.

They stick these in the computer, add some float to the tasks to demonstrate that you are being conservative and bingo; the plan is produced, showing an end date exactly the same as that in the contract.

The contract schedule was of course developed by estimators who had no intention whatsoever of having to prove their vastly out-of-date norms were out by a factor of twenty-five, as they never end up running the project and become accountable for their estimate. They stay in corporate headquarters and decry the poor demented project manager who is failing miserably to achieve their fantasy schedule and budget. The estimators know the project planners would have to fit the project plan to the contract plan. And they do, every time.

Of course, they are the only ones who understand the mumbo jumbo. The last time most project managers were on site, or in the drawing office, Nixon was President of the USA and a 6G welding qualification was the class grade they were in when they found their first girl/boyfriend, and Primavera was an Italian opera singer. So the project manager would never question how they got to their plan, just the end date, and as long as the end date never moved, they were safe from corporate fury and the sack.

When the job goes to rat shit within the first month because obviously no one can actually meet the plan, the planners blame the lack of productivity or design change, and insist that they must reschedule and then the pièce de résistance, they rebase the time line. This will require more planners, preferably with experience (western foreigners on large day rates. Note: the two, experienced and western foreigners are immutably linked according to planning managers and also the body shops of Harry, T Squared and Abe, where they get them from).

They plan using exactly the same norms, providing what is known in the trade as a new baseline, or in any other business, as a cheat or blatant lie.

So it goes on re-baselining with the same end date until even the deluded and demented project manager realises that with two months to go, five million man-hours to burn and only 55% through an original two-year plan, the planners have been conning him for twenty-two months.

He has no option but to hire even more planners to plan the remaining work because he can't be seen to be out of control. 'If you've got a plan, you are in control' is the mantra in real contracting and all business these days. Like the engineering department and the commissioning crème, the planning department grows in size and they all manage to get one more turkey and two Easter eggs out of the job.

The project manager survives because he has been wily enough to ensure he has a plan, however ridiculous and false; no one in corporate understands opera and Primavera anyway. His cost budget, however, is massively overspent. This was the exactly the case Jack was reviewing in the Philippines and Tim had his own views after several years working with Passionate.

"This job is ******, mate, no one understands planning here. Everyone thinks they do and everyone wants me to solve their own bloody problems. The crazy man in the office down there thinks I can pull a plan out the hat. For God's sake if the contractor tells us lies, more lies and more statistics that are lies, how the hell can I provide him with a rev 3.145 recurring that means anything? And don't get me on about the crazy German in Singapore, he threatens me every week with the sack and it's not my plan!"

Jack looked sympathetically at the tortured man.

"But surely, Tim, if we get the teams integrated and you can get one of your planners in the team we can manage to get a schedule that we can all agree on and keep the two crazy men off our backs?"

"Do you really think a schedule will fix this mess, mate? No one wants it to end except me!" Tim wailed and held his head in his hands. "I can't take much more of the torture."

He looked up and fixed Jack a quizzical stare.

"I know you are supposed to be a miracle worker but you have no idea how it all works, have you?"

He asked this rhetorically as he went straight into the answer and gave Jack yet another lesson on real contracting.

'A schedule is an artificial device created without knowledge of the future. Guesses are used as surrogates for knowledge. Project deadlines are tied to corporate review dates. Initially management cuts the budget until failure is assured, then hires many more real contractors to accelerate totally out of control of time and cost.'

"And they expect me to fix that."

He continued his rant and lesson.

"A good project manager will always have a significant level of contract claims dreamt up by Steed or Lord Paul that exactly balances the increase in expat wages caused by his myriad of plans and hordes of new contractors. And of course you don't get many expats to the million dollars, so the claims never match the costs."

Tim took both hands and clasped them over his slightly balding head and was quiet for a while. Jack just sat there contemplating whether to refer him to the HR ladies for more counselling or pay for him to go to The Outback and see the Doc, when Tim suddenly looked up from his misery and came out with a personal revelation.

"I always wanted to be a claims and forensic planner and defend the plan in court. For most of the time as a learned professor of prolongation and acceleration I would never actually be on site, or, indeed ever develop a plan. I'd be held in reserve like the seventh cavalry riding to the rescue long after the job is finished. My hero was my old planning boss, who never left his office except to visit the toilet or attend meetings on the plan, at which he would say nothing in case it incriminated him. The right to remain silent is absolute for a real claims planner!"

He looked morosely at Jack and picked up his empty cup of coffee and finished his soliloquy.

"Now look at me, banished to do real work producing reams of key performance figures, pleading every day to the contractors to tell me the truth and getting dogs abuse from the crazy man. Do you want another cup of coffee?"

Jack looked at the tortured soul and decided that after a life of working for Passionate and the like in jungles and deserts, he was probably a hopeless case and decided to end the interview there.

"Yes, thanks Tim. Can I have one of the nice biscuits you keep in the kitchen?"

"Sure," answered Tim, "I think I'll need to get a box out the safe."

Jack pondered why he would keep biscuits in a safe and particularly why he had a safe the size of one of De Beer's corporate diamond safes in his office.

"What's it for, Tim? Holding the petty cash, confidential reports or something?"

"Hell no, Jack, it contains the cookies. I am damned certain if I didn't have them secure they would be eaten," he replied confidently and proudly.

"Aren't they supposed to be eaten?" Jack enquired, a bit puzzled.

He answered laconically: "Hell yes, but one of those bloody people eats the whole box every time I put them out."

"Oh dear, that is heinous. I can't believe they'd do that to you, buddy," Jack said sympathetically, consoling this icon of cookie management.

"Come out of the office and I'll show you," he said.

They walked out and down towards the kitchen. Dan, who was a huge African American of equal size and bulk to Gator Tom and Big Pat, was sat next to the kitchen, diligently knocking out toilet-flushing procedures and purchase requisitions for containers of cookies. The project services man went through to the kitchen and looked into the biscuit box which he had just put onto the worktops an hour ago, and finding it empty yet again he shouted from the kitchen: "OK, who has been eating the cookies again?"

He walked out holding the empty box and walking towards Dan he shouted so all could hear: "Heh, Dan, have you been eating these cookies again?"

"No sir. I have not, never had one today," Dan replied with a hint of annoyance that yet again he was the alleged culprit.

The project services man, satisfied with Dan's denial, strode up and down his team sitting in their cubicles and asked the same question: "Who has been eating the cookies?"

Receiving nothing but, "Not me, sir," from the national staff," and "**** off," from the American, Brit and Aussie real contractors, he shrugged his shoulders, came back and said:

"See, Jack, that's why I keep the cookies in the safe."

Jack nodded his head at this example of sound man management, cost control and budgeting and went over to Dan, following a trail of cookie crumbs from the kitchen to his desk. Dan was gently brushing off cookie crumbs from his overalls and Jack asked rhetorically: "Heh, Dan, another day in paradise, my man?"

"Sure is, Jack, sure is," he answered, brushing off the last crumb with a big smile, standing up with crumbs falling from his ample waist and giving Jack a high five with his huge hand.

So it wasn't too hard to realise that things were not particularly stressful living here, and that the participants had undoubtedly fallen into real contracting behaviours. Jack had his work cut out again.

On the final evening before he had to return to face his nemesis, Jon, sans Rev 3.142, which was still being ripped up by Passionate into the face of Tim every time he tried to pass it across the desk, Jack met a few like-minded friends in the Union Jack Tavern to drink and forget the horrors of the project and Jon's inquisition.

As he sat waiting for Big Pat to arrive and also Digger, who curiously had called to say he was in town after a meeting with some gangsters masquerading as owners of a site he had supplied the digging machines to south of Manila. He had told Jack that he had arrived on site to have a meeting with the big bosses from all parties to agree that the project was now ready to change momentum. Just as the client was about to present his new strategy the lights and power went out in the offices. Frantically the site owners phoned around to find out what had happened. They finally told the astonished client that the local heavy plant supplier had walked on site (despite tens of security officers) and taken the keys from all the diggers, cranes, generators, compressors. It seemed he wanted a few more shekels now he had been informed the project client was in town and approving the go ahead.

Digger explained that after a fierce argument the client had agreed to pay but only when they were informed that this man was indeed probably Don Corleone's grandson and linked to the local government too, and that unless terms were agreed then Digger's machines would end up in the China Sea and all the client's equipment and nice new steel and copper wire disappear, along with all their scrap and small fabricated items which were deemed scrap anyway, that had not already been appropriated.

Jack sat drinking a cold St Miguel light and reflected on the three Gs that he'd been told earlier, Gold, Guns and Gooks, and remembered that on his own site they had signs everywhere saying to hand in their firearms before starting work. Then he looked at the picture on his phone he'd taken in the club house reception from the first golf course he'd attended.

Yet another lesson learnt.

'Any place where you have to hand your firearms in at the golf club or place of work was indeed a worry.'

Both his friends arrived. Big Pat had shipped his Philippine wife down to Manila on a fourteen-hour bus journey, given her a couple of hundred dollars and sent her out shopping. The big man's personal life was complicated as he had a divorced wife and family in England, a surrogate wife in the Philippines, and he had a strange relationship with the Queer One, a Hong Kong lady, who was always threatening to cut his throat when he was asleep. She was his nemesis, it seems, and that night she proved how dangerous it would be to upset this oriental pussycat.

This leviathan lived and drank mainly on Lamma Island, Hong Kong, in Ama Singh's bar and curry house. The Commodore, Pat and Jack, when visiting for another series of attempts at aligning a Chinese and French manufacturer, would while away hours drinking and eating the Punjabi chef's red hot Vindaloo.

One sultry day some weeks before that night's meeting in the UJT in Manila, Pat had a run-in with 'Pierre the French Kick Boxer'. This man had set himself up as the best fighter in Hong Kong and had come looking for the big fellow. It seems the kicks around Pat's head were like flies to him and he swatted them off before laying the Gallic Asterix out with one punch.

Two weeks later, a Russian hard man and known drug mastermind entered the bar looking for a quiet man and after threatening everyone else in the bar, was put to sleep in as sound a peace as the Frenchman had been the week before, after yet another well directed and forceful Big Pat headbutt. For this service the big man was duly asked if he wanted a beer and his favourite red hot vindaloo curry and he had said in the affirmative, "Aye."

Several beers later he was staggering home and putting his key in the lock, when the Russian attacked him from behind and dug the top of a Heineken bottle straight into the top of Pat's head, dropping him to the floor. The Russian proceeded to jump and stamp on the barely conscious leviathan's head.

Luckily for the big man, some German tourists spotted this and phoned the police who, again luckily for Pat, were in the next street.

Result was that Russian was arrested and Pat taken to hospital. He was discharged a couple of hours later, much to the amazement of the German tourists, who expected him to be dead after the stamping and kicking plus the bottle dug halfway into his huge skull. Not for the faint hearted, taking on a head that would need a jackhammer to crack it.

Despite the Hong Kong police wanting Pat to press charges as the Russian was a dangerous known gangster, Pat wouldn't agree, so the Russian was released. Pat had to come to Manila for work but he anticipated a reckoning some time. Indeed, it was not long coming. After a few beers and some mince, Pat's phone rang.

He answered and said – you can guess by now, "Aye."

He continued after a few minutes. "Aye."

And again after another few minutes, "Aye," and then he switched off.

He looked down, his huge head hanging on his chest, neck muscles straining to hold it and his large furrowed forehead and face twisted in pain. Digger asked the distressed man what was wrong.

"She's had the Russian wasted. Her Triad mates waited for him coming off the morning ferry. Beat the shit out of him and he's now floating in Hong Kong harbour. He's been told to leave town for good or he's the meat in a number 35 Chop Suey and Fried Rice"

"Bloody hell, that's great, man. He's best long gone, mate." Digger stated what was obvious to sane people; he was well rid of that enemy. "What's wrong, man?" he continued.

He replied laconically: "Ah wanted to do that myself."

All agreed that this event was perhaps not good news for Pat because he'd wanted to top the Russian himself and because Digger reminded him that given her Triad affiliations and her 'queer one' ways with the knife, his Chinese pussycat may easily do the same to him one day if he upset her. In that marvellous book *Catch 22*, Hungry Red used to dream all night that Huple's cat was sleeping on his face and one morning he would never wake up as the cat would have suffocated him. One morning he never woke up and Huple's cat was sitting on his face.

Big Pat doesn't sleep well in Hong Kong.

But in Singapore, Thailand and the Philippines he does, especially when he has his Philippine wife with him. Mind you that may well be only every three years that he renews his marriage vows but when she comes, he is a new man. You may have seen it before where people can calm raging dogs, whisper to horses, and even they could soothe the raging Doc with the magic molecule sometimes, but Big Pat's wife came in from the mall and seemed to calm the man into a transcendental state. The sight of her stroking his massive head with loving affection, like Ernst Stavro Blofeld would his stroke his Persian pussy in Bond movies, and the big man, was purring, but sounding more like a wildebeest which doesn't purr but makes a *harrumph, harrumph, ggrr'ng* type noise (so Buffalo Alf reckons), was the most wonderful thing to behold. But Digger whispered to Jack the Scandinavians, Russians, French and Kiwis best beware if she stops.

Pat's wife went out again to Festival Mall to spend more of his money, and Digger began talking about his most favourite subject, in which he and also Martin the Oblate Spheroid in Singapore, were experts, namely pornography.

Jack had found it quite astonishing to listen to Digger, and also the totally spherical Martin when they met in Asia, discuss the relative theatrical skills of the actors and actresses on the pirated porn DVDs that the local girls brought around the bars. What really amazed most normal people was that each one of these very different men knew and would want to argue which director was the most innovative, creative or incredulously, romantic.

Most doubted few of the world's aficionados of the noble art of pornography knew who had actually directed it. Worryingly, these two did – which led to Digger's conversation with Big Pat that evening in the UJT.

"If you want to make a filly ejaculate, you must take your fingers thus, and place them lightly thus and then gently massage whilst doing this."

This, you may well gather (or may well not depending on how sheltered your life has been), was Digger explaining to Pat how he was a master at achieving female orgasm and fountain-like ejaculation of vaginal fluid. A physiological and anatomical myth according to the Doc, but to Digger a sound fact, he'd researched it himself from his early courting in his debauched school days and major porn movie dissertations and reckoned he'd mastered the art. All the Doc's studies of *Grey's Anatomy, Physiology* and his own transgender operational experience were nothing compared to Digger's knowledge of sexual perversion.

Big Pat was interested and took notice of Digger's advice to make sure you laid a nice clean towel on the bed to catch any fluid and headed off to try this new technique with his lovely wife. The next day in the airport bar Digger asked Pat if he had had any success with his attempt achieving what the Doc said was physically and anatomically impossible.

"Nah."

This was his only response, which was the negative of 'aye', the only other word he normally uttered, and it was all the disappointed man could muster. Digger was about to ask why, when the big man took his glass of beer and surrounded it with his immense appendages and swallowed it whole again, and Digger just shut up, with a smile on his face.

Digger told Jack later after Pat left for the bathroom the revelation he'd had.

"Jack, I just looked at those fingers, every one of which was the size of my wrist, calloused and worn with laying bricks over the years, and imagined the poor forty-four kilo filly having this huge beast lying next to her, his nice new towel in place, one of those huge digits wiggling around her intimate parts, and I guess not with the finesse of a practised lover like myself. I realised that maybe I should have kept quiet about the ways of the *Kama Sutra* and *Debbie Does Dallas* to our Pat."

They all enjoyed a few beers and mince. Jack had decided not to eat that evening as he really fancied the Vindaloo curry and had been eating Philippine food for weeks and fancied a real British Indian curry. Even mince was turned down in his addiction to the brilliant Asian UJT cook's Vindaloo. He ordered a take away as his pleasure was to eat this in the comparative luxury of a clean, safe hotel unlike that he had lived in for the weeks previously which had resembled the CIA's hotel on Guantanamo Bay.

He left his mates feeling happy that he had survived some of the more life-threatening events in the Philippines and tried to take a taxi from the Union Jack Tavern to the hotel. After many beers and having waited thirty minutes for anything to turn up, he had to bribe a security guard to bring his brother-in-law or someone's cab, pay for the fuel as the twat didn't even have any in his tank, pay 700 pesos for a 250-peso ride as he wouldn't switch the meter on, and he got so angry with him that he threw his money at him on the front seat and stormed out of his dirty cab.

He shrugged, satisfied, and thought, *I've shown him* – only to realise he had left his Union Jack Tavern bought and paid for take away meal of beef Vindaloo, rice, poppadums and naan bread on the back seat, which he'd had been waiting for lonely weeks to get and had not eaten all day, just so he could enjoy eating in his posh bed in luxury. Jack stormed through the glass doors ignoring the security guards who were carrying more arms than Charlton Heston, but only the wise people knew they couldn't afford the bullets for them, and muttered to himself, "The thieving bugger, he got an Indian supper as well as ripping his starving customer off. The bastard."

As he sat on his bed in tears, eating a Snickers bar from the vastly expensive mini bar, he thought about what a shit day it had been and hoped tomorrow would be better as he was heading home to a place where things actually worked, there were no firearms and people were hit with long sticks in Changi Jail if they ripped you off.

So as he climbed into the taxi the next day to head to the dodgy airport, he was determined this one would be a good last day. The driver, having been booked by the Marriott hotel, was not the usual bandit as he had to charge what was on the meter and not what he made up and extorted out of you.

He was wrong. This driver took the back roads and decided for some reason he would not take the skyway. Jack asked why he didn't; the smiling taxi man said he didn't want to cost him more money. *Nice,* Jack thought, *an honest Filipino taxi driver,* but advised him that he was in a hurry and would he try to get there quick. A mistake: as he then accelerated and screamed around the crowded roads like a poor man's Lewis Hamilton.

The back seats had no seatbelts so Jack was thrown around like a rag doll; well, not so much like that, as rag dolls aren't 110 kilos, but it was disturbing, to say the least. At last they got to near the airport and he then let out a cry, in some Tagalog expletive, screeched into a handbrake turn and headed off back down the road they had just come down. He apologised in broken English that he had missed the turning and it would take more time. Jack told him to get a move on: not a wise move.

He nearly hit several people, cars, stalls and jeepneys (Filipino equivalent of tuk-tuks in Thailand). Jack was sweating, his heart racing, and asking him to slow down.

He continued and hurtled around a corner. Disaster – facing them was a police car in the middle of the road and two police officers with hands in the air asking them to stop. Why? Jack had no idea, but it was plain his taxi man didn't see them as he headed straight for them. Jack shouted for him to stop but he just went straight at them and suddenly he must have realised as he swerved the cab to the left, across another carriageway, just missing a bus, and then back onto our original carriageway ahead of the police car road block. Jack turned round to see the policemen taking guns from their holsters and levelling them at the rapidly receding cab. As he was the target between them and the driver Jack ducked down onto the back seat. They were just about to fire, when the taxi man screeched around a corner and safety beckoned.

When Jack dared to look up, they had reached the airport and his nemesis was driving slower and smiling. Jack was trying not to have a coronary and his heart was beating out of his chest. He tried to refrain from battering him around the head as it didn't seem as if it would do the driver or the distraught consultant any good. As they pulled up the taxi driver smiled and turned around.

"Sir, very sorry, sir, but can you see my name?" And he pointed to his city badge as a licensed taxi, which was a large laminated rectangular sheet with a smiling photograph of his driver.

Jack looked and noticed his name in large letters: Perfecto.

The taxi man laughed as he pointed and said: "My mother, she call me Perfecto, but I think not, sir. You think so?"

"My friend, Perfecto in name you may be, but in nature you certainly are not," Jack replied and laughed with the jovial Perfecto.

He even gave the smiling bugger a tip.

Perfecto indeed.

As he sat in the airport drinking beer with Pat and Digger he reflected upon his assignment. He was never sure about this project and why most there told him that they wanted out when in reality they were in heaven. After three years of meeting all forms of contracting life he started to form the theory that down there in the Philippines he had met the crème de la crème of real contractors. He was duped, they just all lied; a collective Stockholm Syndrome. But never mind, even genius can be defeated sometimes. This was merely a statistical glitch in his wonderful theory soon to make him famous.

Puzzled but happy with the progress made and also the lovely non-armed Philippine people he had met and became friends with, he went back to a gun- and extortion-free Singaporean paradise and copious amounts of Tiger beer to recuperate from Perfecto and his kind.

However, the contractors are still there and still eating cookies, all wearing L'Oréal and Nivea factor 50 sunscreens, eating mince and cookies, playing golf and hoping for yet another turkey out of the next project.

CHAPTER SIXTEEN

Paris, France

Whispering John

Early year four...

The Iron Chancellor was in usual form when he gave Jack his latest assignment.

"You will go to Paris and attempt to get that systems supplier to conform to our Supplier Assurance Program or I will have to take action myself with both them and you. Do not fall into your normal paradigm of bars, women and golf days; I will expect a report every night from you and a conference call every night. Your flights and hotel have been booked for next week. You will stay there until we have a recovery execution plan. We cannot risk failure this late in the project."

"OK Jon. Do you need me to go Russia after as I will be over in Europe? I thought you may like to see what progress has made there with the Supplier Assurance Program and cultural alignment of the supplier team that you attempted on your last visit."

Jack was hoping he could keep himself out of the demanding German's line of fire by taking even more time away from his office and the inquisitions and work discipline imposed by the demanding man. Jon waved him aside.

"No, I believe I have sorted that myself on my last visit there. Did I show you the PR video I made?"

"No Jon, you didn't."

Sadly, Jack was worried as Jon had been on his on his own when he went there. He did not have his tortured consultant coaching him on cultural alignment and hopefully preventing him from causing the next Winter War.

It was very unsettling as he sat in the tropics for Jack to watch Jon on screen far away in the frozen land of Mafia, snow and vodka as Jon showed him on his computer the PR video he had made. He was sat upright behind his desk, wearing his ubiquitous white, long-sleeved shirt and tie, staring fixedly into the camera as he uttered yet another Iron Chancellor classic.

"Working in Russia is difficult; these people don't speak English and their manners and meetings are atrocious. We have had to educate them in how to run projects. We have had to eliminate a few of them and I replaced them with articulate, intelligent engineers and after some effort it is now on track."

Jack watched the rest of the movie in silence, which was as he would have expected a series of progress curves, histograms, key performance figures and one picture of the actual equipment. He noted that there were no Russians in the video, or any human beings. And this was a public relations video! Jon was pleased, however.

"I believe my efforts have not gone unnoticed by the Russians and they assure me I will not be needed to go back. In fact they have insisted. So you will not waste your time there. You will try to sort the French. They are all like you and your friends, debauched, decadent and indolent. You should be able to get on with them and sort it out. Do not come back until I have agreed your plan. Goodbye…"

Jack spent the next week preparing and arranging his schedule and meetings in Paris. He also spent much time in the bars as usual, especially The Outback as he had become fascinated with a newcomer to the bar who he had named Tony Four Fingers.

Tony arrived out of the blue one Christmas. Curiously he said he had lost his finger in a woodworking accident, or so he told everyone. Like innumerable people Jack had met out in Asia, 'he had to leave the UK in a hurry'. As usual, he claimed that he was a contractor of some sort. He told everyone that he was on holiday. He was a large squat man, main digitless on one hand, shaved head and he lived on Aussie mince pies and Tiger. He pulled out big wads of dollars and peeled them off the roll easily, a technique perfected by Robert De Niro or all people you ever met who were used to having money given to them by unfortunate kneecapless victims; bookies, drug cartels, or literary agents.

He was all by himself over Christmas and New Year for four weeks. He had never left the bar, never saw any of the sights, he never ate in any of the amazing restaurants and hawker stalls that this wonderful city of all cultures has. He only ate Aussie mince pies and drank Tiger.

He said he came from the Portsmouth on the South Coast of England, but the Londoners in the bar knew his accent and that he was from the East End of London where all were gangsters, football hooligans or actors on TV soap shows. There was a big gangland case going on at the Old Bailey at the time and those in the know reckon Tony Four Fingers was hiding from that famous criminal court's subpoena.

He left, just like Kneecap some weeks before the day Jack was being sent to France, and never said goodbye to anybody. Jack was sad as he was one more link in his research. However, when he entered the bar that day Jack received a package sent from Tony Four Fingers. Shah the lovely barmaid gave it to him with a letter he'd supposedly written to her, or he had had written for reasons of incrimination or illiteracy.

The package purported to contain a different album copy of a jazz band that he had liked when Dawn played them on her ageing, lethal sound system. It also contained spare CDs and he wanted Dawn to copy another favourite CD that he'd heard in the bar. Jack was naturally cautious because he always remembered when Tom Hagen in *The Godfather* was asked by Michael Corleone's girlfriend – remember the dumb blonde one who believed him when he told her he hadn't killed anyone – if he'd give Michael a letter from her. Tom Hagen said, 'If I accept that it could be proved in a court of law, habeas corpus, in nomine Patris, in flagrante and Hail Mary Mother of God that I have evidence of Michael's whereabouts.'

Needless to say, Jack didn't accept it. His legs and middle fingers were more important than the British Legal System.

There were many strange people in The Outback that week, some he'd met many times, others who like Tony Four Fingers arrived and left 'in a hurry'. As Jack stood drinking several Tigers with Captain Abe, Dawn and the Doc he looked around at the strange clientele around him and wondered how on earth they all arrived in this one spot. He asked Abe of one new face who he'd seen for a few nights: "Abe, who is that and what does he do for a living?"

"He lifts heavy weights," Abe replied, habitual cigarette in mouth and Bundaberg rum at his side.

Seemingly this large young man had intelligence, but his parents were rich so work was a bit of an anathema to him. He didn't speak much about his past – or speak at all, to come to that. For a few free beers he lifted the heavy beer barrels that Abe and Dawn need moving to the bar. Jack was suitably impressed with the young man's qualifications and wondered if he should recruit him into real contracting.

A slim Caribbean-looking black guy, with tightly curled Rasta hair came into the bar, high fiving everyone, carrying an amplifier and microphone. He waved hello to Abe and Dawn. This was 'Bongo Man'. He was the Caribbean singer who played most nights. He played endless Bob Marley. Intermittently, his sexy little Singaporean girl backing singer (she became a Singapore Idol by the way) would sing something they all liked but inevitably Bongo Man would revert back to his native roots and they'd get 'We're Jammin'' again and again, while he bashed away on his bongos.

Of obvious Caribbean descent, no one knew how he arrived in Singapore. He was instantly recognisable by the deformity on his nose which looked very much like a young Ganja seedling (so the Dutch customers reckoned). He may have been the only man to flout the draconian Singapore drug laws by literally growing his own.

Jack said hello to another small local man, very slightly built, very like Father Bob with his trousers hanging off his backside. This was Chris the Insurance Man, a Chinese Singaporean, who was perpetually pissed morning, noon and night. Jack asked Dawn: "What does Chris actually do for a living?"

"It was rumoured he was 'Big' in insurance," Dawn answered.

The Doc, in jovial mood after a few Crown beers shouted across the bar: "He mustn't have a bloody office coz he's never in the bugger."

He was correct, because like the English Indian who was yet to enter the bar, no one knew what Chris really did.

He was, however, a very kind and generous man. Chris had a propensity to buy his favourite people very odd local candy and snacks. They all smelled of fish. Big Marc reckoned, "The bag smells like my wife's laundry basket."

He loved to give these to Gator's son, who was four or five at the time. He never took offence when the boy, sensibly preferring Snickers bars or chips, spat the 'foreign shit' out all over the floor and proceeded to kick him in the shins.

As Bongo Man started his Caribbean racket, a few patrons started dancing on the septic tank that was the Outback carpet. One of these was 'Meester Flintstone', so called because that is all he ever called Jack, due to him once getting pissed in a Fred Flintstone outfit with Danny the demented project manager who was dressed in a neoprene suit as Dino the dinosaur for a project Christmas party. Both of whom entered The Outback pissed after walking up Orchard Road for a mile in ninety-five degree heat and ninety-eight per cent humidity. Danny's red heed was covered in oceans of sweat and his body temperature had reached boiling point in the neoprene suit.

They recovered after several Tigers and Danny told all of the assembled lunatics the story of Jack's supernatural rescue.

"We got to the junction of Orchard and Scott Road, which as you all know is something like thirty metres wide and the traffic lights have a thirty-second timer. We started to hurry across, getting weird looks from the local Singaporeans. The clock was ticking and we were only about three quarters of the way over when it started to count down to ten. As you know if you are caught on the road when the lights turn red the cars keep coming so despite the sweat teeming out of us we hurried up. Then a small boy fell over in front of us; his parents were several steps ahead and didn't see him and the clock went to five seconds and the boy was never going to make it as he lay down crying. His parents got to the other side and turned around. His mother screamed when she realised her boy was imminently about to get squashed by the hordes of commuters heading home along Scott Road. She pointed to the boy and asked for help and the only two behind him were a Dinosaur and Fred Flintstone. Fred accelerated, stepped over the boy and grabbed him and lifted him up in his arms and ran across to the screaming mother and deposited him in her arms."

Everyone laughed at this, while Danny took a breath and another Tiger beer.

"Both parents and boy and many Singaporeans just stood and looked astonished at the large Fred and his Dino standing there who had just performed a superhuman feat of human kindness. The boy's father looked up at Fred and said, 'Thank you, lah,' and held out his hand. Fred took it and shouted, 'Yabba, dabba, doo! Come on Dino, we gotta put that cat out for the night,' and walked down Orchard Road with Dino trotting behind, sweat pissing out of his costume down his legs."

Tonight the surrogate Meester Flintstone was beginning his nightly courtship. He worked in the Four Floors, selling electronic equipment all day. Thinner and wirier than Father Bob, with a bald head, trousers hanging of him like a bag of rags, he looked bit like an Asian Sammy Davies Jr. He was a master groper. He was always pissed and asked all women to dance. The local girls would tell him to piss off because they knew he was a pervert.

Any new Caucasian tourist entering this asylum was immediately offered a dance. Of course they all accepted the local hospitality and husbands and lovers were delighted to take the holiday snaps of 'Gladys dancing with a native'.

Many locals often wondered when the visitors got back to Australia, Europe or where ever and looked at the photos, how they explained to the family the fact that Aunty Gladys had a dusky arm up her skirt and 'Meester Flintstone' was pushing a rapidly hardening bulge in his trousers into her back.

Tonight he was courting a rather large Danish lady and she was seemingly enjoying both his attentions and Bongo Man's wailing. Jack shook his head and turned to talk to another local who had stood next to him, poking his arm to get his attention and standing with a large vodka and Coke in his hand.

This was 'Syndicate Man' who was another Malay-origin

Singaporean who was always reluctant to speak too much about the past. He constantly wanted foreigners to engage in gambling on the English Premiership Football League. This fascinated most UK citizens because they remembered years ago when matches were rigged by the Malaysian Betting Syndicate in Asia. Goalkeepers were videoed by private detectives, taking brown paper envelopes stuffed full of ringgits or Singapore dollars and subsequently they'd drop the ball at the feet of the grateful opposing centre forward with only one minute to go in the match. In one match, they paid someone off to turn off the floodlights at a crucial time when the result was not going their way. None ever expected to end up in the company of the man who did it!

That evening Syndicate Man was explaining to Jack in whispers, over the incessant Reggae music, the reason why David Beckham, England football captain, had missed three penalties in row.

"Jack, he did so to save his famous pop star wife being sold off to T Squared and the Asian sex trade. I put five hundred on for half a goal and won a fortune."

Syndicate Man constantly went on about giving someone half a goal, or two goals, he was offering Jack another bet that evening.

"It's a certainty, Jack, you know what I mean."

Jack had no clue what half a goal was but all he knew was that when he and his mates risked hard-earned contractors' wedge they always won. So that evening, mainly to get rid of the mercurial gambler and syndicate fixer before the Singapore secret police collared him and had him beaten with sticks in Changi, he gave him fifty dollars for a half goal. Syndicate Man left to talk to a shady-looking Malaysian in the corner who was carrying a Spice Girls CD!

'The man with no eyes' scared Jack most nights because just like the name sake in *Cool Hand Luke*, he never ever took off his dark glasses. It was pitch black sometimes in there when Dawn hadn't paid the electricity bill and he would sit with his black shades on, staring blankly at the wall. Just like 'he who lifts heavy weights', Jack never heard him speak. Dawn explained to him that he was a hairdresser and that he never takes his dark glasses off at work either, which makes you wonder how he can tell what colour he has used on anyone's hair. Needless to say, there are some strange hair colours in and around Tanglin Road.

As usual around nine o'clock the English Indian arrived in the bar. He leaned against the space that Syndicate Man had left and greeted Jack with a polite 'good evening' and ordered his Tiger beer. Jack answered and began talking to the man as he liked him a lot, but had no idea who the hell he was. This was because the English Indian was a particularly secretive individual. He was quite a loner, always came in to the Down Under every evening at around 9 p.m. He sat at the end of the bar by himself, smoking, and drank steadily. Jack got into conversation with him on a few occasions and found him very articulate and very humorous.

He was a people watcher like Jack and had some very similar observations. He was liked by most. He told everyone that he was English, and surprisingly he could talk lucidly about cricket, rugby, football etc. and get angry about the various failures of the English at practically everything.

"We English…" He would start the conversation, though plainly with an Indian accent and definitely looks.

Or, "The old country is going to dogs, Dawn, too many coloureds."

His son, he said, had returned to public school there. Plainly he was a man of some means. However, he refused to tell anyone what he did for a living or why he left the homeland, or what he did back home. He just smiled and said, "One day I might."

Jack baited him continually on his past and present but he steadfastly refused to bite. That was until one humid Sunday evening. It had been a particularly long one; the usual inmates had started at 10 a.m. with the Australian Grand Prix. Big Marc provided bacon, sausages, smoked salmon and scrambled eggs, and also for the Francophiles, croissants and brioche (nobody ate them of course, except Marc's beautiful but tormented Gallic wife) cooked in Captain Abe's Aussie pie warmer, with lashings of champagne and Tiger.

It went on through a particularly traumatic defeat, for some, but not the rest of the world's flotsam in the bar, of the English rugby team by Kneecap's mates from the Emerald Isle and was going to close at 1 p.m. after a high-scoring English Premier League soccer game. At about 3 p.m. there entered the bar a particularly smart-looking gentleman, military looking, who proceeded to drink beer and watch the rugby. He did not look like a real contractor so all were puzzled. Ever the nosey one, and hoping he might get a sale of bodies, Captain Abe asked him his name, got into a few beers with him and tried to find out who he was. The stranger said that he was, "in international business development" and on his way back to the UK and had stopped off for a few days' holiday.

"Where are you coming from?" Abe enquired.

"Vladivostok," he replied.

And so it went on over a few more beers. It appeared he'd worked in the same places that Kneecap had, but not quite, his had all been war zones: Bosnia, Chechnya, Kosovo etc. and his latest posting had been Moscow. No one knew if Kneecap had been to Moscow.

To cut a long evening short, the Doc gave him a truth serum in his Tiger and he finally confessed that he belonged to a, "division of the British Foreign Office." That was enough for Kneecap, who 'left in hurry' again; a British spy, obviously. The Doc had a good chuckle with him over the material he could find in the Down Under and having enjoyed a few Tigers the spook went on his way, via Kneecap's house, car and bank accounts.

When the English Indian came in Abe told him about this reconnoitre by the spook and he just happened to drop casually into the conversation, "I told him about you!"

Our Britannic Moghul promptly spat a whole mouthful of his Tiger all over the ample breast of Siti, the lovely barmaid.

"Please, Abe, don't do that, please no. It's not funny."

He pleaded a little too forcefully for all of the bar. Still no one knows what the English Indian is or was but like Kneecap, he moves in some very strange circles.

Jack liked the English Indian, and most Indians he'd met and worked with. However, he had managed to miss working in India. Big Hansie had educated him about the place and the food. Like his dislike of all things kaffir – put simply, non-Boer – he was not keen on our Moghul cousins and in light of his venom on all things Indian, it's probably not difficult to see why they may be paranoid like the Paranoid Indian and the English Indian.

However, Hansie had a rabid dislike for most races other than his own. Norwegians were snow kaffirs; Arabs, sand kaffirs; Indians, curry kaffirs and so on. That evening he arrived with his lovely lady and joined Jack, Dawn and Abe and the English Indian at the bar. He was quite fond of the English Indian, mainly because they could talk rugby, but he loved to bait the small, very thin Indian gentleman who came in later, Manju, the cook.

This guy was sadly not like Steed, he was not well trousered; because like Father Bob and Bill the Argument, Manju's trousers hung around his very thin, bony ass and he wore flip flops which the trouser bottoms covered up. He had a habit of picking his sockless toes, which were covered with brown horny protrusions like one of Buffalo Alf's now extinct gazelles, and absolutely mucky. He smoked roll-your-own cigarettes in which he placed one thread of his baccy he had shipped in from India for two rupees a kilo. He offered Hansie a smoke, much to the big man's disgust.

"**** right off! That baccy is just your own shit and grass. Smells like the shithole you live in. Filthy, all of you: you make kaffirs look clean."

Hansie was never keen on taking up his offer of Indian cigarettes a la Manju, nor was he very compliant with racial abuse laws and all that good-world citizen stuff as you may gather. He offered Jack advice yet again about avoiding India for work.

"Jack, never ever go to where this ****** comes from. Gujarat is the worst place on earth and I've been to many of them, all over the planet."

And picking up a Tiger beer in his huge hand, he shook his flowing blond locks and looked down at Manju and gave his final statement on India.

"It's a shithole, and like you, it's filthy dirty."

Our mild-mannered Indian cook just sat there smoking and drinking, smiling. Jack wondered often what he was thinking about regarding his cultural enlightenment in the Down Under.

Hansie was actually fond of him and used to buy him beer as the poor guy was perpetually skint. His wages he sent to India, except a few dollars for his bus and his couple of beers. Jack lent him money often in the certainty he would never return it. And indeed he never did as several months before that evening when Jack had entered the bar they were all excited. Jack asked: "What's the craic? Why are you all happy?'"

"That Indian curry kaffir won the lotto for ****'s sake," Hansie exclaimed.

"He's bought the beer all afternoon, and has now gone back to India," a delighted Dawn said, as her takings expanded. He then paid his bar bill as well and to Dawn, that was her own personal lotto, as he owed her a couple of thousand from over a couple of years.

"I know you loaned the curry kaffir money, mate, but you can say goodbye to that, you daft ******. I told you not to trust a curry kaffir," Hansie laughed. And he continued in full abuse mode: "Sixty grand makes him a millionaire in that shithole he calls home. You're ******."

For Jack it was yet another few hundred gone on his research for his next thesis. Maybe one day, he thought, he might get the loan back from sales of a book, which his children and family and those of limited cognitive abilities might buy.

But interestingly, like Kneecap Dara, Manju had returned and was ensconced amongst them that evening again.

It seems his relatives took his money and dispersed it amongst many of them across Gujarat and they were lifted from poverty, whilst Manju was kept in a world of excessive cheap liquor and toenail manicures. He was skint when he came back, now working again for his old boss in the Indian restaurant next to the Oz bar.

He had the same flip flops and trousers and they all still kept him in beer. Big Hansie had abused him most days on his return, and that night after the ritual abuse he bought him beer and gave him his bus fare home and the money for a toenail cut.

The Outback was full of people like Kneecap, Tony Four Fingers, Manju, The Commodore and the English Indian. Many people who had 'left in a hurry' or just refused to tell you why they were there and left without a goodbye. Many were contractors, many not.

Dawn's asylum was always getting strange people turning up and staying for periods of time varying from thirty seconds for more intelligent ones, to three years for those that turned native. Dawn could indeed 'bind them all in the darkness'.

Sometimes Dawn captured academics, whose purpose in life was to observe the strange behaviours of her customers. In quantum mechanics there is a theory that if you observe something, you change it. Latest reality theory tries to align the paradox of Bell's Theorem and the fact that it is the consciousness that observes and changes quantum effects. All of this is of no use to the observer of the inhabitants of The Outback, as such observation can never change such perverse behaviour. Only a baseball bat or narcotics can do that. One of the academics who was entrapped by Dawn's Shelob-type web, was Dingo Dave, who came in the bar just after Manju.

Dingo Dave, another Australian tourist, had turned up several weeks before. This was not unusual for the bar purported to be an Australian bar, even though every disenfranchised nation and creed throughout the known, and also the unknown worlds, were ensconced in their regular positions at the bars and tables. This person was unusual in that after a few Tigers and glasses of Dawn's Australian red plonk he declared himself an anthropologist.

The Doc's ears had pricked up like a dingo smelling an Australian mince pie. This was great news. The Doc, though not qualified to study and comment on social evolution, suspected many in The Outback had not evolved from New Guinea head hunter tribal customs or the Great African Rift Valley, but from some unknown tribes in Arkansas or Wales.

The Doc was convinced that The Outback was the cradle of biological evolution; the primordial soup that produced the first amino acids was to be found oozing from its carpet floor. He had no experience to analyse the non-biomedical traits of inmates of The Outback and needed an expert to reference their relationship to hominid evolution.

Here in Dingo Dave was the perfect opportunity to test the influence of social evolution on customers. Did certain tribal influences, racial characteristics, social bonding etc. have an influence on the behaviour of the western foreigner at work? Did the size of the cranium or the optic chiasmata have any influence on the antisocial habits of the characters inhabiting the bars and workplaces? Should, and could they be exterminated by the indigenous population who had to put up with their riotous and depraved behaviours?

The good Doc hoped this Professor of Anthropology may find some of these answers to these questions.

After a few visits the Doc began to doubt the Australian's qualifications to live and work with the indigenous species in the bar. He was no Richard Leaky, Attenborough or Dianne Fossey. Our own gorilla in the mist was quickly sussed out, for when he tried to smell the arse of Boring Rod, the hairy Aussie business lecturer, Rod smacked him with a warm mince pie.

Not for macho Australians the subtlety of primate bonding and subjugation of adolescent males. Moving on to courtship; this diminutive academic made a fatal mistake by scratching his balls and displaying his chest, enticing a much larger female of the species – Dawn.

The landlady was more horny than usual and she gave him one of her New Guinea hugs and he was found days later in her ample bosom by the Singapore Heath and Environment Agency, still searching for the lost health inspector who disappeared in a similar manner months before, during his annual inspection of the bar.

Our intrepid researcher was from the University of NSW, Sydney, Australia. He was not particularly incognito in his dress or mannerisms. He looked like Wolfie from the UK 1970s series *Citizen Smith* or 'Che' Guevara. He wore khaki clothes and a military red beret.

He informed everyone that he was doing a study of the expat community in Singapore. Obviously, he believed that he had entered the Tutankhamen's Tomb of Anthropology when he'd stumbled on The Outback Bar.

He spent hours monitoring and researching in the bar whilst getting pissed, drinking copious vats of red wine. He even began to exhibit the worst excesses of foreign behaviour himself and began to make journeys to the Four Floors of Whores, supposedly carrying out research, but he ended up screwing the local girls, and probably to ensure he had an unbiased sample, the boys. He even had a bash at the more liberated male Caucasian customers in the bar.

The Doc began to realise that he could be of little use to him and may actually harm the perfect ecosystem that had evolved in the Down Under. So he began to dissuade him from such interventionist behaviour.

The Doc asked him one early day during his research, what were his initial observations on Dawn's microcosm of life?

"Strewth, mate! It's rather surreal!"

'In what way?" the medic asked.

"Strewth: I've never seen so many different socially inadequate or culturally diverse individuals in my life." And Dingo continued, "Do you have any idea what we've stumbled upon in here?"

"Yes. I believe they are not here by accident. So you shouldn't get too excited about a Richard Leaky type of anthropological find. These people don't follow known scientific fact, man," the Doc said.

The good Doc continued excitedly.

"For ****'s sake don't you start a dig here. You never know what creature you might unearth from below that bloody carpet. All of Pandora's horrors might exist in that."

All looked down at the oozing mass, beginning to feel afraid, very afraid.

"You see," continued the demonic Welsh medic, "these, shall we call them subjects, are only here because the local mental hospital has a Care in the Community scheme and this place is home to most of the displaced patients," and glancing around guiltily, he whispered even quieter, "even some of the doctors who need help end up in this bar."

He carried on.

"You see, it's not a social evolution thing in here. It's just that everyone is raving mad. Really, mate, you should give up on this bar if you expect to see what foreign culture in Singapore is really like. In here no one cares if you're an expat, local, tourist, arms dealer, spy, bookie, teak dealer or if you're actually sane. We are a corrupted sample, mate. Get out before it's too late."

And he did. But not before going native in the Four Floors of Whores, research on hold.

He frequently returned to the bar as he had that evening, but sadly he was out of favour with most for his unwelcome sexual proclivity and anal sniffing habits, and he sat at the back, watching Meester Flintstone get the kicks that he really thought he should have had...

and Bongo Man played on…

Jack flew off to Paris. He stayed near St Germaine en Laye and spent some time there with the supplier of wires, valves and computer bytes.

There were few real contractors to provide any new data for his research or indeed enlighten him on the cultural nuances of the French. He realised after a few days in France that certain truisms existed about the French and their behaviours, and that they were as directly opposite to Asian behaviours as you could get. He noted a few down for future reference to counsel and dissuade anyone thinking of moving from Asia to France.

In Asia most establishments always make the drinking and eating pleasurable. That normally means having unlimited girls play with the customers' aching limbs and nether regions after a hard day in the office. This means that you can charge extortionate money for cheap drink and enhance your home country's economy in a symbiotic way. Note: unlike in Paris, where the French have not learnt this lesson, and believe it's much better to treat foreign customers like shit and hope they never come back to interfere with their undoubted superior culture. Note: France is in an economic and social mess whilst Asia continues to grow faster than a French politician can drop his trousers.

If you are Asian, even if you are not typically friendly and smile a lot, like Leroy in The Excalibur Bar, Singapore, and you wish to set up a customer-oriented enterprise (oxymoron) in France then you must remember that the French customer does not expect to see you smile or serve them on time and with the correct quality. They will be confused and disoriented, and leave to be verbally abused by your competition and happily wait for hours for their product, not yours.

It is best to learn the body language first. The language is incomprehensible, stick to nonverbal communication; no smiles, just shrugs of shoulders will do, they understand that more that verbal communication. Practise regularly the shrug and never open your business when the customer may actually want your service i.e. between 12 and 3 p.m., Mondays, Sundays, 150 Saint's Days, and the whole of July and August or after 5 p.m.

Yes, it's strange for an Asian to adapt to this non-service culture but it's the only way to survive and live there – well at least until China takes over in the Élysée Palace, then you can open up a dried tiger penis or white rhino horn outlet for all the redundant French politicians who will need a boost to their male ego for sure.

But it was in France that Jack met Tony Four Finger's doppelganger. He was Whispering John.

He was a very thin and pallid, a drawn-out man of very quiet nature and demeanour. He turned up very discreetly on a particularly boring Sunday lunchtime at the end of Giles's bar in St Germaine en Laye, which was aptly named, if Jack couldn't appease his boss Jon. It was called The Bitter End. He spoke very softly and only in whispers in Jack's ear as if the world, or the police, were listening to everything he may say. He had a broad East End London cockney accent. Needless to say, Jack had to get close to this man despite his temporary insanity of agreeing to go to France. There was obviously so much research material here and he longed for and so missed the other lunatics and sociopaths from The Outback. He was also sick of being treated like shit by Parisian waiters, so he really made an attempt to bond with this enigmatic man.

After a week of intense research and gallons of Aspels Suffolk Cider he realised that he had met a friend of Tony Four Fingers: after all the weeks since he disappeared. He was never wrong about people who had issues; as the Doc was often heard to say he was an expert in hangovers because, 'I have had millions myself.' It seemed to Jack that Whispering John was of similar background to Tony Four Fingers. He was pleased that his theory was proven correct.

Whispering was from the East End, London, and was a founder member of the notorious Inter City Firm (ICF), West Ham Football Hooligans. Whispering showed Jack two bullet holes in his bony body, which by the way made Father Bob's body look like Arnie's, and also a sword scar from his knee to mid-abdomen, a leftover of a little ruck with some Millwall supporters. He would not discuss how he got the bullet holes.

He explained that he was studying law in Paris. But it took Jack a few days to drum up the courage to tell him that he thought this was improbable. He told him that he had met many guys who had 'left home in a hurry' and wouldn't grass him up, and that he was 'a diamond geezer'. Jack tried unsuccessfully to sound like a 'real naughty' cockney hard man. But he told the secretive, quiet man that if he was on the run, like Four Fingers, then it was no bother to him, but just to tell the truth, as they had become passing mates.

Whispering would not budge on his story and insisted that he was studying there for a degree and the next day brought three books, stamped inside with 'Property of Nanterre University'. Jack being naturally paranoid after living in The Outback and The Sportsman's for years, never really believed this story fully and was sure he was on the run like Four Fingers. He never believed him totally, even when he asked Jack to take him from his digs in the student residence at Nanterre University to Charles de Gaulle airport at term end, as he could not carry his case too far because of the emphysema caused by the bullet in his lungs and the millions of cigarettes he still smoked. But when Jack turned up at Nanterre University, true to Whispering John's word, he did indeed have a room there.

Jack considered briefly that he should be less suspicious and doubting about his academic studies, but as he had heard a small amount of his chequered past (as he was a diamond geezer and no grass, he could never tell) he said goodbye, still very sceptical. However, as he waved goodbye to his newfound friend, just like Four Fingers, Jack speculated that maybe the trial was over now, hence his return from his Nanterre University hiding place – or the chief witness was dead. He decided the best course of action was to rest his case.

The Bitter End was a very British of pub, owned and run by Giles, that raconteur and most English of men and his hard-working Yorkshire wife, Gina, and in any other world it would have been delightful. However, Jack spent every night and all weekends in it surrounded by normal people and the French, and he began moping for real contractors and the dusky, friendly bar ladies of Asia and Tiger beer. The Bitter End served real beer, cider and cooked mince, so that was a bonus. The mince was only in burgers, but it was still mince. As moules, hors d'oeuvres, escargots or bull's penis were not real contractor bait, and a lot of French food seemed to be very much like the Chinese, that is, it had no backbones, he avoided the other more Gallic establishments and stayed in his comfort zone.

During his first visit to Giles' mission station he had met Youssef. This lovely man was attempting to persuade Giles to give him work in the kitchen supplementing Bernie the usual cook, a rather large Papua New Guinea head-hunter who turned from tribal cannibalism to chef de cuisine (as you do, you may say).

Bernie's talents lay in cooking a menu that erred towards standard western food with a nice French influence; burgers, chicken, French salads, fried Camembert cheese, fish and chips, curries. Youssef was proposing that he could bring in a more North African menu that French customers would enjoy. This caused consternation for Bernie as he began to worry for his job and Youssef would try to fuel this by suggesting that Bernie was not really as good a cook as he would be. Petty, you may say, but it worried Giles and his patrons as they all suspected Bernie had not lost his natural Papuan culinary instincts.

Youssef fuelled this paranoia by calling Bernie and himself 'just n*****s who serve white people', and he was always calling Bernie a cannibal, and always told him that 'we white n*****s should stick together against the Infidel.'

He always said he said this in his form of jest and all hoped that Bernie enjoyed the banter, but given Bernie's size and origin they worried that one day they may find Youssef in a large pan of bouillabaisse and Bernie smiling and chewing betel nut, flipping burgers, pouring Youssef's North African couscous in the bin.

Youssef would talk and have a drink with Jack in the bar trying to recruit his help to convince Giles that he could win him a Michelin star with his talents, and when this inevitably failed, he would move on to the evils of the western world.

He spoke perfect English, came from Tunisia, and had lived in France for some years. He manically disliked the Americans, the Israelis, the French (the white French) and French police. He tried to educate Jack in the ways of Islam.

Jack feared he may well become radicalised in The Bitter End and he would try to head out to escape Youssef's Islamic indoctrination. He'd try to hide in Jackie's bar on la Rue de Paris, St Germain en Laye, and Youssef would follow him, sneak up next to him and whisper his thoughts on all things western (he was like Whispering John in that he thought everyone was listening to him: indeed as things evolved Jack realised they probably were).

He would whisper, leaning up at his theology pupil's ear, looking one way and then the other for anyone who may be listening.

"Everyone in here is a racist, Jack, except you. I hate these people, all of them. They hate us North African Arab n*****s. Look, a racist, I know that."

He repeated this each visit about the barman and owner Jackie, who was as French as you could get and from Brittany and very socialist and liberal in his politics. One time he pointed to another old white Frenchman, sitting at the bar sipping his vin rose and staring into space.

"He is Le Front Nationale. He loves Le Penn. I just know this, Jack. You will too, when you understand and join us in our fight."

He would continue: "Let's get out of here, Jack. I can't stay in here, they are right-wing racists as they all hate me and you shouldn't drink with people like these."

He would walk with Jack to the RER station and they'd continue the education in the bar next to station, run by the browner and more Mediterranean-looking Frenchmen or Portuguese that he felt more comfortable with.

Many times he whispered the various verses of the Qur'an and gave Jack references to Cambridge and Oxford Arab and Muslim clerics and professors, internet links to their papers and dissertations and who he should read to become more enlightened. He would talk about Christianity and have educated discussions about Jesus being a beloved Muslim prophet and that he had no problems with the forgiveness aspects of Jesus's teaching: a tenet that he seemly misunderstood, as he always ended his lesson by suggesting that Jack should embrace the Muslim faith more and then join with him to convert everyone to Islam and eliminate all unbelievers, the West and all things right-wing French!

In fact, Jack always enjoyed the less radical and more rational discussions with Youssef. He found that he was an intelligent man but he feared that he verged on jihad most of time and may have had connections to carry it out, it seemed.

And he grew fond of Jack.

"Jack, I like you. You are non-racist and understand about faith. If you ever need help then my family will look after you and if anyone ever tries to harm you or the family, we put them in cellar, and torture them. Jack, no one messes with us. I will put anyone in cellar that hurt your family."

His nephews seemingly had a propensity to kidnap people that he disagreed with and then they seemed to follow the Terry Waite way of indoctrination. Whilst this was reassuring and a compliment to Jack's ecumenical relationship with this new friend, it was a bit worrying if he broke apart on their theological debates so he tried, sadly in vain, to avoid Youssef's preaching.

Interestingly, Whispering John also had promised Jack he and his West Ham lads would protect his son when he went to London to attend university, and that various appendages of anyone who threatened him would be lost forever. He never mentioned cellars and torture, mind, one may guess that is an Arab cultural thing; East End gangsters must have different values.

Indeed, Jack came to realise he was continuing his cross-cultural training here with these two newfound French chums, each different in their culture, but similar in their behaviour, both of whom communicated only in whispers and extreme violence. He was reminded again about the different interpretation to correct corporate culture and that Steven Covey once wrote: 'even criminals have values.'

Perversely, Youssef would drink and he liked and talked about screwing many women and he really had a black sense of humour mirroring western culture, so Jack was never sure about his real fundamentalist leanings or indeed if he was not throwing bait at him and watching the reaction with joy.

On reflection back in Singapore, he was certain that his Muslim friend was more like the Paranoid Indian; he was probably motivated to angst because he thought all westerners hated him because he was North African. Not unfairly given some of the personal, racist and discriminatory experiences shown in a lot of white right-wing France, he was probably pretty much correct.

On return to the wrath and torture from the Iron Chancellor for spending far too much time in Paris and spending far too much money on beer and mince, Jack awaited the emails that Youssef said he'd exchange as he wanted to send writings from his favourite academics, clerics and friends. But Jack never received anything; nor did he ever receive any answers to the e-mails he sent him.

He checked several times with him in Paris that all was correct and he was sure both e-mails were correct, and he was told that they certainly were. After a period, however, he stopped all contact through this medium as he became convinced all messages were intercepted by the DST, DGSE, CIA, Singapore secret service and MI5. He feared that he was now irrevocably placed on a European possible Islamic radical sympathiser list and may be hauled off to be beaten by sticks again in Changi Jail. Youssef stopped texting him also, which was almost certainly a blessing and hopefully dispensation from deportation to Guantanamo Bay.

However, as a postscript, some months later, Jack's son met the Islamic preacher on a visit to Paris and to see Giles and Gina as recommended by his father. Introduced by Giles to Youssef as Jack's son, Youssef was delighted and he kindly asked after Jack and his family and reaffirmed to his lad his promise to protect him and his kin. He whispered to the young and innocent boy, looking cautiously in many directions, and asked him if he had anyone 'he wanted locked in cellar'.

Jack's son wisely said: "No."

It seems that he had left the pub for pastures new and hopefully to persuade those sympathetic to his religious and North African Michelin star potential culinary causes to take him on. Thankfully his head was intact and not shrunken as Bernie was much happier, now back to flipping burgers and listening to rap at lunchtime, rather than Youssef's lectures on the Qur'an and his tales of subterranean terror.

Jack sat in The Outback on his return looking at the host of multinational faces, each with their own stories and faiths or non-faith, and remembered with fondness his short friendship with Youssef. He had liked him despite his paranoia about potential racists; he had a perverse sense of humour. He was certainly cleverer and more fun than many he'd met and had to listen to their own western racist and bigoted beliefs and one day he thought he may take him up on his subterranean offer; a few came to mind, and after his thrashing by the Iron Chancellor, he chuckled to himself thinking his German boss may well enjoy the delights of a bit of seclusion a la cave chez Youssef and his novel North African hospitality.

As he sat at the bar drinking yet another Tiger and reminiscing about his four years in Asia he realised that, apart from 'Osama Bin Laden's niece', he had never met any person here who was anything but polite, respectful and good humoured. Sitting here in Singapore, and surrounded by the largest Muslim nation in the world and also Malaysia, western people he knew were sometimes paranoid about that, but Jack pondered that everyone he had met, worked and lived with who followed Islam, everyone bar none, had been wonderful, respectful and humble.

He told this to Dawn who was sitting next to him, periodically giving him a huge hug and losing him in her immense bosom. She agreed but laughed when remembering Jack's first experience of cross-cultural dysfunction some years before and she reminded him.

"Jack, can you remember the story you told us of your first trip to Malaysia and the bacon sandwiches?"

She gave him another body-absorbing hug and when Jack emerged, with the delighted emancipated and emaciated food inspector, she told everyone in the bar who wanted to listen the story.

"Jack nearly had a cultural and diplomatic faux pas in Malaysia when he and his wife and two boys were driving the twelve hours from Singapore travelling up to the Perhentian Islands, where his daughter was ensconced as a diving instructor. Having driven across the causeway from Singapore to Johor Bahru, they were looking for somewhere to stop and eat their breakfast picnic that his poor wife had made up at the condo at the crack of dawn. About an hour up the road towards Mersing Jack spotted a car park with a nice new wooden shelter where it looked perfect to sit down inside and eat the picnic. He duly pulled over and they all walked into the shelter. It conveniently had separate small decorated woven mats on the floor to sit on and place the food. How thoughtful of our Muslim hosts, Jack said to his family, to provide home comforts for us all, and they sat down on the mats and opened up the parcels of food and drink from the picnic bag.

"As the family were avid eaters of the bacon sandwiches his wife had made some earlier, covered with HP brown sauce for her and boys, Heinz Tomato for him. There was a flask of coffee for her and soda for boys and Jack cracked a tin of Tiger beer and he thought, *A great start to our Malaysian adventure.*

"They sat talking and enjoying these western delights when Jack looked up at the roof of the wooden building and spotted a black arrow on the ceiling, pointing west of the rising sun, which was pouring its rays through the windowless hut. He seemed to remember somewhere in his cultural awareness seminars that Igor the henchman had informed him about this arrow. He took another bite of bacon sandwich and swallowed the last dregs of the excellent Tiger and strained his memory of what that bloody arrow was.

"It came to him in a flash of fear and dread; it was a qiblah compass. It pointed to Mecca and they were sitting on prayer mats, in a pseudo mosque kindly constructed for travelling devotees of Islam and their daily prayers and they were sitting guzzling cured porcine meat and drinking alcohol by the tin.

"Jack immediately thought of what Igor had told the project team of the Malaysian retribution about anyone who crossed their path and quickly gathered up the blasphemous evidence in the picnic bag, hurried the family out and into the car, driving off in a screech of tyres, hoping they had not been spotted by anyone of Youssef-like ilk. He did not fancy a stretch in the cellar for sure."

Everyone laughed and Dawn gave one more hug and absorbed Jack into her ample chest, more Tiger beers were ordered and the fun began. Jack lay back and thought, *Ralph was correct; let's hope I get one more Easter egg out of this.*

CHAPTER SEVENTEEN

Singapore

The Commodore

Nearing the end...

Jack entered The Sportsman's Bar and was greeted by Ralph, Billy and Father Bob and a host of real contractors who were in good spirits. Billy and Ralph had returned from South America where the project that they had originally been on in Singapore those years before had finally ended and everyone was celebrating the start of yet another project in paradise, this time in Malaysia. As he was offered yet another Tiger, Jack reflected on Ralph's original ideas and revelations on turkeys and Easter eggs. Since that day he had endured nights of constant Tiger, endless mince and tatties, Scottish history, the Glasgow Chanter and much sectarian banter. He was a martyr to the cause of effective communication and delivery of projects, all at no cost to his client, but only to his beta liver cells and funding Harry's next racehorse.

He had not seen the great men since they had sailed off to Brazil with their delighted fellow real contractors. Ralph had eventually lasted till the following July after meeting Jack for the first time in September four years ago. He had cooked his turkey and he eaten his Easter egg.

He outlasted two project managers along with a multitude of other delighted contractors, and as a totally expected economic boost to the local economy, they had funded many working girls, taxi drivers and bar owners. Symbiosis again: This symbiosis now clearly demonstrated to Jack the unerring principle of real contracting, that these projects and businesses that fail abjectly can mutually benefit economically and sociologically all concerned in society. But not for some: At the time Ralph was hoping for his various holiday bonuses, his company was allegedly losing on this project approximately a nine-figure sum.

Jack also had discovered the fact that company financial results in paradise do not correlate to employees' bank accounts or their lawyers' divorce fees. Poor Tiny Tim got a turkey, a wooden crutch; not even an exotic metal or stainless steel one that he could have been sold for scrap money, as most wise contractors do. However, he did get a bonus; a Christmas pudding with a few pennies in it. Ralph got a loyalty bonus of six months' pay for staying put on the job for his undoubted loyalty as well as six months of highly paid day rates and also, never forget his promised Easter egg.

But Tiny Tim's dad was Bob Cratchit and he wasn't a welder, plumber or electrician: he was a book keeper. Lesson for youngsters here; forget formal education or finance-related work (unless it is in an investment bank like Big Marc, and then you can earn even more money in your business career for global economic abject failure). Get a vocational-based trade qualification, apprenticeship or heaven forbid a degree in mechanical engineering and get your CV to Captain Abe or Harry, quick.

Over many months of research Jack had observed that the most proficient exponents of this type of motivation can even survive when there is no project at all. They can survive until the next loss-making project comes along, financed by some deranged business development team in the company who believe they can build a big steel structure, bigger, faster, lower cost and shorter time than the last one which ended up years late and massively over budget.

They last until an equally deranged global engineering contractor bites the deluded operator's hand off for the contract, which will have delay penalty clauses and liquidated damages large enough to close another corporate investment bank or pay back the Greek debt.

The delay and cost escalation of Ralph's project was the result of trying to do just that, which the corporate participants had committed to yet again; that is, build faster, cheaper and quicker than the last one which had failed to do the same thing without changing anything but reduce the price and the schedule.

Einstein said: "The definition of insanity is to keep doing the same thing and expect a different result." Who could question the sanity of this business?

In Ralph's case, as with all the projects in paradise, in an attempt to bring the project on schedule and rescue the Greek debt size penalty clause, Ralph and Billy had been brought in with a host of foreign real contractors one year previously.

They, along with hundreds more, were given huge day rates to 'motivate and incentivise them'. The project was then six months later than anticipated when the first rescue plan was put in place and would go on for another year; the motivation really worked, didn't it?

This is a classic oil company motivational behavioural model that continues to be applied to this day.

They brought famous names like Mechanical Ali, glad to get back into paradise contracting after a very poor choice of working in the Algerian desert. Mechanical Ali was so called because he had spent most of his work in the desert regions of the Middle East with little booze, no women and an abundance of camels and goats.

He could believe his luck when he came to SE Asia and immediately committed himself to making up for lost time. He crammed about twenty-five years of extracurricular screwing into about twelve months. He was in his late fifties or early sixties and quite looking forward to his retirement. He was rather a handsome, dapper man for his age and could charm the knickers off a nun.

With these Robert Redford looks and a commissioning engineer's wallet and per diem expense allowance, funny enough he never failed to pick up a girl. In fact, he held a record because during the past few weeks in Singapore he took home a girl every night for last forty-plus days he was working there.

The Naked Jock was also brought in. The Naked Jock, liked to sit naked in the cabin, cleverly avoiding any inquisitive and squeamish homophobic project managers.

A host of others were lured onto the project, mainly by their mates who told them it would never leave these shores for years and they all kept Harry, the Four Floors of Whores and The Outback Bar in clover for months.

This was classic project management; if you're in trouble throw more foreign expats at it and thousands of unskilled labourers, but this project manager couldn't convince his corporate auditors that he could recover. He made a fundamental mistake of actually telling them that he needed another US$200 million and nine months to get back on track. Sadly for him, he never had a plan. His client lost faith and he was history.

Of course the project manager was the only fatality; the real contractors he'd given a life of debauchery and sunshine to, carried on until finally it all had to end as the company gave up the battle and sailed the boat away to be finished somewhere else where they foolishly believed it would be cheaper. But they took the majority of the real lads with them – where? To the hell of South America! What a magic finesse. Those who had benefited from its Singapore failure, or success, whichever contractual hat you wore or bank balance you had, were rewarded with more money and the Copacabana and Ipanema beaches, surrounded by even more beautiful girls, rather than be sent to Sakhalin Island or Baghdad.

The choice is yours.

Jack was coming up with his own lessons now and now didn't need lecturing to by his real contractor research subjects. He quickly realised that one clear lesson was:

'Projects that are losing mega millions will pay millions to those people who can do little to change the outcome. If you wish to benefit from this, give up your job in financial admin or corporate life and become a real contractor. Always get onto a project where it's warm, sunny and the girls like wallets. Look for a project that's losing its ass.'

It was during these long nights of sweat and mental fatigue in bars of South East Asia and during his research in The Sportsman's that his theory and the behaviours necessary to survive in such a multiverse began to crystallise and he realised a simple fact that was: why would anyone want this life to end? The alternate argument was simple.

'If you lived and worked in an arsehole place, locked up in barracks for three months at a time and drinking nothing but tepid water, without any female company but the odd woman dressed head to foot in a bed sheet who may well want to saw your head off with a bread knife, you would very likely want it to end quickly – and indeed, if you check the success of many mega projects and business ventures in the arse ends of the world, they are actually successful.'

This led to Jack's next lessons learnt:

'Only projects in the ass ends of the world keep to the schedule and budget.'

'Real contractors won't work in these places; the projects that take place in them are profitable and end on time.'

The solution to this algorithm of perverse behaviours was simple, once the reality had set in. After all, if you're paid tax free for each day you attend work and you're living life as a Robert Redford lookalike, despite having a rotund wife and six kids back home, or in many cases six great grandchildren and a pensioner of a wife, and are screwing twenty-year-old beauty queens who will do whatever fantasy you may have dreamed of during your past long, cold, sexless nights of watching *Friends, Neighbours* or *Coronation Street* with the wife – and eating endless mince and tatties – then you really wouldn't want it to end, would you?

It was becoming obvious that the oil industry, or any other come to that, has never understood this paradigm. They invest amazing amounts of shareholders' capital into mega projects and business development, and set totally unrealistic schedules and budgets. They pay everyone mega bucks for each day they work in the liberated sex capitals of the world and then wonder why the days turn into weeks, weeks in months and years into millennia and the workers never seem to get the job finished. Jack had developed his own Catch Twenty Two.

'Catch 22.147 recurring again: only a sane man would question the insanity of motivating people to improve performance and subsequently end their time prematurely in paradise by paying them for every day they spend there.'

Jack, during tortured sleep and fierce hangovers, questioned this moral dilemma ever since his enlightenment and epiphany, and it is probably why he planned to follow Kneecap to the Inuit camp and hide from the many thousands of people who had tried valiantly to keep this esoteric secret from coming out.

His visit to Paris had given him insight into how Langdon from *The Da Vinci Code* felt, being chased all over Europe by esoteric secret-keeping madmen. He also thought he'd bury his thesis, under the Louvre like the Priory of Sion did, mainly because like most French public buildings it's never open when you want to go, i.e. weekdays and weekends and holidays. In hindsight, the Templars got it wrong; a French public building was a great place to bury Mary Magdalene and the Templars' secret. It's a lot safer than Roslyn Chapel or the Temple on the Mount if you want no one to be able to see it during their days off work.

Jack decided he'd have to rethink all theories of motivational behaviour in organisations. Maslow long ago determined that people were motivated through a pyramid of human needs, the most primitive being a need for food, shelter (which, in many places on this earth still motivates the majority of people) and the highest motivator is achievement and the recognition given for that achievement.

In the case of Jack's research none of the hierarchal motivators seemed to be apparent in the world of real projects. His epic motivational theory of people who are lucky enough to work in paradise he was hoping to publish in the Harvard Journal followed as sure as night followed day:

'People are motivated by a need for failure, not achievement, in the sure faith that in failure they will receive salvation, in the form of an extension to contract and a longer time in paradise.'

As the night wore on in The Sportsman's, Father Bob got quite nostalgic and Jack's thoughts turned away from his management theory, more to the behaviours which influenced the very lessons he had determined.

"Bonny lad, remember all those nights and weekends sat here, son, watching the pigeons screw? Those were the days. Danny being chased by the lady boys, you were drowned on Sentosa, Harry buying a beer. Aye those were happy days and you learned a lot, son, from your fatha and from Ralph and Billy, didn't you?"

He winked at Ralph and the gang, so Jack having learned from Big Pat too, kept his council and just said: "Aye."

He turned away from the gang as they returned to talking about day rates, body shops and scrap and reflected on those weekends years before.

They'd while away the best part of eight hours sitting drinking, bantering and watching the sights on Orchard Road out of the window until the first soccer (footie) match came on live from England. They'd ogle the usual gorgeous Asian girls out shopping with their Robert Redford lookalike western boyfriends. Everyone knows that once you are past the International Date Line you turn into Robert Redford: well, you do to the Asian bar girls, if not your mates or your wives or to normal local women. But to those girls/boys/hermaphrodites to whom size really matters, you are a Robert Redford – size in this context being the wallet.

A wife of a friend of Danny's in Thailand said that all the girls in the Paradigm look at men as ATM machines.

"These girls use their various orifices as ATMs; you stick your dick in them and out pops your cash."

Jack in a moment of disillusionment with it all reflected that sticking food in their mouths should in a perfect world be far more helpful and less demeaning but this was not a perfect world. Most of the girls were working only to use their only assets to earn money to pay for their estranged children and elderly families who were living in absolute poverty, and to try to gain a long-term partner who would take them away from desperation. An awful lot of the people he'd met had done just that and they were living happily, in respectful and healthy partnerships. Others were not so lucky and stuck with their life and struggled to survive by the only means they knew. Others were very happy with the life and to earn the money and move on to other ventures. Most were just earning money in foreign bars for being there, being pretty, friendly and good company to lonely men without any sexual relationship or potential abuse whatsoever. A bonus was to meet a partner who would love and support them and take them away from a six to seven day a week life of low wages and long hours.

As Jack considered the experiences he was documenting he now knew that in many cities and towns across Asia the pleasures of the flesh were never far from offer for anyone who walked into the areas or facilities where they were offered. It is indeed an industry that is abused by some, loved by some, hated by a lot and tolerated by many. But it's there and has been for hundreds of years. In the moment of reflection he was experiencing, his hope was that maybe, as consumer wealth grows and economies grow and education through social media and legislation of the rights of women increases, that there will be a fundamental change to the future of the poor across Asia and the consequent need for vulnerable women and also men, to fall into the only way they see or are forced into to survive.

However, sitting in The Sportsman's where no pleasures of the flesh would ever be contemplated by Harry, indeed no pleasure whatsoever if he had his stoic, grim, Scottish way, Jack remembered there was always some fantasy. The highlight to the tedium, or torture, of listening to Father Bob's lessons on life and Danny's wailings about his bad heed after Friday night's Here and Now bar bill and Anywhere's early morning finish, was the Pigeon Screwing Extravaganza.

Every day pigeons would settle on the wall adjacent to Perverts' Window, as it became fondly known, and court each other in loving rituals of avian fantasy, then the male would jump on the lucky female and jump off in two seconds flat.

The suitably satisfied female of the species would then light up a cigarette – fantasising again – she'd fly off, leaving the male to loud applause from all the male human perverts in the window. Their dusky lady girlfriends, and the odd wife on vacation, just looked on, aghast at the male pigeon's staying power.

This ritual was not unlike that followed by most paradise players, played out to similar courting rituals and 'happy endings' in areas of the world where you didn't have to live in fortified barracks or igloos.

Watching the sexual antics of pigeons and their courtship rituals and then observing the human male equivalents in their hundreds, who paraded up such cultural oases as Pat Pong, Walking Street Pattaya, Angels' City, the Philippines, the whole of Batam and Jakarta, Indonesia and their own Four Floors of Whores on Orchard Road, waggling their oversized wallets, guts upstanding, bald pates and hinged hair, just waiting for some innocent young girl to be attracted to the crisp new notes, reinforced Jack's views on what drove working behaviour and cultural integration in such places.

Those long sessions on a weekend, watching pigeons screw, was where he discovered the secret Father Bob always said he'd tell him about, and he determined the fundamental constant of nature, more fundamental that the Cosmological Constant, Plank's Constant and The Real Constant, that was the constant nagging of his wife to get off his computer and get a real job, namely:

'Real contracting has nothing to do with delivering a project on time, within budget and without hurting anyone. It's about how long can you make it last.'

As he sat there watching all the happy faces and listening to the laughter and joy from his subjects in The Sportsman's and he had received another knowing wink from Father Bob and Harry shook his hand and grabbed his metatarsal in his masonic bonding ritual, he knew that he had finally made it; he was a real contractor.

But his days were numbered. Jon called him into the office the very next day as if he'd been a fly on The Sportsman's wall and decided that he could not allow him his moment of pleasure and enlightenment.

"I am running off many of the team now. You will be run off after you have helped me with the celebrations for first gas and oil and have completed the lessons learnt and written the project close out report. You will be contacted by HR and they will sort the human things I have no interest in. We will sit down soon and I will appraise your performance one last time to determine whether we will be interested using you again. Depending on your final performance, I may give you a reference or I may not. Please do not spend the next few months in the bars across Asia. You will also go to Australia again and I do not wish you to get tied in with those morons as you did last time. I have heard reports of you, Richie, that other Australian caveman Digger and that large, fat accountant fellow spending far too much time in the bar every time you visit. Please stop that. Now go and provide me with a plan for first gas celebrations and a PR plan. I will meet with you in one week's time. Thank you and goodbye."

Jack sat in his office and shed a little tear. He was now an official real contractor but was about to be run off. It was a tragedy of apocryphal proportions. Back to a land where they ate you for lunch and the girls all wore triple-x duffel coats and donkey jackets. God, he may end up back again in Aberdeen, eating porridge and freezing his nuts off. The irony of it all was not lost on him. He decided to go drown his sorrows early that day and risk the wrath of the Iron Prussian...

He phoned the Doc to see if he fancied a beer and told him he wished to talk with someone not connected with the project. The Doc indeed was already out and was in Muddy Murphy's, the Irish bar they often met in. The Doc was in with Muse, a real contractor who had married a lovely Chinese girl half his age and was between real contracts and had become a good friend. Also in their company was Bobby, who today seemed to be alive for once.

Bobby was a morose Aussie who one day arrived in Muddy Murphy's and used to sit staring at the television, drinking Tiger and topping up with a bottle of his own lemonade. He surprised everyone when he told them that he had taken a Thai girl from the Four Floors home the night before. They were surprised because the Doc had declared him dead the day before!

To explain: Bobby was well in his sixties, overweight, very red-faced and wheezed and coughed like a grampus. Muse and the Doc would watch him regularly just close his eyes and go into a coma.

If he got up to go to bathroom, he did it as slow as a Galapagos tortoise, with deliberate steps and wheezing. Muse eventually decided in his helpful way he would befriend this poor lonely guy. so he shook him awake one day and asked him to join them. The Doc, who had during his lunch break watched Bobby on a few occasions from afar, was livid with Muse.

"For ****'s sake don't give him my card or introduce him to me. I don't want that bastard as my patient," he ranted. "It's bad enough I have you lot. You are all not long for this earth but he's only got days. I'm not bloody giving that the kiss of life." He was howling now. "He's a walking bloody coronary!"

As it was, ever the collector of the dregs of society, the Doc took on Bobby as his patient, one more hopeless case like the rest of his bar patients for this caring man to look after.

The day before Bobby's encounter in Four Floors, he had dozed off again, this time the Doc was worried as his breathing appeared to have stopped and his normally fat, florid face was pale. The Doc quietly walked over to where Bobby was sat under the telly with his usual burger and chips (mince again) lunch under his large stomach. He gently took hold of his arm and took his pulse. They all were anxious and a bit sad, as Bobby had become one of the characters, pissed when he arrived, boring as hell, knew nothing about the world except Australian sport but was a good mate to a few of usual reprobates in there. The Doc, nodded, looked up and shouted to all who hear in the bar.

"He's bloody well alive. Would you bloody believe it? He should be dead like you lot. It's not fair!"

Again, it was the Doc showing his profound angst about his patients who defied his prediction of their impending death. Bobby duly woke up, ate his mince and chips, and supped another five pints and left.

Everyone was very surprised to think that he could get up the escalators in the Four Floors, never mind carry out any nocturnal cavorting. Even more surprised when he told them of his problem with the wife.

It appears the girl he had attracted with his great looks and body, being Asian and Thai, had left one long black hair under the pillow and also one in the shower. (Real players in the menagerie that is Asia know this, and so do their real wives! So they always take the drain cover off and check that there are never black hairs in the hole, a good free tip for those of you with Sherlock Holmes as a partner.) His wife had arrived back from business and despite Bobby cleaning the house thoroughly he had missed these two tell-tale signs.

He told them that he told his wife that they must have blown in through the window. Surprisingly, for they were told she was an intelligent and astute person, she didn't take him to task, accepted his implausible lie, just showered and went to work. On quiet reflection, Bobby was puzzled by his wife's response and asked the Doc what he thought. Being quite straight with people, the Doc told him that only two things could explain this paradox.

1) She, like him, couldn't believe he could screw anything without the need of coronary care and his explanation was true.

2) She was being screwed herself and really didn't care.

Bobby, after his usual minute's silence between sentences, agreed on number two, drank several more lagers and staggered very slowly to the Four Floors – very sad story, really.

But today when Jack entered he was alive but now comatose again with his head drooped and fast asleep. Jack asked the Doc what he'd been up to that afternoon. The Doc said that he'd visited Big Marc in hospital as he had had a serious penile problem for weeks and was losing weight, with a strange fatigue over the final week. Two days ago, strange pustules appeared from within his gonads and his John Thomas began to bleed in the toilets of The Outback. The good doctor took him to his surgery upstairs and duly diagnosed the problem, that he had raging diabetes.

His drinking days were over, poor sod. The Doc diligently treated the big man in hospital. Jack had visited him of course and the good doctor was there, and always the pragmatist and caring man that he was, he changed Big Marc's blood pressure tablets, telling anyone who asked why: "So that they will help him deal with the alcohol withdrawal symptoms of course."

He also had said to Jack: "I suppose you're off now to that hell hole to carry on your debauched lifestyle?"

Curiously, he was, and he answered in the affirmative. In classic Doc style he pleaded, worrying about his bar patient income again.

"Jack, do me a favour. Please don't tell any of those drunken lunatic mates of yours in that hell hole that I've taken Marc off the drink. I'll never get any of you buggers to come to see me again!"

Jack duly returned to the bar and drummed up the real barmaids to go to visit the big man the following day. He would need cheering up and probably need his decaying genitals brought back to life, he told them.

Without hesitation, they volunteered to go and cheer him up in their own particular Asian way. The Doc went crazy when he returned to check his patient and he was being cuddled in bed by the dusky maidens and his John Thomas regeneration put back weeks by their attentions. He was confined to bread and water and no genital stimulation.

The Doc was happy that afternoon as he was a much richer man, as he was actually paid Marc's bank's insurance money for this treatment and not just paid in the bottled beer that his bar patients normally donated the great medic for the various self-induced ailments he cured.

"At last, I get what I deserve for keeping you drunken lot alive when you should be ******* dead. Real money, not bloody beer."

He ranted and ranted and then when he noticed that Bobby had gone comatose, "Oh dear God, he's ******* died again. I am not resuscitating that Aussie bastard. He's shagged his way through the whole of the Four Floors; God knows what he's caught. I'm ******* off to The Sportsman's."

Jack decided that maybe he would go too and left Muse to stare at the Australian corpse and wait for any signs of life to appear before he reported his death to the head barman, the very camp Iz the puff, who being infinitely more caring than the three Brits, would no doubt give him his own kiss of life.

In The Sportsman's were the usual inmates. The Commodore was also there, in town from Hong Kong, Arun the Indian IT man with the one internal organ left and Big Pat. They greeted each other and the ubiquitous Tiger was bought.

The Commodore loved to talk of the days before Singapore became modern and freer of its colonial past and people like him were still respected as masters and rulers. The Doc had been there before the Commodore and actually had married and lived there so there were often arguments over each of the irascible men's memories and understandings. Tonight the Commodore was holding the stage, the Doc becalmed after his near escape from giving Bobby the kiss of life. The Commodore was waxing on about the old colonial days.

"When I first visited Singapore only the best of the best could get residency and work permits. A solid upper-class background were needed in the good old days to gain residency."

He took a drink of his Tiger and he turned and looked down at Pat sat at the bar, and said: "Of course, those days people like Pat would never have got onto the island at all, never mind work here."

He said this without any bad feeling, just a statement of fact to the Commodore. Big Pat was used to such bombastic direct statements from the old mariner. He accepted his place.

They were in The Sportsman's, having decamped from The

Outback as the American 6th fleet was in town. When the Commodore was in town and it also coincided with his American cousins, he couldn't cope with their rap music and Dawn's fawning over the full wallets that the hordes of young Americans would hopefully throw over her bar. Also that day Pat had returned from the UK with goodies, as most did when returning from leave. These goodies always included black pudding, pork pies and kippers.

Hansie loved it when his Dutch cousins brought back raw herring and he could swallow them whole just like a sea lion. He said to the Brits around him after swallowing a whole seine net of raw fish: "None of that Soutie kaffir meat food for me, only fish and biltong, real Boer meat."

Big Pat had brought a black bin bag of kippers through the Changi customs that day, God knows what the plane smelt like or sniffer dogs would have thought of the smell from kippers that had been in his case for 1.5 days.

Big Pat hailed from the picturesque North Yorkshire town of Whitby, famous for two things, Dracula and kippers. His dad had been a miner from Durham, but now was a fisherman. Pat described himself as a smaller version of his dad. Everyone wondered how his pater could get onto a small fishing boat if that was so. It seems his dad had to eat rather a lot to maintain his size.

Pat told them of his dad's favourite and perpetual meals; the first was a full English breakfast. He ate this every day of his life as long as Pat had known him. It comprised enough fat and meat to fill a self-made frying pan that actually spanned the four cooking rings on a gas cooker, about half a metre in diameter. His next meal was fish and chips for tea every day from The Magpie fish and chip shop where his daughter worked. He ate nothing else, it seemed, and was a fit as butcher's dog. The Doc was in apoplexy every time he heard of his Big Pat's dad's diet. Repeating his mantra: "He should be *******
dead. Like you lot, how the hell do you survive? It beggars bloody belief, you defy medical science, why did I get you lot as patients? Get me a Crown lager, Dawn."

Pat's dad had got Pat the bag of kippers from his fishing mates. Whitby was famous for kippers and they all ate them there, as did a large proportion of the UK take kippers from Whitby. Pat duly plucked out of the seething mass of smelly fish in the bin bag pairs of kippers with his huge hands and handed them to the grateful patrons of the bar. Arun, the token Moghul, and naïve about the ways of British food, asked politely if he could have some.

"How do I cook these, Pat?"

"Stick them in a pan and boil them for ten minutes, mate," Pat said.

At which point the Commodore, standing erect and high and mightier than most, twisted his face and his voice exploded, shouting in his stentorian way: "Boil them! Boil them! You don't boil kippers, you fool. You grill kippers. Only the dregs of the country or a ****** idiot would boil a kipper."

He continued his roaring: "And these are not real kippers, by God. The best kippers come from Craster, from Robson's. It's the only kipper worth eating; these are second rate from Whitby – and you grill the buggers, not boil them! Even these poor imitations will be wasted on an Indian, so I'll have your pair, Arun, you stick to curry and leave good British food alone."

Despite deriding Whitby kippers as second rate, he still took Arun's and his own pair of kippers. A free pair of kippers, even if in his expert judgement they were second rate, was never looked in the mouth by the Commodore.

Big Pat suitably humbled, and also his intelligence, family and his home town, just shrugged his huge shoulders and supped yet another Tiger in one swallow. Arun shrunk another few inches, reminded of his place in this small perverse Society of Friends. Pat, always the gentle man with friends and well used to Commodore's blunt ways, handed out the pork pies to all, including the Commodore.

The Commodore and Pat got into a discussion about how Hong Kong had changed so much. Pat was lamenting that Amar Singh's place, where he spent most of his life, ate his red hot Vindaloos, and where he normally met the Commodore, was not the same these days as lots of old friends had left town and sometimes he was lonely and all by himself in the bar. The Commodore agreed and said: "Yes, I only go there now when Kjell or Digger is in town, otherwise it would be no use going there as there isn't anyone else worth drinking with."

That made Pat feel very wanted and liked indeed and very humble. The Commodore left kippers in hand to move onto The Outback and humiliate someone else. Arun collapsed as his one and only organ failed. The Doc prescribed him more vodka and then exited the bar at speed after his phone rang and his lovely wife had tracked him down again.

As he ran out of the bar, medical bag in hand screaming, "Bloody woman! Why do I have her? What did I do to deserve this life?" Jack and Pat sat and talked. Well, Jack talked, Pat either said, 'aye' or 'nah'.

They talked about Pat's new love in Thailand and Jack drifted off to ponder a question he'd asked himself many times before. Why were there no real woman contractors? He had long ago worried that his business case and thesis may seem heavily biased towards men, and heaven forbid, to some women and liberal men it may even seem to support gender inequality in the 'bidness'.

He had tried valiantly to remove any suggestion of gender inequality in his opus magnus and also include some elements of the research that may amuse and enlighten a potential female reader, but he had come to the conclusion it is by necessity difficult because:

1) The males he had researched normally behaved in a manner that is frowned upon in polite society these days by respectable people. Their exploits may not actually appear amusing, enlightening or entertaining to them. He concluded, however, that they should read his conclusions and attend his Harvard lectures as it may explain why the male gender is destined to extinction and the female gender will eventually take over. All they will need the male for is one small strand of DNA. If they want real sex in the future then they can do what they probably do anyway when their contractors are away in far-off lands, use mechanical devices or their girlfriends.

2) The females in these his business case stories tended to be barmaids or performing acrobats, none of which normal women have an awful lot of time for.

3) The expatriate wives of the men who worked (oxymoron again) are too busy to read the study or attend the lectures because their daily diaries won't allow them the time for such unnecessary things. When they do read it's normally a menu or a flight schedule to anywhere expensive and hot.

He was pondering how to overcome the fact that fifty per cent of the world market for his theory was made up of females and he must make some effort, when in to the bar came Father Bob and his neighbour from his condo, Aberdeen Steve.

After a few beers he discussed this dilemma with Father Bob that he'd never met many females in the business.

"Bonny lad, I've told yeah hundreds of times man, women are dangerous, be careful out here, stick with ya fatha and avoid the honey traps, and nivva have them in the business, man. They might find out what we are up to and some for God's sake actually know what they are doing and might get the job done on time, that's why we keep them out. For ****'s sake they are now starting to get into engineering, that's one step away from construction. If we ever get them on a site, we are doomed, bonny lad. Listen to your fatha, keep them photocopying and tell them nowt."

He took a large drink of his Tiger and continued in his lecture on the merits of female real contractors in the bidness.

"Mind you I've warned you many times about the evils of the East and to stay away from the lasses."

Jack nodded took a drink and agreed.

"Aye, Fatha, you may well have been right given what happened to Ralph."

"For ****'s sake she was a boil-your-rabbit job, that one, Jack. Didn't I tell yeah? I bet you're pleased you listened to me now aren't you?"

Jack winced as Bob recalled this relationship and the fatal attraction that led to Ralph's demise. Those unaware of this analogy, the boiling of children's rabbits being an indicator of a shunned frenzied female's sanity, as in the movie, *Fatal Attraction*. After watching Glenn Close and her rabbit stew Jack had not even spoken to a woman for years and never let his kids keep anything but invertebrates.

"I told you that one of Ralph's could boil a whole menagerie, if Ralph wasn't careful," he reminded about a rather aggressive western female who had taken a fancy to Ralph of Easter egg fame, and indeed some months later he was proved very correct as she tried to claw his eyes out whist he was driving her home, for no reason at all, it seems.

Jack considered this latest advice and lesson. Father Bob was the wisest man Jack had met but even though he thought he had been accepted as a real contractor he was sure Bob never would reveal the 'real secret'. Probably he was wiser than Jack thought.

Steve, on overhearing Father Bob's ranting on Ralph's problems above, and Bob's certain knowledge that Ralph's grandchildren's pets were in danger of ending up as a nice chow mein, asked Jack who the boil-the-rabbit lady was.

"Why do you want to know?" Jack asked.

"Because if I give her a screw she might come and boil our lass's cat!"

He was not well pleased with the orphan cat his wife had taken in and which kept him awake with howling all night.

Expatriate wives did some silly things to keep their minds off the sexual depravity that greeted them every time they walked their credit cards down Orchard Road. It was a constant battle for expat wives to see the Robert Redfords with their amazingly young and beautiful bodied girls sitting on their laps in bars, walking hand in hand or just gazing across a plate of chicken rice. These men, the term is loosely correct, with false teeth chattering and their walking sticks propping them up, white bony legs sticking out of thick woollen socks, tucked into brown shoes. All with baggy khaki shorts and loud batik shirts and bald heads shining in the neon light, with beautiful nurse on hand.

The expat wives spend all day, after giving the maid the cleaning and cooking instructions and their kids to watch over, while they spend quality time lunching, exercising, pooling and shopping in expensive stores to overcome their boredom. It is the way of the expat wife, unfortunately. It's a hard life for them.

However, those with their partners with them kept them all in check without doubt, as without their dearest they'd have lost all control of their bodily functions, or so the ladies say.

Jack took a long drink and pondered the risks of expatriate life in paradise and realised how fortunate he had been that his wife had been with him most of his tortuous time and had kept him going even through the long periods of the hell of his extracurricular research. He decided to offer lessons to potential real contractors through his lecture tours and recommend those who wish to live in paradise long-term, and retain their worldly possessions, that they keep their partner with them at all times.

His lesson would be:

'Remember, the wooden or straw hut that your current little brown girlfriend came from is worth a lot less than your Ferrari and five bedroomed house with pool in Houston, Aberdeen, Surrey, Bergen, Copenhagen, or Perth that your wife is now about to take.'

Jack smiled to himself, called the lovely Loraine over to order even more Tiger and as he mused that the players in his story were mostly in the minority and their wives and lovers back home should relax, as 'their man' would never appeal to the beautiful young brown things that roam these tropical lands – he's too old, grey and fat – that's what his wife thought and said to him when she came home after his first leave, until she arrived to visit him in Asia for a vacation one fine day. She never went back home.

CHAPTER EIGHTEEN

Walkabout, Australia

Hoy the Heed-san

The fifth year and near the end…

"You will make one last trip to Australia and sort out the first gas ceremony. That will be your last piece of staff work as I expect your project close out to be signed off finally next week after the many revisions I have had to make to your work yet again. Do not get drunk and upset the dignitaries and those hangers-on from corporate. Try to put some culture into it, it will not be easy as Australians are Visigoths, uncouth and obtuse, and their country is a barren featureless desert, but I gather some people like it. I will be there of course to observe your performance and if you make a mess of it I will run you off without your end-of-contract bonus. Let's try to put some fun into the process. You know I like a good laugh. I will see you there, goodbye and close the door please."

Jack closed the Iron Chancellor's door, shook his head at another encounter with Jon and looked around the project office as he walked out. He saw many empty desks in a once busy and bustling office, as many had already been 'run off' and many had gone off to Australia to actually fit together the Lego bricks of steel, pipes and wires that had been sent from paradise to the Far Shore and finally for Jim and his commissioning boys. Well, not Jim as he was still planning the next one, to press the buttons to hopefully make the thing work. Jack hoped he'd bump into Kneecap Dara maybe, commissioning things and maybe living in a corrugated iron shack with the native Aboriginals.

Big Richie was ready to actually run the thing and sell liquid gas to the Chinese bar man from the Here and Now and also to the Japanese. He had left his many 'partners' in the various locations across Asia and had married and settled on a lovely Japanese girl to comfort him in his labours and trials in the desert and swamps. He had taken up wrestling bulls again in his native town, throwing himself off 4x4 trucks onto the raging, running beasts and wrestling them to the ground. He found it a soothing therapy after meetings with the Iron Chancellor and he'd told Jack he should try it to help his twitching and nervous breakdowns after his own counselling sessions with Jon. Jack, like Michael Corleone in *Godfather Two*, when asked: "Would you like a banana daquiri, sir?" answered, "No."

Thank you for the offer, he told Richie, but he would just continue on his daily therapy of Tiger beer. It had helped the psychoses and depression induced by Jon for five years up to now so he would continue to the end.

Jack flew off to the Lucky Country, looking forward to meeting his Australian friends again and enjoying the company of those he'd lived and worked with for five years across Asia.

The first night he met Danny in Perth and also Digger in the Subiacco Inn. Danny had been in Australia for some time and was missing The Sportsman's Tiger beer and mince, but not as much as he did during his moths of purgatory in Japan.

Sadly due to Jack's coaching, Danny had built a growing reputation as a renowned leader of multicultural mega project management but this had meant he was sent to places far away from Glasgow and the haven of Singapore and he had to assimilate with weird people and eat "foreign shit bait." He had lost weight and was almost Father Bob's build due to being offered raw fish and live invertebrates as his only sustenance. Sake did not contain the calories of fifteen pints of Tiger, and his 'red heed' had shown no signs of mellowing with his newfound multicultural ecumenism.

Danny was with the Welsh subcontracts manager from Batam who now worked on the Australian project and had grown no kinder or empathetic to his fellow man. A small altercation grew between Danny and one of his loyal followers. This gentleman had a polished English accent and to Jack it seemed that he was upset with some comments that the great Scot had said at a meeting that day. Jack was listening and hoped that this man had not been an Insulator, Safety Engineer, Metallurgist or Piping Engineer, but he also hoped the Danny had mellowed over his five-year coaching of the correct behaviours to our fellow inhabitants of God's great earth. Sadly it seemed he hadn't, or certainly the Welsh contracts wizard hadn't, because the Welshman pushed Danny aside and threw a punch at the slightly built gentleman and cold cocked him.

Looking down at the sleeping man he said: "Don't you call my boss a racist, you English bastard."

Jack shook his head, but he'd long given up on his quest to understand the Celtic people and save the known world. He shivered when he thought of even trying that with the Doc.

The unfortunate man woke up and amazingly apologised for his behaviour. Danny bought him several beers and everyone seemed to be happy again. A madhouse was all Jack could think. Danny introduced a very large Japanese man to him. He was as round as he was high, a bit like Martin the Oblate Spheroid, very sumo wrestler like.

"Jack this is Hoy the Heed-san. He's worked with me many times. He's a real contractor, more Scots than Japanese. I love him, mate."

Hoy the Heed-san bowed and held out his hand to Jack.

"Hoh, Jack-san, Danny-san has told me about you. Velly good man, you help Danny-san velly much with Jon-san, yes?"

Jack took his hand, bowed slightly and confirmed that he did indeed try to stop Danny losing the red heed with the Iron Teuton and acted very much as a mediator between the two diametrically opposed leaders of real contractors.

"Hoh, that is what we all hear in Japan. Jon-san is what we say there, misunderstood. He is velly direct and forceful. That is not our way. Jack-san, you feel he would like to come and work more with us and learn our culture on the next project maybe?"

Jack looked aghast at the rotund oriental. A vision of Jon and his white shirt and red tie, lecturing the Russians on their behaviour in his latest PR video came into his mind. God knows what he'd think of the Japanese. But he was in full Japanese politeness and face-giving mode so he replied positively to Hoy the Heed-san.

"Well maybe; we'll see. Jon always speaks highly of the Japanese company and what you have done for the project."

Hoy the Heed-san nodded and went off to order some more drinks, feeling satisfied that he had done his bit to firm up another Nippon and German axis.

Jack shook his head again and finished off his schooner. Danny looked at him astonished.

"For ****'s sake, Jack, Jon put his boss into hospital. He was a VP for ****'s sake and their sponsor with us. Jon kept asking me to sack him as Jon looked into his office every morning and saw the poor distraught man looking at the dire financial figures and KPIs, head in hands about to top himself. Jon thought he should be doing plans, staff work or site work. So we had to send him to site to check isometrics for ****'s sake with his minions. He had a breakdown! The shame of it nearly made him commit sepukko for ****'s sake. And you want to send Jon to Japan!"

Jack smiled at the thought.

"Aye Danny, I'd love to be a fly on wall when Jon makes the President of the Japanese company provide him with an execution plan!"

They both chuckled at the thought.

Later on Jack was puzzled though.

"It's a strange name for a Japanese, Danny. Hoy the Heed-san. How did he get that?"

Danny explained, his red heed getting redder.

"Well, a year ago he was on site here and in a meeting which was going a bit angry. As you know the Japanese never get angry, it's not their way. They smile and they calmly try to come to an agreement. Drove me ****** mental of course, at first, as you'd guess."

Jack nodded, knowing that Japanese culture was indeed different to Glaswegian. Danny continued: "Well, this English twat from the

315

subcontractor kept antagonising the Japanese and being abusive. I'd have nutted the ******."

Jack nodded again – nothing new to see here.

"Anyway," Danny continued, "the meeting got hotter and the Japanese were getting quieter but still calm, then the English **** stood up to shout something at them, when all of sudden Hoy the Heed-san stood up and just threw a headbutt on the twat. Knocked him clean out."

They both laughed out loud at the thought but Jack then had to ask Danny what were the consequences.

"For ****'s sake, Jack, it was a nightmare. You can imagine how the Japanese felt and Hoy the Heed-san was mortified, wanted to top himself there and then, had to take the paper knife off him!"

He took a drink and concluded the story.

"If HR got involved he'd have been ******, of course. Not company policy to nut the contractor. But I intervened as Hoy the Heed came to see me and he was so distraught that he had broken the Japanese code, may lose his job, and his face, that I felt sorry for him. He was good lad, Jack. So I used up a bit of clout and saved his arse. The bloke he nutted was only a posh English twat anyway."

Jack pondered this final sentence and realised that Danny had two henchmen now, the Welsh terrier and Hoy the Heed-san, and they were all on a mission to rid the world of posh English twats. He concluded that his cultural and team building had not all been in vain and at least he had built a cross-cultural team of genocidal xenophobic maniacs.

The talk turned as it does to more friendly pursuits than headbutting, that was golf, drink, day rates and how long they all could last now the project was about to go 'live'. Digger, who was the most familiar with Australian working methods, gave them all some reassurance that their end was not yet nigh.

"Mates, I will bet you a day's pay that the unions will stop the job next week just as first gas is supposed to happen. Always happens. They'll use some excuse that you're using too many foreigners, the salt in their canteen is too damp, the wage agreement is redundant, a union man has died in Papua New Guinea on one of your projects and they are off in sympathy with the widow as you killed him. Of course a dead dugong or whale will be washed up and they will walk because of toxic chemicals that you have hidden from them. In fact they really don't need an excuse, you see they are just like you, this is the fatted cow and they will milk it forever. Another six months at least: happy days for you all."

Danny held his head in his hands at this news. Only he was demented because only he wanted it to end. His two henchmen comforted him, looking threateningly each way at anyone who may come near to upset the great, tormented man. Digger decided to cheer him up.

"Heh mate, no worries, eh! Look at this photo of my friend who's coming to take me to dinner. Of course she's just a friend, nothing more lads."

And he showed everyone a photo on his smart phone of a lovely girl indeed who had taken a selfie picture of her naked private parts up through her skirt.

"She loves to send me photos of her body to make me horny, but that's all it is. Lovely girl, you'll all love her."

They all shook their heads, they had got to know Digger well.

The night wore on and into the bar came a legend in real contracting. He'd been walkabout across the town meeting his various acolytes and fan clubs. He came up to Danny and Danny was delighted to see him, and he introduced him to assembled menagerie as Clive: The Seeker.

Danny whispered to Jack.

"Jack, this guy is THE master of real contracting and you should try to emulate him in all things he does. Possibly he will become President of the Society of Real Contractors soon."

Jack said hello and The Seeker held his hand and offered to buy him a drink along with all of the hordes who had followed the legend into the bar. He spoke in soft American accent.

"Nice to meet you, Jack. Do you play golf, buddy? I've got two four balls going tomorrow if you want to join Danny and me?"

Jack thought carefully, delighted to be asked to play a game he was pretty bad at but the opportunity to learn more from a master of real contracting was too good to miss. He was about to say yes when he remembered the Iron Chancellor's threat about running him off without his large end-of-contract bonus.

"Sorry Clive, I have to work. My boss is coming into town."

Clive nodded and then astonished Jack with his response, "I know. He's going to play with me the next day. I'll talk to him and tell him to let you off. No one should work every day, man."

Jack was dumbfounded. He'd never known Jon do anything but work and torture people. Fun and days off were for people after he'd run them off. He certainly didn't want to upset his nemesis this late in the day so he had to turn The Seeker's offer down. The Seeker looked surprised as if someone would be mental to turn down a day's golf but he smiled and turned to talk to others.

Jack, excited by this new find, pushed in close to Danny and asked him who this person really was and listened for some time as Danny adoringly extolled the talents of the American.

"Jack, The Seeker is big in materials management and like T Squared, is idolised by his clients, team and staff; Seeker for his amazing ability to find, store, deliver and sell materials and gain the many stamps needed for this mind bogglingly boring and complex process. In two projects I observed that that he was so efficient and professional that he had mastered this process by the third month of his three years' tenure on the projects. The next two years nine months, he managed his staff of nationals by feeding them lunch, supplying cakes, chocolates, golf days and pay rises as they keep the whole thing ticking while The Seeker leads the team in his spare time from the golf course or bar. This is brilliant and effective leadership that Jim Collins or you should write another book about: *From Pipe Fittings to Ping*."

He was in full adoration now.

"The Seeker is constantly in touch with his team and his bosses by handheld communications devices on which he continually presses buttons and gazes at whilst sitting in project meetings, progress meetings, one-to-one communication or just gazing reflectively at a beautiful girl over a Tiger beer. If for one moment an e-mail, text or call arises that needs his attention, he can at a moment get his team to answer it; even from the ninth tee. He is a master at finding lost material or sourcing material that no one can get, normally because someone had forgotten to order it. Jack, remember you taught me that this is classic real contracting from Procurement: *'don't order things on time, or ensure they are the wrong things and then the hordes of quality inspectors will condemn them and that will delay the thing even more.'*

Jack nodded; that was indeed a fruit of one of his early research findings.

Danny continued his beatitude.

"I began to realise that in all probability after three months he had already anticipated the cunning procurement plan for delay and he had sourced, hidden and stored this material himself. I suspect that his team actually hide key materials in readiness for the time when he has to display his exceptional talents for his bosses and then at his call or e-mail from the golf course, they miraculously deliver it to the astonishment and awe of all in the project team."

Danny took Jack's arm and moved him away from the team somewhat and told him more confidential stuff.

"Because of this ability to save demented project managers' arses he is always the last to leave the project, apart from the contract managers who are still fighting the legal battles that are the direct result of placing the late, over-budget projects in paradise. Given the materials have been welded, stuck, laid, screwed onto the big steel things years before, it is a feat of amazing endurance and skill for The Seeker to convince his project managers that he is still vitally important for a successful project which sailed away six months before. I am employing him on my next one."

Danny took a breath and began again.

"If you arrive at any bar in town, anywhere at any time of the day or night, you'd be always amazed to see the Seeker there, surrounded by persons of renown, all in respect of the man. He sits or stands as an alpha male type with his fawning subjects in awe, as he types texts and e-mails into his handheld devices, managing his team, not saying much but just looking up every now and then to drink another beer and smoke another cigarette. His audience sits waiting in anticipation of some wise statement on golf or sex or, on rare occasions, material management."

Danny took a drink, his red face beaming.

"He has contacts like T Squared across Asia and is well respected in all aspects of his profession by the many broken and lost project managers who he has rescued from disaster many times in his esteemed career. He would be essential to any budding project manager looking to establish a materials management system and a dynamic, cohesive functioning project team that delivers results. Just send me a message, I'll have a word with the great man in the clubhouse bar tomorrow and I'll send your CV to him for when Jon runs you off."

Jack looked across at the real contractors fawning over the great American forager and remembered the part that *James Garner'* played in *'The Great Escape'*, The Scrounger. He had a feeling that Clive may well have been playing golf with the German commandant the day they all escaped. No tunnels and firing squads for him.

Jack flew to site in the desert and island swamps the next morning where the unions had, as Digger predicted, gone on strike for damp salt in the canteen and no Netflix on their forty-inch smart TV screens in their dongas (portable homes in the labour camp) and then he flew off to visit another office in Brisbane as due to the strike, the first gas ceremony was off. Jon told him to spend the time touring the sites and offices and facilitate the project lessons learnt.

During this walk about Australia Jack did indeed begin to understand why people wished to live there, but after a huge argument at Perth airport with a Border Security lady over why his toothpaste had foreign writing on it (Vietnamese) and her threatening to put her large bony hand up his rectum, he sat feeling elated that he was on his way back to Singapore on Singapore Airlines with beautiful, brown, dusky ladies who smiled, massaged his aching shoulders and served him Tiger beer and were not proctologists or sadists by nature.

CHAPTER NINETEEN

Singapore

The Green Jelly Man

The end...

"This finger has been up more arseholes than Oscar Wilde."

The Doc had had a busy morning with his errant patients. The first to arrive had been Martin the Oblate Spheroid and his new girlfriend from Vietnam. The Doc was explaining to Martin that he had the most educated finger in medicine.

He always exclaimed loudly this comparison with Oscar's digit to anyone in bars who would listen as he stuck his middle finger up, shouting and cackling insanely with laughter. This was of course the triumph of the Doc. It doesn't matter who you are, or how many times you may take the piss out of him, one day you will need a prostate examination – and then he can get his own back – and he did.

The Doc had named Martin this geometrical term because this very Lancashire, basic man, of porn movie PhD fame, and the Batam dung beetle story, had grown rather rotund over the last few years and being rather short, he did indeed look like something from Euclid's geometrical theorems. Indeed, the Doc was sure he was totally round.

This day he had brought his Vietnamese girlfriend to the Doc's surgery as she was struggling with problems in her rear end. Her English was pretty non-existent at that time so Martin had to try to explain the symptoms to the good Doc second-hand, and the Doc had to physically examine the unfortunate lady. He asked Martin to get her onto the examination table and to try to ask her to remove her panties. Martin was in the process of doing so when the Doc stuck his fingers out and took a pair of surgical rubber gloves out of a box and proceeded to put them on.

The girlfriend looked aghast and Martin tried to turn her over onto her stomach and remove the panties. The Doc moved closer and extended his 'Oscar Wilde' finger and added KY jelly lubricant to the finger. The girlfriend, by now realising what was going to happen, screamed and shouted in Vietnamese and began trying to turn over and pull her panties up. It must be pointed out that Martin had not found this lady in the Dating for Professionals Agency nor sitting in Starbucks over a cup of coffee and her reading *The Economist* or *Vogue*, but in the usual place, the Four Floors of Whores, and she had been working there at the time, all night, most nights and overtime when the American carrier the *Nimitz* came into town. So all assumed, unfairly one may guess, that she was well prepared for what she was facing but this time she also had probable haemorrhoids to face as well.

Martin had to hold her down and attempt to get the panties off whilst the Doc stood over with middle finger erect, ready to make his diagnosis. All this while his lady struggled and hissed and spat in Vietnamese, turning behind her to pull her panties back up again and again. The Doc and Martin finally gave up. The Doc was sure it was haemorrhoids and treated her accordingly. Digger and T Squared videoed the whole thing!

After the examination the Doc chuckled and said to Martin: "The way she hissed and spat, lucky I didn't give this pussy cat a dose of chloralose like the last one."

He cackled and wrote out a prescription for the unfortunate lady. Martin, puzzled, asked what he meant. The Doc explained. When he was a young undergraduate in medical school in Cardiff, Wales, to earn some extra money he worked in a veterinary surgeon's surgery, helping out treating sick animals. Martin thought, *No wonder he practised on us in Singapore!*

One day he was given a pedigree cat and asked by the vet to trim its claws. This cat belonged to Lady Ponsonby, the local landowner and magistrate's wife. She was naturally very fond of her pussy, and asked the good Doc to take extra care of it. He duly told her he was well able to do this and proceeded to carry out this simple procedure.

He looked up from his desk at Martin and continued the story:

"I looked at this bloody cat, and I'm not that fond of them, and it was big, white and fluffy, obviously very expensive but it didn't like me, I knew that. I tried to pick it up but it exploded into a blur of white fur and claws and left scratches all down my arm and flew off to sit on the book shelf."

He took his glasses off and wiped them.

"'OK,' I thought, 'I'll get you, you bugger.' So I put on some long leather bike-riding gloves that protected my hands and arms, after making up a jar and mask soaked with chloralose solution to anesthetise the bloody thing. Made sure I stuck enough in the jar. As I walked towards it, it raised its back and started hissing again. Expecting it to attack any minute, I leapt at it and grabbed the bloody thing by the neck. It was a great attack, caught the thing by surprise. I pinned it down with it hissing and spitting and clawing and clamped the mask over its face and waited till it relaxed."

He took a breath and continued, "It took about a minute of trying to hold a banshee down when she relaxed and I thought, 'Marvellous, that's that over with.' I took the mask off and laid it in on the table and picked up the nail clippers. I looked down and noticed no chest rising and thought, 'Bloody hell, it's dead.' I checked its heart beat with a stethoscope and sure enough the bloody thing was dead."

He was getting excited now, Martin was sure he needed another magic molecule to calm him as he remembered this euthanasia. After taking a long pause he continued.

"I pumped the bugger's heart, bashed its chest and stuck an injection of adrenaline into it but it was dead. I stood looking around, big gloves on, syringe and clippers strewn on the floor and the Lady of the Manor's white fluffy pussy lying stone dead on the table."

He laughed in that usual loud, piercing way.

"What the hell was I going to do now? I've sent Her Ladyship's prize pussy to the knacker's yard. The boss would kill me, I thought."

He was still giggling and cackling insanely.

"What happened? You daft old bugger," Martin asked, trying to be concerned but finding it impossible to stop laughing with the smiling pussy murderer.

"Ah, the vet partner had to console Her Ladyship, said it was a heart attack. I got my pay docked and I think she was carried into her Rolls by her chauffeur."

He continued cackling with laughter: "It just came in for its bloody nails cut. Ha, ha, ha."

Martin left with his unfortunate girlfriend and into the Doc's lair walked Big Hansie the South African marine man.

"What the **** do you want? You should be dead, not walking in here."

Hansie, used to the abuse, sat down and explained that he needed to attend an offshore medical and needed a check-up to see if could pass and if the Doc could help him in case his tests might show some anomaly. The Doc was apoplectic.

"For ****'s sake, man, last time your results should have been all red the amount you drink and smoke. They were normal. I couldn't believe it. You defy medical logic."

Hansie quietly agreed but he was worried.

"My blood pressure seems high, Doc."

"Of course it is, you drink gallons, don't sleep, exercise and smoke like a ******* steam train. Let me take it and we'll see how long you have to live."

He looked at his monitor and screamed: "For God's sake, man, it's only 130 over 80, you should have broken the monitor. It's still too high for your medical certificate. When is the medical?"

Hanise told him the next day and the Welsh medic threw his monitor on his desk shouting as if in pain: "What the **** do you expect to change by then? You will no doubt go to that Australian hell hole after this as you are off work and drink all day and night."

Hansie nodded in the affirmative, scared to answer verbally. The Doc calmed and sat there for some time and then concluded the consultation.

"Right, do what I tell Kjell, that Norwegian piss pot, to get through his medical. He is worse than that bloody Captain Abe and both, by the way, are worse than you. Kjell's liver tests are all always all red but alcohol abuse doesn't seem to bother Norwegian marine companies. In fact I think they won't pass you if you have no liver damage! It's only his blood pressure they worry about. I tell him to drink three large vodkas before his test. Alcohol in moderation will lower the blood pressure. You do the same and you'll be fine."

Hansie thanked the Doc and went out to be held in the unerring grasp of his dear wife Rose, who extracted a real fee from him. She was having a good morning as she'd collared Martin too. If only she could keep him out of The Outback, they could retire at last.

Meanwhile, Jack was sitting in the Colbar just off Portsdown Road drinking a cold bottle of Tiger beer supplied by the owner, the lovely Mrs Limm. He was waiting for Ironman to arrive as he was in town yet again and they were meeting up for a liver and onions early brunch at the great bar where real food was served along with an Asian mix. They were then heading into town for Jack's wake as he had finally been run off by his German nemesis after five years of hedonistic pleasure and masochistic work.

He had been unemployed for two weeks and was now settling into his daily routine of meeting his old friends and networking in the hope he could stay in this paradise for eternity and hopefully never return to the barren and bleak lands of the West. He had been unsuccessful up to now.

Ironman arrived and they ate and drank and took a taxi into the golden triangle of pubs on Orchard Road; The Outback, The Sportsman's and Muddy Murphy's. Ironman was in buoyant mood as he was sure he'd finally raised the squillion-dollar letter of credit for the iron mine and he promised with true altruism, to help fund Jack writing his thesis on real contracting as soon as the money was through.

Jack felt there was more hope for him by convincing another demented project manager that his project needed resurrecting and getting back to earning real money than waiting for Ironman's squillions to appear. He was becoming concerned that his promise to his wife, a true heroine as he pleaded with her nightly after returning from his research in the bars, that one day she could live a life the same as the expatriate female parents whose children she taught to pay the bills. Sadly, but lovingly, she was still working and waiting.

They arrived in Orchard Road and Jack told Shaun that he had to go and see the Doc as he had his MRI results on his bad back which had been killing him for months, and he had developed a worrying shake of his hand. Shaun retired to The Outback and they agreed to meet after Jack's consultation.

Jack climbed the stairs in pain to the Welsh medic's eyrie and said hello and kissed Rose, careful that she didn't take his fee off him before he'd seen the Doc. He entered the 'pain locker' not realising that the Doc had already seen and talked to many of his fellow piss pots, so he expected he'd be in more empathetic mode. He was wrong.

The medic was reading his favourite book, *Madness Explained*, but he reckoned the author had never had to deal with his wife or his patients from The Outback. As Jack entered the Doc's mobile rang and Jack watched his reaction as he struggled to find the correct phone key. The vagaries of mobile technology had left our great mind behind. The spoken word was the intrepid medic's strength. He put the phone down swore and looked up at Jack.

"Oh, it's you," he said, "I suppose you've been that that bloody Scottish hell hole."

"No Doc, not yet: I needed to talk to you, Doc," his sorry patient said. "I've been worried about a constant twitching of my right thumb. I believe it may be signs of motor neurone disease."

He asked this of the master in diagnosis, hoping for some less disturbing diagnosis than a neurological syndrome and hoping for some comfort from his caring physician.

The Doc lamented and shouted so all the patients waiting in his reception area could hear through the closed door.

"For ****'s sake, there are only two things wrong with you. One – alcohol, and two – you're ****** English."

And he collapsed into a cackling heap of insane laughter.

Touché, the Doc yet again, a differential diagnosis in a nutshell. Eat your heart out, Doctor Gregory House; this doctor would make you look like Florence Nightingale, you wimp.

The Doc feeling happy now offered Jack a beer. These meetings in his surgery with Jack were always a bit more informal as they had become friends and were made more sociable than normal doctor-patient consultations because the Welsh wizard always cracked open a couple of bottles of Speckled Hen for before lunch which he kept in his vaccine fridge for such occasions. He was as one may say a bit unconventional, tendering to his piss-pot flock.

They sat drinking and the Doc consoled Jack for his tragic loss, that he may now have to work for a living like him.

"For ****'s sake, seventy year old and still working to keep all my bloody extended family. I'll be here when they carry me out."

Jack sympathised with his plight and asked him if he'd ever been lucky enough to have been left anything from his elderly patients, as he once knew a doctor who had treated a woman in her nineties and was left a million pounds Sterling in her will.

"Jack, I'll tell you how lucky I am. I have been treating an ex-doctor for some years now. I have to get up in the night, leave my surgery, leave my dinner and go to her whenever she calls. All of this for no fee."

"Why?" his patient asked.

He explained.

"Because it's doctor ethics, unwritten rule, we don't charge ex-doctors. The other day she told me she'd left me something in her will. I was bloody pleased and delighted. I said, 'Thank you very much. I hope you haven't left any significant material things, as this would not be necessary.'"

"'It's nothing like that,' she said. 'I've left you my eighty-year-old sister to look after as well.'"

He wailed: "I get the bloody old sister to treat in the middle of the night for nothing and she thinks that's a thank you."

He then began to cackle demonically into his Speckled Hen beer. He took another call and from the tone of the conversation it was obvious something had made him apoplectic again. Jack considered the mania and decided that he did indeed get himself in a pickle with his deranged patients.

"Big Pat, that big bugger mate of yours, recently decided he will become the latest of my piss-pot patients. He has more bloody red lines on his blood tests than you! I have to give the big bugger mega doses of pharmaceuticals; the normal doses don't touch him."

He continued, taking a drink from his bottle of ale.

"I sent him off for an MRI just before you came in. What a bloody morning! All you bloody drunken buggers have turned up. That phone call was the bloody MRI people. Do you know what's happened at the MRI?

"No," Jack said. "Enlighten me."

"The big bugger broke it. He broke the bloody table. He is so bloody huge; he's bent the bloody thing. It'll cost thousands to fix. Now they want to charge me for sending him to them!"

"You lot," he screamed manically at no one in particular. "You should all be bloody dead by now. How did I get you bunch of piss pots!"

He calmed down and took another drink.

"Do you know he defies genetics, that big bastard. He must have gigantic genome syndrome. His recent partner has just delivered a baby boy and sadly they couldn't find any mittens or bootees to fit him and he had to wear a three-year-old's gloves and socks. He never said how his diminutive Asian wife's labour had gone attempting to deliver this twenty-pound mini Pat. Poor bloody lass…"

The Doc's phone rang again.

"Oh, it's you," he answered. "What the **** do you want?"

He listened for a moment then exploded.

"You want me to meet you in the bar and give you a shot! For ****'s sake man can you not walk here?"

He listened again and then slammed the phone down and turning to Jack, he shouted: "It's that big American mate of yours. God knows why you gave him and his massive brood to me. He has gout and can't walk here but he can walk to the bloody bar. He wants me to inject him down in the bar for ****'s sake."

The Doc sat staring at Jack and finally calmed again. He took out a shot of diclofenac from his fridge and placed it in his doc's bag.

The bag contained his little pet dog's food and also the instruments of his profession, mainly shots of penicillin for his more sexually liberated peripatetic bar patients.

"Let's head down to that mad Australian woman's hell hole and get pissed and I'll see Tom and stick the bastard with the extra-large needle I save for all you incorrigible bastards in the hope the pain will stop you coming back to me."

Jack winced; he too had had a shot for the gout from the huge needle, but he was thirsty, so gratefully agreed but reminded the Doc of the main reason he came: "Doc, you haven't told me the result of my back MRI."

The Doc cursed and took the MRI films out of a large envelope and read the results. He walked over to his light box, switched it on and placed one of the photograph films. He pointed to something on the film and Jack asked him what it showed.

"It shows that you are ******."

"Oh dear," Jack murmured. "What next, Doc?"

"An operation and then a huge credit card bill."

Jack looked downtrodden at the abrupt, uncompassionate answer. His insurance had been cancelled after his exit from the project.

"I can't afford the time now, Doc, as I have to get working and I can't afford to piss that sum away with no work."

The Doc stood up and gave his final medical advice, cackling in joy.

"Well then, we may as well get pissed."

And he gently opened the door and looked through to reception and seeing Rose's empty chair he perked up, waved to Jack and said: "Brilliant, there may be a God. She's ***** off for lunch. Quick, let's escape down the back stairs to the bar. You can buy me a Crown for the consultation."

They quickly exited before the dear long-suffering Singaporean lady could extract the fee from Jack and stop the Doc going to his liquid surgery below. With Jack in pain from his back, the Doc tried to help him down the stairs. On entering, they were greeted by Dawn and the girls, who were in the process of stripping all fixtures and fittings off the walls and bar.

"What's up?" Jack enquired.

"I'm out, my dear. She's taken the lease off me."

This was Dawn's despairing answer, tears filling her big brown eyes. She then grasped Jack to her ample bosom, finally crushing the last disc left in the lumbar region. Howling with pain, which she took for ecstasy, she absorbed the rest of his body into that vast chasm from which few returned. Seemingly thinking his muffled screams were signs of understanding and comfort, she said, with tears pouring down her cheeks: "Thanks, darling, I knew you'd understand," and thankfully released him from the pseudopodia-like breasts.

She was pissed, of course, both pissed off and tipsy, and had been on the piss most of the day. She had been given three days' notice that her lease was now owned by her bar manager, the Hobbit, who had performed a Trump-like takeover whilst Dawn was off on her habitual trips to Aussie to stash cash or avoid creditors. And on her return she had been told she had to leave. Today was the last day.

In good old Outback spirit, she told everyone that she would shut the bar when they had drunk the bar dry, for free. Already many of the Doc's reprobate patients had heard of the disaster and had turned up to console their dear friend and landlady and drink copious amounts of free piss of course.

Ironman was already there and greeted the two refugees from Rose's financial grasp with his friendly smile and soft Bostonian accent. Waiting over in the corner at the bar was Gator, he shouted over to the Doc in his loud Dixieland accent.

"Heh Doc, over here buddy. Ah got a foot that's throbbing like a two-tablet Viagra hard on, boy. Come and cure me, mah old friend."

He then turned to Zooby Doo behind the bar.

"Get the Doc two bottles of Crown and me a large Jack and Coke, my angel. I'll soon be able to pole vault over that bar and give you an American Viagra-fuelled smooth dance; coon ass style. Get the grease ready…"

The Doc took Tom off to a darker corner and the Big Man dropped his trousers, his huge white ass glowing in Dawn's dim neon-lighted space. The Doc took out his shot of anti-inflammatory and inserted a huge needle onto the syringe, drew the liquid out of the bottle and then stuck the big American forcefully.

Tom howled: "Goddam Doc, you're prodding mah ass like a duck on a dune bug. ****! That hurts, boy."

He pulled his trousers up and the Doc took one of the bottles of Crown off Zoobie and drank a large swig. He laughed loudly and shouted so everyone could hear: "Maybe it'll stop you and your deviant behaviour in future."

And holding up his bottle he cried to the assembled masses: "Why did I get you all? I don't deserve this bloody life."

Dawn went back to sit with a muscled, youthful American man who was a stranger to the regulars of her asylum. Curiously she had wet hair, and that was very unusual as Dawn always had a full perm and coiffure. She asked the Doc, Jack, Gator and Ironman to join them. The Commodore was in town and was standing nearby. Big Pat came back from his MRI and apologised to the Doc for his misfortune and promised to refund him the money when he got his next pay check. Dawn gave them all a beer and introduced them to the Hulk, or Chuck.

"Chuck's been stopping with me in my flat upstairs for a couple of days," she said, giggling like a schoolgirl.

"Yeah, baby and we are getting it on real nice," Chuck mooched out whilst fondling Dawn's very large ass.

Jesus, they thought, *surely he's not screwing Dawn.* The Commodore, who was in town with his yacht, swallowed a draft of his Tiger and just looked, disgusted, down his weather-beaten aristocratic face at the antics of the romance being enacted out in their place of worship.

"We just got out of the flat," Dawn said, glowing like a glow worm thing.

"Yeah, we sure did, she sure is some babe."

Chuck then tried to stick his hand up Dawn's ample skirts and Dawn shrieked, pushing his large hand away.

"No, you big boy, I'm working…"

The Commodore ran off to be sick. The rest stayed. The Doc was feeling nauseous, given his affection for his patient and Dawn's age, size, his long friendship with her and this young Arnie Schwarzenegger-like stud's affections. He could spot a fraud a mile off and this guy's intentions didn't feel genuine to him or the rest.

"What are you doing here?" he asked the stud, not particularly very friendly like.

"I'm going into business with Dawn, man," he answered happily.

Oh no, Jack thought, *not another one.* Dawn had a million schemes to make money and had introduced him to thousands of budding entrepreneurs (con men) who she had entrapped under gallons of Tiger and Bundaberg rum in her spider's web that was The Outback. She had always ended up in tears.

The patrons had a growing dislike for this man who kept squeezing Dawn's nether regions and whispering suggestive comments into her ear, while she giggled like a schoolgirl.

Ironman asked, "What's your business?"

By this time the Commodore had returned and was shaking his head when he heard the word 'business'. Before Chuck could answer, Dawn extracted her hand from near his nether regions and pulled out of her large handbag a jar of green-looking jelly and gleefully answered Ironman's question for Chuck.

"It's green jelly, Shaun; it'll make us all a fortune."

God, Shaun thought. How many times had he heard that? Especially from the host of Dawn's patrons he drank with.

The Commodore harrumphed like Buffalo Alf's dying buffalo and just turned away. He had heard a lot more than all of them in his long life in the Orient of such confidence tricks and plain extortion.

"Hum," the Doc said, "so what does that do?"

Chuck took his hands off Dawn's ample body for the first time and grabbed the jar.

"Heh man, it's a super hydroscopic polymer. I make it and it can rehydrate the deserts of the world. This jar holds enough water to irrigate a whole avocado orchard."

He continued. The Doc shook his head.

"I am going to sell it to Australia and rehydrate the desert and turn the whole place into a California."

"Disneyland more like it," Jack whispered to Gator.

Dawn interjected: "Doc, I'm going to put money into it. What about you and the Commodore?"

The Commodore, who had been listening but not facing them, turned and in his usual blunt way told the budding billionaires: "Are you insane, woman? The man is a con man, a thief; just get wise, woman, for once in your bloody stupid life."

Aye, all thought, all true but maybe he could have said it in a kinder way perhaps. The Commodore's advice was not taken as you may guess. He had made many a cutting comment on most things in Dawn's strange business world so she was very used to his ways and just carried on, whilst Chuck was attempting to grapple with her huge bosom. Dawn, thankfully and reassuringly for all who loved her was fending him off.

"Jack, you were a chemist or something. What do you think of this stuff? Smashing stuff, eh, can we make it here in Singapore?"

At the sound of the word 'chemist', Chuck started. He stopped his amorous and illegal-in-Singapore molestation of Dawn and said hesitantly: "So you are a chemist, Jack?"

"Well, not a chemist but near enough," he confirmed. "I have a PhD also. Where did you study and what?"

Jack thought it was time to draw this farce to an end. The Commodore nodded to him approvingly.

"Err, chemistry at – err, Wisconsin University," Chuck stuttered, not so confidently.

The Doc butted in and enquired mischievously, "So what is the hydroscopic polymer? Do you have three or four monomers? What is your amphipathic monomer?"

He avoided the question and grabbed Dawn by her huge waist and picking her up off her bar stool said: "Hell, man, I just can't listen to these guys all day. Let's go upstairs and party, baby."

He was a rather large and muscled; he had to be to pick Dawn up.

Dawn just giggled, swept her still-damp hair back with her hand and said to Zoobie the bar girl: "Get the boys a drink on me, my dear, send a bottle up for us and see you boys later," and she was about to be whisked upstairs (well, dragged; Dawn didn't whisk!) by the Green Jelly Man.

The Commodore was pleased and so they all were that they may have seen off the Green Jelly Man, but obviously Dawn sadly had not yet seen through this latest fabricator of truth. She, they hoped, was more interested in making money than his body or his corrupt non-scientific brain. However, she had left the Green Jelly on the bar. Tom opened up and smelled and felt it; it was Swarfega, the universal grease and oil hand cleaner.

Tom decided enough was enough so he went over to Chuck who was whisking Dawn around the septic tank which masqueraded for a floor, and took him to one side. They both left to go outside to the where the toilets were; Shaun followed. Some moments later the two Americans returned minus the Green Jelly Man who was sleeping soundly on the floor of the toilet. Dawn was consoled by several Tigers and large glasses of her rapidly diminishing stocks of red wine. The green jelly was very good at taking the blood stains off Gator's hands.

Jack sat and talked with Dawn while the mayhem continued around the bar. Zoobie and her lovely lady friends had dusted off Chuck, given him his travel bag and jar of green jelly and farewell kiss each and sent him on his way. Dawn was not that sad. She had lost an initial small investment for the green jelly business but she had enjoyed her few days of being wooed, even at a cost. She explained that he had been the only man she had invited to her home except for her lost and errant husband Captain Abe. She had waited until they were legally divorced and she hoped that someone might come along one day for her.

She said nothing happened between her and the Green Jelly Man except a bit of long-lost youthful courting, a few drinks and some time on her own with someone out with her bar customers. She was quite lonely without her family around her after Abe had left for the Black Isle, so a few days of someone showing affection and attention were worth the few pennies thrown away again on the latest mega business deal. Jack comforted her that she may one day get her money back when the Western desert was full of avocados and could live finally in luxury on the green jelly venture.

She reflected on good Captain Abe's demise.

"Jack, he has made his bed but I miss him some days. Maybe I should take the injunction off him and we can start again in business again."

Jack was surprised because after Captain Abe relocated his vast empire to Batam to create PT Captain Abe and to live with his young chum, Dawn was not amused so she took an injunction and restraining order on him. However, he made the odd return to the Lion City as he still had a share of the bar and he had his subsidiaries of Captain Abe PTE to look after. Nevertheless, he had a problem with running his Singaporean enterprise from his usual office in The Outback as Dawn, having grown tired of the wrestling matches on the WMD floor of the bar, and the subsequent visits to the Doc for both of them to be stitched up after the WWF bouts, had also placed the restraining order on him. He was not to come within a kilometre of the bar, or Dawn. Given Dawn's bosom size this was more restrictive and difficult than the boundary of the bar.

Nevertheless, this intrepid entrepreneur was seen by the Doc one day with his briefcase in one hand, cigarette in another and laptop propped on the wall outside the largest department store on Orchard Road, Takashimaya. He was diligently operating as 'Captain Abe's Trading Company PTE' again; 1.1 kilometres from Dawn's ample chest and the unusual regulars of his old bar.

Dawn was in a mothering and reflective mood and gave Jack another huge, back-crunching bosom hug and with red wine in her hand she made her decision.

"Jack, I'm heading back to Aussie and I'll spend time with the kids and grandkids. Then, after a break playing the pokies and enjoying the sun, I will come back and set up another Outback bar. **** the Hobbit. I am the Queen of this place and I'll take all her customers. I'll bankrupt the ****."

Jack was delighted she was in her old sprits again and that her use of the Australian language was still as fluent as when he'd first met her.

He always thought that Dawn was a great lass, very kind in many ways that many people never saw. Always looking for a dime or two, but that was life for entrepreneurs who live by the hard facts of financial life. She gave a lot more than many others in the trade. He had grown to love her in a filial way, a lot like the Doc. He'd miss them both.

Ironman shook him out of his nostalgia and sadness.

"Jack, let's head off to The Sportsman's. I've got to meet a man there. He might be able to move us both forward and save you leaving us, buddy."

Shaun had become a great friend to Jack and despite his perennial mega deals, squillions and CIA sleeper inferences, he liked him. The American had a good heart and practiced his Christian Catholic faith as he preached, helping lots of unfortunate Asian children. If he had money, he spent it. Problem was, his lovely wife had grip on it as hard as the iron mine he purported to own so little was passed his way. Jack told him he'd follow him to Harry's temple of body trading after a couple more Tigers. The free bar was running out anyway.

Jack surveyed the mayhem again. Gator was balancing one of the girls in one hand, gnawing ground nuts with the other. He shouted over to Jack.

"Heh buddy, you'll not see the like of this back in limey land. Send me your CV; I'll give Jim a call in Houston. We'll see if Jim can work something out for you. You keep strong, buddy..."

He turned back to the more important matter in hand and exclaimed: "Goddamn, she's gotta tongue like an electric eel. Dawn, throw me another Jack and Coke and two Viagra quick."

Jack laughed but knew it was all a bit of a show from the Big Man, but he'd miss Tom, the man and the fun.

Tom was off to another company project soon to start in the Philippines. He spoke to Jack about this many times.

"Hell, Jack, I've got that many houses now in the place and ex-wives that I sure hope the ninja don't meet any one of them. She'll claw mah eyes out."

Jack did indeed fear for the Big Man's sight. He pondered what it would be like to work for Radar Jim in Houston. The one-eyed stare, the imminent death from lethal weapons, the battles with HR girls, the slaughtering of the last rare sheep and the huge lunches. He concluded he'd persevere with his attempts to stay in paradise.

He watched as the Doc took a call on his hand phone. He saw the face twist into apoplexy, gesticulate angrily to Big Pat and The Commodore and then rapidly drink off his last bottle of Crown, pick up his bag and run out of the bar into the glare and grasp of his personal nemesis, his loving wife. He would miss him terribly and couldn't imagine what it would be like to visit a doctor in the future without receiving a beer and a hollering.

Big Hansie was throwing his long blond locks around with his gorgeous Indonesian girl by his side and talking with Big Marc. He was berating Manju the Indian cook from next door again.

"It's an absolute shit hole, man. Never ever go there. This curry kaffir thinks it's heaven. And never ever smoke one his cigarettes. Elephant shite and his own shite mixed together. Have I never told you this?"

Jack laughed again as he watched Manju roll one of his one-stranded cigarettes and just smile up at the huge Boer. He noticed that he still had the same baggy trousers on him and his toes had grown nails the size of Buffalo Alf's elephant but he wouldn't have needed his Nitro Express to shoot Manju and he chuckled at the thought; an air rifle would have gone straight through his bony body.

The Commodore was talking to Big Pat about days on the ocean wave. "Until you've tried shagging a boiler stoker, Pat, you've never really served in the navy. Mind you, the British navy had standards then. The likes of you wouldn't have had a chance of joining."

Jack giggled to himself as he watched the big man's huge head with no ears drop onto his chest after another humiliation from the Commodore, taking a moment's pause from battering the great matelot senseless, but knowing he never would.

Digger was in town and popped in to say goodbye to Jack. He had now sired a young daughter and his father had decided he should give up his time of debauchery and hedonism in Asia and move back to Sydney to take over the family business. He was sad of course but consoled himself by drinking the last bottle of Bundaberg on Dawn's shelf and taking a slow, sad walk to the Four Floors of Whores where his now lovely wife was entertaining the Philippine girl band in Crazy Horses.

Before he left he said to Jack: "Mate, any time you are in Sydney or I'm back up in Asia please give me a call. I know a nice place down near the Rocks in Sydney. The fillies there are all friends of mine. Platonic, of course: I'll send you a few photos of them dogging on Bondi beach. Have to go now, got to be up early for the one thirty afternoon flight. Gudday mate, and keep in touch."

As he walked out of the bar Jack thought that it was unlikely they'd meet again. He felt melancholy again. Dawn, noticing his gloom came over and gave him the familiar spine-wrenching hug and a bottle of Crème de Menthe.

"Sup this, Jack, it'll help, dear. I'll always be here for you and we'll get you another project soon. Don't fear, my dear."

Jack decided that a bottle of mint juice on top of a gallon of Tiger may not help his melancholia so he took a drink and managed to get away from the pseudopodia breasts of his surrogate mum by heading for the toilet and then heading out of the building by the rear exit. He walked along Orchard Road in the early evening heat and humidity, the bright lights temporarily blinding his Outback-dulled senses. He focussed slowly and passed familiar haunts as he headed along to The Sportsman's and Ironman's latest mega deal.

He walked past the Four Seasons hotel, scene of Kneecap's drowning on the ninth floor. He wondered where the mercurial Irishman was now. He missed Kneecap.

He passed Black Angus where he'd eaten delicious Australian beef steak many times with Big Marc and his tortured wife before the break, both the marital breakup and the leg break of the unfortunate expat who upset him one night in Leroy's fine establishment Excalibur.

He wondered how Laconic Leroy's gout was and if he had finally found a reason to smile in his retirement from his bar, and which became an iconic music sanctuary for Jack from the nightly dodgy handshakes, bodies and endless Scottish folk songs in The Sportsman's sung by Jim the Glasgow Chanter.

He crossed over to look into Muddy Murphy's. He saw Iz the Puff mincing around the tables, as usual smiling and helping anyone he met. He smiled as he remembered times he'd sat there with Big Pat, Muse, Bruce and the Doc watching Iz on St Patrick's Day in his skin-tight, Lycra, luminous green leprechaun suit, his face painted like David Bowie in 'Ziggy Stardust'. He remembered the Aussie tourists looking aghast at the man and remembered the same day when Big Pat had knocked a large Danish shipping agent clean out, who had started to verbally abuse Iz for his overt sexuality. He grinned to himself, thinking of the perverse irony of it all. He waved hello to Iz who blew him an affectionate kiss and he walked across to the Four Floors of Whores.

He glanced across to Harry's bar and remembered the day Kneecap turned up yet again. He turned up yet again one sultry November evening in Harry's Bar next to the Four Floors. Harry's (not Harry of Sportsman's fame) is a franchise of bars across Singapore that is upmarket from the usual dens of iniquity they frequented, hence it was high priced, served pretty well real bait, and played music from bands in some.

That day Hansie and his lovely girl were in Harry's and they were just chilling out with a beer or two when in walked Kneecap and he greeted them and they asked where had he been this time. They were only slightly surprised at his answer.

"Oi've been to Patagonia for the last few years."

Now to Hansie, who had travelled the world, there aren't many Mechano sets to commission around Tierra Del Fuego and the Cape, but all were used to Kneecap's remote and frozen work places – remember the igloo and his chilly Inuit romance? And amazingly, this time he had brought evidence.

She was in the form of an amazingly attractive native lady from that chilly, barren region, who stunned the whole paradigm players for two days with her beauty and sexuality whilst Kneecap went on his habitual bender and Indian bashing in the Four Floors of Whores.

Before he left that night, Kneecap met Jack in The Outback and told him that he had found out what a P and ID was and was feeling at peace with the world. Jack wished him and his Patagonian lady friend well and one day later he disappeared again without saying goodbye. He hasn't been seen for some time now but if MI6 or the FBI want to catch him, or the indeed the English Indian, well, you know where they'll be – on a bender.

Outside the Four Floors Jack was asked if he wanted the usual massage by old haggled lady who masqueraded as a lady of the night but also was really a pickpocket. He was wise to her after five years but she never recognised him even after trying each night and she was still trying valiantly to get close enough to dip into his now rapidly emptying wallet.

Meester Flintstone was standing on the steps outside his electronics emporium. He greeted Jack and tried in vain, yet again, to get him to come into the shop to buy a new toy. Jack said as he had every night for five years: "Not tonight, Mr Lee, maybe tomorrow night."

He looked up at the windows of the Country Jamboree, thinking about nights of fun and laughter with Gator Tom and his commissioning dandies as they watched the old lady pickpocket steal more from the unsuspecting tourists and ogle the lovely Singaporean girls who walked the streets of Orchard Road each evening, shopping or heading home from a long day's work. Steed had stood always to the side of them, in disgust and in frozen horror at the Big Man's crude Cajun behaviours and humour. It was always all a bit too trite for the aristocratic Steed.

The two same massage girls that he'd met night after night over the years asked him yet again if he wanted a massage. He smiled and refused their services yet again. They smiled back and he actually believed that this time they had really recognised him... but maybe not.

An old friend stumbled down the steps and greeted him.

"Hi Jack. You on your way upstairs? I'll go back with you."

"No, Greg. I'm off to The Sportsman's. You been to the Bali bar?"

"Aye: I'm pissed mind."

Jack decided that he was indeed pissed as he wobbled on the outside steps of the Floors. This was Greg the Miner, a man who had gained more college degrees than a thermometer after leaving the North East England coal mines and became a long-established expert on Thai wives and the culture of the place.

"Jack, we just had a great laugh in the Bali bar, mate."

And he stammered out that a friend of his, who was now confined periodically to a wheelchair because of a serious illness which caused him to have a colostomy and wore a bag under his shirt to hold his faeces, had decided in his suffering that a Thai 'massage' with 'happy ending' may well help his well-being; alternative medicine that the NHS, Medicare etc. or his medical insurance may not have approved of. So along he rolled to the Four Floors of Whores to negotiate such a thing.

He duly met a lovely-looking girl (or boy, not sure) who took to caressing and fondling him as they do in that place. What he didn't know was the girl was trying to lift his wallet and then subsequently do a runner, as he was wheelchair bound and he was not likely to be able to catch her.

Unfortunately for the girl, she mistook the colostomy bag for a huge wallet full of folding dollars and a ticket back to Bangkok. With a quick yank she pulled the full 'wallet' from under the loose shirt and because it was attached to the tube which remained inside his abdomen, pulled the poor guy out of his chair onto the floor. The bag burst open and she was covered in his bodily functions, and him also. The girl screamed and ran off, most likely the end of her earning for that night. Customers scattered at the smell and the mess and the poor guy was left lying covered in his own excreta.

"******* great craic, Jack. You should have been there. Let's go back and take the piss out of him."

Jack said sorry but left Greg with his views on the subject.

"Greg, if there is a moral to this story, well, I guess it's just that – shit happens. All is not what it seems in many countries. I'll see you around, mate."

He walked past the Thai embassy and crossed the road to the Far East Shopping centre and walked up the two flights of stairs to The Sportsman's.

He took the short walk past the golf shop to the toilet first. He looked in the window of the antiques shop next to Mr Ali's suit place. He always looked in the window only to see if the 1,000-year-old Chinese coffin had been sold. It had been in the window since he'd been there and the Commodore told him it had been there years before that. He smiled again and wondered yet again why they never reduced the price; obviously the rules of supply and demand didn't work with these crafty owners.

Mr Ali was sat outside his tailor's shop and greeted him warmly and affectionately as he always had, nightly and at weekends for five years.

"Mr Jack. How are you my friend? Have a tin of tiger please?"

He always offered Jack cans of Tiger in an attempt to lure him into the shop and be fitted for the usual suits, trousers, shirts that he peddled each and every day 365 days a year.

"No thanks, Ali, I'm off to meet Shaun in the bar. Maybe tomorrow I'll pop in, or maybe the weekend, my good friend. I'll see if anyone new people in the bar fancy a new suit for you though."

Mr Ali shook his hand. Jack had persuaded several people over the years to go to Mr Ali and be fitted for suits. Possibly this could be his next career move, he reflected as he opened the toilet door.

He passed Shaun on his way from the bathroom, busy talking calls on his hand phone. Shaun whispered to him that he was close to a big deal and he'd tell him what it was when he came back into the bar.

He entered The Sportsman's which was already busy with the nightly custom of real contractors and normal people. He waved to Father Bob and to Ralph who were sat in secret talks at the corner table by the pigeon-screwing window. Bob had long been run off by the Iron Chancellor as Batam eventually ground to a halt. He had remained living native in the jungle and now had taken up a position over in a Malaysian shipyard running the construction.

Ralph had thrived in South America, finally free of the boil-your-rabbit, eye-gouging lady at last, but sadly for his wallet and gonads the project had finally completed, years late and hundreds of millions over budget but Ralph, Billy and the lads got their completion bonuses and extended day rates and Ralph had returned to paradise to join Father Bob still living native in the jungles of Indonesia. He too was working in Malaysia; masters of survival for sure.

Father Bob shouted over.

"Heh Jack, come over and join us, bonny lad. Ralph's got a few more stories to tell yeah. You'll love them."

Jack shouted over that he'd be there in a while and walked to the bar. Loraine ran around the bar and gave him a big hug; a nice one that didn't snap his spine asunder.

"Oh my dear, I've heard the terrible news," she said, tears rolling down her cheeks. "Harry says come and talk to him. He can help you, my petal, get a new project."

Jack duly walked over to the end of the small bar where Harry stood with gin and tonic in his hand. His regal presence was presiding over the bar and his gimlet eye searching for punters for his bodies or to spot clandestine Fenians he could evict. Before he got to Harry, Sharon, his head-hunter wife, ran around and hugged him and kissed him, wailing in her Borneo/Glasgow accent: "Oh, me bonny lad! Yeah must be fair greet'n with the pain of it arl. Come and share a dram wi' Harry and me."

Harry held out his hand, grabbed it in some 15th degree ritual metatarsal grip and shook his head.

"Big man: terrible news, terrible news. Ah canna believe that they'd finish yeah. And only five years, man. It's ****** criminal. Here, have a beer on me, son."

Jack took the beer while Sharon and Loraine stroked his back and shoulders in comfort. Harry's face was a cold as a witch's bosom, to coin a phrase. He kept shaking his head and growling.

"Big man, send me your CV. Can you weld, son?"

"No, Harry. I didn't study welding."

"No worries. Just put down on it that you worked with Big Jamie on the Clyde, on the BP Forties jobs. The big man is the construction manager on the Malaysian job that your Geordie mates over there are on."

He pointed to Father Bob and Ralph.

"Ah managed to get them on there. There are a lot of oor friends on there." He winked knowingly. "You kna wit ah mean, son."

Jack nodded, as by now he did.

"Yeah'll not have to dee too much welding, son, just turn up and you'll be supervising the locals anyway. They'll dee the work. Day rate could be better, but talk to Big Jamie. You'll start on aboot a grand and a half US dollars a day. Shite money, ah kna, but the job's ****** arlready so should be about ten months late and by then I'll have got yoos all a decent day rate on the Petrobras job that's ganning intaeh Sembawang. And that'll be tax paid, son."

Jack stood and looked at the great man. Harry was in his element placing bodies on jobs, helping friends and taking his per cent. The fact that Jack had as much welding skill and knowledge as Mother Theresa was irrelevant. The fact that 1,500-plus dollars a day, minimum tax, all living expense paid, was 'shite'. The fact that the job was already ****** and expected to run for another turkey and possibly an Easter egg did not surprise him anymore. He had indeed learned the secret.

But he still felt morose. In his sadness his mind drifted away from Harry's bodies as he recalled his last meeting with his boss, Jon, the Iron Chancellor.

"You have done a decent job. Despite you looking like a bricklayer with a PhD, you appear to have helped me get this project over the line. Your staff work was terrible and you will never make an engineer but you seem to be able to change people's behaviour. Pity you couldn't have changed yours as it was atrocious. However, despite that, I will sanction your completion bonus and will allow you a month to relocate your family back to wherever you live in that Stone Age country you call home. Take my advice; never live anywhere where there are more ethnics than you.

"If you wish to stay away from your brutish countrymen and terrible weather, I will try to get you fixed up in Houston with that crazy red-haired Jim or on the project in the Philippines with that big American Neanderthal you call 'crocodile' or something inane and common like that. You appear to have the learned same idiotic behaviours as him. But I wouldn't build your hopes up. The project manager there has nothing like my superior intelligence, support or outstanding vision for the things you may be good at. He is from Texas.

"I have enjoyed our little consultations. I hope you have learned something about how to run projects. But on projects, the contractors get run off, the staff stay.

"Goodbye Jack, and how do you northern English morons say it in my language? ...Auf wiedersehen, pet... ha, ha, ha..."

Jack cheered up a little and smiled at the memory of Jon's last words and the first raucous laugh at work he'd ever heard from the amazing man... but German humour? You can stick it up...

Sharon spoke to him: "Cheer up, Jack. It's nae over yet, man; remember the last time yeah thought yeah were deed?"

"Aye, for sure Sharon, I was deed and then I was alive." Jack smiled at the memory.

He remembered the day Sharon comforted him on the day he died, as only an Asian woman who has seen real hardship can, with words spoken in a Glaswegian accent.

"Cheer up, Jack, two hours ago you were deed and now you're alive."

This was the day when Danny, his daughter and her friend and Jack took a day trip in Jack's bright, shining company-supplied car to Sentosa Island. A very unusual event as those days they always spent weekends in work and the bar. Danny was nervous as he was not used to sun or places with normal people. And he lost Jack on Singapore's holiday resort after Jack had gone for a swim, leaving his shirt and sandals on the sand. Jack had given him his wallet, phone, car keys and cable car tickets to keep until he got back. They lost each other. Danny came back and thought his friend and colleague had drowned. Jack thought he'd buggered off to the bar and left him.

Jack conned his way off the island's chair lift access as he had no money. As he had no car keys, he hijacked a taxi, dragged the irate and confused non-English-speaking taxi driver into The Sportsman's by his collar and Sharon paid him.

He began to drink many beers, feeling very upset with this friend who'd left him without money, car, phone and exit pass. This drinking episode started at three in the afternoon. By nine at night Jack received a call from Father Bob, who curiously enough was not drinking that night, who told him that Danny had phoned to see if he was there. He told him that Danny was still on the island with the police, coastguards and the helicopters were searching for him. Danny had asked his brother-in-law, a chief constable in the UK, to get a local policeman to tell his wife still in England that he was deed.

Danny phoned. Harsh words between them.

"I have been here for four ******* hours. The police want to arrest you for wasting police time now they know you are sat in a

******* bar, pissed."

"Why didn't you realise that when my shirt and sandals had gone that I wasn't belly up in South China?"

"Why didn't you phone me?"

"You had me ******* mobile."

"Surely you could have borrowed a phone, you'd managed to con your way across the bloody island and into the bar without any ******* money at all."

Needless to say, Jack felt like a twat, to coin a phrase, and awaited Danny's return with his car, the police and the eventual Changi Jail and a good caning. Danny returned and they began arguing again, then Sharon in her calming, Borneo/Scottish accent said: "Cheer up, lads. Once you were deed, now you are alive."

Sharon's words were cold comfort then but by the time they'd paid off the police (a joke, Mr Lee Kwan Yew) and they were soon maudlin drunk at two in the morning, two grown men cuddling each other and crying, and: "Yah were deed, now yah alive... yah saved me."

Those words reminded him of Sharon's comfort and how life can be so simple to Asians, yet so bloody complicated to daft westerners.

Harry spoke.

"Jack, cheer up, son. Have I told yah aboot getting a call from the TV to go on the ESPN sports TV channel?

"No Harry, you haven't told me, mate."

"Aye, I'm fair chuffed. Pleased about that. But ah divn't kna whit tae dee, son. Should I tak' the Scottish Saltire Flag or Union Jack? What dae ya think, son?"

"Don't know, Harry, just follow your heart, mate. Remember your dear friends from Celtic might be invited on next week. Why not maybe take the Saltire? A bit of reconciliation would be good after all these years."

After a few moments' thought looking at Jack, puzzled and scowling at what Jack had heretically proposed, Jack thinking maybe finally his evangelism had worked on Harry and it was time to forgive and forget, he lifted his dour face and scowled. "**** that, Ah'll tak the Union Jack."

He looked at Jack with what purported to be a smile, this time with a knowing gleam in his eye.

"There's only one flag for the Billy Boys."

As they say, some things never change.

Jack sat back on a bar stool. He really didn't fancy that night listening to lectures from Father Bob on real contracting anymore, besides, he now was one; an unemployed one, but a lot wiser. As he sat he reflected on the project again and thought what a good one it had been.

Despite re-baselining (cheating) several times, and the Australian Unions going on strike again for koala bear protection, it was nearly on schedule to complete on time, much to the dismay of the real contractors and especially planners.

The main engineering contractor might lose a little money, but not as huge as normal, so everyone was pretty well happy in their corporate ranks. It wouldn't be a real project if they made mega money, as all of the real contractors would have failed. And Lord Paul, Steed and the hordes of lawyers had yet to do battle over the claims and ultimately buy another super yacht each from their day rates.

Danny, unlike most project managers wasn't fired and rumour had it he was being asked to run yet another mega project after this one, this time using all his cultural alignment skills with a dangerous mix of Chinese/Americans/French and worryingly Indian money. But he always had a plan, kept his team and the Here and Now staff motivated and aligned and he maintained a sustainable relationship with the Iron Chancellor, so he may well survive for even greater things.

The Iron Chancellor would probably survive too and would see it through to a successful end, despite not relenting and paying Mr X and his cohorts for all the stamps he received. A unique project: a unique success, and a unique man. He always was cleverer than most.

Jack must have had too many Tigers as he jotted down on his habitual note pad for his research, a Tiger beer mat, that he would drop Jon a line tomorrow and say that he deserved a medal for this achievement. Jack was sure that he was the principle architect of its success. His leadership was direct, tough, but on reflection, fair. The fact that he hadn't run Jack off and had allowed him to stay all through the project-building teams, aligning warring parties, recovering dysfunctional schedules and generally communicating good news, albeit torturing him every step of way, showed he had the vision to think outside of his engineering and procedure box. Jack realised in his misery and the drink that he was in great debt to the irascible man.

The oil company would get its big steel structure, on reasonable time, close to its budget, of acceptable quality and, thanks to the good Lord and excellent HSE leadership, they had harmed no one up to now (except the Batam Cat and the project team through the usual drink, mental and sexually related illnesses). So the oil company was ready to extract an immense amount of profit from this investment over the next thirty years, some of which might Jack wished could support him in his enforced retirement if he had been wise and rich enough to invest in their shares.

Curiously enough, sat in the temple of real contracting with some of the best practitioners of the noble art in attendance, he smiled again as he realised that the project had actually beaten some of the iron rules of real contracting. Maybe the Iron Chancellor was correct to hire him; maybe he had done a good job after all. The irony of this last thought was not lost on him when Father Bob, the grand wizard of the art came over.

"Bonny lad, howay man, come and see ya fatha and Ralph, man. Yeah wouldn't believe the job we're on noo, man."

Jack grinned and thought, *I bet I do. I bet I do, my old friend.*

Bob continued: "The safety is terrible, man. I audited them last week. I took Popeye with me."

Jack grinned again as he remembered his first meeting with Popeye all those years ago. It was in the office on a Saturday morning and normally only the contractor worked Saturdays. Clients had more important things like golf, roller blading, sailing and drinking to do, but Jack used to go in as in his role was to work closely with the contractor. He noticed that the office next to his had no light on but there was a man sat at the desk through the open door. He popped his head in to say hello as he knew this was the new safety manager.

The old one had gone off to earn even more money as a management consultant. He had been very polished, articulate and intelligent and the Iron Chancellor thought he was of the right stuff because of those traits. Danny thought he was too posh, so wasn't too bothered when he left. Jon told Danny he wanted a similar man of his stature in the integrated team Jack had helped him develop. Jack was looking forward to meeting the replacement.

Sitting in the darkness was a small but massive man. He was punching away with two fingers at his laptop keyboard. Each jab was like a blow from Mike Tyson and the laptop rattled. He was dressed just in a loose athlete's vest and very short shorts that were cut up to his gonads. He had muscles like Arnie Schwarzenegger and his whole body was covered in tattoos.

Jack wondered if he'd escaped from Changi Jail or he had taken a wrong turn and should have gone straight to site as a scaffolder. But wonder of wonders, he introduced himself as the new safety manager. He looked more like Popeye to Jack than a safety manager but they made pleasantries and sat and had a coffee together.

"You might have noticed, Jack, that I am not very good with the computer stuff. I can't type at all, buddy."

"I noticed," Jack replied. "What did you do before?"

"Well I've been in safety for a few years now but I was a postman for over twenty-five years. Before that I was in the American navy. I was given a choice by the juvenile judge, join the military or go to jail. So I joined the navy as a stoker."

Jack pondered that facts that the last safety man had several degrees, always wore a suit and tie just like the Iron Chancellor and produced document after document for him and presentation after presentation. He could charm the birds from the trees. This did not bode well.

They talked for a while and Jack came to the conclusion that Popeye was a very practical man and like Buffalo Alf's buffalo, which he resembled, he should be kept on the veldt, not caged in the zoo which was the project office. Popeye agreed with him when Jack explained the risk of him being the quickest person ever to be run off by the crazy Teuton. He said he wanted to be on site, not in the office; he liked kicking ass, not kicking megabytes.

Jack went to inform and counsel his red-headed patient Danny of his discovery and thoughts. Danny had not seen Popeye yet as he had been a corporate drop in recommended from Radar Jim. He went to talk to him. Not long after he came into Jack's office, he closed the door ready for his habitual sore heed nap but before he slept he thanked Jack for his astuteness.

"For ****'s sake Jack, if Jon sees him, he'll run me off. I've agreed he can **** off to Batam first thing Monday morning. I've told him to stay on site all day every day, never come into the office or attend meetings. That was a close shave... Oh, me ******* heed. Wake me up when it's time to go to the pub."

Now after Popeye had survived and was hiding from Jon in the Batam jungle for three years, Father Bob told his new story. It seems Bob asked a meeting of high-level Malaysian managers about their safety performance.

"It is good, we are safe," replied the chief executive. Father Bob, standing up and smoking (what else) next to the window overlooking the huge dry dock, looked out and saw a man in blue overalls floating face-down in the water in the dock, slowly moving down the dock.

"Why man, what's that, then?" Father Bob asked, pointing at the unconscious or dead worker. The Malaysians got up and looked out the window.

"Ah! It is a dolphin," the boss exclaimed jubilantly.

"It's a blue dolphin! How way, bonny lad, dee ya tek me as a coming here on a banana boat, man?" said Father Bob, in full Geordie speak, which no doubt the Malaysians warmed to immensely.

Bob finished this tale with the usual education to his adopted son.

"It'll tek yors to get these right, we'll be there for yors, man, loads of wedge and the day rates will just go up and up. I've sent Popeye in with a baseball bat to sort the buggers. Just lesten to what I tell ya about running sites and foreigners, and ya'll nivva gan far wrong, marra. Come on, let's gan and see Ralph. Billy's back in toon the morn too."

Jack told Bob he'd be over soon and he wanted some time on his own. He sat looking at the assembled masses and realised that this was his life now. He really could not go back home to the rain-sodden streets, perpetual gales and relegation from the football league. He suddenly had a vision: he'd become a missionary. He'd use the management and behavioural lessons that he had discovered and become a roving disciple in an attempt to motivate unfortunate people across the globe to leave their current job and region of the globe where there were currently living in purgatory and get a job as a real contractor in paradise.

His only risk would be if the corporate oil companies and their banks – well, more worryingly, their investors – read his theories and finally cottoned on to what his research had proven and as a result move the jobs from paradise to their frozen homelands.

Or heaven forbid they incentivise for actual results and only pay contractors for delivering on time, something that works and for what they originally thought it would cost. Surely they couldn't be so cruel and sensible?

Just at that moment Shaun arrived back. He looked pleased and ordered two Tigers.

"Cheer up, Jack, buddy; it's time to celebrate. I've just spoken to Ang Sung Sui Chi in Myanmar. We've got a contract to resurface the Road to Mandalay and build a new bridge over the River Kwai. You can be project manager for both. I'll manage the generals and the Thai bank. This will make us millions, my old friend. We just need someone to lay the T Flex. Do you know anyone?"

Jack looked at his old friend, put his head in his hands and thought momentarily in great despair, *I just can't keep taking this…* but after one more sup of Tiger and a comforting hug and cuddle from Loraine, he slowly picked his head up, looked at his iconic friend and then smiling profusely said: "Let's go for it, Shaun. I think I still have Jungle Jim's phone number."

They both raised their glasses full of Tiger beer and toasted:

"Next year we will be squillionaires."

Made in the USA
Lexington, KY
03 September 2018